FROM MALICE
TO
ASHES

Forest of No Mercy

FROM MALICE TO ASHES
Forest of No Mercy

By Gary W. Toyn

American
Legacy
Media

Softcover ISBN : 978-1-7364576-2-7

ebook ISBN: 978-1-7364576-9-6

Library of Congress Control Number: 2025939712

For Danita
My eternal companion and dearest friend

Soviet Union – 1941

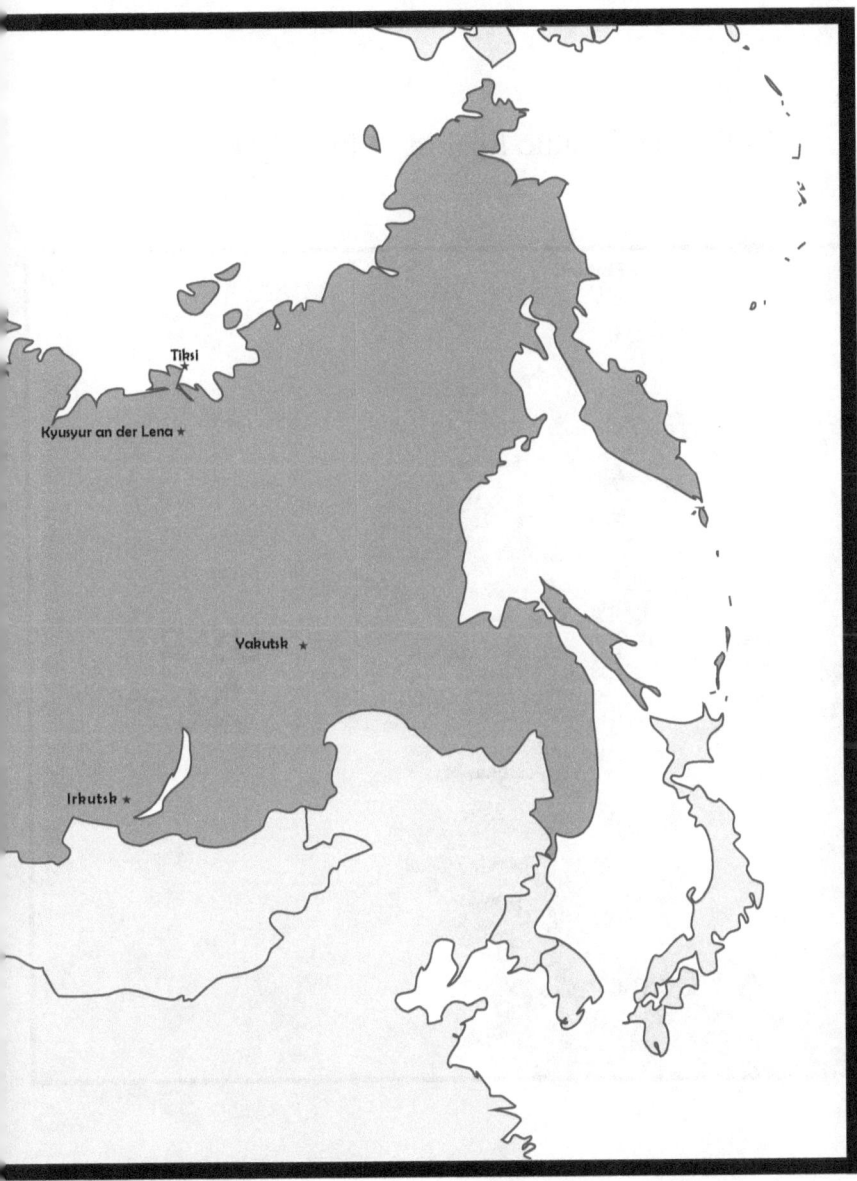

Tiksi

Kyusyur an der Lena ★

Yakutsk ★

Irkutsk ★

Lithuania / Baltic Region – June 1941

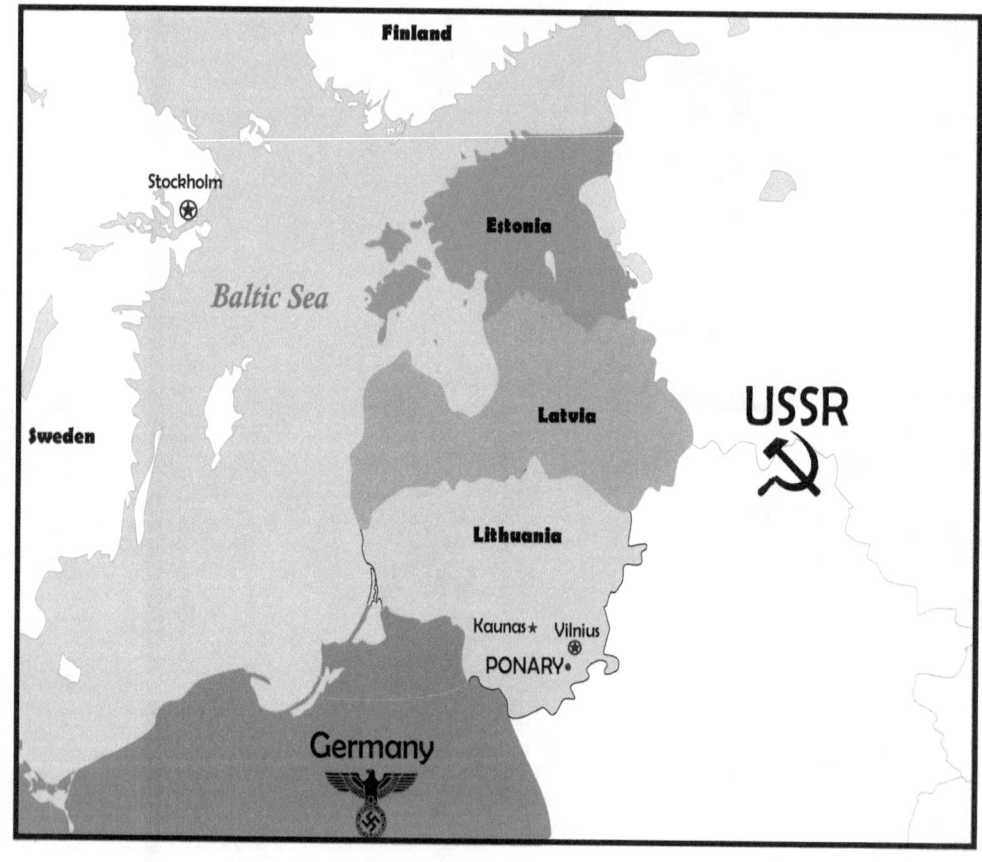

PROLOGUE

Many historians and World War II scholars overlook the magnitude of the tragedies that unfolded in the Baltic countries—especially in Lithuania.

This story sheds light on the unique and profound challenges faced by Lithuanians, who carried an extraordinary burden before, during, and after the war. They were thrust into some of the most complex social and political struggles of the era.

Their experiences reveal how ordinary people wrestle with deeply ingrained biases—and the devastating consequences when those fears are manipulated by forces with darker agendas.

Although Jews made up less than two percent of Europe's population, many Europeans were convinced they wielded excessive control and posed a threat to peace and prosperity. This lie, at the root of the Holocaust, was merely a symptom of deeper issues. This book explores Lithuania's unique connection to the Holocaust—but first, some context:

Lithuania lies in the heart of Europe. With ice-free seaports, natural resources, and a highly educated population, it was a prime target for expansionist neighbors like Russia, Germany, and Poland.

Historically, Lithuania was a formidable warrior state and one of the last in Europe to adopt Christianity. By the 15th century, it had become the largest country in Europe, stretching from the Baltic to the Black Sea. Lithuanians remain proud of this noble past, emphasizing that for much of the last 800 years, they lived as a sovereign nation.

Yet modern history tells a different story. In 1795, Lithuania was conquered by the Russian Empire. It wasn't until the early 20th century, during the 1905 Russian Revolution, that Lithuanians began to openly demand cultural and political autonomy—though true sovereignty would not come until later.

After centuries under foreign domination, Lithuania declared its independence on February 16, 1918, as World War I drew to a close and Germany's hold on the region weakened. Although Germany had occupied Lithuania during the war, its defeat left a power vacuum. In 1920, Poland seized Vilnius, Lithuania's historic capital, and incorporated it into Polish territory—a move that Lithuania never recognized. Meanwhile, the fledgling Lithuanian state faced additional threats from Bolshevik Russia, which sought to reclaim former imperial lands. After a series of military and diplomatic struggles, Lithuania secured de facto independence and gained international recognition in 1922.

During the interwar period, the country's fragile democracy faced economic turmoil and territorial disputes. Like much of Europe, Lithuania was not immune to the rising tide of antisemitism. Jewish citizens faced increasing restrictions and efforts to exclude them from full participation in society. By 1937, antisemitic laws had spread throughout Central and Eastern Europe—not just in Nazi Germany.

In Lithuania, these laws were fueled by economic rivalries, nationalist fervor, religious differences, and antisemitic propaganda. Negative stereotypes and resentment grew, and Jews became convenient scapegoats for national hardships. While many Lithuanians defended their Jewish neighbors, the political momentum favored discrimination. Legalized antisemitism laid the groundwork for even more brutal efforts to purge Jews from the country.

On June 15, 1940, the Soviet Union annexed Lithuania and began executing or deporting members of the so-called "intelligentsia"— anyone deemed a threat to Soviet authority. This campaign led to the mass removal of political leaders, professionals, clergy, and educators, causing a significant disruption to the country's skilled workforce.

To staff local administrations, the Soviets turned to those they considered politically reliable, including some Jews, alongside ethnic Russians and others. A portion of Lithuania's Jewish population— estimated at over 200,000 at the time—were appointed to clerical or educational roles, which contributed to the perception that Jews were aligned with the Soviet regime.

These perceptions—fueled by long-standing antisemitism and ampli- fied by propaganda—led to a dangerous myth of "Jewish Bolshevism." While individual motivations varied, the narrative that Jews wielded disproportionate power under Soviet rule, whether grounded in truth or distorted by fear, only deepened resentment and further inflamed antisemitic attitudes across Lithuania.

By June 1941, as Nazi Germany made quiet preparations for its next great offensive, Lithuania stood unknowingly at the threshold of one of its darkest chapters.

CHAPTER 1

20 June 1941—14:00
Kaunas, Soviet-Occupied Lithuania

Leva Koslowski stuffed her stockings and a pair of shoes into her already bulging leather suitcase. Her heart racing with a mix of panic and resolve. She scanned the small, two-bedroom apartment she shared with her little brother, Al. The room, a familiar space now echoed with the necessity of their escape. Her eyes couldn't focus as they darted from one item to another. She ignored Al tapping his foot, his eyes flitting from his pocket watch to her face. His sighs grew louder and more annoying.

"Where are my letters from Olek?" she said more to herself than to Al. Her thoughts were a whirlwind, each memory a tie to the life she was abandoning.

"Leva, you've got to hurry." His voice was infused with urgency as he scolded. "The train leaves in fifteen minutes!"

"Oh," she muttered under her breath, ignoring Al. "I already packed them."

She stole a glance at the pile of fashionable clothes and jewelry she was leaving behind. "I'll bet Olek can sell it. He needs the money," she said, trying to gain solace in the thought.

"Where'd you put that letter for him?" Al asked as he tightened the grip on his suitcase.

Leva held up the envelope. "Got it. I just hope he understands why we're leaving in such a hurry."

Al breathed in deeply. His eyes filled with both anxiety and impatience. "Your letter should explain it."

Leva met Al's gaze; determination etched on her face. "I just wanted to tell him goodbye."

"We can't take the risk," Al shot back. "He's not stupid. He'll understand."

"I've got the other letter from Mama right here."

She watched as Al reached into his coat pocket, revealing the sealed envelope with their mother's handwriting. *Don't open until your train has left for Vilnius.* He gave a determined nod and stuffed it back into his coat.

"How long before someone at the university realizes we're missing?"

Leva was unconcerned. "It won't matter. They won't miss us until we're long gone."

They locked eyes, sharing a gaze of silent acknowledgment transcending words. Inhaling slowly, Al stepped with purpose toward the door. Leva followed close behind, her heart pounding as she took one last glance at the chaos they were leaving behind.

Leva pulled on the door handle and locked the door; the click of the latch had a finality belying her inner turmoil. Not only were they desperate to board the train, but she felt conflicted about the abrupt disruption to her life. Everything was in commotion. Her dreams, her education. Most of all, her relationship with Olek, the man she once despised, but came to like because of his wit and sarcastic flair. She and Olek expected to get married sooner or later. They even made plans to elope but couldn't quite pull it off with school and family obligations.

Glancing at the empty hallway, her gaze fixed on Olek's apartment six doors down. Seeing his closed door, knowing he was still in the study hall preparing for final exams, she crouched down with his letter gripped firmly between her fingers. Lingering to make sure she was ready to commit.

"Leva. Please." She winced as Al begged.

"I'm coming. I'm coming."

She slid the envelope under his door and turned away, shaking her head in disbelief. With each step, she was leaving behind a life of certainty for uncertainty. The weight of each step was a physical reminder of everything familiar and predictable she was leaving behind. Al appeared oblivious to the risks of what lay ahead. Why didn't he seem concerned about the Russians arresting and deporting them to Siberia?

As they rushed toward the station, Leva knew this journey was fraught with risks. Still, she trusted her father, who knew something she didn't. He had political deep connections and was aware of an impending Nazi invasion. She wouldn't dare contradict him. At least not this time.

As Leva and Al disappeared into the bustling streets of Kaunas, Leva darted around strangers strolling along the cobblestone path. She knew they were fleeing her beloved country, which was now scarred by the extensive Soviet purges of the "intelligentsia," where thousands of educated and wealthy Lithuanians had already been killed or exiled to Siberia.

This was not just a sprint to catch a train. With each stride forward, they were committing to their decision to flee Lithuania. To confront the untold number of risks that could forever change the course of their lives.

CHAPTER 2

20 June 1941—14:10
Kaunas, Soviet-Occupied Lithuania

O lek swung the door open to his apartment; his eyes drawn to the white envelope lying on the floor. The sight of his name, penned in Leva's distinctive handwriting, sent a jolt of anticipation through his veins. What was her letter about this time? Was she breaking up with him? Was she angry at him for some stupid comment he made trying to make her laugh? Was it another one of her mischievous letters where she toyed with him like an adoring, wide-eyed puppy?

Trembling, he reached for the envelope and tore it open, his eyes scanning the words frantically.

Olek's stomach churned. He folded the letter and slapped it into his other hand. Driven by a mix of desperation and resolve, he sprinted down the hallway toward Leva's apartment. His knuckles pounded against the door, clinging to a slim hope that she might still be home. She was notoriously, almost predictably late for everything. What if she was still doddering about in her room, second-guessing herself about what to pack and what to leave behind?

Hearing nothing, he kicked away the doormat and lifted the spare key from the crack in the floor, fumbling to unlock the door. It swung open, its haunting squeak echoing through the empty room. What he discovered inside tore at his soul. The once-organized apartment had been transformed into madness. Papers and keepsakes were scattered on the floor. Ashes filled the kitchen sink, remnants of letters and documents burnt beyond recognition.

Leva's bedroom offered no solace either; her always well-tailored clothes were strewn on the floor, and drawers were left open in disarray. Then he caught her scent. Her perfume lingered in the air, evoking a flood of delicious memories.

Glancing at his watch, the realization struck him. "It's leaving right now." He rushed to the door, slamming it behind him. "I can make it to the rail terminal before the train leaves for Vilnius," he said to himself, more to fuel his desperation than to believe he would make it in time.

Down two flights of stairs, through the double entryway doors, he raced across the bustling Laisvės Alėja (Freedom Avenue), his strides carrying him with a newfound urgency. He pushed himself to run faster, his lungs burning, his muscles protesting the relentless tempo. Clinging to the slim chance their train would somehow be delayed, he picked up his pace, hoping to reach the terminal before the clock struck 14:15.

Turning a corner, hope glimmered, only to be shattered in a flash. The dark green train moved away from him, picking up speed with each passing second. The last car faded into the distance, leaving him behind in a swirl of frustration and despair.

Gasping for air, he doubled over, his fists slamming against his thighs, anger coursing through him. Seeing this unusual public display of emotion, an approaching woman gave an unapproving glare and reached for her young child's hand to steer clear of him.

Those few minutes he spent in the library, studying and then resting his eyes, now seemed like a lifetime lost.

Returning to Leva and Al's abandoned apartment, Olek shook his head, his gaze sweeping across the remnants they left behind. Their father's wealth had never defined them, but it still pained him to witness the disregard for valuable belongings. His eyes traced the handcrafted bookcase, filled with book treasures from around the world. Normally, the allure of those books would have beckoned to him, but his thoughts were too consumed by Leva, her absence tearing at his heart. Memories flooded his mind the day they met in that humanities class at Vytautas Magnus University, where he felt unworthy of her. Her brilliance, her beauty, her charisma all overwhelmed him. Longing to feel her touch again, to have her by his side, he yearned for her presence.

Should he heed Leva's father's urgent instructions that he leave Lithuania? What about his apartment, his belongings, his books? Would he have time to sell anything? And why was he at risk? He was a Pole with family in Ukraine. He had no clear affiliation with the Lithuanian ruling class. Questions swirled in his mind, demanding answers he couldn't yet grasp.

He kept his Jewish heritage secret. He and his family converted to Catholicism when he was very young. He also went to catechism as a child. No one in Lithuania knew that his parents were Jews, not even Leva. He would be stupid to tell anyone. The Lithuanians, the Poles, and the Russians all hated the Jews. Since the Germans occupied Poland more than a year ago, tens of thousands of Jewish refugees had fled and settled in Lithuania. Their arrival escalated the bitter hatred many Lithuanians already had for the Jews.

So why did Leva's father believe he was at risk? Leva's father, the enigmatic figure who urged their departure, held the key to his understanding. What did he know that Olek didn't? He overheard the ridiculous rumors of Nazi forces gathering in Eastern Poland, the whispers of an impending German invasion of Russia—it was utter madness, but it was something that troubled her father deeply. Olek couldn't ignore the urgency in his words, the weight of his recommendation written in Leva's careful handwriting in her letter.

If only he could talk to Leva's father. He and Leva visited her parents' home in Vilnius several times before all this. He resolved to go have a quick

5

chat. His plan took root in his mind. It was the only way to find a glimmer of clarity amidst all the uncertainty. Tomorrow morning, he will catch the next train and go talk to him.

With a resolute nod, Olek committed to himself to stick to his plan. To trust his instincts. It was his only hope of getting some much-needed insight into the whole situation, as so much was riding on his making the right decision.

CHAPTER 3

20 June 1941—19:00
Border Crossing of Lithuania and Latvia

A road sign revealed the Latvian border was only a few kilometers away. Leva glanced at Al, shooting him an optimistic grin. So far, they have avoided any run-ins with the Soviets. They were eager to escape the hazards of Lithuania but fully aware that the same dangers existed in Soviet-occupied Latvia.

As the sun dipped below the horizon, painting the Lithuanian countryside in shades of gold, the train gradually decelerated. Leva bobbed her head to peer over the headrests, and as the train negotiated a slight curve, she caught a glimpse of armed guards eyeing the train as it slowed, ready to step aboard.

Leva rolled her eyes at Al. Her voice filled with anxiety. "They're going to board the train and check our papers."

"Don't worry, Leva. It doesn't seem like they're detaining anyone. It shouldn't take us too long."

Leva bit her fingernails—a habit from her childhood that her mother often scolded her for, but the nerves got the best of her. As the train came to a stop, the heavy doors opened, and a Soviet Red Army guard stepped aboard, clinging to his rifle. He approached the first row of passengers.

"Where are your documents?" he barked in Russian to a terrified woman, a colorful scarf wrapped around her head and tied beneath her chin. Her breathing quickened and her wrinkled cheeks blushed as she fumbled through her bags, retrieving the required documents.

Leva was a few rows behind the woman, yet her upper body tightened in anticipation. The older woman's hands trembled as she presented her credentials to the guard. Grabbing them, he skimmed over the details, his gaze sweeping over the other passengers when his eyes locked onto Leva. Her face burned as the unattractive man gave her a half smile as he scrutinized her—her defiant blue eyes, her hair pulled back tightly in a bun, then he stopped to gawk at her chest. Unsettled, a wave of nausea came over her.

After inspecting the papers of a few more passengers, the guard again fixed his eyes on Leva. His heavy boots thundered through the train as he approached her, smirking to reveal his gray teeth. His voice was raspy and threatening. "And what is your name, my gorgeous Lithuanian sweetheart?"

Leva's heart pounded, yet she pretended not to understand, discreetly reaching into her purse to retrieve her Swedish passport.

Before she could present it, the guard swiftly slapped her hand away. He bent down to whisper in her ear, his breath smelling of stale tobacco and vodka. "I don't care about your passport. I need someone to keep me warm tonight," he stood and sneered, followed by a crude laugh.

He glanced at the other guard as he caressed Leva's hair.

Leva recoiled. He smirked in satisfaction at provoking a reaction.

"Do I scare you, my love?" he taunted, his breathy voice laced with both mockery and menace.

Leva nodded, her fear palpable.

The second guard remained silent, but his slow blink aimed at the first guard conveyed his disapproval. Leva felt a rush of adrenaline through her veins, seeing a spark of hope that she would not be detained.

"Well," he exhaled dramatically. "The boss says I have to spend another night alone." He reached again and caressed her shoulder, lingering while his eyes ogled her longingly. "Consider this a missed opportunity."

He turned and went to the next train car, the door shut behind him.

Leva bit her lip, keeping herself together despite her urge to vomit. Al reached over to hug her, but she pushed him away. "I'm okay," Leva's voice squeaked, and she mustered a feeble smile, determined not to let the guard's contemptible behavior break her spirit.

The terrifying incident replayed in her mind. She'd heard countless stories of Soviet soldiers detaining and raping Lithuanian and Latvian women. Many had been tortured and killed. She had narrowly escaped such a fate, saved by the disapproving guard's silent intervention. The what-ifs gnawed at her. What if he hadn't been there? What if he succumbed to this vile man's desires? Would she be so lucky if something similar happened again?

Hours passed. It was well past midnight when she awoke from a fitful sleep and glanced out the window. She let out a quiet exhale, relieved after spotting a sign for the approaching Riga Central Train Terminal. Exhausted from the ordeal, she held on to the handrail as she disembarked. She and Al watched as other passengers scattered in all directions.

Stepping outside, a cool breeze brushed against their faces, and the fresh air was reinvigorating, helping her push the events on the train out of her mind.

They strolled along the pedestrian path next to the flowing Daugava River. Not far ahead, Leva saw buildings adorned with flashing signs reading "*Viesnīca*," which bore a resemblance to the Lithuanian word for hotel, "*Viešbutis*." They walked with renewed determination, eager to find a bed for the night.

Arriving at the nearest hotel, Al rang the bell. After what felt like an interminable wait, the door cracked open, revealing a short, plump, gray-haired lady peering out at them. She blinked a few times, saying nothing.

"I need a room for two," Leva said quietly.

The woman nodded, motioning for Leva and Al to step inside the metal door.

After Leva paid for the room and completed the registration form, the woman reached out to hand the key to Al. Leva grabbed the keys from the woman instead, giving her a glare of impatience, then asked, "Can you tell us the best way for us to catch the ferry to Stockholm?"

The woman glared at Leva, struggling to lift her arm to point out directions. "Stay on this road and go about three kilometers in this direction," she grumbled. "You can't miss it."

"Can you tell me when the ferry leaves for Stockholm?"

"No idea."

"Do you know, by chance, if it leaves in the morning or afternoon?" Leva knew she was pushing her luck with the woman.

"I said I have no idea. Good night." Leva felt the woman's hand shoving her in the direction of the room up the staircase.

Leva nodded. "I hope there's a ferry tomorrow," she said to Al. "I don't want to stay here any longer than necessary."

Al smiled at Leva's persistence and said, "I guess we'll just have to wake up early and find out."

CHAPTER 4

21 June 1941—08:05
Vilnius Train Terminal, Soviet-Occupied Lithuania

After two bus transfers, Olek was finally headed toward the Žvėrynas district on the bend of the Neris River, an upscale Vilnius neighborhood known for its colorfully painted wooden homes. If he remembered correctly, the Koslowski's beautiful house was near the intersection of Latviu Street and the central street Kęstučio, not far from where the bus would drop him off. He would easily recognize the two-story house for its bright paint and fancy wood carvings on the gables.

Approaching the Koslowski residence, Olek spotted their car parked in the driveway, adjacent to the house's elegant facade. Stepping onto the porch, he strained to hear muffled voices on the other side of the door. He lifted the door knocker and rapped it three times. The voices abruptly fell silent. As the seconds stretched into an uncomfortable wait, Olek contemplated whether to knock again, risking being an annoyance. Unable to endure the silence any longer, he knocked once more and then raised his voice. "Hello? Mr. and Mrs. Koslowski? This is Olek Kosmen, Leva's boyfriend. May I speak with you for a minute?"

Without warning, the door swung open, revealing Mrs. Koslowski's startled expression on her weary face. "Olek, what are you doing here? Come in, quickly," she said with urgency, nearly dragging him inside by his arm. She slammed the door and re-locked the deadbolt. Olek felt his shoulders stiffen.

"I didn't mean to startle you," she said. "But how did you know we were here?"

"I'm so sorry, Mrs. Koslowski. I . . . I . . ."

"Please," she interrupted. "Call me Zeneta."

Olek nodded.

"We haven't been here for weeks," she said. "We just stopped here a few minutes ago to pack some things before we leave to catch up to Leva and Algirdas."

"So, you're leaving too?" Olek's eyebrows raised in curiosity.

Just then a man emerged from behind a door and reached out to shake hands. "Hi, Olek."

"Oh, hello, Mr. Koslowski," Olek said with respect.

"You can call me Matis." He gave a wry smile. "Mr. Koslowski is my father."

Olek felt his warm, strong grip on his hand, and they smiled warmly at each other as Matis turned toward Zeneta. "We're in a bit of a hurry if you'll forgive us for not answering the door. We weren't expecting anyone."

"I apologize. I hope I'm not delaying you in any way."

"You're fine," Matis said with an anxious grin. "You just startled us. So, what brings you here?"

Olek cleared his throat slightly. "I'll be quick. So, Leva left me a letter yesterday, and she wrote that you suggested that I should also leave Lithuania now. Go back to Ukraine or just go hide somewhere."

Matis stood tall and replied. "I really can't share many details with you. But a lot is going on politically. I'll just put it this way: if you think the Soviets are bad, I'm afraid it'll be much worse."

"I assumed it had something to do with Germany, given what Leva said." Matis nodded in agreement. "And I understand why you and your family should leave the Soviet Union. But I'm not Lithuanian. I'm half Polish and half Ukrainian. I'm a student with the papers that allow me to be here. Why is it that I need to leave so quickly?"

Matis paused, choosing his words carefully. "Apart from the concern that the Nazis might arrest all students for being Communists, your biggest risk is because you're Jewish."

Olek's eyes widened in astonishment. "Who said I was Jewish?"

Matis cast a hesitant glance at Zeneta before answering, his voice trailing off, "Leva."

"Why would she think I'm Jewish? I'm Catholic. I was baptized as a Catholic. I had my first confession and Holy Communion when I was seven."

"I'm only relaying what Leva told us. She mentioned that you inadvertently spoke about your Jewish parents and grandparents," Matis said.

Olek searched his memory, hoping he had not let it slip somehow. "No," he said with a nervous laugh. "I think I would remember a conversation like that." His voice trembled, belying his words. "But it's not true."

"In any case," Matis glanced at Zeneta and paused, feeling the awkwardness of Olek's awkward lie. "I strongly advise you to leave Lithuania as soon as possible. Or, at the least, find a place to hide somewhere."

Olek hesitated, absorbing the weight of the revelation, and gazed up at the ceiling. "Well, okay," his voice softened. "Yes. My parents are Jewish, but they're not practicing. My grandmother attends synagogue, but she lives in Kyiv. But honestly, I was raised a Catholic, and I still attend mass when I can."

"The Germans are skilled at identifying Jews. They've been known to make men drop their trousers to check for circumcision," Matis said with disdain.

Olek's face flushed with shock. "I had no idea."

"If they suspect you're Jewish, they will stop at nothing to eliminate you," Matis said.

Matis wondered how was he going to hide from the Nazis? He had just finished his classes and had plans to continue his studies at Vilnius University. "I have nowhere else to go," Olek said, his concern obvious.

Matis whispered something to his wife. Zeneta tilted her head back and forth, appearing to consider all the ramifications of what her husband said, then gave a cautious nod. "The reason we haven't been here is that we've been staying at our cabin in the Ponary forest. Perhaps you would like to stay there? Look after the place for us?"

Matis turned to Olek, a flash of hope in his voice. "Have you ever been to Ponary?"

The tensions melted during their half-hour-long drive toward Ponary. They discussed politics and the political situation. Olek had an important question he hadn't dared ask yet. "So, if you don't want to tell me, I'll understand, but can you tell me where Leva and Al are going? I'd love to have her address if you would share it."

Matis didn't hesitate. "Sure. We have it right here, don't we, dear?"

Zeneta nodded and reached for her purse. She pulled out a little notebook to copy the address, then handed it to Olek. "They're going to live with their Babcia Koslowski in Stockholm," she added.

"That's my mother," Matis interjected as he drove. "She's been living in Sweden for many years now. It should be much safer than here."

Olek glanced upward to consider all that it would entail to travel to Stockholm. "That's going to be quite a little journey."

"Yes. That's why we're hoping they made it to Riga last night," Matis nodded.

"But we couldn't leave until we got our new passports," Zeneta said. "That's why we were at the house, or we would have left sooner."

"Your passports?" Olek asked. "I thought you had a diplomatic passport?"

"I do, but Zeneta doesn't." Matis motioned toward his wife. "We'll have fewer problems if we both have Swedish passports."

Olek stared at Matis, understanding the implication that their Swedish passports were forged.

Matis slowed as he pulled off the busy Wilno-Grodno High Road. The thick, green foliage encroached on the rutted dirt lane. The smell of pine and elm, and ash trees filled the air. He turned into their gravel driveway through a wall of trees and parked next to the cabin.

They exited their car and walked around the cabin to inspect the surrounding area.

"I love it out here because it's so isolated," Matis said with confidence.

Yes, Olek thought. It was hidden away from just about everyone and everything. All that a city boy had grown accustomed to. Would he be able to adapt to such a countrified environment? Would he miss going to the library? Could he adjust to this new, rural life, even if it was temporary?

"We have a shallow well for water," Matis said, "and our electricity comes from a line near the train tracks out back."

Zeneta unlocked the back door and walked in. "Sorry about the mess."

Olek and Matis stepped into the kitchen and living area, inspecting the stove and icebox.

"You'll find eggs and milk in the icebox. Help yourself," Zeneta said, smiling. "I'm glad I don't have to throw it all away before we leave. And that goes for the pantry, too. Use it all." Olek looked over the living room, admiring an inviting leather sofa, chair, and loveseat.

"This is wonderful," Olek turned to inspect the room.

"Down this hall, there's a bathroom and two bedrooms. One room has two beds, the other only has one," Zeneta said.

"Come up here," Matis motioned. "The biggest bedroom is upstairs. It's got a cozy feather bed and a gorgeous view from the balcony."

Entering the upstairs bedroom, Olek smiled at the oversized down mattress and feather blankets. "I wish we could take these with us, but we just can't," Zeneta said with regret in her voice.

Matis opened the door to the balcony and stepped outside, saying, "Take a look at this."

Olek followed, admiring the view. "Oh, this is wonderful!"

Then Olek pointed toward some massive dirt piles through the thicket of the forest. "What are those huge holes for?"

Matis shrugged. "Never seen them before. Probably something to do with the power lines for the trains. Who knows?"

Olek squinted, not fully accepting Matis's theory that these enormous pits were for power lines.

"We sure have a good view of everything from up here," Matis said.

13

"You sure do," Olek said with a smile.

"And see the shed out back and the garden area?" Zeneta pointed. "The property line goes back to the train tracks way back there. And that little shed has a few tools and some other things that I can't remember since I haven't been out there in a while." She turned to Matis. "What else is in there?"

"Let's see, a couple of bicycles, a shovel, some tarps, and some other garden tools," he answered.

"We've had some wonderful memories here, haven't we, dear?" She looked at Matis and smiled, wiping her eyes with the back of her hand.

As they walked back inside, Olek asked, "Where do you pick up your mail? Is there a way?"

"Oh, I forgot to tell you about that. We bought a post office box," Matis said. "We'll give you the key. The post office is just a few kilometers from here in Vaidotai, going south on the main Wilno-Grodno Road we drove in on. There's also a small grocery store close by as well. Make sure you talk to Max; he owns that little store. Tell him you're taking care of this place for us, and he'll be your friend for life."

Zeneta laughed. "He's a friendly guy with a big heart."

Matis added, "Oh, you can use a bicycle. One of them has a good-sized basket on the front of it."

After descending the stairs, Olek continued inspecting the cabin. He leaned over to glance out the window at the garden area, wondering what type of vegetables he could grow this late in the season. As he wandered around, dragging his fingers along the woodstove, he reveled in the idea of being isolated enough to start the novel he'd always dreamed of writing.

"Well, Olek, I'm sorry to be so rushed, but we're in a hurry to go," Matis said. "What do you think? Do you like it?

"I love it. But it may take me a day or two so I can move out of my apartment. There's just a lot I still need to do."

"Don't waste any time," Matis said with concern. "You'll have no more than a day. The more time you take, the bigger the risk you face. You'll have to trust me on this."

Matis turned away and began loading their suitcases into their car.

"Move in whenever you're ready," Zeneta said. "But be careful who you trust, except for Max, of course. But other than him, you never know what can happen."

Olek helped Matis load their car, and Zeneta locked the back door of the cabin and reached out to Olek. "Take these keys. This should have every key, even the post office box."

"Great! Thank you."

He counted three keys. "What's this key for?"

Zeneta inspected the key, then looked at Olek and smiled with recognition. "Oh, that's to the attic. You can get there from the hallway. We didn't have time to show you, but feel free to go exploring."

Matis opened the driver's side door to the car. Olek could tell he was anxious to leave.

"One more thing before you go," Olek smiled. "Can you point me in the direction of the train station? I'm a little lost out here, and I need to be back in Kaunas tonight."

Matis laughed. "Sorry. I wasn't thinking. Squeeze in the back seat, you should have room. We'll drop you off at the train station. It's only a few minutes from here."

CHAPTER 5

21 June 1941—08:55
Riga, Soviet-Occupied Latvia

"Al. Wake up." Leva's voice cracked from being in a deep slumber. She rubbed her eyes to focus better on the wall clock. "Al, it's almost nine o'clock."

Al didn't move. He was face down on his pillow, his mouth open and his pillowcase wet with drool.

"Al! Wake up!"

15

His uncovered feet stirred.

"Come on, Al." She removed her covers and jumped to her feet. She reached down to dig her fingernail into the ticklish part of Al's bare feet.

Al recoiled and moaned, "Leave me alone."

"Al, it's nine o'clock. We have to go to the ferry terminal. What happened with you waking up early?"

Al grunted and rolled over in bed, his back to Leva. "Ten more minutes."

Leva turned away and opened the window shades, letting in the bright summer sunlight.

"Oh, come on, Leva," Al said. "Why'd you have to do that?"

"Wow, would you look at that," Leva said with amazement. "There's a ferry coming into port. I'll bet that's ours to Stockholm, but you're too lazy to get out of bed." She grabbed a pillow and tossed it at Al. It missed Al's head, but landed on his nightstand, knocking off the glass vase with flowers, spilling water onto Al's head. She laughed as Al jumped from his bed, his hair dripping.

"Serves you right." She giggled at her errant throw. "I meant to do that."

Al rubbed his eyes with the palm of his hand, wiping away the moisture from his face. "With the way you throw, you're lucky you didn't break the lamp or the clock or my head, for that matter."

Leva turned again to the window, admiring a small fishing boat disturbing the mirror-like glaze on the Daugava River. "This is such a beautiful place." She paused as she analyzed the ferry port. "There are two ferries out there. We should go find out what time the ferry leaves for Stockholm."

Al reached down to pick up his trousers. "Where's the bathroom?"

"Someone's already in there." Leva pointed at the bathroom door. "I can hear them using the water faucet."

He shook his head, then sat on his bed, resting his face in his palms. "I have to pee."

"You'll just have to wait until whoever's in there gets finished." She said with disdain, "We're lucky we only share the bathroom with one other room. It could have been worse."

Just then, the noise of the toilet flushing prompted Al to leap from his bed. He rushed to the bathroom door. After hearing the opposite door open and close, he knocked briefly.

"Looks like it's all yours," Leva added.

Hearing no response, Al opened the door and closed it behind him.

Ieva surveyed the room to find her clothes. She pulled off her nightgown, put on her bra, and lifted her arms to pull her dress over her head.

"I'm going down to the desk to take a look around," she called. "Be back in a minute."

Al grunted.

The wooden floor creaked with each of her steps. She peered down the stairwell where several people were milling around the room. As she descended the uneven stairs, all eyes turned to stare at her. She felt her face flush as she clung to the railing, watching her feet closely until she reached the final stair.

"*Labas rytas*," she said in a singsong voice, hoping her Lithuanian "good morning" would be greeted kindly by what she assumed were mostly Latvians.

A gray-haired man in coveralls behind the desk cleared his throat. "Good morning to you, too, young lady."

"Oh, you speak Lithuanian?" She smiled. "That's wonderful."

"Born in Klaipėda," he said. "There are some similarities between Lithuanian and Latvian, but they're more cousins than siblings. But with a little work, anyone can pick it up if you're here long enough."

"Oh, I wish I could stay, but I'm hoping you or someone else can tell me when the ferry to Stockholm leaves today?"

"It already sailed. It usually leaves around seven in the morning every day."

Ieva couldn't hide her disappointment, and she gasped. "Seven this morning?" She looked at her feet as her mind raced to devise a solution. "I guess we'll have to stay another night."

"Which room are you in?" the man asked.

"Room seven."

"No problem. You may want to pay before the end of the day. That way, you can leave early and just drop your key on that little shelf over there." He pointed to a receptacle for room keys. "But you and your husband are free to come and have breakfast. It's open for another fifteen minutes. And it's free."

"Oh, that's not my husband," Leva said. "That's my little brother. But he'll be thrilled to have something for breakfast." The man behind the desk rubbed his chin.

"Do you mind if I give you a little friendly advice?"

Leva shrugged. "Sure."

"You said you're going to Stockholm?"

Leva nodded.

"By the way you're dressed, the Soviets will keep a very close eye on you."

Leva's heart jumped. "Oh, why's that?"

"They're on the lookout for people taking money out of the USSR." He raised one eyebrow and lowered his chin. "They'll search your bags, and your pockets, all the places you'd usually carry money. If you've got a lot of money on you, hide some in your shoes, hide some in the seams of your clothes, or hide it some other place they're not likely to search, but not in your bags."

Leva nodded.

"And they don't like the Poles. You're not Polish, are you?"

Leva shook her head, hoping her lie was convincing. "Oh, no. We're going back to help my grandmother in Sweden. She's getting up there in years, and she needs help taking care of her house. It's a massive house and—"

"Don't tell them that!" His voice was loud and forceful. Leva stepped back, startled by his tone.

"They'll assume you're from some rich family, and they'll for sure search every inch of you for any money or jewelry they can find." His warning voice caused Leva's chest to tighten.

"They also don't like smart people," he said. "By the way you're dressed, you're probably one of those smart college girls, aren't you?"

"Is it that obvious?"

"Yes, so I'd be careful about looking too smart and too rich. They might think you are an anti-communist revolutionary of some kind."

"Now you've got me terrified." Leva couldn't hide her concern.

"Well, you need to be careful, but you'll likely be all right," he said with little conviction.

Leva took a shaky breath. "So, can you or anyone else tell me about how long the trip is? Is there a restaurant or a place to buy food on board? Is there anything else I should know?" Leva scanned the room to see if somebody else could answer her question.

Another middle-aged man in a worn-out coat, slightly tattered vest, and weather-beaten cap hesitated until he was sure no one else was willing to answer. "Well, it is a long trip, about thirteen or fourteen hours, depending on how rough the sea is. Pack some food and water. There's not much to eat or drink on board. At least that's what I hear, especially with all the shortages of everything."

"One last question. I promise," Leva said with an apology in her voice. "We are traveling on Swedish passports. If I have a problem, is there a Swedish consulate here in Riga that I can call? What do you think my options are?" She scrutinized the group, searching for anyone to give her an answer that could put her at ease.

The man behind the desk chimed in. "Well, if you're Swedish citizens, then you shouldn't have any problems. But I thought you said you were Lithuanian."

Leva hesitated and shook her head unconvincingly. "I guess we're a little of both," she shot him an innocent smile, knowing her answer wasn't completely honest.

"You and your brother ought to make sure you've got your story straight because you're far better off being from Sweden than Lithuania."

Her eyes blinked quickly. "I can't thank you enough for your advice." She offered a quick wave.

"My pleasure," he said with a toothless grin as she rushed up the stairs.

CHAPTER 6

21 June 1941—14:00
USSR Lithuanian-Latvian Border

Matis and Zeneta slowed to a stop and pulled off on a small bend just out of sight of the Soviet guards at the Lithuanian-Latvian border. Turning off the car and getting out, they walked a few meters to peek around the trees to better assess the situation.

"It seems like there are a lot more guards than what we were told to expect. What's going on?" she asked.

Matis said nothing, rubbing the stubble on his chin as he thought. "I'm not entirely sure. Probably nothing but a shift change or something simple like that."

Returning to their car, they closed the door and sat in silence. Zeneta's left foot bounced anxiously as she contemplated the situation ahead.

As they looked at the checkpoint ahead, Matis's mind raced through their precarious plan. His diplomatic passport—once a symbol of his position and security—was now worse than useless. The Soviets had immediately invalidated all Lithuanian diplomatic credentials upon occupation. Using his passport would surely make him a target as a counter-revolutionary. He would face immediate arrest and execution should they find it.

These Swedish passports were their only hope. Risky, yes, but less dangerous than the truth. The price he paid for each forged passport was worth a year's salary. So far, he didn't need to use them. The real test would be at this checkpoint ahead. The guards were sure to inspect them closely. He could only hope they were good enough.

He then glanced at his luggage where they'd concealed a large stash of cash and jewelry. Another calculated risk. Because the Soviets had frozen their accounts, carrying cash seemed to be their best option. Zeneta argued to leave it all behind, but what then? The compromise was to leave some of it hidden in the cabin in Ponary and hope someday they could come back and retrieve it.

Both of their bags had Swedish Krona sewn into hidden compartments inside. If they were separated for some reason, each would have some resources to survive.

They were also carrying a small stack of Russian Rubles. While Rubles were worthless outside the country, they needed some Soviet money to make it out of the USSR.

Just to be safe, Zeneta had sewn her most precious pieces of jewelry in the seams of her coat, pants and other clothing. If they made it to Sweden, it would all go to support themselves and their children.

"Are you sure our plan is good enough? Have we forgotten anything?" Matis looked at Zeneta with concern.

"Better to risk everything than arrive with nothing," she replied. Her fingers instinctively brushing along the hidden stitching of her coat sleeve where she could feel a concealed emerald brooch.

Matis prayed they hadn't miscalculated. He inhaled through his nose and looked at Zeneta for reassurance. "Are we ready for this?" he asked with gentleness in his eyes.

"As ready as we'll ever be." Her eyes fastened on her passport.

"This is one of many security stops," he said. "We'd best not offer any information we're not asked. I know we've talked about it before, but I just needed to say it to be sure."

"I know," she said. They'd been through this a hundred times. "Let's just get it over with."

He started the car and accelerated. As they drew closer to the border marker, a guard with a rifle slung over his shoulder held up his hand. Matis slowed and approached with caution. He rolled down his driver's side window.

"Papers, please," the guard said without emotion.

Matis reached over to Zeneta and collected their Swedish passports, vehicle registration, and authorization to travel by private vehicle to Riga and by ferry to Stockholm. He handed the papers obediently to the guard but said nothing.

"Matis Barsauskas?" he said as he compared the photograph on the passport. Zeneta flinched at hearing her maiden name attached to her husband's forged passport.

"Yes, sir."

"And you are Zeneta Barsauskas?" The guard glared at Zeneta.

She nodded. "Yes."

"Where are you coming from?" He asked Zeneta directly.

Her eyes widened as she replied. "Vilnius."

"What is your business in Vilnius?" his voice rang with authority.

"We were attending to an urgent family matter," she said, her eyes locked on his.

"What type of urgent family matter?"

"My sister was ill. She ended up passing away."

The guard gave no reaction but pointed to the back seat of the car. "What's all this you have back here?"

"This is what she left behind. We're taking it back to Sweden for my family."

"Are you from Sweden?"

"Yes."

He turned to Matis with steeled eyes. "Where did you get this car?"

"A friend allowed us to use it during our visit. That's why it isn't in our name."

The guard focused on the vehicle registration and asked, "Who is Algirdas Koslowski?"

"A dear friend," Matis said truthfully, knowing it was his son's true name.

"Why would he allow you to borrow his car for such a long trip?"

"He made arrangements for us to leave it in Riga, where he hopes to sell it," Matis said confidently. "He can no longer afford to keep it."

"Turn your vehicle off and give me the keys."

Matis dutifully complied, expecting they would need his keys as the decisive step before letting them proceed. Within minutes, the guard handed the keys and other papers back to Matis and motioned for him to move along. "You're free to go."

Matis started the car and gently pulled away. As they accelerated, both were afraid to look at each other until they were far out of sight of the Soviet guards.

"Well, that went okay," Zeneta was the first to break the tension.

"It's never easy, though." Matis gripped the wheel with both hands, his knuckles white with worry.

For the next forty minutes, they continued driving through scenic forests bursting with lush ferns and other fauna that encroached on the well-kept gravel road. As they neared a small town, they noticed a few locals out in the fields tending to their crops. Occasionally, the smell of fresh strawberries was tempting enough that Matis considered stopping at a field and asking a farmer if they could buy a box of berries. They decided it was too risky and pressed on toward Riga.

Nearing the village of *Plakanciems*, close to Riga, they noticed several military vehicles parked on the shoulder, limiting traffic to only one car at a time.

"Matis, what's this?" Zeneta couldn't hide her fear as her eyes blinked nervously.

As they approached, a Soviet border guard in his green uniform held up his hand.

Matis slowed the vehicle, stopping a few meters in front of the guard.

Two other guards approached the car on either side. They nodded to each other, and one moved toward the driver's side window.

"Paperwork, please."

"What's going on?" Matis asked firmly, but with as much calmness as he could muster.

"Your paperwork. Give it to me," the guard demanded.

Zeneta reached for the documents and handed them to the guard. He studied them for an uncomfortable moment, then snapped, "Turn off your vehicle and give me the keys."

"You are Matis Barsauskas?" The guard looked like a teenager, his ruddy cheeks and deep brown eyes stared piercingly.

"Yes."

The guard glanced over at his supervisor and nodded. The supervisor tilted his head, giving the guard a command he fully understood.

"Get out of the car," he said as he opened the driver's side door and latched onto Matis's upper arm.

"What did I do?" Matis said pleadingly.

Another guard approached Zeneta's door and opened it quickly, grabbing her arm and pulling her from the car.

"You're hurting me," she protested.

The supervisor walked up to Matis, but gave a sweeping motion with his hands to the other guards, "Search every inch of this car and let me know what you find."

Matis felt a guard push him toward a black official-looking car and throw him into the back seat. Matis cringed as they manhandled Zeneta roughly, shoving her into another car. Both doors slammed shut and were locked.

Within minutes, the guards produced several papers, including a stack of Russian rubles, some Swedish krona, and a paper bag full of watches, rings, and other jewelry.

Both Zeneta and Matis saw the guards smile as they strutted with their confiscated items. Zeneta leaned back, covering her face. Unable to stop herself, she burst into tears. Her shoulders heaved as she was powerless to control her sobs. Matis stared out his window, his head shaking with disgust. How could he put his wife in such a dangerous situation? Where did he go wrong? Why did he overestimate his chances of getting away with all his cash and jewelry? How did he miscalculate everything so badly? His mind raced as he tried to conjure up a reason for having so much cash.

The supervising guard approached, giving Matis an expressionless stare. "Well, Mr. Koslowski. We know your last name is not"—he inspected the passport again— "Barsauskas. We have been waiting for you and your wife since you left the border station about an hour ago. We've been looking for you for weeks now. You are both under arrest."

CHAPTER 7

22 June 1941—10:15
Kaunas, Soviet-Occupied Lithuania

Olek's two suitcases contained all that he owned. Less than twenty-four hours after visiting the cabin in Ponary, he scrambled to sell or give away everything from his apartment. He had also sold what he could from Leva and Al's apartment, making a few hundred rubles. One suitcase was filled with valuable items like a heavy wool blanket, a down pillow, Al's wool coat, and a small wooden box full of assorted jewelry he could sell later. His other suitcase was packed mostly with the leather-bound books from Leva's bookcase. He figured he would rather lug around this incredibly heavy suitcase than endure the prospect of having these books thrown away.

The Kaunas train station was bedlam as news of the German invasion caused panic, particularly among Lithuanian Communists and other collaborators. They were scrambling to escape Kaunas before the Germans arrived, knowing they would be the first targets of the new Nazi regime.

Olek rushed to the bus station, but quickly realized the chaos was even worse than the rumors he had heard from the people at the train station. He watched as passengers scrambled to and fro in a panic. Children collapsed on the floor, screaming, while their parents could do nothing but wait for the next bus to arrive. Other hopeful passengers stared on in a daze, searching for anyone looking like a Soviet official willing to help or give answers. Yet they had all abandoned their posts. No one was there. Even the ticket office was closed. Olek boiled with anger, frustrated with himself for not trusting Matis to leave earlier. If only he listened.

He checked his watch and started walking eastward. He hoped he wouldn't have to walk the entire ninety kilometers to Ponary, and that someone going that way would pick him up. Now he had no other options.

Olek walked for almost two hours on residential roads and rural dirt roads. He met little traffic. As he entered the city limits of *Biruliškės*, he was only seven miles from the outskirts of Kaunas. He couldn't travel far because he kept stopping to rest his back from his heavy suitcases.

He decided he would have better luck walking on the busy highway between Kaunas and Vilnius and felt relieved to see many more cars coming his way. Within minutes, a produce delivery truck slowed to give him a ride. Olek rushed to catch up to the truck as fast as his weary legs would take him.

"Thank you for stopping," Olek said out of breath.

"No problem," the man said.

Olek lifted his heavy suitcases into the bed of the truck.

"So, where you headed?"

"To Ponary, just off the Wilno-Grodno High Road outside Vilnius."
Olek hoped the man knew what he was talking about.

"I'm going right by there." The man accelerated as he shifted gears.

Olek adjusted himself in his lumpy seat for the hour-long ride.

"Running away from the Germans?" The man's voice had a hint of accusation.

"Well, yes and no. I don't want to be in Kaunas if the Germans are coming, but I just finished at Vytautas Magnus University, and I am headed to Vilnius to continue my studies."

"Oh, so you're one of those college boys, are you? What did you study?" he asked.

"My degree is in humanities, but before the Russians changed everything, I studied literature. I'm also trained as a journalist."

"How did you like school, especially after the Soviets took over?" Olek could feel the man probing for information about his political leanings, but he didn't want to reveal too much just yet.

"It was okay."

"Just okay?" His tone was dubious. "Didn't everything change when the Russians took over?"

"Yes." Olek studied him, hesitating before continuing, hoping the man wasn't a Soviet apparatchik. "They offered me a job teaching Marxism and Leninism in the schools, but I haven't made up my mind yet. To be honest, it really wasn't to my liking after the school was Sovietized. Most of the focus was on political topics, and I would rather have studied more about literature."

The man let out an exhale of relief. "Oh, good. So, it's safe to assume you're not a Communist then, right?"

"Are you a Communist?" Olek shot back.

"No, never!" the man said with emphasis.

"I'm not either," Olek said without hesitating.

"Are you Polish?" The man glanced at Olek to watch his face.

Olek knew it was risky to admit to being a Pole because many Lithuanians hated the Poles after decades of war and occupation. "No, I'm from Ukraine."

"So, are you a Jew?" The man looked again to see if Olek squirmed.

"I was born and raised Catholic."

The man reached over and patted Olek on the shoulder. "Had to ask." He gave a menacing laugh. "I would have kicked you out if you were a Jew."

Olek felt his chest tighten.

"Since the Russians came, I'll bet at least half of the Communist Party is made up of Jews. Maybe more. Like cockroaches, they scampered over to the Soviets once they took over and then used that power to show their true, disgusting nature. We had some Jews come to our village and threaten us if we didn't give them food. All the Jews are corrupt. It's how they're raised." He turned to face Olek again, trying to assess whether he agreed or disagreed with his views on the Jews.

Olek feared that if he answered wrong, the man would stop and let him out. "Well, now that the Germans are here," his words were cautious and measured, "it's certainly going to get worse for the Jews if the Germans end up staying for very long."

"Damn right," the man said emphatically. "That's why I'm going to Vilnius. I'm part of the Lithuanian Activist Front. We've been fighting against the Communists since the Russians took over. Now that the Russians are leaving, we're going to free our brothers from those prisons. And then we're going to fill them up again with all those dirty Communist Jews before they scamper away to Russia."

Olek readjusted himself in his seat, straining to hide his discomfort as the man grew angrier and more intense about wanting to rid the country of all the Jews.

"With the Germans coming, we would be stupid not to take advantage of this chance to purge this country of the Jews. We have to create such an anti-Jewish climate in this country that not a single Jew would even dare to assume they have any rights or any chance for subsistence in the new Lithuania."

Olek said nothing but tried to be polite, nodding at times to acknowledge that he understood him.

"Do you want to join us? The Lithuanian Activists Front? I can make it happen."

"I probably couldn't because I'm Ukrainian."

The man smiled at Olek and asked, "How did you learn to speak Lithuanian so well?"

Olek didn't want to admit that he was born in Lithuania and that his family moved to Kyiv because of Jewish persecution. Instead, he said, "I just picked it up. It's a beautiful language."

The man gleamed with pride, then gave a puzzled stare. "Why did you come to Lithuania?"

"Vilnius University has an outstanding reputation in the humanities. But they ended up moving that program to Vytautas Magnus a few years ago, so I had to finish my degree in Kaunas."

Approaching the road where Olek needed to stop, his hand held the door handle ready to step out the moment the truck stopped. Still about ten kilometers from the cabin, he didn't care if his arm fell off carrying his heavy suitcases. He just wanted to get out of the truck and put an end to this horrible conversation.

As they neared the Wilno-Grodno intersection, Olek blurted. "You can let me off right here." Olek smiled with as much cheerfulness as his face could muster and said in a rush as he closed the door. "Thank you."

Once he retrieved his luggage from the back, Olek waited for a few moments until he was sure the truck driver was out of earshot. Then he screamed out: "You're a pig."

CHAPTER 8

23 June 1941—08:40
Hotel Kung Karl - Stockholm, Sweden

"How are you feeling?" Al asked Leva, who was on her bed, bundled up in her feather mattress.

"I think I'll be okay." Leva's voice squeaked. Even though she had a night's rest, her throat still felt raw from vomiting for most of their voyage across the Baltic Sea.

"Do you want to eat some breakfast?"

"I think so." Leva lifted her head off her pillow and rested on her elbow, facing Al. "I don't know why you weren't seasick, but I wouldn't wish it on my worst enemy."

Their hotel room was a welcome gift from Babcia Koslowski because she expected they would arrive very late. What she couldn't have known was how miserable Leva would be after being on the ferry and how welcomed it would be to have the hotel so close to the ferry dock. It took every ounce of her energy to make the short walk from the pier to the hotel. Al was patient, stopping many times to let her rest.

"I've never seen another human puke so much for so long." Al laughed, but Leva wasn't amused. "And we thought dealing with the Soviet guards was going to be the worst part." He shook his head in amazement. "They asked me a few questions. It was almost anticlimactic!"

"But I will say that going to that thrift store was a stroke of genius." Al smiled to acknowledge Leva's idea.

Leva and Al stumbled upon a thrift store not far from their hotel, and Leva suggested they each buy some worn travel clothes, hoping to lower their chances of drawing the attention of the Soviets.

"You could have passed for a street urchin," Al chuckled. "Your curly hair is still everywhere. I could hardly see your face."

Leva smiled, then said with mock accusation, "You were quite pathetic looking yourself."

"It certainly did the trick," Al said with a grin.

"After they split us up, they only asked me a few questions about where I was headed and why I was in Riga. What did they ask you?" Al hadn't been able to ask such questions of Leva yet because she was sick most of the time on the ferry.

"They asked me some questions about living in Sweden, and a few others about my thoughts about Marxism and Leninism. I just tried to repeat all the twaddle they made us learn at university, and he was convinced I was a good Communist, so they let me go."

As Al sat on his bed, he pushed the curtains aside to gaze out the window. Looking out over the city from their fourth-floor window, he smiled broadly. "Can you believe we're really here at this amazing hotel?"

The Hotel Kung Karl was a famous landmark in the heart of Stockholm, known for being the hotel of royalty. The rooms were stunning and luxurious, and the private bathroom was just what Leva needed, fearing she would continue to be sick throughout the night. Fortunately, once she got her land legs, she felt better and slept well.

As Al opened the window, the commotion of street cars and taxi cabs roared in the street below, and the cool, fresh air streamed into their room. After a minute, he grabbed the room service menu from his bedside stand and read it again.

"When did you say Babcia was going to be here?" Al glanced at his watch and then at Leva.

"The clerk said she'd be here sometime this morning to pick us up. That's all she told me."

"Well, I'm going to order breakfast."

"Okay, what have they got?" Leva asked.

Al read over the menu: "Let's see what sounds pretty mild for your weak little tummy."

He glanced at Leva to see if she caught his little dig, but she ignored him. "You could have *knäckebröd* and *kalles caviar*." He eyed Leva and added with a tease. "It says it's a delightful combination of fish paste on crispy bread. And you can have eggs on it too if you want."

"What else is there?"

"How about Swedish pancakes with fresh strawberries?"

"That sounds delicious. I'll do that," Leva said.

"Oh, they can even add some bananas!"

"Okay, both strawberries and bananas. I haven't had a banana in years."

"What else do they have here?" Al mumbled to himself as he kept reading. "This looks interesting. Mackerel filet in a tomato sauce on a piece of soft bread and topped with cucumber. I think that'll be delicious. I'll have that." Al smiled. "Do you want coffee, tea, or juice?"

"Tea, please."

Al called in his breakfast order to the kitchen, speaking in English for the first time in many years. After a few minutes, they confirmed his order and hung up. "My English is rusty. It's been a while," he said.

After half an hour, Al heard three taps on the door, followed by a woman's voice in broken English, "Room service."

He jumped to his feet and answered the door. A tall, blond woman in her early thirties smiled at Al, pushing a cart with their breakfast. She rolled it past Al and parked it next to the table beneath the window.

"Please sign," she pointed to the bill with a kind smile.

Al took the paper and signed his name at the bottom.

"*Tack*," she said in Swedish. "Enjoy your breakfast."

Al eyed Leva and whispered, "Do you have any money for a tip?"

"Nothing but these useless rubles," she replied. Al took a few bills and showed the woman his money.

"I'm so sorry," Al said kindly. "But I have only Russian rubles."

The woman rolled her eyes and said with a laugh. "No, no, no. It okay. Rubles no good."

Al and Leva watched the woman bow slightly and wave as she shut the door behind her.

As Al unloaded the cart with their breakfast, he spotted two newspapers on the middle shelf, the *London Standard Examiner* and the *Stockholm Tribune*.

"Look, Leva. Some newspapers." He handed the Swedish paper to Leva, who could also read enough Swedish to get by.

Her eyes widened as she translated the headline. "Al, listen to this: Hitler begins war on Soviet Russia."

Al's head jerked toward Leva. He picked up the London paper and scanned the headline. "This one says the same thing; *Nazis Launch Surprise Attack on Stalin's Red Army*."

His eyes bulged as he read the article and translated it into Lithuanian. "It says the Nazis invaded Soviet-occupied Lithuania, with intense fighting happening in Raseiniai."

"Raseiniai?" Leva interrupted as she stared at Al. She had been there many times, as it was only an hour from Kaunas.

"That's what it says," Al reread the English words. "But the attack also went south to Soviet-occupied eastern Poland all the way to Romania and Bulgaria."

Al eyed Leva as he realized why their father was so eager for them to leave the Soviet Union with so little warning. "That's what Tata was so worried about. He predicted this was going to happen."

Al watched Leva's hand cover her mouth. "Oh, my poor Olek." She knew Olek was looking for a new apartment somewhere closer to Vilnius. She also knew about her father's letter advising him to leave Lithuania and go back to Ukraine and live with his parents or grandparents. Yet she knew Olek would never do that because he liked his new life as a Lithuanian. If he did go to Ukraine, there would have been no way he could have escaped the Nazis.

"I wonder if Mama and Tata got caught up in it?" Al asked, then regretted it as he watched Leva's face.

"It's so frustrating to have to wait for them." Her voice cracked, and Al glanced at Leva. Her eyes grew red and watery as she fought her emotions.

"They'll be just fine," he tried to be reassuring. "If anyone can stay a step ahead of the Soviets, it's Tata."

Leva nodded, but Al knew she wasn't fully convinced.

"It may take some time, but they'll be here. Mark my word."

Al took a few bites from his fishy breakfast. He wrinkled his nose, "This mackerel sounded a lot better on paper than it tastes. It's like taking a bite of soggy toast dipped in seawater."

"Mine is incredible," Leva said playfully. "And the bananas are amazing."

Al reached with his fork and took a slice of banana from her plate. Leva took a swipe at his hand with her fork. "Get your own bananas," she protested.

"I just wanted a taste before Babcia gets here."

Al took a few more bites of his breakfast, then picked up the telephone and called the kitchen. "Hello, room service, I'd like to order some Swedish pancakes with bananas, please."

After a brief conversation, he nodded, forgetting that the person he was talking to couldn't see him nod. "Yes, yes." He answered. "Room 422. Okay. Thank—" he paused. "So, about how long will that be?" He couldn't help from asking. "Oh, that would be great. *Tack* to you too."

Al turned to Leva. "I assume *tack* means thank you?"

CHAPTER 9

24 June 1941—07:40
Ponary Forest, Nazi-Occupied Lithuania

The Koslowskis' pantry had an ample supply of essentials like eggs, flour, sugar, and oil. Olek also found plenty of other staples like potatoes, onions, carrots, dried apricots, and apples. While this supply could last him for a while, he still wanted to see what the town of Vaidotai had to offer. His most important goal was to visit the post office to check for mail and buy postage stamps. If he could find the grocery store, it would be a bonus.

He walked outside, stepping lightly on the damp, tall grass. The overgrown grass prevented the shed's door from opening, and he gave a quick jerk on the door to flatten the grass. After he pulled the door open, the shed revealed a year's worth of dust and tangled cobwebs dangling from every surface. Two bicycles hung on the wall, both were covered in dust but looked to be in rideable, good condition. As he lifted a bicycle from two nails fastened to the wall, he winced at seeing that both tires were flat.

He searched the shed, looking past an old wheelbarrow and beneath the shelves holding unfinished projects. Behind the stack of garden tools, he spotted a hand-operated tire pump. One of the wooden handles was missing. He unfolded the metal footstep and put his foot on it to hold the pump in place.

With each pump, the tire hissed. Attaching the inflator valve to the bicycle tube, he began pumping the tire, and it quickly inflated. He repeated the process on the back wheel. Within minutes, he was riding around the yard, smiling at himself because he now had a working bicycle for transportation.

Leaning the bike against the house, his next step was to go inside and write a quick letter to Leva. Much had happened that she didn't know yet. He described his luck at finding her parents at their house in Vilnius, despite them being there for only a few minutes. He also explained how and why they suggested he stay at the cabin while they were gone. It was also important for her to know that her parents dropped him off at the train station on their way to Riga.

He described his adventures in traveling from Kaunas to Vilnius and the strange conversation he had on the way. When Olek finished the letter, he copied Leva's address from the piece of scratch paper Zeneta had given him.

As he sealed the letter, it dawned on him, would his letter be intercepted. Would it be censored in some way? Would someone come looking for him if he said something critical? If Leva wrote to him, what would the people in the post office say if he asked for the Koslowskis' mail? Would they question him? If they were suspicious, would they call the authorities?

He began to wonder if he should send anything to her at all. Then he realized he had no choice but to send something. Leva had to know where he was living, that he was okay, and that her parents were too. In the future, however, he had to be cautious about how much he was willing to share with her and how he was going to protect himself from prying eyes. He turned his letter over and added a final warning:

PS I just thought of this as I was about to seal your letter and drop it off at the post office. In the future, I will try to write to you as often as I dare. I don't want to become a target, so don't be surprised if I only write to you once a week or so.

When you write to me, please don't talk about politics or the war. I don't want to prompt any suspicions. If circumstances change and I find out there is no need to be so careful, I'll let you know.

In your letters to me, just tell me how you're doing. How much you love me. How you and your family are getting along. And, of course, tell me how much you miss me.

I love you more than words can say.

I hope to see you soon.

Olek

He sealed the envelope and put it in his pocket for safekeeping while he rode his bicycle into town.

He hadn't been on a bicycle for years, and after just a few kilometers, his thighs were burning. When his forty-minute ride into the town of Vaidotai was over, he noticed a church and decided to take a break. The sign in front said, "The Church of the Conversion of the Apostle Paul," a Catholic Basilica that looked to be recently constructed. He was comforted by knowing a church was so close.

As he dismounted his bicycle, he was a little dizzy and stiff. He nearly fell to the ground, but he caught himself and looked around to see if anyone was watching. Seeing nobody, he opened the gate to the church property and sat on a nearby bench. Taking in a calming breath, he scanned the small town hoping to find a likely place for a post office.

After a ten-minute rest, he found the town's post office. It was a nondescript old brick building that had enjoyed more prosperous days. Leaning his bicycle against a fence, he approached the hefty steel door and pulled it open.

As he walked in, he noticed a window just wide enough for him to poke his head in. A thin, bony-faced middle-aged man sat at a wooden desk that was covered in assorted rubber stamps. The man was dressed in a faded blue postal uniform, the elbows and sleeves threadbare.

Olek cleared his throat to attract the man's attention.

"Yes?" the man said impatiently.

"I'd like to buy ten airmail stamps for postage to Sweden, please."

"Ten stamps?" He shot Olek an incredulous glare.

Olek didn't flinch. "Yes, please."

"I don't have ten." His tone was impatient.

"How many do you have?"

"I'm counting," he shot back, then looked up at Olek. "You're not from around here are you?"

"I just moved into Ponary."

"Ponary?" He said with disdain. "How can you afford to live in Ponary?"

Olek didn't reply, but he stared at the countertop, trying to avoid a confrontation. The postal worker stared menacingly at Olek, then after seeing no reaction, he reached down to a drawer in his desk. He retrieved a small stack of airmail stamps, and with listless speed counted the stamps.

"I have five. Twenty kopeks each. That will be one ruble."

Olek nodded as he pulled out his coin wallet and gave him a coin. "Here. One ruble."

The man took the coin and put it in a drawer in his desk, then turned away as if expecting Olek to go away.

"I also have a letter I would like to send," Olek quickly licked a stamp and attached it to the envelope, then handed the letter to the clerk. "I also have a question about picking up mail."

The man blinked, annoyed by Olek's question. "Well, go ahead?"

"I am picking up mail for Matis and Zeneta Koslowski. I am the new caretaker of their house."

The man looked at Olek with disdain and said, "You can't get any mail unless you have a key."

"Okay." Olek nodded, then produced the key from his pocket. The man yanked the key from Olek and turned toward the wall of small postal boxes. He turned the key over a few times in his hand, holding it as far away as his arms would extend so he could read the number on the key. Finally finding the right box, he pushed in the key, and it clicked open. Bending over to peer inside, he looked to Olek and said coolly, "No mail."

"Okay." Olek smiled. "Thank you."

The man slowly returned, tossed the key on the counter toward Olek, then returned to his chair. He grabbed a rubber stamp and tapped it on the ink pad. With a heavy hand, he pounded Olek's letter, leaving a dark black insignia over the postage stamp Olek had just affixed. The worker then tossed the letter into the outgoing mail bin.

Olek walked out of the post office, rolling his eyes in annoyance at the man's grumpiness. He mounted his bike to continue exploring the town. He found the grocery store, the police station, and a quaint little community park.

Making his way back home, he heard a roar of vehicles a short distance ahead of him. Approaching the main Wilno-Grodno highway, he was stunned to see a steady convoy of armored vehicles, a swastika emblazoned on each vehicle, and stacked up as far as he could see. Unable to cross the road because they were traveling so fast, Olek could only watch as the column of military vehicles raced unchallenged toward the traditional capital city, Vilnius. One after the other, hundreds of tanks, trucks, armored personnel carriers, and even motorcycle-sidecar combinations paraded in front of him in a relentless stream. Seeing no break, Olek could only sit and wait for the convoy to end.

He and everyone else in Lithuania knew the Nazis had attacked Russia a few days earlier, but Olek thought as they stood there, no one could have predicted the rapid collapse of the Soviet Army and the blazing speed of the Nazis' advance. By the sheer number of vehicles, it was clear the Nazis intended to stay in Lithuania for a while, and that terrifying prospect made Olek sick to his stomach.

CHAPTER 10

24 June 1941—21:00
Eastbound Train from Riga, Soviet-Occupied Latvia

During their interrogation in Riga, the Soviet soldiers had beaten Matis mercilessly. The right side of his face was black and blue, his hair was bloody, and bruises covered his body. He complained that the sharpest pain was in his back.

Zeneta felt the train's momentum begin to slow. She and Matis were sharing the cold wooden floor of a cattle car with about eighty other political detainees. The train left Riga only hours before the Nazis launched their surprise attack on Lithuania, Latvia, and other Soviet-held territories. Despite warnings from the Allies, Stalin's Red Army was caught completely off guard. Except for a brief counterattack, the Soviets were routed by the Nazis and fled back to Russia for their lives.

"Matis, we're slowing down again." She nudged him with her elbow to wake him. "Maybe they'll let us relieve ourselves," she said, hoping for Matis to react.

People were lying in every available space, avoiding the hole in the floor that was used as a toilet. Zeneta was mortified the first time she had to use it. She waited for two days until she couldn't hold it any longer, apologizing repeatedly to others around her as she finished. As the days progressed, when someone had to use the toilet, people around them simply turned their heads to avoid direct eye contact.

The smell could have been worse, but this car had a small window near a forward-facing corner. While it was too small for an escape, it did allow for much-needed fresh air. To avoid conflict, they all agreed to a rotation so everyone could take a turn being near the window.

"Do you think they'll give us water this time?" she asked Matis. "Maybe they'll give us something to eat."

She looked at him, waiting for an answer, but he could muster only enough energy to shrug and raise an eyebrow to acknowledge he heard her. With Matis having so little to eat or drink, she was anxious about his rapidly declining health. The skin on his neck and arms was dry and cracking. His lips were parched, too. Matis hated having cracked and dry lips, but he didn't seem to care now. All he could do was lie on the floor, and she couldn't do a thing about it.

Zeneta noticed the diminishing clicking sounds as the train moved along the uneven rails. Within minutes, the train stopped, and everyone grew quiet, the silence broken by an occasional whispered conversation or heavy sigh.

Zeneta's attention turned toward the window as someone announced, "It looks like we're in Moscow."

The announcement caused a stir, many people sat up from their prone positions. A dull roar erupted as detainees muttered in near unison, "Look, we're in Moscow."

"Honey, wake up. We're in Moscow." Zeneta again nudged Matis, but he lay motionless. She ran her fingers through his thinning hair, wondering what would happen if he didn't drink or eat something soon. She grasped his hand, surprised to feel his usually warm, moist skin now cold and dehydrated. She took his hands in hers and rubbed them vigorously. "This should warm them up."

The train sat motionless for what seemed like hours until she heard a clanking noise and their car lunged forward. She realized their car had been detached and reconnected to a different train. Moments later, the train's sudden acceleration sent a few passengers stumbling and reaching for the walls to stabilize themselves.

A man motioned to Zeneta that it was her turn at the window. She worried about leaving Matis, but he rested quietly, and she didn't want to miss her turn to breathe some fresh air. She stood up and from the window, she watched the landscape change from the urbanized city of Moscow to a wall of tall spruce and fir trees. With nothing left to see, she returned to Matis and fell asleep on his shoulder.

Hours after leaving Moscow, Zeneta awoke feeling the train's momentum again slowing to a stop. "Matis." Zeneta poked Matis in the ribs to arouse him. As he lifted his head, she tried to pull him to a sitting position, but he was too weak.

The Soviet guards unlocked the sliding door and opened it. The bright sunlight was a shock. The passengers squinted and covered their eyes with their hands.

"Out! Every one of you!" a Soviet guard shouted in Polish. "Go, do your toilet business. Make it fast. We haven't got all day."

"Come on, Matis, you need to get out and pee. You need to keep moving," Zeneta said pleadingly.

She pulled him to his feet and helped him to the door, but it was too far to jump.

As many women and children jumped easily from the car, Matis shook his head in protest, ashamed of his weakness, as well as the added burden he was placing on Zeneta.

"I'll be okay," Matis's voice was weak. "I don't need to go that bad."

"No," Zeneta demanded. "You're getting out. It will do you good to stretch your legs and start your blood moving." She sat on the floor of the train car, shuffling her way off and landing on the hard ground. "See, that was easy. Now you do it. I'll help you."

"It's too far," Matis said. "I won't be able to climb back up."

"Matis," she insisted, "You have to try. It's not good for you to stay in one place."

With slow, deliberate movement, he sat on the edge of the boxcar door, seeing the long distance to the ground. "Please don't make me jump. It hurts too much."

She reached for his legs and pulled him toward her, shuffling him closer to the edge.

"Stop it, I'm going to fall," he protested.

"I've got you." She reached around his waist and, with all her might, lifted him down to the ground as gently as her small, thin frame would allow.

He winced as he straightened himself, reaching for the discomfort in his back.

She led him by the hand toward a clump of trees.

Matis pulled down his trousers and tried to urinate. He screamed in agony.

"What's the matter?" she asked, seeing that Matis had doubled over and was struggling to breathe. As he finished relieving himself, she winced as she watched him fight to stand upright again.

Zeneta watched as he left a pool of blood on the soil and leaves. She instinctively stepped back and covered her mouth. She had no idea he was in so much pain. Had he peed blood before now? He hadn't let on that he was having any discomfort in his groin. It was so like him not to complain. It was so like him to avoid being a burden on anyone or to cause her to worry about him. A dark sense of sadness and mourning enveloped her as she realized she had pushed him too far.

"I'm so sorry I made you come out here." She watched as Matis turned and walked back toward the train.

"You meant well," he whispered.

At the door of the car, guards were handing out metal cups filled with water. The passengers would share the cups and then hand them back to the guards for refilling. A guard handed a cup to Zeneta, and she helped Matis drink, making sure he didn't spill a drop. She took a drink herself and returned the cup.

"Would you please help my husband get back up?" she asked the guard. Zeneta clung to Matis's arm on one side, but the guard single-handedly tossed Matis up to the floor of the cattle car. Matis landed on his shoulder and let out a painful groan. Zeneta could do nothing to protest. She struggled to lift herself, then crawled over to comfort Matis.

"I'm so sorry I made you get out," she put her hand on his shoulder. "I had no idea."

Matis said nothing but reached for her hand and gave it a gentle squeeze.

For over a week, the relentless train pressed on, its course fixed toward a mysterious fate in the heart of Siberia. Every day, it halted in desolate spots, granting respite to its weary captives. During each reprieve, a haunting ritual unfolded. Soviet soldiers scoured each carriage, alert to the signs of lifelessness, transporting the deceased to a dedicated car for the dead. As the train was in motion, the door remained ajar, vainly attempting to dissipate the stench of decay. As the number of bodies increased, soldiers resorted to flinging bodies into the forest, making room for the influx of souls unable to endure the grueling, interminable journey.

A cruel dance of scarcity played out during these seemingly endless days when water was sporadically offered to the refugees. Hunger gnawed at their increasingly fragile bodies. At one stop, a welcome offering appeared—a lukewarm, watery soup tinged with remnants of potato and beet peels. Grasping her portion, Zeneta settled beside Matis, hoping to give him some nourishment.

"Sit up for a minute." Her voice carried a tender yet determined tone, urging him to rally. "I have some soup for you."

"It hurts too much," he said, his voice strained even though he spoke in a whisper.

She guided the cup to his lips, trying to direct the soup into his parched mouth, but it slipped through his lips, flowing onto his clothes and dripping on the floor.

"Please, Matis, try." She caressed his face, avoiding the sores near his eyes and cheeks. Traces of dried blood clung to his hair and skin, prompting her to gently scrape them away, an act met with a wince and a slight shake of his head.

Throughout the night, she fought the urge to sleep. She needed to stay awake to make sure Matis was all right. Over the unyielding rumble of the train, she heard his breaths growing shallower. His grip on life was slipping away like smoke through trembling fingers. Her attempts to wake him revealed he was teetering on the edge of oblivion.

At some point that night, Zeneta fell asleep, and she was startled awake by the train's abrupt lurch as it negotiated a treacherous curve. In the disorienting moment, her hand reached instinctively for Matis. She was frightened by the intense cold in his lifeless hand. Her stomach dropped.

Tears cascaded down her face. She leaned over and pressed her quivering lips on his icy forehead. She kissed him again on his cheek. On his nose. On his lips. For the first time ever, he didn't respond. She recognized an unfamiliar and overwhelming sense of emptiness. Of being alone. Truly alone.

"Oh, my dear Matis," she wept softly as her tears dripped down her cheek.

CHAPTER 11

26 June 1941—10:30
Vaidotai near Ponary, Nazi-Occupied Lithuania

Olek stepped off his bicycle, rested it on a fence, and opened the door to the grocery store. A wall of canned goods, laundry soap, and other grocery items filled the shelves behind the counter. A brass apothecary scale allowed bulk items to be weighed, and a steel-cast cash register sat on the counter.

He was greeted by a kind shopkeeper. "How can I help you?"

"I just moved into a small cabin over in Ponary, and I just wanted to see what you had."

"Ponary? The only cabin in Ponary belongs to Matis Koslowski."

"That's the one."

"How are you connected to the Koslowskis?"

"I'm dating their daughter, Ieva. I just finished university up in Kaunas, and I needed a place to stay while I work on some writing projects."

"So, are you Polish too?" the man asked.

Olek was surprised at the question but offered a candid reply. "My father is Polish. My mother is from Ukraine."

The man smiled warmly and held out his hand. "Well, a friend of the Koslowskis is a friend of mine. I'm Max Lewandowski."

Olek shook his hand. "Nice to meet you. I'm Olek Kosmen. How long have you lived in Vaidotai?"

"All my life," he said. "This store was started by my grandfather in 1890, then my father took over about thirty years ago. My father and I ran it until he died about five years ago, and I've been running it ever since."

"Then you probably know everyone in town, and you've heard all the gossip too." Olek gave him a mischievous grin.

"Normally, I would say life is mostly quiet and predictable around here, but these past few days have been terrifying."

"You mean with the Nazis taking over?"

"Yes, but also what's happening with all those Lithuanian partisans in Vilnius?" Max seemed truly sad about what was happening.

"I simply haven't heard anything," Olek replied.

"You should have a radio there. At least I ordered an expensive radio for Matis a few years ago."

"Oh?" Olek asked.

"It's an amazing new American radio. One that can pick up stations all around the world."

"I'll have to go explore the place a little better," Olek said.

"Just be careful," Max said with a pointed finger. "I don't think the Nazis like us listening to anything but their version of the war. Just like the Soviets."

"That reminds me." Olek rubbed his chin in deep thought. "I met a man the other day who was going to Vilnius. He said something about being part of . . ." He searched his memory, trying to recall the name. "I think it's called the Lithuanian Activist Front or something like that. Ever heard of them?"

"Yes, they're the partisans that fought the Communists. But it sounds like they don't have an enemy anymore, so their new enemy is the Jews," Max gaped at the wall, taking in the news and shaking his head in frustration.

"That's what it sounds like," Olek said. "So, this man said he and his counterparts were going to free all their friends being held in prison, and then they were going to round up Jews."

"That's exactly what they're doing. They even burned down most of the synagogues last night, and I heard they were just shooting Jews in the streets."

"And the Nazis are helping, I suppose?"

"No, as far as I've heard, it's just Lithuanians doing the shooting. Many of the shooters started wearing white armbands so everyone knows who they are. They're offering ten rubles to anyone who rounds up a Jew. So, teenagers are dragging Jews out of their homes."

Olek gave an astonished glare. "This is right here in Vilnius?"

"And Kaunas, Alytus, and other places all over Lithuania."

"And the Germans don't know what's going on, or they just don't care?"

"I'm sure they know about it, but from everything I've heard, the Lithuanians just started shooting. And they're doing it right out in the open, and people are laughing and cheering, and no one is trying to stop them."

Olek thought intensely about what Max had just said, pausing to choose his words. "It's terrifying that everything has spiraled out of control so quickly."

Olek and Max continued chatting until a customer interrupted them, and Max turned his attention to her.

Olek waved as he walked out. "A pleasure to meet you."

"Likewise, Olek. We'll see you around."

When Olek arrived back at his cabin, he searched for a radio. He inspected every closet, every cupboard, and the shed out back. He even used the key to explore the attic. Still no radio.

As he sat in the chair in his bedroom, the sense of frustration led him to wonder if Matis would have taken extra measures to hide a radio out of fear that the Soviets would arrest him. He stood and inspected every space in his room, looking for a hidden compartment or room that would hide a person or two, or possibly a nook with enough room to hold an illegal radio. He ran his fingers along each wall. He inspected the bookcase and knocked on the walls, listening for a hollow sound.

Just as he was about to give up his search, he noticed the gap between the wall and a two-shelf bookcase that somehow seemed unnatural.

Knocking on the wall again, he noticed a hollow sound that was startling. Not knowing what he was looking for, he continued knocking on every corner of the bookcase, both inside and out, searching for the source of the hollow sound, but he found nothing. Exasperated, he started pulling out books and stacking them on the floor. On the second shelf, he grasped a hardcover book, but it didn't move, and it slipped out of his hand. He tugged at it again, but it wouldn't budge.

His heart raced and his eyes widened, thrilled with new evidence he'd uncovered in this intriguing mystery. As he grasped it again, he somehow tipped the book on its side, and he heard the shelf unlatch, and the entire bookcase swung open slightly from the wall on a hidden hinge. Olek felt a rush of adrenaline.

"What have we here?" Olek said aloud with delight. The bookcase was so ordinary that no one would suspect anything without first knowing what to look for. As he swung the well-balanced bookcase open, he explored the space inside, finding a small room that could fit two chairs, a small table, a Murphy bed, and an American-made Philco two-band AM/shortwave table radio.

Olek was beside himself with excitement as he admired the shiny new radio. It could change his entire existence in these hidden and remote woodlands. He flipped the switch on. The dial lights and band selectors glowed. He inspected the back and followed a long wire that led to an outside antenna. Seconds after the radio's tubes had warmed up, he listened to a static hum and the faint sound of swing music, but it faded to a hiss.

He turned the dial again and heard a Nazi announcer explain in Polish about the rapid advances of the invasion of the Soviet Union. He used the tuning dial again but heard mostly static and an occasional voice in an unrecognized language.

He said aloud, "I'll bet I'll have better reception once the sun goes down. Then I can listen to stations from around the world. I wonder if I can get a signal from London? Or even America? Wouldn't it be a thrill to hear a real American radio station? To enjoy the popular big band music that everyone talks about? Or to hear trustworthy news that wasn't tainted by the government's agenda?"

He ducked out of the tiny room and replaced the books where they belonged on the shelves. Then he carefully swung the bookshelf back in place until he heard it latch.

Tonight was going to be a good night.

CHAPTER 12

27 June 1941—12:15
Stockholm, Sweden

L eva looked in astonishment as Babcia held up an airmail letter with Leva's name on it. "For me?" she asked.

"Who on earth could be writing to you here?" Babcia asked. "It's not your father's handwriting."

Leva took the letter and recognized the handwriting. "It's from Olek."

"Who is Olek?" Babcia asked.

"Her boyfriend," Al said.

Leva turned to Al with a puzzled expression. "How on earth did he get this address?"

"I have no idea." Al shrugged.

Leva carefully removed the letter and read it to herself.

"Wow." She glanced at Al with surprise written on her face.

"He's living in our cabin in Ponary. He somehow found Mama and Tata, and they gave him the keys."

"Very interesting." Al nodded with approval.

"He's going to try to write a book." She smiled, knowing he had the ability. She had encouraged him many times before to start writing his novel, but he simply couldn't find the time to sit down and do it.

"Oh," Leva said, "He also said that Mama and Tata dropped him off at the train station on their way to Riga." She stared at Al. "So, we know they did leave for Riga . . ." She saw the date at the top of the letter. "June 21st. Wasn't that last Saturday?"

"Yes," Babcia said.

"But that only tells us when they were in Vilnius. We don't know if they made it to Riga or not," Al countered.

Leva responded with a nod.

"So, what else does he say?" Al asked.

Leva scanned the letter, mumbling to herself as she read. "Olek met a man who wanted to hunt down Jews. He asked if Olek wanted to join them," she chuckled.

"That's terrifying," Babcia said. "I just can't imagine what I'd do if I knew you were still in Lithuania. I'd be beside myself with worry."

"We have friends there who are Jews," Al glanced at Leva. "Olek included."

Babcia inhaled quickly in surprise, and Leva's head turned instantly to see what had startled her. "Your boyfriend is a Jew?" Babcia asked in disbelief.

"Yes," she said emphatically, looking at her grandmother. "Is there a problem with that?"

"Oh, no. I was just surprised."

"Olek's parents and grandparents are Jews, but they aren't practicing, from what I hear. Olek was raised as Catholic, so I don't think he'll have to worry."

Babcia smiled and turned away.

Leva watched Al as he walked upstairs to his room. Then she sat at the desk in the library to respond to Olek's letter.

My dearest Olek,

I can't tell you how shocked and thrilled I was to receive your letter. I just can't believe that you're in our cabin in Ponary. I love it there. It's one of my favorite places on earth. It's always so peaceful and quiet. I'm sure you'll find it a nice place to work on your book.

We are still waiting to hear from my parents. They should have heard from them by now, so it's frustrating that we can't do anything to help them or even find out where they are. There's no way to know if they were stopped or if they had car troubles, or if they're lying low until the whole Nazi invasion blows over. Mama said we should give them at least a week, but it has been six days. I'm still hoping they were delayed somewhere and will just appear out of nowhere. That's my only hope anyway. Waiting is bad enough, but wondering if they've been arrested or, even worse, is almost too much to bear. It's been hard on both me and Al, and we've lost patience, and our tempers are short with each other. Poor Babcia has been caught in the middle of our arguments. It's not like us to fight like this. We usually get along quite well. Maybe it will take a while for everything to calm down.

For the good news, Al and I have more or less settled in here in my Babcia's house in Stockholm. I doubt I told you, but Babcia's home is an imposing, eighteen-room stately manor. It was built in the mid-1600s for Swedish royalty, but it has seen better days. Throughout the centuries it has survived fires, revolutions, decay, and several royal renovations. Now, most of the bedrooms are sealed off, but we still have six huge bedrooms, along with a banquet room, library, study, and a huge kitchen. Outside, there's an enormous garden that is absolutely gorgeous. We see people out there all the time who just stroll the grounds. They come from all over Sweden and even Finland.

When Babcia first moved into this place a few years ago, she had plans to turn this into a hotel. Back then, she had a staff of ten or so. For one reason or another, she couldn't finish renovations before the war. Now, because of shortages of building materials and manpower, all construction is on hold. Only the housekeeper, cook, and groundskeeper remain. We are truly lucky to be living in such a wonderful place.

I love it here, but Al's not happy at all. I think he feels guilty about living in such a wonderful place while our friends back home are suffering. It could be something else, but he's not letting on what's bothering him.

I assume you know that Sweden has declared neutrality in this war, but they're still calling up all the eligible men for military training. With so many men now mobilized, they're wondering if there will be enough people to harvest the crops this fall. That's one reason Al is concerned because it's likely they're going to call him up for duty. After all, he's considered a Swedish citizen (because he has a Swedish passport).

He has hinted about wanting to go to America. My uncle Jouzas lives in Chicago, and Al thinks he can wait out the war there. He's always wanted to see the States, but I think it's more of a threat because he's so unhappy here. Once he figures out what he wants to do with his life, I'll bet he'll stay here with me and Babcia.

I wish you could tell me all about what you're doing, what it's like living there now, and what has changed. Tell me anything you feel comfortable telling me.

I love you more each day. I miss you every time I think of home, which is all day every day. Please be safe and write me back as soon as you can. I can't wait to see you again.

With love,

Leva

CHAPTER 13

5 July 1941—06:30
Eastbound Train near Cheboksary, USSR

Z eneta's brain was in a fog. Daytime and nighttime were just a blur. Over the next few days, Zeneta wasn't fully aware of where she was or even how she got there—but she knew she was sitting near the exact spot where Matis had died. It was only when the train stopped during the early morning hours that she was able to clear her mind. As the people in the car began to stir that morning, someone announced they were in *Gorky*, or *Nizhny Novgorod*, as the Soviets had recently named it. This sizeable city was about ten hours east of Moscow and had grown into one of the largest centers of production for the Soviet war effort.

Without warning, the guards opened the doors and shouted, "Everyone get off the train now! No exceptions! A new train will be coming for you."

As the guards gave the all-clear sign, Zeneta and the others watched their old train lurch a few times before finally creeping forward. After a short wait, a new train approached but seemed to be taking its time.

Zeneta could tell instantly that the new train engine wasn't as old and battered as their earlier one. As it drew near, the throng of people was eager to get aboard, but the irritable guards continued to shout. "Wait for it to stop. It's not going anywhere without you."

When the train's wheels squealed to a stop, the guards called out, "Keep walking to the last six cars. They are empty, so you won't have to fight for space."

Zeneta walked around the crowd gathering near the first four cars. The last car had no one waiting, so she lifted herself through the door and climbed to her feet. Three levels of wooden bunks were lined up against the wall. Each bunk could fit one or possibly two people if they were small. It was a definite upgrade from sleeping on the cold floor. Zeneta noticed the familiar hole in the floor for the toilet, again with nothing to offer any privacy.

Families with children and teens climbed up to the car, and Zeneta rushed to climb to a top bunk to claim it as her own. She hoped it would allow her a modicum of privacy and a chance to escape some of the noise and chaos of families and children below.

Once the train began to move, Zeneta used her wool coat as her pillow. It wasn't a comfortable pillow because she had sewn cash, jewelry, and other valuables into the seams of the coat. She was also given one of her small suitcases. One of the guards retrieved it from their car the day they were arrested. It contained a blouse, a skirt, a pair of pajamas, and a few pairs of underwear.

From the beginning of this horrible trip, she had no opportunity to change clothes. Now that she had her own bunk, the thought of changing her underwear appealed to her perception of normalcy. It allowed her to feel a little dignity and control over her life. She glanced around to see if anyone was looking, but she realized she was hidden by the darkness. She was energized by this new sense of privacy, yet her ingrained modesty made her fear she would be spotted by someone. Despite her solitude, she quickly changed into a clean pair of underwear and then exhaled with delight. After adjusting her clothes, she rested her head on her suitcase and savored this small yet important victory.

Traveling for hours through a long stretch of trees, the train unexpectedly stopped. Zeneta waited for the door to open, but it took more than a half hour for the guards to finally unlatch the doors and shout, "Hurry and do your business! Make it fast!"

As the detainees scattered throughout the woods for some privacy, another group of guards arrived, escorting eight women detainees. Four women teamed up to carefully carry an oversized pot nearly overflowing with some type of soup. Two other women followed carrying a wooden box filled with loaves of bread.

"Did you see that?" Zeneta said loud enough to get the attention of those nearby. Within seconds, a crowd gathered around the guards. Each detainee was given a metal cup; then a woman dipped her ladle in the pail, drawing out a serving of watery soup. Once the first person in line received their soup, the next woman handed out a small portion of bread. Zeneta was among the first in line, and after receiving her food, she stepped away from the chaos to find a quiet place to eat. She dipped her bread into the soup and took a bite but moaned in pain. The stiff bread was too hard for her to chew.

Looking around she noticed a young, attractive woman with two young children clinging to her. One appeared to be a boy of six or seven years old. The other was a girl who seemed to be four or five. Both were thin and pale, sitting quietly as they devoured their food.

Zeneta asked the young mother, "Would your children like some more bread?"

The mother's eyes widened. Her eyebrows lifted with anticipation.

"Oh, yes. That would be greatly appreciated."

Zeneta smiled back and nodded. "I'll see if they'll give me some more for you."

With as much stealth as she could manage, she made her way to the back of the line. The guard glanced at her, giving her a wary eye, but then turned away, convinced he had not yet seen her in line. As she approached the soup, she took the cup of soup and said a soft 'thank you'.

Stepping forward, Zeneta recognized the woman handing out the bread. She froze in place as the woman was about to alert the guard. Zeneta gave her a pleading glance and said, "It's not for me. It's for those two children over there." Zeneta pointed.

After a brief hesitation, the woman gave a piece of bread to Zeneta.

"Thank you so much." Zeneta smiled and rushed away before the guard could stop her.

The young mother thanked Zeneta through wet eyes. Desperate and hungry, the woman kept the soup but handed the more valuable bread to her children. They shoved the bread in their mouths and chewed on the hard bread with all their might.

"You are so kind." The young mother's voice was raspy. "How can I ever repay you?"

"It's nothing," Zeneta said. She thought of Ieva and Al when they were young. She remembered how much they complained when they were hungry, yet she knew they had never missed a meal and certainly had never lacked for food like these two children.

"Minutes later, the young boy stepped up to Zeneta and tugged on her coat. Thank you." He smiled, looking at his mother as she nodded her approval.

Zeneta squatted to be at the boy's eye level. "What's your name?"

"Mykolas," the boy's voice said in a whisper.

Zeneta smiled. "That's a wonderful name. And how old are you, Mykolas?"

"Seven. But I turn eight next month."

Zeneta tried not to appear too surprised that he seemed much younger. She glanced at his sister. "And what's her name?"

Mykolas' eyes lit up. "Saule. She's four."

"My name is Zeneta. I'm from Lithuania. Where are you from?"

The boy said nothing.

"Can you tell her that you're from Lithuania too?" the mother said with encouragement, but the boy only nodded.

"I'm from Vilnius," Zeneta said, looking at Mykolas, and then at his mother.

"We're from Vilnius too, but we've also lived in Kaunas." She reached out her hand to Zeneta. "My name is Ugna. Ugna Petrauskas."

"It's a pleasure to meet you, Ugna. I know Kaunas quite well. My children attend Vytautas Magnus University."

"Oh, really? My husband attended there before he was taken by the Soviets a few weeks ago." She hesitated as she gathered her composure. "I haven't seen him since."

"I'm so sorry to hear that." Zeneta tried to be reassuring, resisting the thought of consoling her with her own story of tragic loss. It was just too painful to talk about.

Zeneta turned to the boy. "Are you taking good care of your Mama? She really needs your help taking care of your little sister."

Mykolas hid behind his mother.

"He's a little shy sometimes," Ugna said.

"He's a brave little boy," Zeneta said. "And he'll grow up to be big and strong, just like his Papa."

As they continued to chat, the women who served the soup picked up their empty soup pails and disappeared into the crowd. The guards then shouted as they began the process of getting everyone back on the train.

"Everyone, get on the train. Hurry. We don't have time to waste."

Zeneta was impressed with the guard's command of the Polish language, and something in her mind convinced her that she should compliment him. Without thinking, she said, "Where did you learn to speak Polish so well?"

The guard shot Zeneta a glance of bewilderment, stunned that a detainee would voluntarily say anything to a guard. He turned away and said with much less disdain than she expected, "None of your business."

Zeneta was about to step away to a safe distance when he said, "I once thought Poland was our enemy, but after the Germans betrayed Russia, I realized we are now allies fighting a common enemy."

Zeneta was startled by his answer and paused before mustering the courage to reply. "I agree. We are indeed allies. I hope we will be treated as allies when we reach our final stop."

He gave a hesitant nod, not appearing to be annoyed with her. She pressed her luck by asking the question she and everyone else wanted to know. "Where are we going? I would hope allies wouldn't keep such important information a secret."

The guard peered over his shoulder again to see if it was safe to talk. He replied in a quiet voice so only Zeneta could hear. "Our orders are to escort you to the Altai region of Siberia. Where you go from there is anyone's guess."

Zeneta was hoping their trip was almost over, but she knew the Altai region was far away in central Siberia, somewhere between Mongolia and Kazakhstan. "That will take weeks to get there," she said in disbelief.

The guard nodded and replied. "I'm guessing another ten days to two weeks, depending on conditions."

Zeneta said nothing, gathering all her strength so she wouldn't burst into tears.

CHAPTER 14

9 July 1941—09:00
Ponary Forest, Nazi-Occupied Lithuania

Olek sat at his desk in the living room, where he usually sat as he wrote. With the window open, he could hear the birds singing, and the sun would occasionally break through and brighten the room.

Taking out a blank piece of paper, he began his letter to Leva.

> *9 July 1941*
>
> *My dearest Leva,*
>
> *I finally got your letter yesterday.*
>
> *I'm sad that your Mama and Tata hadn't arrived yet in Sweden, or at least they hadn't arrived by the time you sent your letter. Maybe they have arrived by the time you get this letter. I sure hope so.*
>
> *I wish I could provide you with more information about what happened when I last saw them. It was a chaotic scene when they dropped me off at the train station on 21 June. I know the invasion started the next day, but I just don't know if the Germans had made it to Riga by the time your parents were there. It is possible, but I just don't know. It's more likely that the Soviets were still manning the border stations until 24 June, when the Soviets began their retreat. I guess we won't know until we can talk to your parents.*
>
> *On a much less serious note, I've been thinking a lot about the book I want to write, and I think I'd like to write about the Bolshevik Revolution. I've heard about how some of the leaders who first established Communism were accused of treason and imprisoned. Some were forced to confess to crimes they didn't commit. I think there are so many ironies when you think about how the Communists are being accused of betraying the Communists. I think there's a compelling story there. What do you think about that idea?*
>
> *10 July 1941*
>
> *I fell asleep writing last night. I actually started writing my book, so I didn't finish your letter. I decided to keep adding to your letter until I've filled a few pages.*

That way, I'll just write to you as often as I have something to tell you. After the pages are full, I'll mail it so I'm not sending too many letters. I hope that works for you.

It has been a noisy few days here. I thought it was going to be quiet and isolated here. When I first came to the cabin, your Tata showed me around, and he pointed out some large pits. Apparently, they were dug by the Soviets, intended to be oil storage tanks. I'm sure you've seen them because they've been here for a few years. Anyway, the last few days the Germans brought in some heavy equipment and started digging out these storage tanks again. Maybe they're going to use them to store oil, but it looks to me like they are digging them much deeper for some reason. As I look out from the balcony, I can see a few German soldiers, but mostly it's Lithuanians. Most of them have white armbands. I think that means their part of the Lithuanian Activist Front I told you about. They were fighting the Russians, but once the Soviets retreated, these white-arm-banded men started rounding up Jews. Anyway, I'm not sure what to make of it. I can hear a lot of men working in these pits. It's very distracting.

11 July

It was a beautiful day. The weather is warm but not too hot. At about three this afternoon, I heard what sounded like gunshots coming from the forest near the pits. As I went out on the balcony, I was surprised to see a few hundred people out there being herded around by those white armband Lithuanian men carrying rifles. Some of these riflemen appeared to be no older than seventeen or eighteen years old. From what I understand, they belong to the Sauliu Sajunga, or the Shaulists for short. They want to get rid of all the Jews in Lithuania.

Most of the people being herded around are likely to Jews, but a few are not. I assume they are either Communists or Poles. Most of them were men. They are very well dressed. Most were carrying suitcases. About an hour later I could see a group of people taking off their shoes and overcoats, and the Jews were taking off their yarmulkes, but nobody took off their pants. The Shaulists then made about ten of them line up on the edge of the pits, then they started shooting them. These poor souls fell into the pit. I could also see the Shaulists shoot into the pits if they noticed anyone moving. The shooting continued until just before the sun went down, and it finally stopped.

12 July

It started all over again today. By late afternoon, they marched in another big group of mostly Jews into the forest. I would guess there were at least 300 this time, and it was about half men and half women. They appear to be the intelligentsia, because they are well-dressed and appear to be well off financially. After they shoot a group of them, they make the next group shovel dirt over the people they just shot.

So far, I have not seen any Germans doing the shooting. I've seen German officers looking on. Some are even taking pictures. But the Shaulists are doing all the shooting. It has happened for two days in a row now, so I assume it's going to continue. I hope I'm wrong. So far, I don't think they're aware that I'm here. Once they do, who knows what they'll do to me? I'm afraid to leave, but I still need to go to town for groceries.

Frankly, I still can't believe this is happening. Every time I hear a volley of gunfire, I instinctively flinch, terrorized by each gunshot. I wish I knew what I could do to make it stop. If I protested, I would end up at the bottom of that pit. I think the only thing I can do in protest is to be a witness. I will write everything I see with as much detail as possible, then send you a copy. I'll hide another copy outside in the ground. (I'll give you more details later.) That way, if they intercept a letter, there's still a copy here. It will be up to you to protect these letters for posterity.

Somehow, the world needs to be aware of what's happening here. There can be no mistake. This is mass murder, and I'm seeing it happen with my own eyes.

Olek

CHAPTER 15

16 July 1941
Stockholm, Sweden

Since that first exciting letter from Olek, Leva clung to the hope that she would receive regular letters from him. Yet her waiting was in vain. Along with not hearing from Olek again, she still had not heard from her parents. The longer the delay, the more it appeared that something serious had happened to them, but it pained her to think about it.

To help her pass the time, she penned a letter to Olek. Although she knew he asked they not send too many letters, she figured this one letter was worth sending, just to let him know how long it takes for his letters to arrive.

My Dearest Olek,

Since your first letter dated 24 June, I have yet to receive any more letters from you. I thought I'd tell you, so you could calculate how long it takes for a letter to get here.

We still haven't heard anything from my parents. After waiting two weeks from the time they were supposed to arrive, it was clear that they were taken into custody by either the Russians or the Germans. Since we don't know what really happened, we're left to guess. In most scenarios, we just don't want to think about it. It is so hard to think that something could happen to our parents, yet despite our fears, we're not going to give up hope.

The biggest news I have to tell you is that Al left for America yesterday. He took the train to Gothenburg, and in a few days, he'll board a ship bound for New York. Despite my desperate pleas for him to stay, he was determined to go. He's heard so much about America, and nothing I could say would change his mind. Babcia wrote a letter to my Uncle Jouzas a week ago to warn him that Al might be coming. There's a good chance that Al will arrive before that letter does. Al was so determined to go immediately that he was okay with taking his chances that Uncle Jouzas wouldn't be there to greet him at the train station. That's because there are fewer and fewer ships making the transatlantic voyage. If he didn't go now, it's likely there wouldn't be another ship making the trip for the foreseeable future.

It's sad not to have Al here, but he was miserable. He cleared out one of the large bedrooms upstairs and completely refurbished it. He replaced all the rotting wood by taking wood from the walls, floorboards, and trim from other rooms. Babcia was thrilled, but I think Al decided he didn't want to spend the rest of the war fixing up Babcia's house, so that's probably a big reason he wanted to go to America.

I wish I could know more about what you're doing, and how things are going since the Russians left. I understand that you can't tell me much, but that still won't stop me from asking you.

Babcia and I are doing well, and we both try to keep busy working in the gardens or doing some project around this big old castle. Sorry that my life is boring.

I miss you terribly. I would love to hear your voice again and see your beautiful smile. I long to feel your warm caresses. I remember we were walking up and down the sidewalks of Laisves Aleja just before Christmas. It was snowing and we walked and talked and laughed until after midnight. You kept whispering in my ear that you loved me. Those memories keep me going. I can hardly wait to be with you again, and I hope it's very, very soon.

All my love,

Leva

CHAPTER 16

24 July 1941
Novosibirsk, Siberia, USSR

Somewhere outside a place called Cheboksary, Zeneta convinced the people in the bunk below her to trade bunks so Ugna could be nearby. Zeneta helped the best she could to care for Ugna's children, allowing one of the children to sleep on her bunk so Ugna wasn't so crowded. Zeneta also made sure the children could get their share of water and occasionally some soup when it was offered.

The next time the train slowed to a stop, Zeneta peeked between a crack in the wooden slats of the train car. The dazzling city of *Novosibirsk* gleamed after sundown and signaled the final stop of their arduous and fetid trip. Zeneta could see the Ob River bisect the city known as the capital of Siberia.

Being with Ugna and her two children was just what Zeneta needed. She loved having a reason to focus on someone else, rather than her grief. It was therapeutic to cling to the hope that she and Ugna's children would somehow survive their miserable and desperate circumstances. Most of all, helping Ugna and her children gave Zeneta the healing benefits of sacrifice and service.

The travel conditions took a physical toll on all the detainees. With so little to eat or drink, many of the older passengers died, as did some children. Of the others that did survive, they could do little more than sleep the days and nights away.

Getting off the train, the disheveled and emaciated detainees walked for nearly an hour until they arrived at an abandoned cinema. The chairs had been removed, and debris littered the concrete floor. They were instructed to find a place to sleep wherever they could, but with over eight hundred people, there weren't many options.

Seeing the flood of people on the floor, Zeneta took Mykolas by the hand and said, "Come with me. I've got an idea."

As quickly as her tired legs would take her, she walked up the stairs to the balcony. Noticing a secluded corner for the four of them.

"Go tell your mama I've found a better place up here." Zeneta turned him around and directed him toward the stairs, and Mykolas ran down as fast as he could.

"Mama, Zeneta and me found a better place upstairs." He pointed to the staircase.

"Okay, take me there," she said. "Let's see what you and Zeneta found."

Holding Saule by the hand and carrying a small suitcase for each of them, she trudged up the stairs and was bumped and nudged by others who were rushing upstairs to find an open space. Out of breath, she slowed as she finally reached the top.

"She's here somewhere." Mykolas scanned the room, leading his mother and sister by the hand. He led them in the direction of a dark corner by the balcony where he had last seen Zeneta.

"I'm right here, Ugna." Zeneta waved to attract her attention, and Ugna smiled and lifted her head to acknowledge her.

"This should be a little quieter than downstairs." Ugna nodded as she inspected the small corner.

"I even found an old drape we can use for some privacy," Zeneta said. "The only drawback is that the lavatory is downstairs."

"I think I'll like this much better than being downstairs. Hopefully, we won't be here too long."

Zeneta watched as others claimed their space by laying out their tattered blankets and bedding all around them. As people encroached on their little corner, she was losing hope in her plan that most people wouldn't want to deal with the stairs. Within minutes, however, the chaos had lifted, and more people were going down the stairs than were coming up. Once the tired detainees had claimed a place to rest, a stillness soon prevailed throughout the dilapidated theater. Ugna and Mykolas were cuddled up next to each other, and Saule had fallen asleep near Zeneta, and she gently combed Saule's hair with her fingers.

The next morning, Zeneta awoke to a ruckus happening below. As she kneeled to peer over the edge of the balcony, she could see a cluster of women wearing aprons and headscarves, setting up to serve food. A group of them was tending to a dozen or more pots steaming with some type of soup, while another worker carefully hung a clean ladle near each container. Another group was gathered around a table. Loaf after loaf of dark, heavy bread was systematically being torn into smaller chunks. They said nothing to each other as they worked to complete the task.

Ugna awoke and noticed Zeneta on her knees, looking over the rail of the balcony.

"What's going on?" she asked, stroking her messy hair and trying to focus her eyes.

"They've got soup and bread for us. I should probably take Mykolas and get in line." Zeneta smiled at Ugna. "You stay here, and we'll bring you and Saule what we can."

Zeneta reached toward Mykolas and tugged on his shoulder. "Mykolas, wake up. They've got food for us downstairs. Let's go get in line."

Mykolas sat up quickly, looking around, still dazed. "Is there food for us?" he asked, his voice raspy and hoarse.

"Yes, my dear." Ugna reached over and stroked his hair. "Go with Zeneta downstairs and get in line for us, okay?"

Mykolas blinked a few times, still groggy from sleep, then stood and took Zeneta's hand.

When they returned, Mykolas smiled at his mother, grasping a metal cup filled with soup and bread bulging from his coat pocket.

"Mama," Mykolas smiled. "They let me have three pieces of bread." He fumbled around in his coat pocket and retrieved a piece for Saule. She eagerly grabbed it from his hand and took a bite.

"Here's a piece for you, Mama."

Zeneta watched him reach out to his mother. His proud smile brought tears to Ugna's eyes.

"Thank you, son," Ugna beamed. "That was kind of you."

"They should have enough for everyone." Zeneta handed a piece of bread from her pocket and gave it to Ugna. "Here, you want some soup?"

Ugna nodded and took a sip from Zeneta's cup. "It's good. Maybe it's because I'm so hungry that anything with a little flavor seems like a gourmet meal."

They both laughed softly.

A Russian guard arrived at the top of the stairs. He held a small clipboard with some notes. He cleared his throat and said, "I need everyone to listen closely. I'll only say this once. You will be staying here for a few days until we can finish preparing your barracks in a settlement camp on the outskirts of town. While you are here, we will bring you two meals per day. You are not allowed to leave this theater for any reason. If you do, you will be arrested and sent to a gulag."

The guard glared at some detainees to emphasize his point. "There are no exceptions."

CHAPTER 17

7 August 1941
Ponary, German-Occupied Lithuania

Like most evenings, Olek listened to the hidden shortwave radio after dark because the reception was best at night.

When he initially found the radio, he spent much of his day listening to the official German radio and then comparing that news to the BBC's German Service broadcasts. These BBC broadcasts were transmitted daily in English, German, French, Italian, Dutch, Hungarian, as well as other languages he understood, like Polish, Russian, and Lithuanian.

At first, it was confusing to hear conflicting versions of the news. But it didn't take long before he came to rely on the candor of the BBC broadcasts that weren't afraid to report on all things newsworthy, even if it was unflattering to the British. He was surprised by the Western style of reporting, as these daily programs not only covered European news, but he could hear reliable war-related reports, including British, German, and Soviet casualties. He learned about the abundant types of food available in London stores and restaurants because food shortages throughout Europe were becoming worse. He liked to listen to the comedy sketches, although he didn't understand many of the English words, he could tell by the way the audience laughed that they were making fun of Hitler.

One morning, about two weeks into his stay at the cabin, Olek sat down to finish his letter to Leva.

> *Since my last letter, the shooting has continued almost every day. The shooting sometimes goes late into the night. Some nights you can tell when someone tries to escape because I'll hear gunfire at random times throughout the night.*
>
> *As I've said before, I can see almost everything from my vantage point, so it's not hard to notice when people come and go. But it also means I'm able to count all the people who are shot each day. I keep a daily record of what's going on here in the nearby forest. I keep notes of what I hear, what I see, and if I hear something from anyone else, I include their comments in my notes. Every few weeks, I've hidden these detailed notes in a vodka bottle, sealed it with wax, and buried it in a safe and protected place. Hopefully, they will be found by the right people should something happen to me.*
>
> *I have yet to receive any letters from you, so I don't know if you are getting my letters. I'll keep writing to you until I hear otherwise.*
>
> *Don't forget that I love you and miss you terribly.*
> *Olek*

The next morning, Olek mounted his bicycle and made his way toward Vaidotai to drop off his letter to Leva and buy some much-needed groceries.

After dropping his letter off at the post office, he walked into the store.

"I wondered if I'd ever see you again!" Max welcomed Olek with a smile. "Haven't seen you in over a month. I wondered if sooner or later you'd stop by to restock your pantry."

"I was running out of a lot of things," Olek said with a nervous laugh. "I need potatoes, onions, vodka, and flour."

"I'll be happy to help," Max said as he collected the items for Olek. "Why haven't you come sooner?"

Olek cleared his throat. "I have to be careful about being out and about."

"Why's that?" Max gave Olek a confused glance.

Olek wanted to say something to someone, but he didn't know whom he could trust. Max seemed trustworthy, and Matis and Zeneta spoke highly of him. Still, one slip-up and he could find himself in serious trouble.

"Well, I just have to be careful about . . ." Olek paused. "running into some of those *Shaulists* and Nazis that seem to be everywhere out there near my place."

Max shot Olek with a baffled glare. "*Shaulists* and Nazis? What are you talking about?"

Olek checked behind him to make sure he was the only customer in the store.

"You know what I mean when I say Shaulists, right? The *Sauliu Sajunga?* The white armband mercenaries who have been rounding up Jews?"

"Oh. Of course. I see them in here all the time."

"I figured you would. Did you know those Nazi trucks have been hauling Jews out to the forests near my place every day and shooting them one by one?"

"What?" Max's eyes bulged; he stared in disbelief.

"The bodies fall into these huge pits that were originally dug by the Soviets for oil storage tanks."

Max gasped in disbelief. "I see those trucks all the time. How do you know they're not just hauling around Nazi troops?"

"I can see it from my balcony," Olek said. "I've watched these *Shaulists* make the victims strip down to their underwear. Then all the clothing is taken to a nearby barn and sorted. They've got a little side business selling the victims' clothes to the residents of the local villages. They'll sell a sack of clothing for 100 rubles each. And the locals are very aware that these clothes belong to Jews, Poles, and Communists, but they don't care."

Max gasped in disbelief. "And this is happening near your place?"

"Yes! It all started on July 11, and all through the end of July, I've counted roughly five thousand people they've brought in that didn't come out. And from what I can tell," Olek said in a near whisper, "most of the prisoners come from the *Lukiškės* Prison in Vilnius."

"Where did you hear that?" Max asked.

"On the radio," Olek said. "I can also hear them talking to each other. I hear men crying, women screaming for mercy. Max, you have to believe me. I'm not making this up."

Max couldn't hide his skepticism, not wanting to believe him.

"I've seen it with my own eyes. The Nazis just watch and do nothing. Some of the officers take notes, but as far as I can tell, it's been Lithuanians shooting other Lithuanians."

Max gazed at the floor, nervously rubbing his upper arm as he struggled to process the terrifying scene Olek was describing.

"You can't say a word, Max, or I'm a dead man." Olek eyed Max with desperation. "If they know I'm a witness, I'll end up in one of those pits."

Max stared at Olek slack jawed. "Why are you sticking around? You need to leave. Now!"

"I have no place else to go."

"But why are you telling me?" Max asked with a bit of protest in his voice, not wanting the responsibility of knowing what was happening.

Olek's voice cracked with nervousness. "You're the only one I know."

They stood in awkward silence.

"I'm sorry to lay this on you, but I had to tell someone because the situation is changing so fast. Nobody is safe. Nobody is exempt from being targeted."

Olek sensed Max's discomfort but had to finish making his argument. "It's only going to get worse," Olek said. "I know that doesn't sound possible after the hell we went through with the Soviets. The Nazis are just getting started. Did you hear that the Nazis imposed a fine on all the Jews of five million rubles? If the Jews don't come up with the money by today, they will execute all the Jewish leaders in Vilnius."

Max stood in stunned silence. He ran his hand through his hair, exasperated.

"On the radio last night, they said the Nazis just removed the Lithuanian military government and replaced it with a new German civilian administration. So much for giving back Lithuania its independence."

"You better be careful with listening to that radio," Max gave Olek a stern glare. "I heard the Nazis are looking for shortwave radios and they've threatened to execute anyone found with one."

Olek contemplated the thought of Nazis searching his house for his radio. "I had no idea they—" Olek's head turned instantly as another customer opened the door.

Max leaned over to Olek and said, "We can talk later."

Olek paid for his groceries and gathered them in his knapsack, his hands shaking with fear.

CHAPTER 18

17 August 1941
Novosibirsk, Siberia, USSR

Zeneta, Ugna, and her children shared a barracks with four beds. When they first arrived at this settlement camp on 24 July, they were assigned two middle-aged Estonian women as their bunkmates. The next day, the two women moved out to live with another Estonian family in a different building. So far, the supervisors either didn't know or didn't care that only four people were in a room, instead of six, like all the other barracks.

Each of the ten rooms in the barracks was sparse. Between the sixty residents, they shared two common washrooms, each with a basin, a toilet, and a shower. Each barrack also had a small kitchen to prepare food with a single stove and not much else.

The morning after their arrival, Ugna was forced to leave her children with Zeneta, as everyone aged sixteen to fifty was needed to walk to a field somewhere and dig irrigation ditches. Each was issued a shovel and was told to dig at least four meters per day or face being beaten by one of the guards. Ugna's hands were covered in blisters, but she had to return the next five days or risk being assigned an even more difficult assignment in the nearby brick factory.

As September rolled around, the nights suddenly turned bitterly cold, and the ground was too hard for ditch digging. When Ugna showed up for work, she and the other workers were led to the brick factory and given jobs according to their strength and size. Ugna was assigned to stacking bricks onto a train car with seven other Lithuanian women. It was back-breaking work that took a toll on Ugna's health. She was petite before she was captured by the Soviets, but she was becoming even thinner and frailer with each passing day.

Zeneta did her best to keep Mykolas and Saule busy while Ugna was away working. The children had cleaning assignments and couldn't go outside and play with other children until they finished their work.

Ugna was paid nothing for working in the factory, leaving Zeneta to turn to a vigorous black market to buy or trade for food. Zeneta used the rubles she had sewn into the seams of her clothing. She was also a shrewd negotiator, obtaining flour, along with some oil, a few potatoes, and even some rice that helped feed the four of them. Others who didn't have any cash were forced to trade their jewelry, furs, and even shoes to get the food they needed.

As autumn temperatures plummeted, wood and coal grew to be more valuable and difficult to find. Because the barracks were unheated, residents spent much of their time in the kitchen huddling around the stove, even if it wasn't their turn to cook. Most shared in the cost of keeping the stove fired up throughout the day until after everyone had gone to bed. Those who gave little or no wood or coal were ostracized and became a constant source of contention. The freeloaders were made to leave the warmth of the kitchen until they contributed to the cause.

Sunday was Ugna's only day to recover both in mind and spirit from the toll of such physically demanding work. But it was also the day that all detainees were required to attend a political lecture in a nearby theater.

Finding a seat in the sizable theater, Zeneta and Ugna sat with Mykolas and Saule between them. The lecturer was a Soviet officer wearing a button-down khaki green tunic with red trim and a leather belt with a square brass buckle that framed the Soviet star. Medals covered his chest.

The room was quiet because they had been warned to be respectful to the Soviet officer or risk severe punishment.

The officer said, "The bloodthirsty fascist rulers in Germany have embarked upon this great patriotic war by attacking our beloved homeland. We refuse to allow these predators to erase the gains we have made against similar exploiters like landowners, capitalists, and the tsars, whose goal was to enslave the working class.

"As our great leader, Comrade Josef Stalin, has declared, 'The distinctiveness of today's Soviet society is unlike any capitalist society because there are no more antagonistic and hostile classes in it. We have liquidated the exploiting classes that once existed, and now our Soviet society lives and works based on friendly cooperation. While capitalist societies are torn apart by irreconcilable contradictions between workers and capitalists, between peasants and landowners, which leads to the instability of their internal situation, Soviet society is freed from the yoke of exploitation. We no longer face such glaring contradictions, as we are free from class conflicts, and that will always plague the capitalists and fascists who oppose us'."

Zeneta turned her head slowly to Ugna and rolled her eyes, trying to hide her slight smile.

"Imagine how difficult it was for the Soviet state to build a formidable army after having so recently been devastated by the imperialist war and the subsequent civil war. We Soviets made the necessary sacrifices to build our army into a significant force with heroic strength. It was the Soviet Army that refused to allow the aggressive Finnish White Guards to prevail in their illegal land grab in 1939 and 1940. They have since shown their criminal tendencies by joining with the fascist Germans and attacking our beloved Soviet lands. It wasn't long ago that the Soviet army sacrificed itself to liberate the peoples of Western Belarus and Ukraine, Bessarabia, Estonia, Latvia, and Lithuania."

Zeneta covered her mouth, fighting the urge to chuckle at his silly propaganda, but suddenly realized she was at risk if someone nearby noticed her laughing in disbelief.

"With the cry 'For the Motherland, for Stalin, and for the brave fighters,' the Red Army is now demolishing the fascist Germans, along with their evil co-conspirators, and removing them from our country. It is because of you, the workers, who have volunteered to contribute your time and efforts to the cause, that we are now successful.

"It will not be long before we can end this subscription to the state loan, and we'll be able to pay off that loan and reinstitute the salary payments made to the workers who have so willingly sacrificed themselves at this critical time. The state will continue to give you a home to live in, but it is still necessary to mobilize all our efforts in the service of the army. We are relying on your continued efforts to work on collective farms and state factories to build our defense capabilities, because although we are succeeding, our work is not complete.

"When history is written, it will be said of the great people of the USSR that you gave all your efforts, resources, and energy to defeating the enemy. As this inevitable great victory nears, our great family of peoples will rally around the great Soviet government, around our benevolent and powerful Communist Bolshevik Party, and our wise and gracious leader, our Comrade Stalin."

As the officer sat, the audience nervously applauded, fearing retribution from the hovering Soviet guards.

Three more officers stood to speak, each repeating the call for greater sacrifices from the heroic working class to strengthen the Red Army and guarantee their success.

As they returned to their barracks, Ugna held her children's hands but said nothing, looking only at the ground, her eyebrows furrowed as they walked. Zeneta noticed her and said, "Don't let it bother you. You can't trust a thing they say."

"Oh, I know it's all lies, but I still look forward to the day when I'm no longer a slave working for my family instead of for the glory of the Soviet Union."

Zeneta didn't reply. She didn't want to give Ugna false hope that someday she would not be forced to work for nothing. She also didn't want to ruin the small scrap of hope Ugna clung to, that her situation would improve once the war ended.

The next Friday, after another long week, Ugna came home after work. Zeneta was quick to notice Ugna's clothes were not as dirty as usual and that she was walking with a skip in her step.

"Why are you so happy?"

"They told me today I don't have to work loading bricks anymore," Ugna said, hugging her children. "The supervisor is this nice, middle-aged man who called me into his office and asked if I had any experience in an office. I told him I could type and do bookkeeping, and he told me my new job was being his assistant."

"That's wonderful news." Zeneta smiled awkwardly, then asked, "And you trust this man?"

Ugna paused. Knowing the true answer had been thrust far into the back of her mind. As she walked out of his office, she knew the supervisor's eyes had lingered too long when he'd offered her the position. That familiar, appraising look—she'd seen it before, from guards at checkpoints and soldiers who came to inspect their barracks. The way he'd commented on her "delicate hands" being better suited for office work than hauling bricks. The casual brush of his fingers against hers when handing her the paperwork.

"You'll be perfect for this position," he said, his eyes holding hers a beat too long. Warning bells rang softly in her mind, but her desperation shoved them aside. Her hands were already broken and bleeding from weeks of loading the heavy bricks. Just yesterday, she almost collapsed from exhaustion. Her vision darkened at the edges as she struggled to gain her bearings. The doctor had warned her—women her size weren't meant for such hard physical labor. Without better nutrition, her petite body would fail within weeks.

And the children—what would happen to them then? A desk job meant survival. It meant better food. It meant warmth in the coming winter. She had handled compromising situations before. Besides, maybe these red flags were just a fleeting impression," she whispered to herself. "Maybe I'm wrong."

For now, she had to think of Mykolas and Saule. But even as she said it, she knew. Women in camps learned to recognize certain truths without being told. The knowledge settled into her bones like the Siberian cold—inescapable, inevitable.

"I have to trust him. What other choice do I have?" Ugna protested, tears welling up in her eyes.

"He has three teenage daughters! He also doesn't seem to be one of those Communist cheerleaders." She chuckled awkwardly at her own words.

Zeneta could sense the discomfort in her voice, understanding fully that Ugna was clever enough to know that this new position was a calculated risk.

"I can't tell you how glad I am I don't have to work so hard anymore." Ugna rubbed the calluses on her hands. "But he said he would train me how to do my job, and he even said he could make sure I get extra food and wood if I worked hard."

Zeneta's eyebrows raised with hope. "That would be nice, wouldn't it?"

Ugna was relieved that she could finally provide something to help support her children and not rely on Zeneta for everything. Yet was it all too good to be true?

"I feel so bad that you keep giving so much to keep us going. I want to be able to contribute something."

"You've given me a purpose in life, Ugna," Zeneta took Ugna's hand in hers. "Before I met you, I was about to give up. I had no reason to keep going."

"You're like my second mother." A few tears fell from the corner of Ugna's eyes. "I rely on you for everything. I'd have never made it without you."

Zeneta smiled. "We'll make it through this. We're tough old Lithuanians."

CHAPTER 19

4 September 1941
Ponary, Nazi-Occupied Lithuania

As was his routine, Olek awoke and ate breakfast, then prepared to write his journal entry for the previous day. As he took out his notebook, he noticed he had only a page left to describe the unusual events he saw that still needed to be documented. He wrote in small, deliberate letters to make sure he could squeeze in everything he wanted to say.

Wednesday, 3 September

It was a miserable, windy, and overcast day. The rain was heavy, but despite the weather, I was awoken to shots ringing out at 7 in the morning. Unusually early.

At about 7:30, I could see out on the main road a long procession of people at least two kilometers long. As I watched them trudge their way toward Ponary, I could tell they were exhausted. Even though the Shaulists were yelling at them, it didn't appear they were able to walk any faster. As they grew nearer, I could tell that generally these people were Jews, mostly by the way they were dressed, as the men were wearing yarmulkes. But there weren't that many men. (I can only assume that there weren't many men because they have killed mostly men over the past two months.) This group consisted primarily of women and children, many with young babies still in diapers. This is the largest group I've ever seen on a single day. I estimate there are between two to three thousand Jews in total.

As I understand it from a radio bulletin, this large group of Jews was rounded up in response to an incident on Sunday (31 August) where they claimed some German soldiers were attacked by two Jews. The two culprits were summarily killed, but the bulletin also said that no Germans were hurt. Still, the Nazi officer in charge wanted to make an example of these two "cowardly bandits," to avoid such attacks in the future. He said the "responsibility (for the attack) lies with the entire Jewish community."

Monday and Tuesday, the Nazis report said they have removed almost 40,000 Jews from their homes and forced them into a ghetto. Roughly six thousand Jews were taken to Lukiškės prison. Today, about half of them were marched here to Ponary.

As the long line of people approached the pits, many of them began to understand what was going to happen. Some were calling out in desperation, "Help us!" and "Please don't do this!"

I counted about eighty to a hundred Shaulists who were lined up to do the shooting. Another hundred or so were guarding the fence that surrounded the pits. Many of the Shaulists were still drunk from the night before, so some of the women were beaten and brutalized while they stood in line. The men were taken to another pit, so they were out of sight of the women. The women, however, were forced to take off their clothes and stand in their underwear. Many of these women had expensive clothes. Some even had furs because they believed they were being moved from their homes to the new ghetto. Others had jewelry and other valuables. I'm sure there will be many local women who will be dressing well after today.

With the Germans now exerting their authority, they are proving to be fast learners. They are implementing the lessons they learned from watching how the Shaulists have been able to round up Jews without a mass revolt. By depriving Jews of food, water, and sleep, then forcing them to march to the point of physical exhaustion, they can control the Jews more easily. Some of the Jews seem to be resigned to their fate.

The shooting was constant throughout the day, and continued until late after dark, almost to ten. I could see them using the headlights from some trucks to illuminate the pits so they could finish the job.

Olek removed his journal pages from his notebook and gently rolled them up so they would fit into a vodka bottle. He had already washed the bottle and left it to dry, just to make sure no moisture spoiled his papers. After sealing the bottle with the cork, he lit a candle and dripped the wax over it to ensure the bottle was completely sealed.

The door to the shed creaked as he opened it. He shut the door just enough to see what he was doing inside. The ground was softened after he had previously dug a hole to hide his first bottle that held his initial journal entry.

Using a small hand shovel, he lifted the soil, carefully stacking it nearby. Once the hole was sufficiently deep, he placed the bottle in the hole and quickly piled the dirt over it. He then tamped it down with his feet to pack it tight. He reached for the rake and did his best to blend the freshly dug dirt with the surrounding soil. Finally, he lifted two heavy earthen planters over the site to disguise it even further.

As he stood to admire his work, something outside caught his attention. He held his breath to listen for any commotion. He was convinced he heard footsteps in the overgrown grass. Terrified, he bobbed his head back and forth, looking through the small crack in the door to see whatever was outside. After a few tense moments, he stepped cautiously toward the door, listening intently for any other sounds. Hearing nothing, he tiptoed toward the door, careful not to touch it so the squeaky hinges would give away his presence. As the minutes passed without hearing anything, his heart felt like it was about to burst. As he mustered the courage to step outside, he breathed a deep sigh, comforted that nobody was waiting for him.

As his breathing returned to normal, he inspected the grass around the shed. About to chide himself for his wild imagination, his heart jumped at seeing some grass compressed with footsteps. Spinning himself in a circle searching for the culprit, he saw nothing. Then he realized he could have made the impression with his steps, but he couldn't remember. Walking out to the shed, his mind was preoccupied with burying the bottle, so he couldn't recall the exact path he took to the shed.

With only this single impression in the grass, Olek walked back to the house with care, searching for any other evidence of someone nearby. As he opened the back door, he shook his head and said to himself, "I must be going crazy."

CHAPTER 20

11 October 1941
Stockholm, Sweden

Babcia knocked on her bedroom door. "Leva, are you awake? It's ten o'clock in the morning."

Leva said nothing, covering her head with her blanket, hoping to disappear.

Babcia opened the door.

"Leva, honey." Her gentle voice landed soothing and kind in Leva's ears. "You can't spend all day in bed again. You have to get going."

Babcia sat on the bed next to Leva, caressing her hair. "I know you're sad. But you can't just stop living."

"Why?" Leva's voice croaked, and she cleared her throat. "What's to live for? Everyone important to me has—"

Babcia interrupted. "Everyone? And I'm just an unimportant nobody?"

Leva removed the covers from her head and sat up on her elbow. "Babcia, you know what I mean. I miss my parents. I miss Olek. And I miss Al a lot more than I ever thought possible. I've gotten no letters, no telegrams. Nothing. I don't know if they're dead or alive."

Babcia continued to run her fingers through Leva's hair. "Why won't Olek write to me? He said he would. Why won't Al write to us? He's been gone for almost three months."

"It just takes time for letters to arrive from overseas." Babcia tried to be encouraging. "You just have to be patient. I've heard letters from America can take six months."

Leva lifted her feet to the floor, stopping herself from bringing up the subject of her missing parents. It was just too painful.

"I'm sorry that things have worked out this way." Babcia tried to be comforting yet firm. "But do you think your parents would want you to just lie around and do nothing? I understand that you're sad. You have every right to be. But do you think your father would want you to sit around feeling sorry for yourself, or would he tell you to get off your arse and do something productive?"

Ieva couldn't help herself, and she smirked at Babcia's uncharacteristic word choice. "I don't think he'd say arse," she joked.

"He'd probably say the real word. Plus a few more I don't dare say or you'd think a lot less of me."

"You can swear all you want, Babcia. I'd never think any less of you." She reached toward Babcia and gave her a thankful embrace.

Ieva watched the postman stop at their mailbox and deposit a letter. She dashed outside. Opening the mailbox, she instantly recognized the red and blue alternating colors on the edge of the envelope, the words "air mail" emblazoned in blue. She hesitated as she saw the return address from "Algirdas Barsauskas," but then realized that was his new identity since leaving Lithuania. The postmark was a little blurred, but the words "Chicago, Ill." were clear.

Caring little about tearing the envelope apart, she pulled out a one-page letter. Al's sloppy penmanship made her smile.

31 August 1941

Dear Ieva

Well, I finally made it to America. It took me a little longer than I expected. Our ship had to make a stop in England to make some repairs. We spent a few days in Southampton, and I met a cute little British girl at a pub. It was hard to say goodbye to her. After a long journey across the Atlantic, we arrived in New York, and I spent a few days there figuring out the best train to Chicago. I arrived about a week ago.

I love Chicago. It's amazing. Uncle Jouzas says there are almost a hundred thousand Lithuanians here in Chicago. It's called Little Lithuania because there are the most Lithuanians here except for Lithuania.

Uncle Jouzas told me I had to pay rent. I'm happy to contribute. He said I could get a job at the meat-packing plant because they're always hiring, and they especially like Lithuanians. Instead, I got a job at a place called Southport Bowling Lanes. It's just around the corner from our house. I'm a pin setter. I set up the pins whenever someone knocks them down. I have to work fast, or else the bowlers are upset. They pay me thirty-five cents an hour. I started at twenty cents the first day I started. That's because they thought I was only sixteen years old. When I told them I was twenty, they made me a supervisor over the other pin setters. So far, I like it.

What amazes me about America is how big it is. Everything is so spread out. The streets are wider. The cars are bigger. Oh, and their food is really good. I've tried a hot dog, a hamburger, fried potatoes, which they call French fries, and pizza. It's all very tasty, and I think I've gained weight since I got here.

Leva, you should come here. You would love it. There's enough room in the house, and Uncle Jouzas said he'd love to have you, as long as you paid some rent. Think it over and let me know so I can make the arrangements. If you don't want to leave Babcia all alone, I understand, even though she's lived on her own all these years before we got there.

Have you heard anything from Mama and Tata? What about Olek? Write to me soon.

Love,

Al

After reading the letter to Babcia, Leva looked at her. Babcia looked down. "I've lived on my own before. I can do it again."

"But what about taking care of this place? There's just so much that needs to be done."

"I've got enough help, I'll be okay."

Leva contemplated Al's proposal to go to America, then shook her head. She just wasn't ready to go on such an adventure. "It may be safe for Al to travel alone, but it's a different thing for a girl like me."

Babcia nodded. "Well, you do what you think is best."

"What I do like about what Al said was the idea of getting a job. Maybe that's what I need to do to keep myself busy and occupy my thoughts with other things besides missing everyone so much. I think it would be good for me. Don't you?"

"Unquestionably," Babcia said. "And if you're serious, I have a friend who's looking to hire a waitress at her restaurant. It's not that far away. You could probably walk there."

"A waitress?" Leva's eyes lit up with excitement. "I could do that. I'm sure it's a lot of work, but I'd get accustomed to it."

"I'm sure she'd be happy to teach you everything you need to know."

CHAPTER 21

17 November 1941
Novosibirsk, Siberia, USSR

The bitter, autumn air grew even colder with the dwindling daylight hours. The constant bitter winds swept through the barracks, making it miserable for Mykolas and especially Saule to keep warm at night. Despite wearing layers of clothes to bed, their thin, cotton blankets were no match for the Siberian weather.

After three nights of listening to Saule cry herself to sleep because she was cold, Zeneta stood and lifted Saule from her bed and put her down next to her to share each other's warmth and blankets. After a while, Saule drifted off to sleep.

Lying in the cold, Zeneta devised a plan to find warmer blankets for the children. She had seen others in her barracks with surplus army blankets and hoped to find out where they got them.

In the morning, she learned where she could buy or trade for the wool blankets. The man who sold them lived nearby, but he had a reputation for striking a hard bargain. She planned to take the two children, hoping their faces would wear down his resolve.

She waited until Ugna left for the factory, then said, "Mykolas, Saule, do you want to go on an adventure?"

"Where are we going?" Mykolas asked politely.

"To see a man about getting some blankets for you two."

Mykolas turned to Saule with wide eyes. "Really? For us?"

Zeneta smiled as she touched his head kindly. "Yes, you need a good blanket."

"Is that because you don't want to help me get warm at night anymore?" Saule's voice was laced with disappointment.

"No, dear. That's not the reason. It's because I want you to sleep better and not be so cold at night."

Saule smiled and buttoned up her coat.

After walking for half an hour, they approached a sea of three-story concrete apartments. The buildings appeared to be shabbily constructed—likely, Zeneta thought, because the Soviets were still rapidly expanding their industrialization efforts. Zeneta couldn't help but wonder how much the rent would be to live here. Probably nothing by the looks of them. She had read somewhere that the Soviets provided farmers with a small, sparsely furnished apartment. This was because the Soviets had stripped them of their homes and farms. After all, they outlawed ownership of private property. She wondered how these people adjusted to this gray and dark city and living in these hideous, tiny apartments.

After trudging through the footworn snow path, past one concrete building after another, at long last, they found the right building. They stepped into a dark, wet stairwell, expecting to be protected from the breeze, but found it was still even colder. At the top of two flights of wind-blown stairs, Zeneta squinted in the poorly lit hallway to better read the apartment numbers. Saule and Mykolas clung to her. At last, they noticed the apartment at the end of the hall. Zeneta knocked gently on the hollow wooden door.

When they had waited for a moment, Mykolas shuffled his feet. "Let's go."

"Let's give them a chance to answer the door. They may not be expecting any visitors."

They heard the dead bolt clank. The door opened a few inches, and a round elderly woman wearing a headscarf said, "How can I help you?"

"I understand you may have some surplus wool blankets for sale?" Instantly, the door shut tight.

Zeneta stepped back with surprise, turning to the children about to leave when she heard the rattle of the door's safety chain, and the door flung open.

"Come in, please," the woman said with a heavy dialect she could only assume was Mongolian. "My husband will help you."

Just then, a man's voice rang out abruptly from the darkness of the back room. "How many do you want? They're a thousand rubles each."

Looking in the man's direction, Zeneta could see his silhouette but not his face.

"I'd like to see one to see if they're worth a thousand rubles."

He disappeared for a moment, then returned with a small blanket rolled up as if it had just taken off a soldier's rucksack.

"A hundred percent wool. Made in Romania. See how soft it is?"

Zeneta reached out and stroked the wool blanket, sizing it up to see if it would cover her bed. She nodded to Mykolas and Saule. "Feel it for yourself. Both of you. See if you like it or not because they're for you. If you don't like it, there's no sense paying a thousand rubles apiece."

"It's kind of soft, even if it feels a little itchy," Saule whispered.

Zeneta caressed her shoulder. "That's very nice of you, Saule. What about you, Mykolas?" she asked. "What do you think?"

"It's nice," he said, feigning enthusiasm. "It's a lot better than what I've got."

Zeneta turned to the man. "What's your best price for four?"

The man rubbed his chin, then glanced at his wife. "We have four, but I don't give discounts."

Zeneta stared at her feet as she thought of her next strategy, "Would you be willing to trade?"

"Depends on what?"

"How much do you know about jewelry?" Zeneta held her gaze.

"Enough to get by. Why? What do you have?"

Zeneta reached into her pocket and grasped the piece of jewelry, but before pulling it out for him to inspect, she said, "This belonged to my grandmother. It's made of fourteen-carat gold, and it's worth at least ten thousand rubles if it's worth a kopek. But I need blankets for these two children."

She produced a gold brooch from her pocket, and the man's eyes lit up. "It was made in 1821."

The man stepped closer to inspect it.

"I sewed it into the seam of my coat when the Soviets first—" She stopped herself from saying too much. "Those two small diamonds are not quite a carat each. That big central diamond has two carats. We had it appraised a few years ago. In today's rubles, it would be worth about twelve to fifteen thousand."

The man looked at Zeneta. "Can I see it?"

She put it in his hand. He looked closely, then turned it over to study the inscription on the back. "Why would you trade this for four blankets if it's worth fifteen thousand rubles?"

"Because it's doing me no good now when we need these warm blankets to stay alive. And we expect that it's only going to get colder."

The man continued to examine the brooch. His wife interrupted. "We'll take it. And we'll throw in four pairs of gloves too. Although we don't have children's gloves, maybe you can trade them for some gloves more their size."

"That's very kind of you." Zeneta reached out and hugged the woman. "I can't say thank you enough."

The man retrieved the blankets and gloves from a hall closet. Saying nothing, he handed the items to Zeneta, then held out his hand to receive the brooch.

"Here you go." Zeneta turned to the children. "Tell these two good people goodbye and thank you."

Mykolas and Saule waved, saying goodbye in near unison.

As the door closed, Zeneta said, "Do me a favor. Tell your mother these people gave us the blankets and the gloves because they were kind. You don't have to say anything about the jewelry. That's our little secret. Okay?"

When Ugna arrived home, the children were excited to show off their new blankets.

"Look what Zeneta got for us today," Saule beamed.

"Where did you get those?" Ugna took a blanket from Saule to inspect it. "That's a nice blanket."

Mykolas answered. "Saule and me went to see some people, and they gave us the blankets. And look at this, we got gloves too."

Ugna glanced at Zeneta to verify his story.

Zeneta's face gave nothing away.

"That's what happened. We heard a man and his wife had some surplus military blankets, so we went to see them. We got a really good deal, didn't we?" She dipped her chin, eying the children with a subtle prompt. They both responded with a nod.

"Well, I have good news too," Ugna said, jumping in place. "My boss told me today that he would allow us to write a letter home, and he would make sure it got approved by the censors and sent in the official mail pouch."

Zeneta's knees grew weak, and she rushed to sit on her bed.

Ugna smiled at her. "He said he would do it this once, and he said I need to bring the letters tomorrow."

"Can I write Leva in Sweden? Or does it have to go to someone in Lithuania?"

"He knows your children are living with your mother-in-law in Stockholm, so I'm sure he expects you to write to them," Ugna said.

Zeneta's mind raced about what she could tell her children that would not catch the attention of the censors. How was she going to tell Leva and Al about the death of their father? And after all the threats about their not disclosing their location to anyone, how was she going to give convincing clues that she was in Siberia? They have no idea she was in the Soviet Union. She certainly can't say she's in Siberia. She can't even say they were arrested by the Soviets. She settled on writing a cryptic letter. She figured they were smart enough to read between the lines.

Zeneta crossed her arms and locked her ankles as she thought. Ugna watched as Zeneta's mind raced. "We must be very careful about what we say," Ugna said. "If our letters end up getting my boss in trouble, I'll lose my job... or worse. It's safer if we say as little as possible."

Zeneta uncrossed her arms and smiled. "I agree. That makes sense to me."

"I'll go ask one of the neighbors if they can give us paper."

A month after the letters were sent, Ugna arrived home late again. This time, two hours after Zeneta had already put the children to bed.

Zeneta could see Ugna's eyes were red and puffy. Strands of her hair were dangling out of her usually tidy bun. Her shoulders drooped as she struggled to speak, but she couldn't utter a word.

"Is everything okay?"

Tears welled up in Ugna's eyes as she sat on the edge of her bed. Zeneta sat next to Ugna and put her arm around her. "What happened? Tell me. Please."

Ugna wiped her nose, then burst into tears. "I'm so ashamed. But I had no choice."

"What happened? Tell me."

Ugna sobbed as she fought to collect her emotions. She sniffed and dabbed her nose with her handkerchief.

Zeneta said softly, "Take a deep breath and tell me what happened."

Ugna paused for a moment, then said, "He told me that if I report it, he will report me to the police and say I have stolen from the government, and he would see to it that I get sent to a gulag, or maybe I'd even hang for it."

"Report what? You mean our letters?"

"No. My supervisor—that he was making me have…" she hesitated. "Intimate relations with him."

"What?"

"Tonight?" Zeneta said with a gasp, both hands were quick to cover her mouth.

"It's been going on for a month now. It started the day we gave him our letters."

Zeneta covered her mouth in shock.

"That's not the worst of it," Ugna again struggled to stop sobbing so she could talk. "I am two weeks late for my period."

CHAPTER 22

1 December 1941
Ponary, Nazi-Occupied Lithuania

What had changed over the past month was the uniforms. During November, the *Shaulists* were no longer wearing their old uniforms but now wearing Gestapo uniforms. While he couldn't be sure they were the same people, he could see that many behaved similarly in their cruelty toward Jewish women and children.

He could also hear when someone tried to escape. Once the Jews realized they had arrived at Ponary, some would dash into the forest. Most wouldn't make it very far before being shot.

Throughout the day, some people were shot but not mortally wounded, yet they still fell into the pit and pretended to be dead. If it were early in the day, most would suffocate under the crush of bodies from later killings. If it were late in the day, they had a better chance of staying hidden among all the bodies until the *Shaulists* and the Nazis left for the day. In the darkness, they would crawl out of the pits and make their way through the forest, hoping to find the anti-Nazi partisans living nearby. Most who escaped were unable to make the arduous trip, and their bodies were found in the forest. A few, however, managed to find the partisans and were eventually nursed back to health.

After Olek finished his last journal entry for November, he readied another vodka bottle to seal the papers inside. Then he applied the wax to further seal it from the elements, put on his coat, and headed outside to the shed.

The morning hoarfrost was yet to melt in the early morning sun. On his path to the shed, his feet left distinct footprints in the overgrown grass that had turned brown and dry.

Repeating the process of the last two months, he removed the earthen planter and dug the frozen earth to reveal the previous bottles holding his journal entries. After tamping down the dirt, raking it, and replacing the planters, he turned to leave and stumbled on the rake, stepping on an old, folded tarpaulin. From beneath the tarp, a small voice gave a strained, high-pitched whimper.

Instinctively, he grabbed the shovel with both hands, ready to swing it to defend himself.

"Come out," he said. "Show yourself now, or I'll stab you with this shovel."

"No!" the tiny voice begged. "Don't hurt me."

Olek used the end of the shovel to lift the tarp just enough to reveal a small, gaunt-looking boy who was naked except for his underwear.

"Please don't hurt me." The boy's bony arms and bloody hands were raised above his head.

Olek put his shovel down and lifted the tarp completely off him, revealing his abdomen covered in blood from a gunshot wound. The dark, bloody wound had stopped bleeding, but the boy clenched his stomach as he lowered his arms.

Olek looked at the boy's emaciated face and sunken stomach. His eyes widened, assuming he was about to be killed at any moment.

"I'm not going to hurt you. Come inside with me." Olek's voice was soft, and his eyes were wet with pity at seeing this small skeleton of a child. "I promise I won't hurt you. Will you come with me inside? It is much warmer." Olek motioned toward the house.

The boy's nod was barely perceptible, yet enough that Olek reached out his hand to help him. The boy refused. He wanted to stand without help, despite wincing in pain.

"I'll take care of you. Come with me."

Olek took off his coat and wrapped it around the boy, who stepped barefoot out of the shed and toward the back door. The boy shuffled along carefully, ignoring the frozen grass as if he had no sense of feeling in his feet.

Olek put his arm around him, steadying him as he wobbled. As the boy lifted his foot to the stairs, he lost his balance. Olek's arm was at the ready, keeping him upright and lifting him effortlessly to the top of the stairs.

"There you go. Take it slow if you need to. I've got you." As the boy stepped inside the door, he nearly collapsed, and he grabbed Olek's arm to steady himself. Olek directed him to a kitchen chair.

Olek helped him settle into the chair, but the boy cried out in pain again. Olek went to the back bedroom and yanked a blanket from the bed. Running back, he draped the bedspread around him. The boy breathed in deeply, enjoying the instant comfort and warmth.

After a few minutes, Olek knelt before the boy, trying to lift the blanket to reveal his stomach wound.

"Let me take a look at this," Olek said, but the boy pushed his hand away.

"Okay," Olek said kindly. "Maybe in a minute. So, I told you my name is Olek. What's your name?"

The boy said nothing.

"That's okay if you don't want to tell me your name. Can you tell me where you live? Are you from Lithuania?"

Again, he didn't respond, as if he didn't understand anything Olek was saying.

Olek then asked in Polish, "Are you from Poland?"

He said nothing in reply, but the terror in his eyes spoke volumes.

Olek rubbed his chin as he tried to think of a way to encourage him to say something. Anything.

"Would you like some bread?" Olek pointed to a half-eaten loaf of bread on the counter.

The boy nodded with as much energy as he could muster.

"Oh, so you do speak Lithuanian. That's good to know." Olek stepped to the counter and tore off a small piece of bread. As he presented it, the boy grabbed the bread and shoved it whole inside his mouth. He stopped chewing to rest for a moment, then continued chewing until he swallowed.

The boy pointed to the bread.

"You want some more? Okay. First, however, I need to look at your wounds so I can put a bandage on it. Can I see your stomach?" As he asked, Olek removed the blanket, and the boy did nothing to stop him.

"Oh, my!"

The deep, dark-red hole was surrounded by a purplish-red entrance wound a little larger than a coin. Yet with how deep it was, how on earth did he not bleed to death? Olek shook his head in astonishment as he undraped the blanket from the boy's back, revealing an even more grotesque exit wound. It was a miracle this small child was able to get out of the pit, let alone survive. How long has he been hiding here? What would have happened had he waited a few days or even a week to go out to the shed? Olek couldn't think about it now. He draped the blanket around the boy again and asked, "Can you tell me if you were shot more than once?"

The boy pointed to his shoulder, revealing a bullet that grazed his upper arm. The blood was dried, but the wound didn't seem to do much else but break the skin.

"Are there any other wounds I need to look at?"

The boy shook his head.

"I'm going to let you lie down, and I can take a closer look and see if you have anything else I need to see, okay?"

He stared at the loaf of bread, longing for more.

"Okay. I'll give you some more bread."

Olek ripped off another small morsel of bread and handed it to him.

"Let's be careful about you eating too much, at least until we know your stomach can handle it, okay? But I'd like you to drink something too."

Olek poured a small glass of water from a pitcher and handed it to the boy, who drank it up, spilling some on the blanket.

"I don't know what I should call you. What's your name?"

The boy turned his head away, mouthing his name in a whisper, "Mordecai."

Olek smiled. "Did you say Mordecai?"

The boy gave a quick nod.

"That's a fine and honorable Jewish name. Mordecai is a hero of mine from the Torah. What's your last name?"

Mordecai hesitated but relented, saying, "Goldberg."

"How old are you?"

"Ten," he said a little louder than before.

Olek stifled a gasp of surprise as he figured the boy was about six or seven, given how small and skinny he was.

"Well, Mordecai, I want to take you back to your parents or family. Can you help me contact your family?" Olek cringed as the words spilled from his mouth, realizing his question would likely require a painful reply.

"Everyone in my family was killed over there." He pointed in the direction of the death pits.

CHAPTER 23

10 December 1941
Stockholm, Sweden

With Leva working both afternoons and late evenings at the restaurant, her schedule wasn't predictable. Yet, with all that was happening in the world, Leva and Babcia spent most of their leisure time listening to Swedish radio news bulletins about the fast-moving events of the war—from Japan bombing Pearl Harbor in America, to the Russians pushing back against the Nazis, to Hitler declaring war on the United States. War news dominated their thoughts and conversations.

Mail was the most reliable way to communicate with family and loved ones. Most all the letters they received were from Sweden. Leva rarely received any letters. Hopeful to hear from Al or Olek, she dutifully went to the mailbox each day.

As she opened the mailbox, she noticed an odd-looking envelope with Cyrillic characters and the postmark said: "*Москва.*" The typewritten addressee was Leva Koslowski, which made her even more curious.

She ripped open the letter and recognized her mother's penmanship; then her heart dropped as she read it.

"Babcia!" she shouted. "Where are you? Come quick. My Mama sent a letter!"

Leva sat at the kitchen table and began to sob. The letter from her mother lay next to her hand. Her face was buried in her arms on the table.

She heard Babcia dash in from her bedroom to investigate. "What happened?" Leva sat crying and felt the warmth of Babcia's hand on her shoulder. As she lifted her head, she tossed the letter toward Babcia. "Papa is dead!"

Babcia covered her mouth, then took the letter from the table to read it.

My dearest family,
I have been allowed to write one brief letter so I can let you know that I am alive.

We did not make it to the ferry when we arrived in Riga. We did everything we could to get to you. The same day, your father was severely injured, and we were then put on a train. Unfortunately, he passed away a few days later due to those injuries. I am so sorry that I must tell you about such sad news in a letter like this.

I cannot tell you where I am living now due to war conditions, but I am far away from home. We attend lectures once a week, and we have learned that Comrade Stalin is defeating the fascists. We are all working together to achieve a glorious victory.

I am surrounded by many others who speak my language. I am living with a young mother who has two children, ages four and seven. I watch these children while their mother works in a factory.

With the deepest love and affection,
Mama

As Babcia stood next to Leva, she took out a handkerchief from her pocket and wiped her tears. "My son is dead."

After a moment, Babcia looked at Leva, saying, "I'm glad your mother is alive, though."

Leva nodded as she sat again at the table.

"Matis hated those Soviets with every fiber of his soul." Babcia spat, startling Leva.

"He often told me that he'd probably die at their hands. He was right. Those vile Soviets killed my son."

Leva had never heard Babcia speak with such bitterness and anger, and she lifted her head, offering an alternative explanation. "It could have been the Nazis who did it."

Babcia pointed to the letter. "Read it closely. In the first place, she talks about Stalin. Second, she makes it clear he was injured the same day they were stopped from getting on the ferry. So, it had to be the Soviets. And how else would he be injured? I doubt he just fell somewhere and hurt himself," Babcia reasoned.

"So, you think they beat him or tortured him?" Leva asked.

"Let's hope not," Babcia said, knowing it was unlikely he could escape such treatment.

As Babcia spoke, Leva interrupted. "What do I say to Al? How do I tell him?"

Babcia reached out to embrace Leva, drawing her closer as they both wept. Their tears flowed freely.

"We don't have to send a telegram now. We can wait until you're ready." She whispered tenderly.

Crying softly, they stood and held each other, needing warmth and comfort from each other.

Leva stepped back and wiped the tears from her cheek. "I'm sorry you lost your son," Leva sniffled, wiping her nose with her sleeve.

"I'm sorry you lost your father," Babcia said with a kind smile. "We'll miss him. He was a good man."

CHAPTER 24

17 December 1941
Chicago, Illinois, USA

Al was at his usual position, standing on a ledge, overseeing four younger pin boys doing their job. After each bowler took their turn, a boy would jump down from their ledge, clear away the downed pins, or reset them all for the next bowler. They'd then give the ball a strong heave to send it back to the bowler. If a boy couldn't set the pins fast enough or if a bowler challenged how the pins were set, Al would step in and resolve the conflict.

From his position, Al noticed his manager waving to attract his attention. It was quite unusual, and it signaled that something was wrong.

"Barsauskas," he bellowed over the roar of bowling balls and crashing pins. "Barsauskas, get your butt up here."

He motioned to Al to leave his position and come to the front. Al stepped with care along a narrow path from the back of the bowling lanes. As he approached, he saw standing next to his manager a young boy about thirteen years old. The boy wore a white shirt and tie, a button-down blue uniform, and a three-pointed cap with a black visor. A metal emblem in the center of the hat read "Western Union." The boy held his thick leather gloves under his arms and managed to take back the telegram from the manager, who had taken it from him despite his protest. When the manager finished reading it, he summoned Al.

"Son," he said with unusual kindness.

Al's heart raced, wondering what would make his boss act so uncharacteristically kind as to call him son. "It looks like you've got an important telegram."

The Western Union boy looked at the telegram as he struggled to pronounce the name. "Are you," he asked, then paused. "Al-jerd-us . . . Bar . . . ar," he paused again.

Al interrupted to save the boy from pronouncing his name. "My name is Algirdas . . . Al-Gird-Us," he said slowly. "But everyone just calls me Al. My last name is pronounced Bar-SOW-skuss. Is that who you're looking for?"

Relieved, the boy nodded. "Yes. This telegram is for you." He handed the card to Al, then turned and left. Al skimmed over the codes and other gibberish at the top of the message, recognizing his name and address before the primary message.

10 December 1941
Algirdas Barsauskas
3313 N. Southport Ave
Chicago, Ill.
Letter from Mama says Tata killed by Soviets. She is in Siberia. A detailed letter coming soon. Leva and Babcia

Al felt the manager's hand on his shoulder. "I'm sorry, son. Take the rest of the day off if you'd like."

Al examined the paper, engrossed in his thoughts as he processed the news. He nodded instinctively and replied. "Yeah. Thanks." He read and reread the telegram.

"Where are you from again?" the manager asked Al. "Bavaria or Romania, or something like that?"

"Lithuania," Al said with impatience.

"Where's that?" he asked.

"Near the Baltic Sea."

"Where's that?"

Al rolled his eyes, tired of always explaining European geography to Americans. "East of Poland. West of Russia."

"Oh," he said. "So, you're close to Russia. That makes sense."

"Yes, sir," Al replied mindlessly, a tear dropped from the corner of his eye. "Can I go home now?"

"Sure thing," his boss said. "But we'll see you back tomorrow, right?"

Al walked toward the door and winced at the bright sunlight. As he walked home, his thoughts kept racing. If Tata were dead, then that must mean Mama must be okay. Maybe she escaped somehow? Yet she also said Tata was killed by the Soviets, so that would be why she is in Siberia. She's probably a prisoner. Oh, how can they treat my angel mother like some common hooligan? How long can she survive in those conditions? What if she's already dead? Or maybe she's suffering? Maybe they're going to work her to death? It just hurts too much to think about.

It took a week after receiving the telegram for Al to become convinced he wanted to join the US Army.

With his passport in hand, he walked into the enlistment office and completed the application.

As Al stepped up to the desk of the enlistment officer, he glanced over the application and asked, "So you were born in Lithuania?"

"Yes, sir."

"Do you have any identification?"

"Yes, sir." Al reached into his pocket and pulled out his Swedish passport.

The man nodded politely, then asked, "So you're a Swedish citizen?"

Al hesitated, not knowing how to answer that question truthfully. "Yes, sir, but it's kind of complicated. It doesn't really matter because I want to be an American citizen. I heard America wanted all young men my age to enlist."

The man put the application on the table and set it aside. He smiled. "While I appreciate your willingness to serve, right now we can only accept enlistment applications from U.S. citizens."

"I have a sponsor," Al protested. "I'm here legally. And I also have a job."

"That's all good, son, but you have to be a naturalized U.S. citizen to join the U.S. Army," he said.

"How do I become a U.S. citizen?" Al asked.

The man paused and pretended to look at his watch. Seeing the other men anxiously waiting in line. "I can't tell you how to become a citizen. You'll have to talk to a lawyer or something."

"Where do I go? Who do I talk to?" The man could see that Al was both sincere and ignorant.

"Look here, son, the laws are confusing. It usually takes several years to finish the process."

"Several years?" Al's eyes widened. "The war could be over by then. I just want to do my part."

"I understand, young man. But since you have a sponsor and a work permit, you can contribute in other ways."

Al walked away dejected. It was the first time since coming to America that he longed to be with Leva and Babcia. And with Christmas just a week away, he was feeling unusually lost and alone.

Chapter 25

22 December 1941
Ponary, Nazi-Occupied Lithuania

December was relatively quiet in Ponary. Most days Olek saw no one. Occasionally, guards would unload a truck with a few Jews, usually teenagers or young mothers. Olek wondered how they had been caught. Were these the unlucky souls he'd heard about from Max, who were arrested in the Vilnius ghetto for committing such crimes as forging

"Aryan" papers to escape? Or had they been rounded up for some other reason, like smuggling food from the outside?

Olek also noticed more and more Poles being brought to Ponary for execution. Most wore the green uniform of the Polish resistance. These "freedom fighters" aimed to reinstate Polish control over Lithuania and restore the borders that existed before the Soviets and Nazis invaded. Once the Polish resistance began having some success, the Germans redoubled their efforts to capture and punish anyone who had any connection to the Polish resistance. That included arresting university students, former Polish army officers, and even Catholic priests suspected of being sympathetic to the Polish resistance.

Throughout the month, Olek counted about a hundred and fifty Poles coming from *Lukiškės* prison. However, they weren't being executed by the Shaulists. In fact, since mid-November, all the shooting was done by the German Einsatzgruppen, the SS unit assigned to execute Jews and other enemies.

December's relatively small number of slayings was significantly lower than the previous five months, when executions happened almost daily, with hundreds, and sometimes thousands, of people. While Olek knew his running tally would never be completely accurate, his November journal entry listed more than thirty thousand people who had been killed in the Ponary forest since July.

Since he found Mordecai hiding in his shed three weeks earlier, Olek's morning routine was to clean and dress Mordecai's wounds on his stomach and back. The wounds had mostly closed on their own, but at first, they were draining a greenish fluid that had a nasty smell to it. Olek had made about a dozen bandages from an old bed sheet. After washing the soiled bandages, he would boil them on his stove to make sure they were as sterile as possible.

"Good morning." Olek smiled as he entered the bedroom carrying a bottle of antiseptic and a fresh bandage.

Mordecai said nothing but sat up on the bed so Olek could remove the old bandage wrapped around his stomach. As he removed the bandage with caution, he revealed Mordecai's wounds on his front and back. Olek inspected the wound on his stomach and said, "It looks like it's getting better. Don't you agree?"

Mordecai nodded but, as usual, said nothing.

"It's still draining. I think that's a good thing, as long as the drainage is clear. It looks mostly clear today, wouldn't you agree?"

Again, the boy nodded.

"Now let's look at your back."

Mordecai winced as he stood by his bed, turning around so Olek could inspect the larger wound on his back.

"It's looking good. We still have a little drainage, but not too much. Are you feeling any pain?"

Mordecai gave a slight shake of his head.

"What about when I touch over here?"

Mordecai flinched, startling Olek.

Olek stood and thought for a moment as he ran his fingers through his hair. The wound shouldn't be so tender. It should be healing by now. He wondered what he should do next to help Mordecai.

As Olek walked into the bathroom to put the dirty bandages in the tub, his eyes were drawn to fresh blood in the toilet. He dashed back to the bedroom. "There's blood in your urine again. Has it been getting any worse or better?"

Mordecai's eyes glanced at the floor, and he shrugged. "I guess so."

"There's nothing to be ashamed about," Olek encouraged. "We have to keep an eye on it, so we know if it's getting worse. Will you try to pay attention, and then tell me if you notice that you're seeing more blood when you pee? Please? It's really important. Okay?"

"Yes, sir," he said in a whisper.

"I'm not angry. I just need to know so we can get you better."

Mordecai stepped toward his bed and climbed back under the covers.

Olek rubbed his chin, hoping for some inspiration about what to do. Then the thought hit him to go talk to Max. He didn't know why he trusted Max so much. It didn't make logical sense to trust this man so much. Yet Matis and Zeneta trusted him. Olek and Max seemed to hit it off when they met, and Max seemed to be trustworthy. Talking to Max looked to be the best option. He seemed to know a little bit about a lot of things. If he didn't know what to do, Max would know where to find the answers. Telling him came with risk, too. If he somehow let it slip that Olek was harboring a Jew, Olek would quite likely end up in a pit in Ponary.

He was also concerned about leaving Mordecai alone. Olek had yet to leave him alone since he arrived and was always nearby just in case, he called out for help. With Mordecai now stabilized and able to get around on his own, Olek hoped he could leave him alone for a time so he could ride into town.

As he looked at Mordecai resting in bed, Olek blurted out. "Mordecai, do you think you'll be okay if I go to the grocery store? I need to stock up on a few things."

Mordecai didn't answer, but Olek read fear in his eyes.

"You'll be okay. People never come to our place. It's just too far off the beaten path."

"How long?" Mordecai asked.

"I hope no more than two or three hours."

Mordecai sat up on his bed and asked, "What if those mean men with guns come here?"

Olek paused, then looked up the stairs to his room. "Do you think you can make it up the stairs okay? I need to show you something."

Mordecai said, "I'll try."

He removed the covers, carefully stepping out of bed and standing for a moment to catch his breath.

"I'll help you so you won't fall."

Mordecai held on tight to the banister, groaning softly in pain as he lifted his feet to each stair. With great determination, he smiled as he reached the top of the stairs, inhaling deeply. Olek said, beaming, "You made it. You're here!"

Catching his breath, Mordecai stood at the top of the stairs and glanced at these unfamiliar surroundings with curiosity. Seeing the big bedroom and bathroom, Olek watched Mordecai's eyes widen.

"Come in here," Olek guided. Olek walked toward his bookcase and helped Mordecai stand next to him so he could see the secret opening to his hidden room.

"See these books here," he said. "These aren't real books. These are fake books that are used to unlock a secret room behind this bookcase."

Olek set the books on their side, and the bookcase swung open just enough so that Mordecai could see the darkened room behind it.

Mordecai's eyes popped open with awe. "Come back here so I can show you," Olek swung the bookshelf out of the way, and bent down to walk inside. "Come in and look around."

Mordecai didn't need to bend over much to fit under the tiny doorway. As he entered the room, he stood erect, looking at the shortwave radio.

"I'm not supposed to have this radio, but it allows me to hear what's going on so I can protect us from the bad guys. Promise me you won't say a word about this radio," Olek's eyebrows raised, demanding a reply.

"I won't," Mordecai promised.

"This room is where you can hide. You close the door like this." He pulled a small strap that swung the bookcase closed and he heard it latch.

"When it latches, the books go back to the upright position, so they don't know there's even a hidden room at all," Olek said.

Mordecai nodded his understanding.

"Now, unless you're making noise or listening to the radio, nobody is going to find you in here. There are even a few cans of food and water here over there in the corner. It should keep you going for a few days or even a week if needed. Let's hope you never have to hide here. Okay?"

"You can also pull on this strap here, and you have a small Murphy bed just in case you need a place to rest." Olek pulled the strap and a bed unfolded from the wall.

"Wow," Mordecai said in amazement, smiling as he admired the magically appearing bed.

"I'm glad you like it," Olek said, wearing his broad grin.

Mordecai touched the bed as if making sure it wasn't a dream or illusion.

"Does this make you feel safe enough for me to leave for a little while?" Olek asked.

"Yes."

"Would you rather stay up here while I'm gone?"

"Yes, please."

"That's perfectly fine with me," Olek said cheerfully. "Let me show you how the radio works."

Olek explained his radio in simple terms.

"Make sure you keep the volume down," Olek warned. "We wouldn't want to wake up the neighborhood!"

Mordecai gave Olek a wry smile, letting out a brief giggle before grasping his stomach in pain.

"It hurts to laugh," he said playfully.

"I'm sorry. But it's so nice to see you smile."

Olek waited outside Max's store until all the other customers were gone. As he entered, Max nearly shouted, "Olek, my boy. So glad to see you. Come on in and tell me the latest news."

"It has been a wild month since the last time I was here. And I need your advice on something, but I don't want anyone else to hear. So, I'll talk fast while we're alone."

"Okay…" He paused as he chose his words. "You know about all the Jews, as well as other people that are being killed, right?"

Max nodded. "Yes."

"Sometimes, they shoot a person who falls into the pit, but they don't die. Sometimes these injured people wait until it's dark and they can escape from the pits. Usually, they'll go out into the forest and find some help from the resistance fighters living out there. But a few weeks ago, I was out in my shed, and I stumbled on a ten-year-old little Jewish boy. He had a gunshot wound to his stomach." Olek pointed to his abdomen to the left of his navel. "There's an exit wound on his back."

"What are you doing harboring a Jew?" Max said, slapping his hand on his forehead. "You'll get yourself killed."

"What was I to do? Let him die?"

"No. But a fugitive Jew? My good heavens. That's a death wish."

"I'm fully aware of that, but it's too late now."

Max put one hand on his hip, his other hand scratched his head as he looked around the room, contemplating the predicament he was in. If he said nothing to anyone, he was now an accomplice for harboring a fugitive.

"I don't know, Olek. You put me in a bad spot."

Max shuffled his feet in place, shaking his head as he considered his dilemma.

"I'm sorry, Max, but I had nowhere to turn."

"I understand, but damn it, Olek, I do everything I can, just to steer clear of the Nazis, to make sure I give them no reason to bother me. But now I'm going to be looking over my shoulder every time someone walks into my store. I'm going to wonder anytime someone knocks on my door. You've just sentenced me to sleepless nights and indigestion and who knows what else." Max's eyes focused on his feet, then he stared directly at Olek. "I know you didn't mean to, but..." He stopped.

Olek stepped back in surprise. The mood hung heavy as both said nothing in the awkward silence.

"I'm really sorry, Max. I am. I just didn't realize . . ." he paused. "I just didn't think about how I put you at risk." Olek shook his head in disgust. "I should have thought it through. I'm sorry."

"Well," Max said with resignation in his voice. "I guess there's no going back now, tell me the rest."

Olek's voice was soft. "His wounds don't seem to be getting better. I've done my best to keep them clean and bandaged, but it's still draining. I don't know if that's normal or not. Do you know?"

Olek watched Max's eyes blink a few times, then dart back and forth, a sign that he was thinking.

"Oh, and..." Olek paused as he pointed in the air with emphasis. "He's also got blood in his urine."

Max shook his head at Olek and said, "Son, this is way out of my league. And if he's got blood in his urine, it's possible the bullet hit his kidney. No matter how good you are at dressing his wounds and taking care of him, he needs a doctor."

"It didn't occur to me about his kidneys," Olek looked at the ceiling as he mulled over the new information. "See, that's why I knew I should talk to you. You know so much about so many things."

"I know enough to know that a bullet wound is a serious matter. He certainly needs someone with the right knowledge and tools, no matter how smart you are." Max folded his arms, appearing to be deep in thought.

"What do I do, Max?" Olek asked. "How do I help this little boy and make sure that we both don't end up dead in the process?"

"I'm not sure," Max said.

"I'm so sorry to drag you into this." Olek apologized again. "I promise, I didn't come here to ask you to risk your life for me. I just came because I needed your advice."

"I know. I'm not blaming you for anything," Max said. "Yet if I did nothing, I'd have to live with this little boy's life on my conscience for the rest of my life."

"What can I do for you?" Olek asked. "I'll do anything."

Max glanced at Olek and squinted as he thought.

"Well. I know a doctor—"

Olek interrupted. "And you trust him with your life? With my life?"

"I'm pretty sure we can. I'll call my friend and see if he's willing to come out to your place and look at the boy."

The next week, Mordecai seemed unusually anxious, asking Olek repeatedly when to expect their visitors.

"They're going to be here after dark when there are fewer people out and about," Olek kept reminding him. "Just be patient."

When their visitors finally knocked on the door, Mordecai dashed as quickly as he could into his room.

After answering the door and chatting briefly, Olek walked into Mordecai's room with Max and the doctor followed close behind. Mordecai sat on his bed, rubbing his hands anxiously, looking at Olek as if needing affirmation that these strange men were not going to hurt him.

"Mordecai, this is my friend Max. He works at the grocery store."

Mordecai gave a soft answer, "Yes, sir."

Olek put his hand behind Max and pushed him forward toward the boy. Max offered his hand. Mordecai's eyes were glued to the floor, but he lifted a limp hand toward Max, who grasped it enthusiastically. "Hello, Mordecai. It's a pleasure to meet you, son. Olek and I are good friends, and I'm here to help you. I even brought my doctor friend here who's here to help you. His name is Dr. Avižienis."

Olek stepped in saying, "Dr. Avižienis needs to look at your stomach and back. Can you take your shirt off for him?"

"Hello, Mordecai." The doctor gave a warm smile to Mordecai. "I want to see if I can help your wounds heal better, all right? Can you lie down for me?"

Olek helped Mordecai remove his shirt and directed him to rest his head on his pillow. With great care, the doctor pressed two fingers near the wound, Mordecai holding his breath waiting for the pain. "Did that hurt you when I touched there?" the doctor asked.

Mordecai gave a quick shake of his head. "No."

"Can you turn over on your stomach, please?" Dr. Avižienis helped Mordecai roll over. As he inspected the wound, he pressed around it gently until Mordecai flinched. "That hurts right there. Over your kidney?"

Mordecai said, "A little."

The doctor asked, "How often do you have blood in your pee?"

Mordecai didn't answer, and then Olek asked him with more emphasis. "Is it every time you go? Once a day? Once a week?"

"Once a week. Maybe. I don't remember," Mordecai said meekly.

Dr. Avižienis asked to clarify. "It's not every day or every other day, right?"

"Last week was the first time in a long time," Mordecai said with newfound courage.

"That's good," Olek nodded. "I thought it was more than that."

Dr. Avižienis stood up straight and turned to Olek. "I think you've done an amazing job so far. I wouldn't worry about the drainage. That should go away in a week or two. Keep it clean and keep doing what you're doing until it stops. I think the bullet may have done something to his kidney, but it seems to be healing. I would normally recommend he be outside doing more to be active instead of lying down all the time. I know that's hard given the circumstances, but if there's a way to keep him active, that's what I'd recommend. Otherwise, he's going to be just fine."

"That's great news, doctor. I'm so glad he's doing okay." Olek smiled as he patted Mordecai's head. "What do you think about that, Mordecai?"

The boy gave a tentative smile at Olek. "I'm not going to die?"

Max and Olek gave an enthusiastic said in unison, "No!"

Dr. Avižienis leaned over toward Mordecai for emphasis. "If that's a concern, son, then you can put it out of your mind. You're healing up nicely and you'll be up and about in no time."

Mordecai looked at the doctor, then at Max, then was overcome with emotion. He rushed toward Olek and reached out to embrace him. Olek was stunned by his uncharacteristic show of emotion, feeling the warmth of Mordecai's arms wrapped around him.

"Thank you for taking care of me," Mordecai said. "Thank you for saving my life."

Olek was too choked up to speak. He gave Mordecai a careful squeeze, wanting to return the affection, but also trying to avoid hurting him. This was the first time he had seen Mordecai's raw emotions. He felt the boy's warm, kind embrace and turned his head away so Max and Dr. Avižienis didn't see him cry.

1942

CHAPTER 26

27 September 1942
Stockholm, Sweden

Leva opened the letter from Al and read it aloud for Babcia.

Dear Leva and Babcia,

I can't remember if I told you that I quit my job at the bowling alley. I was offered a great-paying job working on the new Dodge Chicago Aircraft Engine Plant they're building here. My job is in the tooling shop where we build jigs, tools, and fixtures to build engines for a big super bomber called the B-29.

The factory still has a few more months before it's all built, but it's exciting to see how it has all come together. It's a huge factory. It covers about eighty acres or roughly thirty city blocks. The parking lot alone is going to be a block wide and a mile long and will park over thirteen thousand cars.

You can't believe how big this country is. There are also a lot of people too, especially here in Chicago. It's amazing to me that they can build this huge factory where they need to hire fifteen thousand people or so, and they're not worried about getting that many people to apply. That's mind-boggling when you really think about it.

I finally did it. I enlisted in the US Army, and I officially report for duty on the 10th of October at Keesler Field near Biloxi, Mississippi. I was going to enlist in March when they announced that foreigners could get citizenship if they joined the army. But I've been so busy working that I just didn't have time.

When I went in to enlist, I was more or less resigned to the fact that I would be in the Army infantry. But after I had my physical and took a few tests, they said that because I had some familiarity with aircraft tools and engines, they would likely put me in the Army Air Corps. I'll know more once I get through boot camp, but I'm hoping I can be on a crew that flies in one of these huge super bombers.

I also met a girl that I really like. Her name is Maria Galvez. Her family came from Mexico City, but she was born here. We met at the bowling alley where she worked as a waitress. She's very beautiful. She invited me to meet her family. There are twelve children. She is the oldest. She's also a great cook. She and her mama make a dish called tamales. They're made with some type of corn dough that gets wrapped in corn husks. It's filled with spicy meat and then steamed. They're very good. She taught me how to make them, but I'm not very good at it. She also makes tacos. Have you ever heard of them? They're made with a corn flatbread, and they fold them in half. They are usually filled with spicy beef or pork, but you eat them with your hands. There are a lot of Mexicans here in Chicago, and I've tried all types of food here, not just Mexican. There are also a lot of Lithuanian restaurants here, so I'm not too homesick for Mama's cooking.

I told Maria that I was going to join the army, and I wanted to do my part to end this war. She wasn't very happy with me. She wants me to stay here so we can get married. I told her I felt it was my duty to serve, just like all the other boys my age. She asked me to wait for a few months before I decide. I haven't told her yet that I got my letter from the army telling me to report for duty. Who knows what she'll do now? I'll let you know what happens.

Well, that's all I have to say for now. I'll write to you once I arrive in Mississippi.

Love,
Al

CHAPTER 27

20 December 1942
Novosibirsk, Siberia, USSR

Amid the icy grip of the spring thaw, Zeneta surprised Ugna with a daring trade—exchanging some of her cherished jewelry to gain access to a secluded garden plot just a kilometer away from their barracks. Zeneta dutifully tended to the garden. Every weed she uprooted and every bit of tender care she gave her sprouting potatoes, beets, cabbage, and onions were vital to surviving the coming winter months. It was also her small act of resistance against the oppressive Soviets she had grown to despise.

Ugna worked in the factory until the day she delivered her baby. Her labor was an arduous battle, stretching on for twenty grueling hours before delivering a baby girl on 24 July. With Zeneta's unwavering support and the aid of three other women from their barracks, they rallied around to help Ugna, knowing her already frail health made her delivery even more tenuous and dangerous.

She named her baby Audra, a fitting name meaning "storm" in Lithuanian. Although unusually small, the infant was otherwise healthy. Ugna's path to recovery stretched on for nearly three weeks. For the first few days, she was unable to walk or even nurse the baby. Two other mothers nursed Audra until Ugna was finally able to nurse the baby herself.

The community of Lithuanians all knew the circumstances of Ugna's pregnancy and rallied to help ease her burden. Ugna openly wept at receiving gifts of a baby blanket, some cotton fabric for diapers, and a rare set of diaper pins. She also received a small bassinet woven from cornstalk fibers blown off the train cars traveling from Kazakhstan and other warmer climates in the south.

Ugna was given extra food and firewood rations by the baby's father. He continued to threaten her not to tell anyone about their liaisons that he started shortly after she returned to work. However repulsive it was to have intimate relations with a married man more than twice her age, she resigned herself to endure these encounters as a means of survival.

One day in December, Ugna walked home from the factory, her windblown skin burned from the bitter cold and gusty winds gripping *Novosibirsk*. As she walked into the barracks, the relentless wind penetrated the halls and public spaces of their barracks. She walked through the door, seeing her three children resting comfortably in a bundle of blankets, sleeping soundly and not hearing her come in. With each exhalation of her children, a cloud of misty vapor lingered in the air. Ugna was relieved to see them asleep, and she approached Zeneta with her sad news.

"I'm pregnant again." Her voice cracked as she spoke.

"Are you sure?" Zeneta asked with reticence, not knowing what else to say.

Ugna nodded, wiping her eyes with her sleeve. "I'm so afraid," she confided. "I don't know if I'll survive this one."

"We have more food now than we did last time," Zeneta said with strained encouragement.

"But I can hardly take care of myself anymore, let alone Mykolas and Saule," Ugna's tears rolled down her cheeks. "And poor Audra, it's all I can do to keep her fed. And I hate imposing on you to watch my children."

"You know I'm happy to help, and so is everyone else in our barracks," Zeneta said. "We've done it before, and we'll do it again."

"I know," Ugna squeaked between sobs. "I know you will step up again. I know you'll sell your family heirlooms or find some other way to make it all work out, but I just don't want to go through it again. I can't go on anymore. My children would be better off if I just went away."

Ugna's eyes stared at the floor, fearing Zeneta's reaction. As her eyes met Zeneta's, they said nothing.

Zeneta said with confidence, "Ugna, we'll get through it. We have no other choice, do we? Your children have seen enough sadness and misery. They need their mother. Now more than ever."

"You'd be a much better mother than I could ever be. You can be their mother. Just let me die. Please, Zeneta. Will you do that for me? I just want to jump off a building and be done with it, please," she begged. "Please don't try to stop me."

Zeneta guided Ugna's face onto her shoulder while they cried in silence.

On Christmas morning, Ugna rushed into their room and whispered in Zeneta's ear. "I just started my period, and it's a very heavy flow. Do you think I could have had a miscarriage?"

"It's very likely," Zeneta said with caution. "How do you feel otherwise?"

"I had some cramping last night, and my back hurt, but that's all gone away."

"It sounds like a miscarriage," Zeneta said. "Are you okay with that?"

"Yes!" Ugna's enthusiasm woke Mykolas and Saule.

"Merry Christmas, you two!" Ugna said as she reached down to hug her two children. "I have a gift for each of you."

They jumped from their bed and rushed to Ugna's side.

"For Mykolas, we have these wooden building blocks. I asked Mr. Gabraitis to make these. He works in the wood shop at the factory and made these from some scraps of wood."

"Wow," Mykolas' eyes widened as he took the package wrapped in paper. It was filled with about twenty rectangular blocks that were hand-sanded smooth. "Thanks, Mama!"

"For you, Saule, here's this beautiful little sock doll." She handed it to Saule, who smiled brightly and hugged the doll, twisting her torso with delight.

"What are you going to name her?" Zeneta asked.

"Umm," Saule paused as she thought, then smiled as she said, *"Mergaitė."*

CHAPTER 28

21 December 1942
Ponary, Nazi-Occupied Lithuania

From the year up to December 1942, Ponary was comparatively quiet. A few times a month, a truckload of Jews, Poles, or Red Army soldiers would arrive. From Olek's vantage point, he could see that some of the prisoners were allowed to escape, giving the *Shaulists* the thrill of hunting them down. Most prisoners only lasted a few minutes, and the bodies were dragged back and thrown into the pits. Occasionally, one or two men escaped into the dense forest, and Olek could hear the *Shaulists* cursing at each other for their poor marksmanship. He could only assume the escapees somehow linked up with the Polish or Lithuanian resistance hiding out in the woods.

Despite Dr. Avižienis' optimistic predictions, Mordecai's recovery was slow in coming. For most of the year, his persistent infections and abdominal pain were debilitating. His days were spent in bed. He also grew more somber and quieter, making his emotional state more desperate.

After a long summer and into fall, Mordecai at long last began to feel well enough to come out of his bedroom and talk to Olek. The conversations revealed some of Mordecai's long-held secrets about his family and background. He was born in Kraków to Lithuanian-speaking Jews. His parents, two sisters, and an older brother fled and came to Vilnius shortly after the Germans invaded Poland.

Among the many things Mordecai revealed about himself was his love for football. He often played goalkeeper when his neighborhood friends got together to play. He missed playing the game and often reminisced about playing with his friends. As Mordecai's health and attitude improved, Olek recalled seeing an old football in the shed. He pumped it up and watched Mordecai beam when he gave it to him.

Because Mordecai was forbidden to go outside, Olek cleared the furniture from a bedroom so Mordecai could entertain himself with the football. Marking a goal on the wall, he installed wooden slats over the windows and encouraged Mordecai to try to break a window. Still skinny and weak, he hoped kicking the football would help the boy improve his strength and stamina.

Mordecai loved to kick the ball, spending an hour or so each day dribbling and kicking the ball against the walls. While the sound of the ball bouncing off the walls was a distraction at first, Olek learned to ignore the constant pounding as he worked on writing his novel.

On the last day of November, Mordecai surprised Olek with a powerful kick that broke the slats and shattered a window. Olek didn't complain, he was happy to see Mordecai gaining strength. He knew he couldn't ignore the broken window or else the house would be unbearably cold.

Using a slab of wood that he scrounged up from the back side of the shed, he cut the board so it would cover the window from the outside. Waiting until he saw no activity going on around the forest, he hurriedly climbed a ladder with the wood in one arm, and his other arm grasping the ladder. Once he had the wood in position, Mordecai held it in place from inside the house, Olek pounded some nails into the wood until it was secure.

The next day it only took Mordecai a few swift strikes of the ball to send the board crashing to the ground. Again, Olek made his way outside and hammered twice as many nails to secure the board in place. He also cut another board to fit on the inside of the window, and he nailed that to the window frame.

As he returned the ladder to the shed, he was shocked to hear a vehicle approach on the dirt pathway leading to the house. A dark green army field car appeared with a Nazi officer at the wheel.

Olek studied the house, praying that Mordecai heard the car approach, then hid in the room upstairs.

The SS officer turned off the car and opened the small door. He was wearing a gray, double-breasted coat with a dark-green collar, and his high-waisted trousers were tucked into his black leather riding boots. He scrutinized Olek's demeanor, then blurted out, "Was that you making all that noise?"

Olek forced a smile. "If you're asking if it was me pounding nails, yes. That was me."

The man glanced past Olek, eyeing the house.

"We didn't think anyone was living here. How long have you been here?"

"For a few weeks," Olek lied.

"Why are you here?"

"I'm the caretaker. I was asked to take care of this place while the owner was away at war."

"The owner is a Lithuanian?" the officer asked.

"I'm not sure," Olek lied with confidence. "But I think he may have been a German officer during the Great War."

"So, he's German?"

"I think so." Olek nodded. "He married a Lithuanian woman. But as I understand it, he went to Germany when the Soviets first took over a few years ago."

"Oh, so he's been gone for a long time?" the officer asked with less disdain.

"I'm guessing so. I mostly deal with his wife."

The man said nothing more, nodding as he stared into Olek's eyes to assess his trustworthiness.

"My name is *Oberstleutnant* Köhler. I am in charge of operations here at Ponary."

"Would you like to see my papers?" Olek bluffed, hoping that his eagerness would discourage his curiosity.

"No, that's not necessary," he said. "I need to hire someone to work in the guardhouse up the road." His tone was much more pleasant. "Do you know anyone locally who is looking for work?"

"I don't know many people, frankly. I'm not a good one to ask." Olek felt a lump in his throat as he tried to remain calm.

"No one at all?" He pressed.

Olek paused, pretending to think harder. "No, not really. I just don't know many people around here yet."

Köhler scowled, looking around as if he was about to leave, then turned quickly. "What about you? Have you ever shot a rifle?"

Olek giggled. "Not really, maybe a small caliber gun when I was a child."

"Then you're qualified," Köhler announced. "You could use some more money, couldn't you? Or do they pay you an exorbitant salary as a caretaker?" Olek could sense the hint of threat in his voice.

Olek smiled. "No, I'm not getting rich, but I'm from Ukraine. I didn't think you would want to hire someone like me."

"Are you a Communist?" Köhler asked with unmistakable disdain.

"Heavens no! I hate the Soviets," Olek didn't have to lie.

"Then you're hired."

"Wait, wait," Olek protested. "What do you mean I'm hired? What is it that I would do?"

"It's not a hard job. All you have to do is keep people away who don't belong there. We'll train you so you know everything you need to do. Do you think you could do that?"

Olek thought for a moment. He figured he had more to gain from being agreeable. Refusing would cause more suspicion, then he blurted out without thinking, "Do I have to wear a uniform?" The prospect of wearing a Nazi uniform made him shudder.

Köhler paused, rubbing his elbow as he thought. "No. At least for now. But that may change depending upon the circumstances."

Olek felt a wave of relief settle over him, then he asked, "What about a gun?"

"Yes. We'll issue you a weapon and ammunition, and we'll show you how to use it properly."

Olek's heart sunk and his shoulders slumped slightly. "Okay," his voice grew softer. "How often would you need me?"

"Depends on the day. Lately, it's about once a week or so." Köhler shrugged. "Sometimes it's four or five days per week."

"You'd want me to be there five days a week?"

"No, you wouldn't be called on that often," Köhler replied. "We have hired others for this position. But you would live the closest, so we may ask you first because you're so close," he paused and looked at Olek. "If you don't want to do it..."

"No, I'm not saying that. I just wanted to know approximately how often you would need me." Olek didn't want to appear uncooperative, but he needed to know.

Köhler paused giving Olek a sense that he was being judged for his trustworthiness.

"Well. Okay. You can work it out with my subordinate. His name is *Hauptmann* Schröder. I'll have him come to see you and work out the details with pay and scheduling."

"Okay. When will he come here?" Olek asked, wanting to make sure the man didn't learn Mordecai was there.

Köhler turned to walk back to his vehicle and said over his shoulder. "Probably this afternoon sometime."

"Okay. I'll be here," Olek gave a slight nod.

The vehicle roared to life, and Olek stood dumfounded at what just happened. While he would enjoy greater protection because of the new job, at what cost? He didn't choose this job, but he could have said no. Suddenly, he realized he was now in collaboration with the Nazis. While he wasn't required to wear the uniform, he was required to wield a Nazi weapon. That prospect weighed heavily on his conscience. Though he wasn't pulling the trigger, he worried about his culpability. Of how history would judge him. He no longer held the moral high ground over the despised Shaulists he was documenting in his journal. He was now one step from being just like them.

Pushing those thoughts deep inside his mind, he watched as Köhler's car disappeared. He dashed inside and yelled, "Mordecai? Mordecai? Where are you?"

Hearing no answer, he rushed upstairs to his room and called out again, "Mordecai, are you okay?"

Still no answer, so he reached to trip the lock on the hidden door and looked inside.

"You did it!" he raised his hands in victory. "You did everything we practiced. You came in here, closed the door, and didn't respond, even though I called out your name. You kept quiet until I opened the door."

Mordecai beamed as Olek praised him. "You said that I should keep quiet in here no matter what."

"That's right. No matter what." Olek smiled and put his hand warmly on Mordecai's shoulder.

"Who was that man?" Mordecai asked, his voice trembling.

"That was a German officer. He heard me pounding nails on the window and came to investigate. They didn't know I was here, and now they do. That means we have to be extra careful from now on, to make sure they don't accidentally find out you are here."

"Do they know I'm here?" Mordecai's eyes were wide eyed with fear.

"No," Olek shook his head. "They have no idea. And that's the way we want it. But another officer is coming here this afternoon to talk to me about a job they want to hire me to do as a guard in the guard shack over at the pits."

"You're not going to do it, are you? You're not going to work for them, are you?"

"Yes, I am," Olek said. "If I don't do it, they'll be more suspicious of me. And this way, I can make a little money, and I won't have to stay hidden all the time. I can go to town and buy a few more things that we need. Like potatoes and flour, since we're about to run out."

Mordecai nodded, agreeing with Olek's logic.

"I also think we should move your room upstairs permanently. If anyone came here and saw your dirty room, they'd be sure I had an eleven-year-old boy living with me." Olek gave a playful smile, and Mordecai nodded.

"Can I still kick the ball downstairs?"

Olek looked up at nothing on the wall, considering the consequences of what he was asking.

"I'll have to think about that, Mordecai."

"I'll be quieter."

Olek rubbed his hands as he considered Mordecai's appeal. "Let me think about it. For now, we can clear out your room downstairs and move it all up here."

1943

Chapter 29

3 February 1943
Ponary, Nazi–Occupied Lithuania

At nine in the morning, Olek and Mordecai sat transfixed on their shortwave radio, waiting for an official German broadcast to begin. To keep Mordecai entertained, Olek translated the Polish into Lithuanian.

"They said to stand by for a special communique from the *Fuhrer*." He paused. "Today is the third of February, and this message is from the German High Command. Are you with me?"

Mordecai nodded.

"The battle for Stalingrad is over. True to their oath to fight to the last breath," he paused to listen. "The German Sixth Army has capitulated to the enemy." Olek paused. "Wow, can you believe that?"

"What does capitulate mean?"

"Surrender or give up," Olek said.

"What does it all mean?"

"I think this is the first time the official German radio has admitted a military defeat. It's the first time I've heard about it. I'll have to listen to the BBC and see what they say," Olek said.

"When does the BBC broadcast come on?"

Olek glanced at the clock on the wall. "The Polish broadcast starts at about nine o'clock tonight."

"Is what happened to Germany good for us?" Mordecai's question was sincere.

"Yes and no," Olek shrugged. "It's good because it would be nice to get rid of the Germans. But no because it means we'd probably have to deal with the Soviets again."

"The Soviets have to be better than the Germans, right?" Mordecai asked innocently, having had little experience with the Soviets, and knowing that the Nazis killed his family.

"Not necessarily. It's hard to say who is worse." Olek scowled at the prospect of his situation getting any harsher than it is.

"Will the Soviets continue killing Jews and other people in those pits?" Mordecai tipped his head in the general direction of Ponary.

"That I don't know," Olek sat back in his chair to think it through. "Probably not the Jews, but they've been known to kill a lot of people just because they disagree with Communism."

Mordecai's eyes fell, looking at his feet, showing his disappointment.

"How long do I have to stay locked in this room today?" Mordecai asked.

"I shouldn't be long." Olek tried to be comforting. "Maybe a few hours from what they tell me. You'll be okay, won't you?"

Mordecai said nothing but nodded dutifully.

Mordecai grew more and more impatient with having to stay hidden in his room. He usually kept the door open while Olek was there. Seeing no reason to keep the door closed, he started with a small crack in the door, but before long, the door was wide open so he could hear the hundreds of birds singing outside the window. Venturing into the bedroom, he paced around the bed wanting to go downstairs to play football, but he thought better of it. He opened the door to the balcony. Feeling the brisk, cool air, he closed it again. He sat down on Olek's bed, then moved over to unfold the feather blanket that was neatly rolled up at the foot of the bed. His hands were behind his head as he rested on Olek's pillow. He crossed his feet and glanced outside, dreaming of walking in the tall grass or strolling through the thick forest of trees.

As he was about to fall asleep, he was startled by the sound of a thud on the window of the balcony door. He jumped up to investigate and spotted a starling flailing about on the wooden deck of the balcony.

Without thinking, Mordecai opened the door to the balcony and rushed to the aid of the hapless bird. As he reached down, the bird struggled to escape and fell to the ground below.

He examined the massive tree growing next to the house and calculated the best way down. He climbed over the railing and stepped down to a thick tree branch where he easily shimmied himself down the trunk of the tree.

Dashing over to the bird, he cautiously gathered the bird into his hands.

"Are you okay?" he asked in a whisper. "You shouldn't fly into windows like that. Are you trying to kill yourself killed?"

With one hand he held the bird as tight as he dared, and with his other hand stroked the bird's head tenderly. "I hope you're not hurt too bad." As he continued stroking the bird along its back, it struggled to escape. Instantly, the bird jumped from his hands and disappeared into the thicket of trees nearby.

Mordecai smiled, seeing the bird was well enough to fly again. He was completely lost in the moment until he heard the faint voices of two men talking as they patrolled the main road in front of their house.

He looked around the yard, looking for a place to hide. In a flash, he scampered back up the tree, stepped from the tree branch, and over the railing to the balcony deck. Dashing back into the house, he shut the balcony door closed and rushed back into his hidden room. Breathing hard, he rested his arms behind his head. His heart pounded as he lay there, wondering if he had been spotted. In an instant, his tears gushed from the corners of his eyes. He was not only afraid of being discovered, but he was also disappointed with himself for disobeying Olek.

Two SS soldiers approached Olek as he sat in the tiny guard house, and one of the guards said, "Isn't that your house over there?"

"Excuse me?"

"Isn't that where you live?" the other soldier asked again, pointing to Olek's house, his other hand gripping the strap on his rifle draped over his shoulder.

Olek stood from his stool, stepping out of the guardhouse.

"Yes, it is. Why do you ask?"

"We heard something that sounded like a door slamming shut. I thought you lived alone. Are you living with somebody else now?"

"Are you sure it was a door and not a gunshot or something like that?"

The soldiers shook their heads. "No. We're sure it wasn't a gunshot."

"Well, my shift is over now, so I'll go home and investigate," Olek said, trying to downplay the incident.

"You don't want to go alone. It may be a Jew who escaped, and they'll attack you with anything they can get their hands on. We'll go investigate it with you. We know how to handle Jews." He let out a sinister laugh.

"I would like that," Olek said, feigning his agreement. He could feel his pulse throbbing in his temples.

Olek carefully closed the door to the guard shack, double-checking it to make sure it was locked. The two soldiers waited patiently. As they walked in silence, the dwindling twilight obscured the path toward Olek's house, and he led them in single file. Approaching the house, he unlocked the deadbolt on the door. The men gripped their rifles, waiting for him to turn on the lights.

They finished searching each room, using their flashlights to inspect every potential hiding place. Returning to the bottom of the stairs, one of the guards said, "All clear. There's nobody else in here."

"Let's go look upstairs if you don't mind," Olek asked, and they nodded. As they ascended the stairs, he regretted his stupid suggestion, fearing Mordecai had left some evidence of his presence. Maybe they would stumble upon a boy's sock or some other clothing that would reveal his existence. Olek felt a lump in his throat, his heart pounded faster as he climbed each stair.

The men scanned the area upstairs, looking for any sign of movement. Olek noticed his bed wasn't made, evidenced by the indentation on his feather blanket in the form of a small figure. The soldiers were unaware that anything was out of place, but they checked the closet and under the bed to make sure there was nobody there.

Olek held his breath.

"Looks like you're okay," one of the men said. "Just let us know if you see anything suspicious. You never know what a Jew might do to you, so be extra vigilant."

"I will."

The soldiers descended the stairs, and Olek followed close behind.

"I appreciate your coming here and helping me out." Olek held the door as they walked out.

"Not a problem. That's our job."

Olek watched the Nazi soldiers point their flashlights around the yard, giving it one last inspection. As they left the yard, Olek held his breath, exhaling in relief at his narrow escape. At Mordecai's narrow escape. His hands were shaking as he reached to close the front door. Feeling a rare sense of rage at Mordecai, he turned and dashed up the stairs.

"Mordecai!" He shouted as he jerked on the bookcase latch, swinging it open hard enough that it slammed against the wall, leaving a small indent. Olek bent down to clear the small door frame and spotted him on his bed.

"What were you doing out—" he paused as he noticed Mordecai's face buried in his hands.

"I'm sorry," Mordecai said with pleading in his voice. "It all just happened so fast."

Olek paused after hearing him cry.

"What happened so fast?" Olek's voice was softer.

"The bird. There was a bird that hit the window, and I wanted to make sure it was still alive," Mordecai said between sobs.

"Wait," Olek took a deep breath to gather his composure. "How did you know it was a bird that hit the window?"

Mordecai hesitated, then confessed. "I was on your bed."

"So you were on my bed, not in your room like you're supposed to be, right?"

Mordecai looked down and nodded.

"Okay. So, we know you were outside your room. Tell me what happened after that."

Olek listened as Mordecai gathered his composure and explained what happened.

"Oh, so that makes sense," Olek replied. "You were in such a hurry to get back into your room, you didn't realize you slammed the balcony door shut."

"I did?" Mordecai asked.

"Yes, you did. They heard the door slam, and that gave you away. If they thought a Jew was hiding in here, they'd tear down that door in a heartbeat."

Mordecai stared at him, his boyish mind thinking through the scenario Olek had explained.

"Listen, Mordecai, we've got to come up with a codeword that only we know, that when I say it, you know when it's safe to come out."

Mordecai listened and nodded. "Okay. What kind of word?"

Olek rubbed his chin as he thought. "Okay, how about this? When I say the word 'football' then you'll know that it's safe. Would that work?"

"I like football, so I can remember that."

"Good. Then we're all set, right?"

"Yes, Mr. Olek. Are you still angry with me?"

"No, I'm not angry—"

Mordecai interrupted. "I'm sorry, Mr. Olek. I promise I won't do it again. I promise to stay in my room all day if that makes it, so you don't hate me."

"I don't hate you, Mordecai."

Mordecai smiled at him. "I'm glad, Mr. Olek. I'm glad you don't hate me."

CHAPTER 30

2 April 1943
On a Train from Biloxi, Mississippi to Kingman, Arizona

Dear Leva and Babcia,

I'm sorry I'm so lousy at writing. I promised to write to you once I arrived in Mississippi, but they kept us so busy that I just didn't have time to write or do much of anything else. This is really the first time I've had to myself, where I wasn't worried about passing an exam or studying for one.

I've spent the last six months in aircraft and engine school. I learned everything you can imagine about how airplanes work and how to fix them. It's a very intense class where I spend almost every hour from morning until late at night. One of the benefits of such a class is that my English is getting much better. I'm still a little unsure when I'm around some of these fellows, and they start talking so fast that I can't understand them.

There were plenty of guys that washed out because they didn't want to study, and instead go out with their buddies to get drunk. I don't understand their fixation on drinking until they pass out. Silly Americans.

Right now, I'm on a train headed to Kingman, Arizona. I'm traveling with about twenty other guys from my class at Keesler who volunteered for flexible aerial gunnery school. We're all talking about how much we want to fly on one of those big American bombers, like the B-24, or the B-17 Flying Fortress. After five weeks of this school, I'll earn my gunner's wings and automatically become a staff sergeant. They'll assign us to our airplane and crew, and we'll spend a few months learning how to work together, and then we'll be transferred to our duty station. But I'm getting ahead of myself.

Yesterday, when we all finished the graduation ceremony, me, a guy from Mexico, and another guy from Poland, were called into a special ceremony with about ten other guys. Some bigwig from Washington, D.C., was there to give us our naturalization papers to become American citizens. It was an emotional experience because many had escaped from Europe and lost their parents and families. One guy was a Jew from Krakow, and he told the judge that he was the only one from his family of thirteen who got out of Poland just after the Nazis first attacked in 1939. He wanted to come to America so he could fight the Nazis and get revenge. When the judge asked me why I wanted to become an American, I wanted to tell him about Mama and Tata, but I didn't. I just told him that I love America, and I want to do my part. After that, we said the Pledge of allegiance, and they said I was a U.S. citizen.

Well, our train is almost to Kingman, so I'll end my letter here. I can't promise that I'll write more often because I expect we'll be kept busy during these five weeks of training. I'll write as soon as I can.

Love,

Al

CHAPTER 31

6 April 1943
Ponary, Nazi-Occupied Lithuania

Olek was exhausted, yet mustered the energy to write the events he'd seen but also added some details he learned from the radio.

4 April—Working in the guard hut, I've often had run-ins with a man named Trevakis, and I wanted to document my knowledge of his criminal behavior for posterity as he continues to abuse the townspeople in ways that need to be exposed.

Trevakis is one of the original Shaulists and was one of the first men to start killing Jews last June and continued through December of last year. He is a frightening man in his appearance, but his red hair makes him particularly unforgettable.

A few months ago, he showed up wearing a Gestapo uniform, along with many of the other Shaulists. While I never thought someone could become horrible just by donning a uniform, in the case of Trevakis, that's exactly what happened once he put on a Nazi uniform. Trevakis speaks both Lithuanian and German. He is known to stop people on the streets and shout and scream at them in German until he is offered a bribe to let them go.

The other day he stopped a Lithuanian family and pretended to inspect their car for weapons. Meanwhile, the woman asked her husband in Lithuanian what she should do if he found her stash of jewelry in her bra. Fully understanding their conversation, Trevakis finished the mock inspection, and then forced both of them to strip down naked, revealing the woman's heirlooms. He took the jewelry and then sent them on their way.

A few months ago, he went to a local village and befriended some locals in a tavern. After a while, the locals had disclosed much of the town's gossip, like who was brewing moonshine. (The Nazis have issued a decree threatening the death penalty for anyone found brewing alcohol or who had recently butchered an old sow.) The next week, Trevakis showed up in his Gestapo uniform, and threatened each of these families with execution, unless they paid him a tribute. He is now making a tidy sum from all the tributes he has demanded from the locals.

This is just one man that I know about, and I have reasons to believe there are many other Shaulists who are similarly terrorizing the local populations, demanding tributes, and punishing those who oppose them. It seems that wearing the Gestapo uniform has emboldened these men in disturbing ways. To make matters worse, the Shaulists will protect each other, giving the local people few if any alternatives to protect themselves. For many of the locals, their only hope is to turn to the Bolshevik partisans hiding in the nearby forests, who aren't afraid of taking on the Shaulists. The hardest part, however, is finding the Partisans because they are always on the move. The Nazis are relentless about capturing and executing all anti-German partisans. It all makes it very difficult to live in one of the nearby villages.

6 April—I have witnessed one of the worst two days ever here in Ponary. What I've seen are among the most horrific, appalling, and dreadful events since I first started documenting the mass murders here in Ponary.

Last month, I wrote about the frequent arrivals of the ever-familiar passenger cars that carried condemned Soviet partisans, along with their wives and children. The number of passenger cars has declined as of late, along with the number of prisoners they have executed, probably in the number of two or three hundred altogether.

For the past few months, the Nazis have intensified their pursuit of anyone with anti-German sentiments, and they are tracking down any local people who oppose them.

The Germans seem to be more desperate lately. Much of it stems from their repeated battlefield failures since their stunning defeat at Stalingrad. They've been beaten in Rostov, Kursk, and now Karkov, and their prospects in the Caucasus seem hopeless.

In their desperate need for fighting men, the Nazis just announced the conscription of Lithuanians for a new "Lithuanian Legion." Their very public calls for enlistment have fallen on deaf ears. The reasons are obvious. When you couple the Nazis recent losses, along with the fact that most Lithuanians no longer believe the Nazis will ever grant Lithuania any level of independence, many men have gone into hiding in the far-flung forests throughout Lithuania rather than fight with the Nazis. Many of these men are joining the Soviet partisans. Other Lithuanians have simply ignored the German's order of conscription, which has further angered the Nazis against the Lithuanians.

122

In the wake of the Soviet partisans gaining greater traction, the Germans decided to liquidate several ghettos in the outlying regions south of Vilnius and near the Belorussian border. They somehow convinced the local Jewish council leaders (the Judenräte) that they would move the Jews from these four ghettos in these outlying areas of Mikhalishki, Soly, and Oszmiany, and into labor camps or ghettos near Vilnius and Kaunas.

These Jews had heard horror stories about what happened in Ponary, so many refused to board the trains at all. To convince these Jews to go, the Nazis coerced Jacob Gens, the head of the Judenräte, to select who would go to the new labor camps or the ghettos. Gens and his Jewish police officer would escort them there. If they returned, it proved the Nazis could be trusted.

Gens first selected about 1,250 people, consisting of skilled craftsmen and their families. Gens and a group of Jewish policemen escorted these people on the trains to a labor camp and returned as promised. The next day, another 1,400 healthy young men were then escorted to another work camp, and Gens and his police entourage also returned. The remaining people were then convinced they were being transferred to another ghetto, so they signed up and boarded the trains, expecting to go to the ghettos in Kaunas.

That evening the trains arrived in Ponary from these outlying ghettos with about 4,000 Jews. The doors to the freight cars were locked from the outside, and the train was surrounded by armed Nazis and Lithuanians. When Jacob Gens and his police guards realized they were duped by the Nazis, they were arrested and swept away to Vilnius.

That morning, the freight cars were unlocked, and the Jews were led to the shooting pits. When the Jews finally realized they were in Ponary, many tried to escape but there were so many guards standing by that nearly all the escapees were shot on the spot. A few were able to make a getaway. With so many Jews sitting in freight cars, it took almost two full days to finish the job.

On 6 April at the Vilnius ghetto, one of the Nazi Sipo officers (Sicherheitspolizei, or Sipo) demanded that the Judenräte require at least 25 Jewish police to come along with him to Ponary the next day. It caused an uproar because no one believed these policemen would ever return. Still, the officer insisted, and that morning, the Jewish police arrived in Ponary and were appalled at what they found. They gathered and buried as many as 400 Jews who were shot while trying to escape the two previous days. All the Jewish policemen returned to the ghetto that night as promised.

This was the first time that I know about where the Nazis allowed the Jews to witness what was happening in Ponary and be allowed to live to talk about it.

It appears that at least one of the pits is completely full now. They covered it with sand and abandoned it. The other four or five pits still have room for more, but I hope to never see what I've seen these past days.

In the span of these two days, I've seen women being shot with children or infants in their arms. I saw people beaten so badly with a rifle butt that I cannot describe what was left behind. I saw Jews being forced to strip naked before entering the pits, and their clothing was fought over by the Lithuanian and SS guards. I saw several kind Jewish men show their true characters by helping the frail or injured get down into the pit, and then calmly lie next to the others of their group, waiting to be killed by a submachine gun.

I've described so many grisly details in my earlier entries about all the horrible ways people have been killed. I've tried to keep an exact account of how many of these innocent victims have been killed. I've also described the countless incidents of depravity among the perpetrators. Now, after what I've seen these past few days, I have simply exhausted the words of my vocabulary to describe all the gruesome and horrific events that I've seen. After seeing so much unabashed evil, I'm afraid I have come to accept it as part of normal, everyday life, and that it will always be this way. This terrifies me, as I fear I may end up growing numb to it all.

Above all, I wonder about what I've become. I was coerced to become a guard at the guard shack nearby, but I can rationalize away my guilt for only so long. I haven't as much as raised my gun once. It remains sitting in a corner of the shack where I leave it each day. But my hands now tremble with guilt. I am a Jew by birth, but a Nazi guard by necessity. While I've never betrayed my people with the sword, I worry that I have betrayed them with my silence. How can I live with that silence?

After he finished writing, his elbows sat on the desk, his expressionless face rested in both hands. Rolling up the pages of his journal, he gently tapped the papers inside his vodka bottle and sealed it. As he had done before, he carried the bottle out to the shed and buried it.

CHAPTER 32

17 September 1943
Kyusyur an der Lena, Siberia, USSR

"Watch your step." Zeneta helped Mykolas and Saule as they each made the short leap off the steam barge onto the frozen regions near the small Siberian village of Kyusyur. Each of them carried their blankets and what other meager belongings they could strap to their backs. Ugna followed, carrying Audra as they made the short jump to shore.

On 21 June, they had boarded one of five rickety cattle cars, each with sixty other Lithuanians crammed inside. It was standing room only. They endured these miserable conditions for two weeks until they arrived in Irkutsk and boarded another train, this time with twice as many cattle cars, so they didn't have to take turns lying down.

With constant breakdowns, track repairs, and other disruptions, their journey took them from Irkutsk, through Chita, and northward for a 3,000-kilometer journey into the Siberian wilderness, disembarking in Yakutsk, the only permanent city in the world built on permafrost. From there, they boarded another steam barge on the Lena River and, for another two weeks, journeyed beyond the Polar Circle, where they were forced to disembark in an uninhabited area near Kyusyur.

They had passed hundreds of barely inhabited settlements along their three-month-long, 7,000-kilometer journey from Novosibirsk. It was about twice as far to go to Moscow as it was to the North Pole.

What started as a small disagreement with her supervisor about her needing more food for Audra turned out to be her banishment from the factory. On 19 June, Ugna was notified by her supervisor that she and her family were being required to move to a new location in the north, to "labor for the glory of the Soviet Union." He gave her no explanation, other than it was her moral duty to go where she was needed. He said nothing more to her, despite knowing she was destined for a remote, uninhabited location a thousand kilometers north of the Arctic Circle.

Although it was September, the biting, early evening air felt like Novosibirsk in January. Fortunately, Zeneta, Ugna, and her children were well prepared for the cold. Most all the other four hundred Lithuanians traveling with them lacked winter clothing suitable for the bitter and dangerous cold that was soon to come.

Of the entire group of beleaguered travelers, only forty able-bodied men made the trip. Most of the group consisted of women, children, and far too many frail and elderly individuals in no condition to endure the Siberian winters, where temperatures were known to dip as low as -60 degrees Celsius.

As Zeneta surveyed the landscape, she saw no buildings, roads, trees, or any raw materials that could be used for shelter. Nothing existed to protect them from the subfreezing nighttime temperatures. The Soviet plan was to have them build their shelters. The only materials available were stacked inside the barge. Until they could build these shelters, they had no choice but to sleep on the icy tundra in the open air.

Several supervisors stood by, trying to appear important as people milled about waiting for instructions. The head supervisor was a pudgy, middle-aged man named Sikorsky. Whenever he barked orders to the barge's crew, they jumped. Once everyone had finally disembarked from the barge, Sikorsky again demanded that his new subordinates, the Lithuanians, listen and obey.

"Everyone must help to unload the barge," he shouted. "Everyone, including old people and children. No exceptions! Drop your belongings and get to work. The darkness will be here soon."

For almost two hours, they all worked to transfer the tons of cargo to shore, consisting of wooden planks, bricks, and some tools. One by one, a human chain unloaded thousands of bricks buried deep in the lowest parts of the barge.

The last crate held a huge tent and several containers of food. Once it was set aside, an armed guard stood next to it to prevent anyone from pilfering it. These supplies were for the administrators only. Everyone else had to fend for themselves.

Once the barge was emptied, the engines revved. Within minutes, it had turned around and was headed back south to avoid getting stuck in the frozen river. The passengers could do nothing but gaze longingly at the barge, watching as it steamed away in the opposite direction.

Standing motionless on the shore, Mykolas looked up at Zeneta, then to his mother. "Where are we sleeping?" He saw nowhere to sleep.

Zeneta shrugged, then eyed Ugna for an answer.

"I don't know right now, son. We'll have to talk to the others and figure something out."

"We'll probably be sleeping close to everyone else," Zeneta said. "Like we did on the train, remember?"

Then Saule asked. "When are we going to eat?"

"Probably not tonight, my dear," Zeneta couldn't hide her disappointment and softly stroked Saule's tousled hair.

Ugna exhaled in frustration and said, "We'll figure it out by tomorrow, I hope."

The two children sat down on the ground as they waited for the adults to decide what to do. Near the unloaded cargo, a group of men began to lean some of the wooden planks against a pile of bricks. Within a few minutes, they had created a makeshift shelter that could protect themselves from the elements. Once the others saw the pattern, they joined to move the planks and bricks to make better use of the space, allowing for additional shelters to be assembled. Just as it grew too dark to see, they had built enough shelters for everyone to sleep for the night.

As Zeneta, Ugna, and the children bent over to prepare their blankets for bedtime, the children sat on the ground and were surprised by the thin, spongy layer of moss below them.

"Look at this." Mykolas smiled at Zeneta with delight as he pressed his weight into the ground. "It's soft."

Zeneta reached down and touched the moss, letting out a quick giggle. "You're right, Mykolas. It sure is soft."

"It's almost like a feather bed, isn't it?" said Mykolas, pleased with himself for making the connection.

"Maybe so," Zeneta said as she spread out Saule and Audra's blanket. "But it's still going to be very cold tonight because there's nothing but ice below the moss. I'm going to double up our blankets, and we'll have to huddle up real close to each other so we can try to stay warm."

Many of the children cried and fussed throughout the night, making it next to impossible to achieve a restful sleep. While it was still dark, Sikorsky broke the silence with angry shouts. "Get up. It's time to work. We have much to do." He pointed his bright flashlight inside the makeshift shelters and continued shouting until enough people were awake and moving about.

"If you want something to eat, I need a group of women to come here and help prepare the food," Sikorsky said.

"What about building a fire?" a voice from inside a shelter asked.

The supervisor replied. "If you want to burn this wood, we've brought for you to build your shelters, then go ahead. Be my guest. But I would suggest not wasting your wood on a fire until there's another shipment of wood in a few days."

Zeneta listened to Sikorsky's conversation and scanned the scene, noticing a small group of women gathering nearby. She glanced at Ugna and tilted her head to show she was going to see what the supervisor was talking about. "I'm going over to see if I can help,"

As she joined the group of women, she asked Sikorsky with a kind tone, "What are we making?"

"Fish. There's some fish in those burlap bags over there." Sikorsky pointed. "There are some knives and other utensils over by our tent." His voice was condescending, but the women said nothing and went to work.

"You will watch this woman show you how to prepare raw fish. You will need to learn this skill to survive here," he said sharply.

A short, dark-skinned woman with Asian features, a round face, and piercing brown eyes smiled warmly. She held a knife in one hand and a frozen fish in the other, which she pressed to the moss-covered ground.

The woman spoke only in Evenki, an indigenous language that no one understood, not even the supervisor. With ease, she showed the process of slicing off the skin and then cutting small slices of raw fish. The fish was a taimen, a massive trout-like fish native to Northern Siberia and in great abundance in the nearby Lena River. As she cut off a piece, she stabbed the

128

slice of meat with the end of her knife and put the slice in her mouth, smiling as she chewed. She continued cutting off a few more pieces, offering the slices to the other women as they watched. The women were cautious as they stepped forward to take a slice. Grasping the slice with their fingernails, their hunger overcame their first apprehension of eating raw fish.

Zeneta leaned over to another woman and smiled, saying, "It's not bad. I like it. What do you think?"

The woman gave a quick nod but said nothing. Soon, the group of ten women had each taken a fish in their hands and fumbled as they struggled to butcher it.

"She makes it look much easier than it is." Zeneta chuckled as she struggled to hold the fish long enough to sink the blade into its frozen skin. Within minutes, she was skillfully cutting off thin slices of flesh and into a small pile on the ground.

"Mykolas! Saule!" she called. "Come and try this fish. You'll like it." Both children dashed over to Zeneta, eager to eat anything. Even fish. Ugna and Audra followed close behind. They glared at Zeneta as she pointed to the small pile of meat and said, "Try this fish."

The children were wary, but each took a slice, their noses wrinkled as they smelled the fish, holding it between their fingers and thumb.

"You have to be brave and just put it in your mouth," Zeneta admonished. "It's all we have to eat today, so if you don't want it, you'll go hungry all day."

Saule was the first to put it in her mouth. Feeling the texture of raw frozen fish was new to her. It melted in her mouth, and she made funny faces as she gently chewed.

"It's not fishy at all," she said with a smile. "It's good. I like it."

Not to be outdone, Mykolas took some meat and tossed it into his mouth and nodded. "Not bad."

Zeneta kept slicing off pieces, giving them to others as they gathered around her. When she noticed no one was around to watch her, she sliced off a few healthy portions of fish and shoved them in her pocket.

When the last fish was devoured, they cleaned up and went back to their shelters feeling satisfied. Before anyone could rest, Sikorsky roared, "I need all men lined up right here. Immediately."

They obeyed and, one by one, gathered around the Sikorsky awaiting his directions.

"You two over there." Sikorsky pointed at two young teens who were chatting with each other. Surprised, they looked at him like they had been caught stealing something.

"How old are you?" he asked the teens.

"Fourteen," they both said in unison.

"You're old enough. Get your stuff and come with us," he said without emotion.

"Where are we going?" the teenager asked innocently, looking back at his mother with fear in his eyes.

Sikorsky was unable to hide his scorn for the insubordinate question. "They're going fishing up in Tiksi. It's north of here on the Laptev Sea, about 100 kilometers away. You won't be back until it's too dark to see up there, sometime in November." Sikorsky then turned to the rest of the group and said with contempt, "You rich, privileged women will just have to figure out how to build your own shelters. Everyone has to pull their weight up here to survive. You better plan on working hard, because if you don't, you'll die." He walked away, motioning for the men to follow him.

Zeneta and Ugna glared at each other with confusion and panic.

With two younger supervisors leading the way, the men walked away from their wives and children, looking over their shoulders. A few men waved; others wiped away tears as they could do nothing while their families stared on in horror.

Zeneta turned to Ugna as she asked, "They really expect us to build our own shelters?"

Ugna's face was red with anger. "I know nothing about how to build anything."

As the men marched away, Zeneta shook her head and said, "What choice do we have?"

CHAPTER 33

10 September 1943
Ponary, Nazi-Occupied Lithuania

Olek was sleeping soundly when his bedroom door burst open and two *Shaulists* wearing Gestapo uniforms switched on the light and pointed their rifles at Olek's head.

"Get out of bed," the lead soldier shouted. "You are under arrest."

Olek squinted, covering his eyes, trying to make sense of the sudden intrusion. The second soldier grabbed Olek's arm and pushed him out of bed. Olek groaned as he landed.

"What have I done?" Olek protested. "Why are you in my house?"

Once Olek could focus his weary eyes, he recognized both men. The lead man was a Lithuanian named Mosin. The other man was also Lithuanian and was often seen among the execution squads, but Olek didn't know his name.

"You're Mosin, aren't you?" Olek said with authority. "What gives you the right—"

Before Olek could finish his sentence, Mosin stepped forward and landed a blow on Olek's chin, sending him backward, crashing into his nightstand. Olek's head was spinning, and he couldn't see clearly. He blinked a few times, fighting to keep himself from blacking out.

Once his eyes focused, Olek noticed the bookcase wasn't latched closed. His heart dropped. In a split second, he concocted a plan to keep these men from looking at the bookcase and discovering Mordecai's hidden room.

"What have I ever done to you to deserve this?" Olek said with pleading in his voice.

"You are a traitor," Mosin said with contempt. "You are the reason Trevakis was killed by the Bolsheviks. It's because of you he is dead."

"I did no such thing," Olek lied, knowing he had indeed spoken to a Bolshevik partisan. It started when Trevakis discovered a prominent Jewish couple in hiding and, for weeks, compelled them to pay him a tribute. When their money ran dry, he forced them to Ponary, shot them, then went through their pockets for money and removed their clothing. Olek had seen enough, so he sent out the word that he wanted to contact the Soviets and let them know where and when they could find Trevakis and finally put an end to his reign of terror over the local townspeople.

"We have reliable reports that you were seen talking to someone who is connected with the Soviet partisans," Mosin said. "Shortly after that, they chased down Trevakis and tortured him to death."

"Don't blame me." Olek shook his head in protest. "I speak to a lot of people because I work at the guard shack, but the only two places I ever go is here and the guardhouse."

"Not this time. There was no mistaking it," Mosin said.

"It's just not possible that I would somehow venture out somewhere in the forest. I wouldn't know how to find a Bolshevik partisan, let alone talk to one. The Nazis have a hard enough time tracking them down. What makes you think I could do any better?"

"We don't know how you did, but you did," he countered. "And you've always hated Trevakis. You've never made it a secret."

"Everyone hates Trevakis," Olek shot back. "You hated him too. He was cruel to everyone and cared little about anyone else but himself."

Mosin didn't argue, then looked around the room for evidence that Olek was hiding something.

Olek blurted out to distract Mosin from looking closer at the bookcase. "It was probably you who betrayed Trevakis. It could have been anyone."

The other man jumped toward Olek and punched him again. "Shut your mouth."

"We know you spoke to someone with connections to the partisans," Mosin said, putting his hands on his hips. "We know that for a fact."

"Well, they were wrong. It wasn't me," Olek retorted.

"You're always standing up for those Jews. You can't hide it," the other man said with disdain.

"You're out of your mind," Olek said, unable to think of anything more convincing.

As the men continued gazing around the room, looking for something of value they could take.

"You have the wrong guy," Olek said, again trying to redirect their attention.

Just then, the other soldier sneered as he looked at Mosin, "You know what, I'll bet he's so sympathetic to Jews because he is one." he let out a sinister laugh. "I think we ought to check him."

Olek's face flushed, then the color ran from his face, unable to hide his fear.

"Look at his face," the soldier said. "He's terrified we might discover his Jewish secret."

"Are you a Jew?" Mosen asked, fully expecting Olek to admit it.

"Of course, I'm not a Jew," Olek protested. "Why on earth would I work at Ponary if I were a Jew?"

"We heard that there's someone else living with you, but they never found them. It was probably a Jew," Mosin said coldly.

Olek went on the offensive. "I'm going to report both of you to *Hauptmann* Schröder. You are both way out of line. They'll send you both to the Eastern Front for breaking into my house, making false allegations, and accusing me of being a Jew."

Mosin paused as he gaped at Olek, assessing the risk of being reported to their Nazi superior officer and what would happen to them if they were caught threatening Olek without proper cause. Mosin turned to his partner and said, "I'm not worried about *Hauptmann* Schröder." He turned his head again at Olek and sneered. "I'm more worried that you're a Jew. Now drop your pants and let's prove it one way or the other."

Olek stared with defiance at both men, his hands on his waist.

Mosin lifted his rifle and pointed it at Olek's crotch. "One way or another, we're going to see if you're a circumcised Jew or not. You better hope you have some foreskin there. That's all I can say." Mosin laughed, lifting his index finger off the top of the trigger guard and placing it directly on the trigger.

He leered at Olek. "I'll give you to the count of three."

Olek took a shallow breath, then slowly loosened the tie holding up his pajama bottoms.

"One," Mosin counted. "Two."

Olek dropped his pajamas and underwear to the ground.

Mosin gasped and said with disdain, "Will you look at that? He's a Jew."

Olek bowed his head in defeat, reaching down to pull up his pajamas.

Mosin repositioned himself behind Olek and stuck the end of his rifle in Olek's ribs. "We've got just the place for Jews. The ghetto in Vilnius. That's where we keep all you filthy Jews until we're good and ready to send you to hell where you belong." Mosin laughed at what he thought was a clever comment.

"Let me get dressed," Olek's hands were trembling. "It's the least you can do, especially if you're going to take my clothes and sell them after you shoot me. I might as well put on the most expensive clothes I have."

Mosin nodded in agreement and stood while Olek put on pants, a shirt, socks, leather shoes, and a woolen coat over his pajamas. As Olek dressed, he glanced at the bookcase, hoping that Mordecai had heard the entire confrontation. He pleaded under his breath that Mordecai would stay hidden for a few hours until it was safe, then do as they had rehearsed if such a scenario were to ever happen. He hoped Mordecai would remember how to find Max's store.

CHAPTER 34

10 October 1943
Presque Isle, Maine, USA

Al sat on the bed in his barracks, waiting for the snowstorm to subside. He and the others on his B-17 crew were waiting to make their long-awaited transatlantic flight. They were scheduled to leave Maine and make a stop in Greenland. Then on to Iceland, to Ireland, and then they would arrive at their new, yet-to-be-known airbase somewhere in Europe.

They found themselves stuck in Maine for a weather delay, waiting for the gale-forced winds and blizzard to finally break. Once it did, they were instructed that they had to be ready to prepare their plane and leave within an hour. Given how bad it was outside, it was doubtful they would leave anytime soon.

Having nothing better to do, Al sat on his bed and started a letter to his sister and grandmother.

Dear Leva and Babcia,

I can't tell you where I am. And I also can't tell you where I'm headed. But once I'm there, I'll send you a letter, so you have my new address.

Since I last wrote to you, I completed gunnery school. To qualify for my wings, I had to fly in an airplane and shoot at targets being towed by another plane. I had to learn things like how to lead a target, I had to know the trajectory of a bullet so I could predict where it would hit. I also had to know how to identify enemy aircraft just by the silhouette of the plane. There's a bunch of other things I had to learn, and I could spend ten pages explaining it, but I won't bore you. What it all means now is that the United States Army says I'm qualified to shoot down enemy planes. I don't feel qualified. Frankly, I'm a little terrified because I don't feel ready at all.

A few months ago, I reported to my duty assignment, where I met the group of guys in my crew. That's also where we were assigned to fly a B-17G. These are the huge bombers I was telling you about before. The ones they call the "Flying Fortress."

We have a crew of ten men. The pilot's name is Captain Bud Sterner. He's a friendly guy from Texas, and he has a strong accent that I can't understand all the time. He's always giving me advice about one thing or the other. He's twenty-seven years old, but he's going bald, so he looks a lot older. He's from a place called Plano, a small town near Dallas. I tell you that because the captain named our airplane "Plano's Pride" after his hometown. Some of the guys were not happy because they wanted him to name it after a girl, because they wanted to paint a sexy girl on the nose of the plane. That's a tradition they have here with the US Army Air Corps.

Sitting next to the pilot is the copilot, a guy named Henry. Then there's Mel, the bombardier who sits in the nose of the plane. He also mans the chin turret under the nose of the plane. Behind him is Bob, the flight navigator, and he also mans the cheek turrets. George Howell is the flight engineer, and he is usually in the same compartment as the pilots, but he is responsible for manning the top turret gun position. All of these guys are responsible for flying us to and from our target, dropping our bombs, and getting us back home safely.

There's also a guy we call Woody. He's the radio operator, and he sits in the radio room between the bomb bay and the ball turret. At the very end of the plane is the tail gunner, a guy named Howard. Then two guys named Hank and Ray are the waist gunners. They man the guns in the middle section of the plane. The tenth person is me. I am the ball turret gunner. To be a ball turret gunner you have to be pretty small because it's a very cramped space.

The ball turret is kind of like a little bubble on the belly of the airplane. It's made of plexiglass and aluminum, and I have two .50 caliber machine guns. To get into the ball turret, I squeeze through a tiny door about a foot wide, and I have to wriggle my way into this little compartment about four feet in diameter. It's very claustrophobic because I end up lying down almost in a fetal position with the gun sights between my knees. My hands are above my head so I can control the movement of the turret, and it's very uncomfortable, especially when we're flying at high altitude because it gets really cold. The ball turret can swivel around in a complete circle. I can also point the guns straight down if I see an enemy plane coming from below. I'm usually the first to see the enemy, so they rely on me to warn everyone so they can be ready.

All the guys in our crew are really swell guys. They come from all over the country, so they are very different from each other. I told you about Captain Sterner and the other guys. But one of my friends is the waist gunner Ray Montoya. He's from a tough neighborhood in Los Angeles. Although he swears a lot and always talks like he's a tough, mean guy, he's really not. He always talks about his mama and how he wants me to come to his house to taste his mama's Mexican cooking. He's really a mama's boy!

My best friend and bunkmate is Hank Meyer. He's a quiet, Mormon kid from Utah. He keeps to himself, but privately he is a very religious guy. We've bunked together since we first met, and he's always trying to encourage me to speak up more, especially when Ray or some of the other guys tease me. Hank is always reading something. If he's not reading the Bible or the Book of Mormon, he's reading a novel or some other book. And for religious reasons, he doesn't drink alcohol, tea, or coffee. And he doesn't smoke either. He's the only one of our crew who doesn't smoke. He has helped me a lot in dealing with what happened to Papa. I ask Hank questions all the time about things, like what happens when we die and why God lets people suffer. His answers make me do a lot of thinking. He said that I will not only see Papa again, but we can all live together as a family in the next life. That's an interesting idea, mainly because I worry about dying all the time because *of my job. I wonder what will happen if I don't survive, and his ideas give me hope. I sure hope he is right.*

Well, I've got to get to bed. I just heard from Hank that they predict we'll be getting a call sometime early in the morning.

I haven't said this before, but I want to tell you, Sis, that I love you so much and I'm thankful for all you have done for me, for putting up with me and all my crazy ideas, and for letting me leave you there in Sweden. I am very grateful to have a sister like you. And I'm also thankful for Babcia, and for giving us a good Papa. I'm lucky to have a great family like ours.

I'll write to you soon. I promise.

Love,

Al

CHAPTER 35

11 November 1943
Vilnius Ghetto, Nazi-Occupied Lithuania

After tossing Olek through the main gate, the German guards left him to himself. The Vilnius ghetto was swarming with people, as tens of thousands of Jews crammed into an area roughly 1,500 square meters.

Olek had to find a place to sleep, so he wandered around until he discovered a warehouse on *Šiaulių* Street, where several families had settled. He found a corner on the concrete floor and slept there using some discarded papers as his pillow.

As he ventured outside the next day, he discovered how the Jewish prisoners tried to reimagine normal life. Many prisoners were compelled to leave each day as forced laborers outside the ghetto. Everyone else found ways to occupy their time.

The Nazis banned all public gatherings, yet that didn't stop musicians and actors from performing secretly for small groups. Skilled tradesmen, as well as writers and artists, continued their work despite the risks of drawing attention to themselves.

A robust black market offered a vast range of goods and services at the right price. Olek discovered a man with forged papers that allowed him to come and go from the ghetto. This man had a trustworthy contact who would deliver correspondence to people outside the ghetto for the right price.

Olek had sewn money inside the seam of his coat and was willing to spend whatever it took to communicate with Max. He wanted to make sure Max was aware he was in the Vilnius ghetto and would likely not survive. More importantly, he wanted to make sure Mordecai found Max.

Olek also arranged for Dr. Avižienis to find someone to look after the boy he had grown to love. This contingency plan was put in place over a year ago, so someone would take care of Mordecai if something happened to Olek. Despite having a good plan, he knew of so many ways for the plan to fail. He didn't want to die without knowing Mordecai was safe.

The plan was to have the letter delivered on the morning of Wednesday, 19 September. Olek waited for two days, unable to do anything but worry if his letter was delivered or not. Late that evening of 21 September, Olek was shocked to hear not only that his letter was delivered but that Max made the courier stay while he penned a note for Olek.

Olek tore open the envelope, his eyes widened as he skimmed over the cryptic note.

> *Dearest Sir,*
> *Thank you for contacting me.*
> *Your package arrived safely and has been sent to its intended recipient.*
> *We will continue to watch the situation closely.*
> *Sincerely,*
> *Your friend*

Early the next morning, hundreds of soldiers appeared dressed in both Sipo and Gestapo uniforms. Ukrainian security police were stationed strategically outside the gate, should the Jews try a mass breakout from the ghetto. A few guards posted flyers throughout the ghetto that read:

ALL RESIDENTS OF THE JEWISH QUARTER
MUST APPEAR AT THE MAIN GATE AT 12 NOON ON 23 SEPTEMBER.
ABSOLUTELY NO EXCEPTIONS.
EVERYONE MUST APPEAR AND BE COUNTED.
ANYONE WHO REFUSES TO COOPERATE WILL BE EXECUTED.
PREPARE TO TRAVEL TO LABOR CAMPS IN LATVIA AND ESTONIA.
ALL ITEMS OF PERSONAL VALUE MUST BE CARRIED WITH YOU.
ANY ITEMS LEFT BEHIND WILL BE CONFISCATED OR DESTROYED.
BY ORDER OF
HAUPTSTURMFÜHRER RUDOLF NEUGEBAUER,
EINSATZKOMMANDO 3

Olek wasn't about to cooperate, knowing that anytime the Germans rounded up Jews, the outcome usually ended in death. To make sure, he found a place to hide in an upstairs room overlooking the main gate and the huge yard where people were gathering near the gate. Looking out from the window, he could see hundreds of German and Ukrainian security forces lurking about on either side of the ghetto fence.

He knew the Sipo or Gestapo would come looking for every last Jew, including him. Realizing the round-up was happening below him, he looked around his building, wondering about the best place to hide. He searched the upstairs area, trying to find access to the ventilation system where he hoped to conceal himself. Finding nothing, he glanced out the window, and his eyes were drawn to a group of soldiers placing an upright piano in the center of the yard near the main gate. The piano seemed so bizarre and out of place. Olek was drawn to what was happening. Stepping closer to the window, he couldn't take his eyes off this surreal sight.

A Nazi officer stepped up and smiled, stroking the piano like a trusted farm horse. He dipped his head to thank the guards for setting it where he wanted. The officer was a tall, thin man. His immaculate uniform was tailored with precision. His trousers were tucked neatly into his knee-high jackboots. His peaked Nazi officer's hat appeared to be glued to his head.

A Luger pistol was conspicuous, yet safe and secure in a holster on his hip. With a flash of bravado, he stepped in front of the piano bench and sat down, adjusting it so his feet could reach the foot pedals. After a dramatic pause, his hands touched the ivory keys with finesse as he began playing Wagner's Sonata in B-flat major, a bright, happy melody that made the chaotic scene even that much more bizarre.

Meanwhile, Jews were heard screaming in terror. Some were being chased by security guards in hot pursuit. Other guards were violently dragging families from their hiding places and hurling them to the ground. Women and children were sprawled out crying out in pain after being struck by a fist or rifle butt.

Undeterred, the music continued. This well-known composition was a spirited piece, requiring technical skill and artistry, yet the officer played it without flaw.

Olek couldn't tear his eyes away from the frenzied scene. While the man played the piano, Olek watched in horror as a Gestapo soldier herded a few families out from their hiding places and into the yard. One family came out of the door screaming. The father and mother were being beaten, a young boy fled from the guard, and rushed toward the piano, nearly disrupting the musical performance as he begged the piano-playing officer for mercy.

"Please don't make us go. I don't want to die. Please help us," Olek could hear the boy pleading, while tugging on the officer's arm as he continued playing piano.

Unfazed, the officer's left hand continued playing, but effortlessly drew his handgun with his right hand and shot the boy twice. The limp body dropped with a thump against the sturdy piano.

The mother screamed, rushing toward the piano to attend to her son as he lay motionless, his contorted body tangled around the leg of the piano. The Nazi officer continued playing, furrowing his eyebrows to threaten her with the same fate if she interrupted him again. She dragged her bleeding son carefully from the piano leg. The officer continued playing as if nothing else mattered.

Olek had seen enough.

He recognized this action could only be an organized effort to clear all the Jews from the ghetto. He saw trucks lined up as far as he could see.

Armed guards were everywhere. He also knew if he were to cooperate, he would eventually be worked to death in a labor camp or end up in a pit at Ponary.

He ran toward the stairwell and down to the basement, dodging debris and other "malinas," or places where Jews once hid. As he continued rushing in the opposite direction of the main gate, he could go no further. Seeing a window, he peeked his head out into the alleyway to make sure it was safe. Seeing no one, he delicately lifted the window to keep it from squeaking and alerting a guard to his presence. Again, he glanced both ways and saw no one. About fifty meters away, he spotted the doorway leading to his hiding spot and temporary safety. Jumping from his position, he made a dash for it, stumbling on the window ledge but catching himself before tumbling to the cobblestone pavement.

Hearing nothing but his footsteps, he raced toward the safety of the doorway. At the end of the narrow alley, a commanding voice shouted, "Stop or I'll shoot."

Olek ran past his door and toward another door across the narrow street.

A shot rang out with a bang. Olek flinched and bent down as he ran.

"Stop now," the guard said. "Stop now or I will gladly kill you."

Olek rounded a corner out of the line of fire. Stopping to look around, he noticed a door only a few meters away. He threw the door open as a ploy to deceive the guard. Leaving the door open, he rushed to the other side of the street. He tried another door, but it was locked. A few steps away, he reached out to open another door and rushed to step inside. Holding the door handle tightly, he closed the door softly, releasing the doorknob with care so it didn't make a sound. Once inside, he locked the door and stepped back to catch his breath.

As his breathing returned to normal, he stepped toward the window. Glancing through the sheer drapes, he waited for the pursuing guard to appear. As the guard rushed around the corner, spotting the open door, he ran toward it. Drawing his weapon, he dashed inside and disappeared.

After a few minutes, the frustrated guard appeared and stood outside the door, angrily scanning the empty streets for any sign of movement. Seeing nothing, he draped the strap of his rifle over his shoulder and hurried off toward the main gate.

Olek looked out the window until he was sure the guards were gone. With the immediate threat gone, he glanced around the messy apartment he had stumbled upon. It was clear many people were living here, as they had left behind unneeded coats, shoes, clothes, papers, and photos that were strewn on the floor. Bending down, he picked up a crumpled photo of a young Jewish boy holding an open prayer book, wearing a yarmulke and a prayer shawl that draped past his knees. He stood next to a sign in Yiddish, but a handwritten Polish translation said, "*Bar mitzvah of Shmuel Czerniaków,* 1938, Warsaw."

Olek tossed the photo to the floor. He cautiously walked from room to room. The smell of cooking oil lingered in the air, a reminder that people were preparing food here just a few hours beforehand. He glanced up the stairs, then double-checked the streets again through the window. He ascended the steep stairway, holding on to the wooden handrail, wincing as the wooden planks creaked. At the top of the stairs, he saw two bedrooms. He walked toward the closest bedroom. A mattress leaned against the wall, and bedding was tossed haphazardly on the floor where it appeared that at least ten people had slept the night before. Seeing nowhere to hide, he descended the stairs and peeked through the curtains in the front window. The pouring rain was making large puddles on the cobblestone road. The roar of rain and thunder helped to conceal his presence from anyone who might be listening and watching for people to emerge from their hiding places.

Seeing no one nearby, Olek opened the door and dashed to the other side of the street in the shadows of the alley. Listening attentively, he hugged the walls of the building as he made his way back to the door to the warehouse on *Šiaulių* Street.

Olek's hideout was a crawl space beneath the building's sewer pipes. He had to shimmy his way through a small gap in the pipes. Behind these pipes was an open space big enough for him to stretch out. It was so well hidden that he heard other Jews walk within a few centimeters of him, completely oblivious to his presence. Olek wasn't the only one using an unpredictable place for a hiding place. Others were hiding in chimneys, subfloors, attics, drainage pipes, or behind double walls.

◀◆▶

After more than two weeks in hiding, Olek stumbled upon a significant stash of potatoes dug into the basement floor near his malina. He also found a leaky water pipe that dripped enough potable water that he could fill a tin cup a few times a day.

By mid-November, it was clear to Olek that hundreds of other Jews were still in hiding, maybe as many as a thousand or more. But their numbers were dwindling. Week after week, the Sipo's relentless searches extended to every conceivable space in the ghetto to find the last remaining Jews. With few exceptions, every Jew the Gestapo found was dragged out of the ghetto and put on a truck for Ponary.

Sometimes the Sipo were lucky and stumbled on a Jew who was doing everything right to stay hidden but was in the wrong place at the wrong time. Other times, a Jew was careless, letting down their guard and somehow revealing their location.

Yet far too many were betrayed by other Jews. When the Sipo arrested a Jew, they would torture them until they revealed the whereabouts of another Jew in hiding. Olek had heard these stories before and knew that no Jew was spared from dying at the hands of the Nazis, neither the betrayed nor the betrayer.

CHAPTER 36

24 September 1943
Kyusyur an der Lena, Siberia, USSR

The day after all the men left for Tiksi to catch fish for the state, the women, elderly, and children gathered to start construction of their shelters. They had to hurry before being handicapped by the frigid and perpetual polar nights.

Ugna and Zeneta lacked any skills in construction, but so did everyone else, especially when it came to building on permafrost. Together everyone struggled to figure out how to make a sturdy, weatherproof shelter with the limited supplies that were available. Ugna and Zeneta chose to be deliberate about their plan before starting their construction.

"Matis and I lived next door to a man who built a root cellar," Zeneta said, eager to share her idea with Ugna.

"You want us to live in a root cellar?"

"It was a way to keep his potatoes and other produce from freezing over the winter. The ground acts as an insulator, so the temperature was always pretty consistent, and it never got below freezing."

Ugna nodded, trying to understand Zeneta's unusual idea.

"He dug a hole about a meter deep and then built an A-frame over the hole." She touched the tips of her fingers together to show the shape. "After he placed his wooden planks against the center beam for the roof, he put dirt on the top of it to seal it from the elements."

"Do you think we can dig in this dirt?" Ugna asked, digging her toe into the moss. "It's frozen solid beneath the moss."

"They said we could use a shovel." Zeneta motioned to the tools piled up near the supervisor's quarters. "It may take us a little bit longer, but with the two of us, I have to think it will give us more insulation than if we just built on top of the moss. Don't you think that makes sense?"

Ugna studied the area, counting the available bricks and wooden planks that they were given. "We won't be able to make it very big, but it should give us enough room for us all to lie down next to each other and also enough room for that wood stove." She pointed to the stove that they were issued, which sat near the pile of bricks.

"We can take turns digging the hole while the other keeps an eye on Audra," Zeneta said.

Ugna laughed and said, "She's enough to wear anybody out. I don't remember Mykolas or Saule running around as much as Audra when they were fourteen months old. She runs everywhere."

The layer of permafrost soil was harder than they expected. After a few days, they were making slow progress, second-guessing themselves for their ambitious plans, yet they continued to dig.

Sikorsky and one of his assistants were often seen inspecting the progress of the construction efforts. He would strut around, criticizing women for their poor construction skills, but never offered any suggestions or exerted any effort to help. At times, he would point to a shelter, whisper to his assistant, and laugh as they walked away.

As he strolled past Ugna and Zeneta chipping away at the frozen soil, he said nothing, but his slight nod of approval suggested they were on the right track. After a week of exhausting labor, their foundation was finally complete, excavating a full meter deep into the solid tundra. Many of the other Lithuanians recognized the wisdom in using the soil as insulation and decided to change the design of their shelters.

Zeneta finished digging a post hole large enough to place the main pillar that would secure the wooden frame in place. Once in place they both started placing bricks around the pillar to better secure them to the wooden frame. With the frequent gale-force winds that swept through their camp, they worked doubly hard to make sure their walls were steady and reliable.

As they laid a row of bricks, a layer of moss was used as a mortar. Getting enough moss was another constant struggle, as it clung stubbornly to the permafrost despite their efforts to pry it free. Mykolas and Saule worked a short distance away, clawing at the moss with their bare hands while also keeping an eye on Audra as she tottered about exploring the surroundings. Within a few days, the two children had created an impressive pile of moss.

After several failed experiments at using the moss as mortar, Ugna discovered the best combination was combining moss with a little water and sand. As their shelter began taking shape, they were thrilled to see it was more than wide enough for the five of them, along with ample space for the wood stove.

At times, one of the other Lithuanians would stop to admire Ugna and Zeneta's work, often asking questions or seeking advice. Zeneta would go and inspect their work, offering suggestions or even spending an hour showing them the techniques they had learned.

Before long, they were all joining to help finish all the shelters. Once they had teamed up to help each other, the shelters were constructed with much more precision and at a much faster pace. On 25 October, the last shelter was completed. This gave them about a month before the sun went down for good, and the long polar night would continue until mid-January.

Standing to admire their work, they congratulated each other for their efforts. Their hopes soared at being able to survive the bitter elements that were yet to come.

The day after finishing their shelters, Sikorsky gathered the Lithuanians together to inform them of their new responsibilities. He liked being hated by the Lithuanians. He didn't like them because they stood for the bourgeoisie that the Soviets detested. These were the privileged wealth hoarders who used and abused the proletariat, or common workers. As a devout Communist, Sikorsky wanted little to do with them. But he also knew that if it weren't for this job supervising them, he and each of his assistants would be fighting the Nazis on the eastern battlefields. This was a cushy job in comparison. But for him to satisfy his superiors, he had to show he was needed. He created a constant stream of confrontational situations, creating an environment that needed his constant oversight and strict discipline. Otherwise, he was expendable and could be put to better use elsewhere.

Sikorsky and the other Soviet administrators were living in insulated portable apartments that were delivered by barge a few days before this group of Lithuanian exiles arrived. Each apartment was well equipped with all the necessary items they needed to thrive, including a few reams of wood and a full tank of kerosene to give them light and keep them warm. The firewood was fenced off behind barbed wire. It was forbidden for the Lithuanians to use that wood, and anyone caught stealing it would be sentenced to five years of hard labor in a gulag.

The Soviets also delivered the materials to construct a small kitchen, along with all the necessary items needed to bake bread. While the administrators could have as much bread as they liked, each Lithuanian household was allotted one loaf of bread per week. Otherwise, they were on their own to find any additional food they could. Each Lithuanian was required to work for the state, regardless of their age, physical limitations, or fitness to work. A weekly loaf of bread and a monthly salary of six rubles would only be given to those who worked their required number of days.

Much of the work was either tedious or backbreaking and generally involved working on behalf of Sikorsky and his assistants. Most people were given the assignment of fishing on the Lena River, or they were

146

assigned to cleaning and storing fish. None of the fish could be taken by the Lithuanians. It all went to the state. With administrators keeping a close eye on the entire operation, it was difficult for anyone to take a fish for their own needs.

Those not on fishing duty were required to complete other jobs, like cleaning out the administrator's apartments. Others had the unpleasant job of keeping the septic tanks, clearing the pipes of ice so they didn't freeze up. The most feared job was to be part of the log retrieval work group. They were assigned to venture out into the wilderness and search the banks of the Lena River for dead logs that had drifted ashore. As few trees could survive in the tundra, some trees further south would occasionally die and fall into the river. Finding these downed logs was an exhausting and grueling job. To make matters worse, Sikorsky insisted that each search group would be punished if it returned to camp empty-handed. This often meant they were venturing five and ten kilometers away, putting each member of the group at risk of freezing to death.

Upon finding a tree, a team would start chopping away at the ice to free the log. When they were ready to lift the heavy logs onto a huge sled, as many as six women were needed to lift it onto the sled. Four other women were harnessed together to pull the log through the snow. They each took turns in the harness to haul the logs back to camp. Sikorsky earmarked the wood from each log for his use. None of it could be used to heat their shelters, and anyone caught taking this wood was punished.

With so little to eat, symptoms of malnutrition and exhaustion were quick to set in. Scurvy became a significant threat because of the lack of vitamin C in their diet. Scurvy symptoms included lethargy, body aches, swelling in their legs, and open skin ulcers that wouldn't heal. As the disease progressed, scurvy often caused spongy and porous gums and a foul-smelling breath. Eventually, a scurvy victim would wake up and find several teeth on their pillow.

As the Soviets provided no medical supplies, injuries often festered for weeks or months. The sick or injured were often left to themselves. Those unable to care for themselves were not only denied their bread rations, but those who attended to them were also penalized unless they found some way to complete their assigned tasks to earn their weekly salary.

When the sun set at noon on November 22, the bitter cold of the polar nights had begun. For the next two months, they expected average temperatures to range from a high of -25 degrees Celsius to a low of -50 degrees Celsius, and often much colder. In that bitter cold, nothing worked well, more particularly their ability to think and perform everyday tasks. Being outside for too long meant they risked frostbite on any exposed skin.

As the temperatures plummeted, the conditions were much too hard for the weak. Many woke up with frostbite on their ears or noses. Others woke up with their hair frozen to their beds or the brick walls of their shelter. The death count mounted quickly for the frail and the elderly. Small children were the next to succumb to the horrible combination of extreme cold, exhaustion, and malnutrition.

Each morning, corpse collectors carried the deceased to a location outside camp. The ice was too hard to bury the bodies. That task would have to wait until spring. For now, bodies were stacked up unceremoniously, all were frozen stiff in the position they held before their last breath. The bodies of babies and children were put into burlap sacks, and the number of bodies was never counted because the corpse collectors saw no need to open the sacks and count.

With so little wood available, Zeneta hoped to pay or barter for firewood, but her offers fell on deaf ears. It was far too valuable, and no one was willing to part with it, no matter the price.

The next two months of darkness were going to be a threat to everyone, especially the children. Both Ugna and Zeneta worked hard to be prepared, but it was clear they hadn't done enough. Zeneta looked at Ugna and said, "I'm very worried about having enough wood."

"How much do we have?"

Zeneta scanned around their shelter, counting pieces of wood they used under their beds to lift them off the frozen ground. Some wood was hidden in any nook or corner they could find, anywhere but outside, where it could be easily stolen by someone desperate.

"Probably enough for a month." Zeneta gazed upward while she calculated how much wood they were using. "Maybe six weeks if we're careful.

But we're going to run out before long unless we can figure out some way to find more wood."

Ugna shook her head in frustration but said nothing.

Zeneta touched Ugna's arm, saying, "I am most worried about your children, more specifically Audra."

"They're just not getting enough to eat," Ugna said with frustration. "And I'm afraid they'll freeze to death if we don't keep at least a small fire going." A tear dripped down her cheek as she gazed lovingly at her children while they slept.

Zeneta nodded saying, "They've been so good." She knew they rarely complained, despite the condition. Her heart ached for them.

Ugna wiped her eyes and nose with the sleeve of her coat.

"All Audra can do is sleep. She sleeps all day and all night." Her voice choked as she said, "I've tried to wake her up. All she does is squirm a bit whenever I touch her."

Zeneta reached down and caressed Audra's hair, then felt her shoulders, surprised by her withering body. "When's the last time she ate anything?" Zeneta looked at Ugna with concern.

"She hasn't eaten for two days." Ugna's voice was a strained whisper. "I can get her to drink a sip of water now and then, but it's just not enough to keep her going."

"Give her some of my bread ration," Zeneta insisted. "Maybe she'll eat it."

Ugna gave Zeneta a quick shrug. "We can try."

Zeneta reached into her pocket, where she kept her bread warm enough to eat. She broke off a small piece and handed it to Ugna.

"Audra. Are you awake, my dear?" Ugna's high-pitched voice was kind and warm. "I've got something for you to eat."

Zeneta stood nearby, hoping Audra would answer, but she only stirred.

"Audra, dear. You need to eat something." Ugna's voice was pleading. "Here's some of Zeneta's bread. Do you want a piece?"

They both watched as Audra lifted her head slightly to see her mother looking at her adoringly. "Here." Ugna touched the bread under Audra's nose, then to her lips. "Take this, Audra. Please. You need to eat."

Audra lowered her head and closed her eyes. Zeneta watched Ugna as she wiped the tears from her cheeks. Ugna lifted Audra to her chest to embrace her. Audra fussed for a moment but didn't have enough energy to protest much, and she returned to sleep.

Zeneta reached for their largest piece of firewood and nestled it into the simmering embers of the wood stove. Within minutes, the flames reflected from the stove, brightening their little room and waking Mykolas and Saule from deep sleep.

"That feels good." Mykolas smiled at Zeneta and his mother, kneeling near the stove.

"It's a little treat for tonight only." Ugna smiled at her son. "Audra's not doing very well tonight."

"Is she going to die?" Saule lifted herself on her elbow, her voice was laden with fear.

"I don't know, my dear," Ugna said without flinching. "She's very sick right now."

Saule looked at her brother, then at Zeneta, hoping for a more reassuring answer.

"She's not doing too good," Mykolas said unfazed. "We'll have to wait and see."

"We're hoping we can warm it up in here a bit, so it helps her," Zeneta said as she looked at Saule and smiled.

Saule understood the situation, then rested her head back on her bed.

As the heat from the fire waned, the chill returned. Ugna held Audra closer. She fought the intense need to sleep, wanting instead to listen to Audra breathe. Despite her best intentions, Ugna fell asleep, only to be startled awake when she felt Audra stir. Hour after hour, Audra's breathing grew more shallow and less frequent. Ugna knew the end was near, but she could do nothing but hold her, love her, and listen.

Sometime through the night, Ugna was alert enough to hear Audra suddenly inhale. As the seconds passed, despite Ugna's silent pleadings for her to breathe again, Audra didn't exhale. Her tiny body relaxed, surrendering to the extreme elements.

1944

CHAPTER 37

4 January 1944
Kyusyur an der Lena, Siberia, USSR

Blizzards with gale-force winds swept over the Lena River and the surrounding plains around Kyusyur. The extreme conditions tested not only the strength and integrity of the Lithuanians' shelters but also their will to survive. The lack of sun during the polar nights sent temperatures down to -55 degrees Celsius. A mild breeze could send the wind-chill temperatures to -68 degrees Celsius.

The extreme temperatures were deadly. Corpse carriers made a daily visit to each shelter to retrieve the bodies of those who didn't make it through the night. On an average night, they collected about six to ten bodies. Some nights were better. Most were not.

Anyone leaving the protection of the shelter was taking their lives in their hands. Skin exposure to these extreme temperatures, even for only a few minutes, could cause painful, often debilitating frostbite. Inside the shelters, a constant fire was necessary to survive, but the shortage of wood stayed a persistent threat. Many resorted to taking wood from Sikorsky's private stash, knowing the risk was being sent to a gulag. Most people didn't care, and Sikorsky never discovered the thefts because he knew better than to go outside.

While the cold was limiting, the prevalence of scurvy made life almost unbearable. No one escaped scurvy. The lack of essential vitamins resulted in the body's inability to produce collagen, the tissue needed for healthy skin, muscles, and bones.

Zeneta tried to hide her excruciating pain each morning. Her joints and muscles were swollen to the point that she couldn't straighten her legs. Most of her front teeth were also loose and aching. The open sores on both calves were also large and deep, with some of the most extreme sores revealing her muscle tissue.

Ugna's health was also declining; her arms and hands were swollen, so her clothing was too tight and restricting. Along with extreme fatigue,

Mykolas and Saule also suffered from open sores on their lips, ears, and noses. Unlike many others in the camp, they were fortunate to have avoided diarrhea, the final stage of scurvy that always led to a painful death.

Just as everyone was waiting for their turn to die, to their surprise the Lithuanian men returned from their fishing excursion up in Tiksi on the Laptev Sea. Unlike the women and children who remained in Kyusyur, the men had been fed enough to avoid scurvy and malnutrition, yet all were still thin and emaciated. Some were wearing fur coats made from polar foxes bought from the local tribe of Evenks who lived on the Laptev Sea delta.

Among this group of Lithuanian men was Antanas Buchinsky, a physician. After seeing the deplorable state of the women and children, he rushed from shelter to shelter to assess the situation and figure out a plan to save as many as he could.

Seeing so many suffer from scurvy, as well as a host of other ailments and illnesses, he wasted no time. Ignoring his safety and security, he boldly knocked on Sikorsky's apartment door and waited for him to answer.

"Who is it?" Sikorsky shouted through the door.

"Dr. Buchinsky," he said with both respect and urgency. "It's critical that I talk to you now."

"What do you want?" Sikorsky didn't want to open his door to let the cold air into his warm and comfortable apartment.

"Please," Buchinsky said. "I'll be brief."

Sikorsky hesitated, wanting Buchinsky to wait outside and eventually go away. Buchinsky persisted, dancing in place to keep his blood moving.

Sikorsky relented as he realized he wasn't going away, "Oh, all right," he said in exasperation as he unlocked his door. He hastily grasped Buchinsky's coat and dragged him inside. "Make it quick. I don't have all day."

Buchinsky couldn't help but glance around his apartment and notice the fur coats hanging from a coat tree. Fur boots and mittens were tossed on the floor. An open can of pork and beans, sacks of flour, and sugar rested on the counter. Both had labels showing they were gifts from the USA, Russia's ally.

Buchinsky turned to Sikorsky and said with authority. "These Lithuanian women and children are dying, and they could all be saved if we could get some of the food in your storehouse."

"What makes you think we have extra food?" Sikorsky sneered.

"I followed a guard into the warehouse today, and I saw boxes and boxes full of canned food." Buchinsky's tone was direct and unflinching.

"Those things are only for my team of assistant supervisors. We need those to survive."

"There's enough to feed an army. You have plenty," Buchinsky said with confidence. "And then there's all the fish you have stored outside the storehouse. You've got enough to feed you and your assistants for ten years. We need some of that fish too because they need ascorbic acid. They all have scurvy."

Sikorsky furrowed his brow, staring at Buchinsky and assessing him as a boxer who would size up his opponent.

Buchinsky was ready to spar with Sikorsky, believing he knew what truly motivated him. "If too many of these people die, I know that won't bother you. But have you thought about what your supervisor in Moscow would say? Especially if you have no one to supervise? If you let these people die, Moscow would have no choice but to send you to a combat unit. You need these people alive and healthy, if you have any hope of keeping off the front lines and holding on to the power you now have."

"What makes you think I have any power?" Sikorsky said in protest, but his feet shuffled nervously.

Buchinsky gave no reply.

Sikorsky seemed to know he was out of his league trying to argue. He replied in a benign tone, "What do you want from me?"

"What these people need more than anything is vitamin C. They will all die without it. That means I need things like the cans of soup you have in storage. I also need some fresh vegetables if you have them." Buchinsky wasn't sure if they had any frozen vegetables or not, but he figured he'd ask.

"All I have are dried seeds for peas and carrots. If you want to feed them seeds, be my guest." Sikorsky said with disdain.

"Maybe we can figure out a way to sprout some of those seeds, and they can eat the greens."

154

Sikorsky eyed Buchinsky and sneered, "Good luck with that."

"I won't take more than I need. And you'll still have plenty for yourselves. If you want, you can send one of your assistants to escort me through the storeroom, and he can approve whatever I need to take."

Sikorsky nodded. "Are you finished stealing from me?"

"We also need more wood," Buchinsky said without flinching. "They can use some of the wood they've brought back from the river. You have kerosene heaters. They have nothing else to stay warm. Too many have already frozen to death."

Sikorsky shrugged his shoulders but didn't respond verbally.

"I'll also need to use the camp kitchen to prepare meals for the people who are too sick to help themselves. We'd also like to have the bathhouse fixed so we can disinfect people and kill all the fleas that are crawling all over them. We can fix whatever is broken, but they just need your permission. They haven't been able to bathe since August."

"Do you want my clothes? My coat? My hat? What else are you going to take of mine?"

Buchinsky ignored Sikorsky's attempt at sarcasm. "That should be all I need for now. I appreciate your cooperation." Buchinsky bowed slightly as a show of respect, then dashed out the door.

Ugna heard a knock on the door frame. "Hello. Can I come in?"

She was in too much pain to move, let alone crawl out of bed or stand up. She stayed huddled next to Zeneta and her children, saying in a raspy voice, "Yes!" She coughed to clear her throat, then said again, "Yes. Come in."

She watched as a man in a fur coat rushed inside, closing the door tightly behind him.

"I'm Doctor Buchinsky. I'm here to help you get better. I also have some soup for you. It's pea soup, and it's got the vitamins you need to help you with this nasty scurvy."

Buchinsky walked to the stove, pried open the can of soup, and set it on the stove.

Opening the door to the fire, he inserted a small piece of wood he had brought with him. "I brought you some wood for your stove. There's more where this comes from."

"Won't that be nice?" Ugna said as she looked at Buchinsky.

Zeneta said, "How did you convince Sikorsky to let you take wood from his stockpile?"

"Just lucky, I guess," Buchinsky replied modestly.

He turned to Ugna first. "Can you take off your coat for a minute? I'd like to see what's going on with you. It looks like you've got some swelling in your legs and arms."

"Yes," Ugna winced as she struggled to remove her thick coat.

"I can only imagine how painful it is," Buchinsky gently helped her with her coat. As he evaluated her arms, he gave them a gentle squeeze.

"Does that hurt?"

"A little."

"I'm going to press a little harder, so be prepared." With his thumb, he pressed hard into her forearm, leaving a divot.

"Ouch!" Ugna winced. "That hurt."

"I'm sorry, but I had to see if it would leave a pit, and how long it would take for it to return to normal."

"It didn't. It's still there," she studied the divot in her arm.

"Yes, that just means your heart isn't able to pump enough fluid to fill the pit. That tells me a lot about how your organs are working."

"Am I going to die?"

"Not if I can help it," he said, but his eyes couldn't hide his concern.

He turned to Zeneta. "Do you mind if I take a look inside your mouth?"

He tried not to recoil at the smell of her rotten breath, but he couldn't help himself.

"I'm sorry." She shook her head, ashamed.

"It's okay. That's all a natural part of scurvy. I won't think anything less of you." He glanced at Zeneta, trying to be kind.

"It looks like you've lost a couple molars back there, but luckily nothing up front, at least not yet. I'm sorry I can't do anything about the teeth you've already lost, but hopefully some vitamin C will firm up your existing teeth. Okay?"

Zeneta nodded.

"Can you straighten your legs for me?" he asked.

She shook her head. "Not anymore."

"Do what you can to straighten them out. Just keep working at it. It shouldn't be permanent, so anything you can do to loosen them up should help."

He turned to the children, putting his hand on Saule's head, and turning it back and forth so he could assess the open sores on her face and neck.

"Do you have any sores anywhere else?" he asked in a soft voice.

She nodded and pointed to her heels.

"What about you, young man?" he glanced at Mykolas and gave a warm grin.

"The back of my legs," Mykolas replied. "It hurts."

Buchinsky nodded, then bobbed his head back and forth to better inspect the sores on his ears.

"I'll bet those sores make it hard to sleep."

Tears welled up in Mykolas' eyes as he gave a slight nod to the doctor, but stopped because he didn't want his mother to worry about him. "I'll be okay."

"You're a brave young man," Buchinsky said. "It's okay to tell us when you're in pain. We need to know so we can help you feel better, okay?"

Mykolas nodded, wiping the tears from his eyes with the back of his hand.

Seeing the fire had heated the soup, Buchinsky poured a small portion of soup into four mugs.

"Here you go, young lady." He reached out to hand a mug to Saule. She struggled as she sat up in bed but took the mug and felt the warmth on her face, savoring the smell of the soup.

"It's hot, so be careful, especially with those trophic ulcers on your lips," Buchinsky cautioned.

"Is that what you call them?" Ugna asked as she helped Mykolas hold his mug.

"Yes, they're common with scurvy, but they'll go away once you get the nourishment back into your body."

"Do you need me to hold it for you, dear?" Ugna asked Mykolas as he struggled to hold the mug.

Mykolas shook his head, "I can hold it."

As Ugna took a sip of soup and said with a smile, "Oh, that's marvelous!" Tears of gratitude flowed freely down her cheeks.

Zeneta sipped her soup, closing her eyes as she savored it.

"Nice, isn't it?" Ugna smiled as she watched Zeneta enjoy the warm, tasty soup in her mouth.

"It's the most delicious thing I've ever had." Zeneta held the mug with both hands as she admired her nearly full cup of soup.

"Go slow," the doctor cautioned. "Your body needs to adjust to all the calories and nutrients. We don't want you to throw it up. It needs to stay down, so take your time. There's still some soup in the pot. You can have that later if this doesn't make you feel nauseated. Give it about thirty minutes and see if you can keep it down."

A few days after Dr. Buchinsky's visit, Ugna, the two children, and Zeneta were feeling well enough to walk the few meters to the bathhouse. They were escorted by one of Dr. Buchinsky's new assistants, recruited from among the corpse collectors. The doctor taught these boys how to help the sick, what symptoms to watch for, and which symptoms they needed to tell him about.

As they walked and closed the door to the bathhouse, the young man said, "I'll be back in a minute once you've removed all your clothes and are in the tub, okay? I need to check the fire on the water heater outside."

Ugna and Zeneta nodded, then everyone began the slow process of peeling away the layers of coats and clothing that hadn't been removed in months. The two children were still too weak to be embarrassed about being naked in front of each other. Even Zeneta and Ugna were in too much pain to worry about their modesty. Their biggest concern was getting into the warm water. They didn't know if they could tolerate the water on their open wounds.

With great care and apprehension, each descended into the healing mineral water. It was luxurious. They submerged to their necks.

Ugna and Zeneta let out an audible gasp of relief. The water seemed to infuse new life into their tired, sickly bodies.

Once they were all in the water, the attendant returned and said, "Now we're going to put your clothes in that machine over there. All except your coats."

He pointed to a large steel drum with a pressure meter and several pipes leading to and from the lid. "This thing will disinfect your clothes and get rid of all those nasty fleas." He let out a nervous laugh. "You brought some extra clothes, right?"

Ugna nodded as she closed her eyes, overcome with the new feeling of being relaxed. "For months I've felt like I've left my body, but now it feels like I've come alive again." Ugna dipped her head under the water for a moment, then popped her head up. "Oh, that feels so good!"

Mykolas and Saule both plunged their heads under the water, holding their noses. As they appeared, they smiled playfully at each other.

"Do you like that?" Ugna asked. "It feels nice, doesn't it?"

Her children smiled and nodded, then dipped their heads under again.

"Try it, Zeneta," Saule looked at Zeneta with an encouraging smile.

Ugna said with encouragement, "Come on, you'll like it. It feels wonderful."

Zeneta bent down with apprehension and dipped her head into the water. As she emerged, her graying, curly hair covered her eyes, and the children laughed with delight.

Ugna giggled at Zeneta's antics, then bent over and whispered in her ear. "That's the first time I've heard them laugh for more than a year. Isn't it a wonderful sound?"

CHAPTER 38

23 January 1944
RAF Thurleigh, Bedfordshire, England

Al and his crew started their mission briefing at 05:30. By 08:00, they were wheels-up and circling the airfield as they waited to join the main formation for their most dangerous mission yet. Today's assignment was to drop their payload of twelve 500-pound bombs on military targets near Kiel, Germany.

Captain Sterner called out over the interphone, "Please call out 'bombs away' for us. We need to know when we can change course to get out of this flak."

From his position in the ball turret, Al could see the bombs wobble as they cleared the bomb bay doors.

Mel Connors, the bombardier, answered, "Bombs away! All bombs have been jettisoned and cleared the airplane!"

Captain Sterner pushed the control stick to make a sharp forty-five-degree turn to his left. The crew reached out to grab hold of a seat or the bulkhead to stabilize themselves as the plane dipped sideways.

After avoiding flak as they fled their target, they approached the Dutch coastline, expecting an even greater barrage of flak. Al flinched as flak hit the fuselage and wings. The terrifying sound of the flak fragments grew louder as they approached the coastline.

"Captain," Engineer Robert Donny called over the interphone, "I think an engine is leaking oil. We're losing oil pressure in the number four engine."

Sterner noticed a plume of oil spewing out of the cowling. "I'm feathering number four," Sterner said over the interphone. "Adjust our power so we can keep up with the main formation."

Al could see the propeller blades tilt into the airstream and lock in place to lessen the drag.

"We're losing speed, Captain," Donny called. "We can't keep up."

Sterner tried to increase speed to keep up with the main formation, but *Plano's Pride* slipped further behind.

"Bogey at six o'clock," Al echoed the call from Howie and Woody.

"Keep your voice down on the interphone," Sterner reminded. "Stay calm and tell me what kind of plane it is."

"I don't know. What *is* that?" Woody looked out with real curiosity.

"I don't know either." Al strained to identify the plane. "It's too big to be a *Messerschmitt*."

"Maybe it's a Junkers 88?" Montoya added.

"You're right," Woody smiled. "It sure is a Ju-88. Haven't seen one of those yet, have we?"

Woody adjusted his goggles to make sure they weren't mistaken.

"Looks like he's going to attack us?" Howie said under his breath. Sterner peeked over his shoulder to watch the enemy plane.

"That's what he's doing. He's coming around to attack," Woody called out.

"I've got my gun on him." Al squinted to improve his aim at the oncoming plane. "He's coming up at six o'clock! I've got a good shot."

The Ju-88 fired its guns at their crippled B-17, but only a few bullets hit the plane.

Sterner announced on the interphone, "I'm headed down to that bank of clouds below us. Hold on!"

Al felt the tug on his stomach as the plane dropped. The gunners held on tight to keep their balance.

The Ju-88 was too slow to keep up as Sterner plunged to four thousand feet where the protection of cloud cover extended as far as the eye could see.

Al scanned the sky looking for any sign of the enemy plane.

The captain called his name. "Barsauskas, do you see him?"

"I see nothing, Captain. But I can't tell if he's in these clouds or not."

"Keep an eye out."

"Yes, sir."

With no sign of the Junkers for at least fifteen minutes, Sterner said, "I'm going to head for the deck and see if we can't make it home below their radar." He nosed the plane downward, heading for a break in the clouds. Although he risked being spotted by an enemy plane, he needed to see the ocean to help them navigate their way home. Flying just a few hundred feet above the water, Sterner picked up a navigation signal from England and was able to fix his position and direction.

"Captain, look at all those ships!" Woody's eyes were wide with amazement.

"Would you look at that," Al said as he spotted a convoy of merchant ships bobbing in the water below. Sterner pulled up to a thousand feet so he could take a better look at this unusual scene below.

"There must be thirty ships there. Boy, what a submarine captain would do with all those ships in a tidy, little row!" Woody said.

As they passed by the convoy a safe distance away, Woody called out. "Bogey, six o'clock."

The Ju-88 dropped from the clouds and unloaded a barrage of rounds that missed *Plano's Pride.* The German dived toward them but sped by as he drifted past Sterner's window.

The Ju-88 again slowed and set up its attack from two o'clock. Sterner increased his power and made a sharp turn into the attack trajectory of the '88. As hard as the German dive-bomber tried to be in a position to shoot, Sterner pulled hard on the stick to maintain a sharp turn, preventing the Ju-88 from getting a shot off.

"Nice move, Captain!" Woody called out over the interphone.

"That was an amazing bit of flying there, Skipper," Howie said.

Sterner's quick evasive maneuver exposed the Ju-88 to the full, concentrated fire of Connors, Woody, and Montoya. They unloaded a barrage of .50 caliber bullets into it as it passed.

"I think I hit him," Montoya said, "but I'm not sure."

"He's coming around again," Howie's voice was breathless. "Yeah, it looks like you got him. One of his engines is smoking."

Sterner pulled hard and again swung their plane inside of the '88's flight path, keeping the B-17's dead engine on the inside of the turn.

"He's still trying to get a bead on us," Hank said.

"Keep it up, Captain," Woody said with delight. "You're keeping him on his toes."

Sterner dipped his wing to the right, and the B-17 still had enough power to make a hard, tight turn. The '88 was unable to get in a position to shoot and again was exposed to the gunners on the left side. Al, Hank, and

Woody let fly a burst of bullets, hitting the '88 again, causing the second engine to billow with smoke. As it limped away into the clouds, the enemy pilot fired two bright red and yellow flares—a distress signal to the convoy of ships below.

"That was quite a display of piloting there, Skipper," Harris said.

Connors agreed, saying, "Captain, that was amazing."

Sterner aimed his crippled plane back down to the deck, lowering it back to just fifty feet above the water.

For the next two hours, *Plano's Pride* limped across the North Sea, finally arriving at RAF Thurleigh a full hour later than the main formation. Sterner had brought his crew and aircraft back home safely, with battle damage to the fuselage and engine.

Al and Hank inspected their B-17, pointing to hundreds of bullet holes that had ripped through the fuselage. Both had a sense of amazement for having survived this crazy cat-and-mouse game with an enemy plane.

As Al and Hank walked back to their quarters, they talked about their first real encounter with death.

"I think you're right, Hank," Al said, "I think it is a miracle we survived."

Hank nodded, saying, "I don't think any pilot, no matter how good he was, could have survived that encounter, especially on his first combat mission, without a little help from the man upstairs."

Al bobbed his head in agreement. "Maybe all your praying is actually helping us?"

"I do believe in prayer, that's for sure," Hank said.

They continued chatting until they arrived at their bunks. Hank kissed his first two fingers, then touched the photo of his parents and said, "Thanks for your prayers. We made it back safe again."

Al smiled at Hank, having heard him talk to the picture of his parents like they were in the room.

"I've seen you talk to your parents every day. You act like they are really here." Al looked at Hank with curiosity. "Why do you talk to them like that?"

"Oh, I don't know," Hank said sheepishly. "I guess it's because I know my parents are praying for me, so it helps me stay connected to them."

"If you think it would help, I'd be happy to talk to their picture. It seems like I've known them for years, even though I've never met them."

"Maybe someday you can meet them. They're terrific people. You'd like them."

Al nodded with enthusiasm. "Maybe someday I can come to Utah. You can show me around. I'd love to see Yellowstone. Is that close to you?"

"It's in Wyoming, but it's only a few hours away."

Chapter 39

29 January 1944
Vilnius Ghetto, Nazi-Occupied Lithuania

"Get out of there! Now!" a Gestapo soldier shouted. Olek jumped at seeing the end of a German rifle just inches from his nose.

"Come out of there now," the voice demanded in Olek's face.

Olek swallowed hard, knowing just how trigger-happy these guards had been whenever they discovered a Jew hiding in the ghetto.

"I'm coming. Don't shoot me," Olek lifted his hands so the guard could see them.

The guard held his position, gun at the ready, his finger on the trigger.

Olek untangled himself as he came from behind the drainage and water pipes where he had hidden for the past few months. As he stood up, his hands were in the air.

"Please don't shoot. I'll go peacefully. I won't cause you any problems. I promise."

The guard motioned with the end of his gun toward the exit. "Go that way."

Olek kept his hands up, walking at a normal pace, resigned to his fate that he would be just like the tens of thousands of other people he knew who were murdered in Ponary.

"Who told you I was here?" Olek asked, knowing someone had betrayed him.

"It doesn't matter now, does it?" the guard said without emotion. "But we can rely on you Jews to reveal each other's secrets. It's only a matter of time," he sneered as he pointed Olek out the door of the building and toward the main gate.

A light snow covered the narrow cobblestone streets. The ghetto had been quiet for weeks as most of the other residents had been rounded up and taken elsewhere. The able-bodied men were taken to concentration camps in Estonia. Women and children were taken to Ponary and executed.

As they approached the gate, an uncovered military truck waited for the daily roundup of Jews discovered in their hideouts throughout the ghetto. Thrusting the butt of his gun into Olek's side, the guard shouted at Olek, "Get up there!"

Olek groaned in pain at the impact. Weak and exhausted, he did his best to jump up into the bed of the truck to avoid another blow. A pain shot through his shoulder as he landed hard on the truck bed.

After an hour of waiting, two other guards approached the truck, pointing their rifles at three other Jews they had found. After getting them loaded in the truck, the Germans seemed satisfied with the day's success, so they sent the truck with its human cargo on its way.

Olek couldn't see outside, but he could tell they were heading in the direction of *Lukiškės* Prison in central Vilnius. It was only a few kilometers away and took a few minutes to arrive. It was a massive, four-story brick building with reinforced steel bars covering row after row of windows on each floor. Barbed wire wrapped around the length of the building between the first and second floors, in case someone tries to escape by scaling the walls of the prison.

The prison was teeming with inmates, most of them Jews, but Olek could tell many appeared to be peasants by the clothes they were wearing and had been arrested as resistance fighters.

Olek was taken to an interrogation room on the main floor. The long, narrow room was dimly lit, but Olek could see assorted torture devices like sheep shears, chains, whips, and other devices hanging on the wall alongside a photo of Adolf Hitler. A single chair sat in the center of the room. The wooden floor was stained with blood. Thick, concrete walls were painted dark green except for where the paint had been chipped away, exposing the plaster.

The Gestapo guard shoved Olek into the flimsy wooden chair and whacked the side of his head with the back of his hand.

"I have permission to kill you anyway I wish." The officer's voice was low and intimidating. "You have disobeyed the orders of the highest-ranking officer in Lithuania by choosing to hide in the ghetto. Our orders are still to shoot anyone we find in there. But because we are not the beasts that our enemies have made us out to be, we will give you a chance to live. But only if you tell us where we can find the last remaining Jews who are hiding out."

Olek said nothing, looking ahead at the green wall and thinking of his best response.

"I will give you one chance to tell me, and if you do not cooperate, we will take you to the execution wall outside and be done with you. It's your choice."

"I know you won't believe me," Olek tried to be convincing. "But I haven't seen anyone in the ghetto for weeks. I think I was probably the last one."

"Liar!" The officer smacked the back of Olek's head with his truncheon. Olek recoiled in pain. His hands instinctively covered his head as the room began to spin. As the dim light grew even darker, Olek could feel himself slumping in his chair just before he blacked out.

Olek awoke in a cell with three other prisoners. He rubbed the back of his head, feeling a goose egg still oozing with blood. He blinked a few times to focus his eyes on the three men who stood over him.

Olek heard them speak, but he couldn't make sense of any of their words.

"Where am I?" Olek asked.

As one of the men looked at him, he could tell he was speaking some Slavic language, but Olek couldn't understand a word, despite his best efforts to make any sense of the noise coming from this man's lips.

Olek heard the word *Lukiškės*; then he was able to piece together the evidence.

Despite their inability to speak a common language, Olek learned his cellmates were Hungarian Jews. They were trying to get to Russia but were caught in Eastern Poland and imprisoned.

Early on 2 February, prison guards shouted and banged truncheons on the doors to awaken the prisoners. Olek was startled awake after a fitful and restless sleep.

"You are leaving," a guard spat. "Get out quickly."

Cellblock by cellblock, hundreds of other prisoners were escorted at gunpoint outside and to a long line of waiting trucks. Many of the inmates were former Soviet soldiers, now prisoners of war. A few were Polish women and their children. The rest were Jews they had rounded up from throughout Lithuania.

After a short forty-minute trip, Olek could see the familiar young pine forest of Ponary. Approaching the main gate, he recognized the guardhouse where he had once worked and the posted signs warning onlookers, "Do not approach. Deadly land mines."

More than a hundred Sipo soldiers stood as sentinels behind the barbed wire that encircled the entirety of the Ponary killing zone. Nothing else had changed since he had last worked his shift at the guard shack a few months earlier, except it was he who was being herded into the killing pits this time.

The guards shouted at them to hurry, while others used their rifle butts to punish those who were too slow. Olek watched with sadness as the women and children were forced to disrobe. Just then, Olek realized he was part of a group of about forty men being led in the opposite direction from the women and children. Olek scrunched his face in confusion as he headed to one of the pits that he knew was already full and covered in sand.

Trudging up a slight incline, the familiar circular pit came into view. It was about four meters deep and twenty-five meters in diameter, with massive square stones forming a vertical wall.

The only way to reach the muddy surface below was by a rickety wooden ladder. One by one the prisoners descended as the guards screamed "Hurry" and "Don't take so long."

Inside the pit, a group of prisoners was finishing the construction of a smaller bunker hut next to an already finished one. They were constructed with pine boards and lodge poles. A curved, rounded roof was made of mud and straw.

Olek was among the first to climb down the ladder. While he waited for the others, he walked over to inspect the larger bunker hut with its compacted soil floor. Rolls of unused barbed wire sat waiting to be installed around the perimeter of the bunker hut.

Once everyone was down in the pit, the head Gestapo officer stepped forward. He had a pristine uniform, mirror-shined boots, white gloves up to his elbows, and an overinflated sense of importance. He shouted, "Make four lines next to each other! Make it quick or you will be punished!"

Within seconds, the group of men stood in four rows, each man standing shoulder to shoulder. The group consisted of a few boys about eighteen years old and a sizeable group of Red Army officers, some in their fifties. The Nazis selected these men because they seemed healthy enough for hard, physical work. As the men stood at attention, another group of soldiers climbed down a much sturdier ladder, carrying leg irons. One by one, they wrapped the metal collars tightly around each man's shins. The chain between each leg was not quite long enough for a full stride.

"You are here because you have been selected to do a special assignment that is of the utmost importance to the state. Your legs will be chained together to keep you from running away. You would be foolish to even try to escape. No one has ever escaped from Ponary, and you will be stupid to even try."

Olek gave a sudden exhale through his nose. He knew plenty of people had escaped. Mordecai was one among hundreds who escaped, despite the odds.

"If you try to escape, you will be shot," the officer said angrily. "If you try to remove the chains, you will be shot. If you do not work hard, you will be executed for sabotage. If you disobey any order, you will be executed. Do you stupid Jews understand? Anything you do out of line is cause for immediate execution."

168

Olek stood and nodded.

"Another thing you must obey with absolute exactness, and that relates to hygiene." He paused for effect. "Never, under any circumstances, will any of you touch us. EVER!" He shouted. "Even if it's accidental, if you even as much as brush any of us with your filthy skin, you'll be summarily executed. No questions asked."

He stared at Olek, then the man next to him. "You are no better than the vermin that you will find in abundance here in Ponary. To make my point, I'll use these two ladders as an example." He pointed to the ladders they had used moments earlier.

"Your ladder is only for you to use, and only when we have lowered will you use it to go to your work site and return when it's dark. This other ladder is only for Germans and other Aryans. Do not touch this one. Ever! Similarly, do not approach any of us without permission. Do not talk to us without getting permission first. If we need to inspect something you find, you will put it into a glove, a hat, or just leave it on the ground so we can inspect it from there. You must always keep your distance from us. Is that understood?"

Olek and the others stood in stunned silence.

"Good. Now that we have that clear, let's talk about why you are here. Your assignment relates to propaganda from our enemies that claim that one hundred thousand bodies lie here in Ponary. This is nonsense. It's all lies. In a few months, when your work is finished, I will defy anyone to come here and find a single figure buried here in Ponary. It is your responsibility to see that no figure will ever be discovered here."

He walked a few steps away to point to a newly excavated area of another pit a short distance away. It measured about a hundred meters in diameter and seemed to be nothing more than a pile of sand.

"Your job will be to sift through that sand and pull out any figures that you find and see to it that nothing recognizable will remain."

Olek glanced at the others to see if they understood what they were about to do. He also understood the Gestapo soldier's euphemism using the word "figure" to mean a human body.

When he had talked with other Jews who were also hiding in the ghetto, he hadn't believed the rumors that the Nazis were organizing "burning brigades" in Ponary. As the Russians were pushing the Nazis into retreat,

169

the Germans were worried about leaving evidence of their mass murders. Olek believed it was impossible to burn as many as a hundred thousand corpses who had been killed since the summer of 1941, above all because so many of those bodies had surely decayed beyond the point of recovery. Upon hearing the rumor, he dismissed it. Now, however, he was being forced to take part in the Nazis' grim deception.

After a few days, Olek and the others understood the hierarchy of who was in charge. The condemned workers answered directly to the Gestapo soldiers. These Gestapo soldiers directed the day-to-day tasks, supervising the workers, shouting instructions, and beating prisoners when they were displeased. Always standing nearby were the SS security police, or the Sipo. They were the enforcers, ever ready to shoot someone for whatever reason they wished. Other SS officers also stood by to oversee the entire operation.

As the process of exhuming bodies began in earnest, the stench was overpowering. Still, Olek and his fellow workers were forced to ignore the putrefying smell and work without any rest during the daylight hours. At sundown, they were escorted back to their bunker hut, where they ate a small meal. It was prepared by four women who were saved from execution. They were assigned to cook, gather water, and firewood for the seventy-six men returning each day from the day's gruesome labor.

As the days grew into a routine, Olek was given various assignments throughout the entire grisly process. Some days he would be part of a group assigned to pulling the figures from the sand using an iron hook. He would pull out a body and clear away as much sand as he could. Most times, the bodies were nude, with their hands tied behind their backs with barbed wire. Most bore signs of a single gunshot to the nape of their neck.

Occasionally, the corpses wore pants and had items like money and jewelry in their pockets. These items were turned over to the Gestapo. But when a worker found an item they could use, they waited until the guard was distracted before pocketing it. At times, he would come upon a group of priests or nuns, identified by their vestments. Some were still clinging to a cross or rosary.

Once the body was removed, Olek would load it onto a waiting stretcher where two other men would roll over to the "dentist," who used pliers to extract gold fillings. Each body was then taken to an area where hundreds of dry fir tree branches were made into large pyres nearly seven meters high. A heap of combustibles was spread in an area large enough to fit several hundred bodies stacked head to toe. The layer of bodies was then covered with another layer of small, dry logs, and the logs were then coated with a thick layer of kerosene or combustible oil. Once they could fit no more bodies on a layer, they started a new layer of tree branches before stacking on another level of bodies, then more logs and oil, and so forth. The process was repeated until about thirty-five hundred bodies were stacked in place.

The Gestapo would then place Thermite grenades throughout the pile to ensure it burned hot enough to incinerate the bodies. Thermite created a quick burst of heat at very high temperatures. Usually, the fire burned for three days or until a heap of ashes remained. No matter how long it burned, many substantially sized bones would remain, requiring a crew to pound the leftover bones with flat-headed earth rammers.

Once the rammer crew had finished, another crew would use a fine, iron screen to sift out any significant particles of bones or other valuables like gold teeth, jewelry, or gold that wasn't confiscated before execution.

After all the valuables were removed, the remaining bones were again pounded to powder, then the cremated remains were mixed with the sand from the excavation pit. A Gestapo guard watched closely to ensure that the sand with cremated remains was the same color as the sand that covered the bodies still waiting to be cremated.

The work was difficult. Without much food and water, several men grew ill, developing fevers and exhaustion. One of the *Sturmführer* officers was responsible for finding any workers who needed to go to the infirmary. If someone was working below expectations, they would have their chains removed and be pulled from the pit. At gunpoint, the *Sturmführer* would direct the prisoner down a path, deeper into the forest and hidden from sight. A few minutes later, the workers heard a single gunshot, and the officer would return alone, chuckling and saying, "I've cured another man of his terrible illness."

From then on, men would simply not allow themselves to be seen as ill, even though they had fevers, diarrhea, and vomiting. It was clear to everyone how important it was to always appear vigorous and healthy.

A week had passed, and Olek was drained and sore from the intensity of the physical labor. After eating his small portion of potato soup and a slice of bread, he rested in his top bunk, hoping to sleep and find an escape from his torturous existence. Keeping him awake was an impassioned discussion going on in the bunk below him. Olek leaned over to listen as three men discussed the construction of some type of escape tunnel.

The person doing most of the talking was a short, stout young man named Feivel Zalman. He came from a wealthy Jewish family from Vilnius and was comfortable giving orders and making decisions. He had recruited Chayim Lieb, a friendly and studious twenty-year-old who had apprenticed as an engineer. His task was to devise the best plan for building a tunnel and then obtain the tools needed to make it happen. The third person was a lanky, middle-aged man from Kaunas. He introduced himself as Moshe Shamash. He wore a perpetually annoyed expression on his face. As far as Olek could surmise, his skill was to criticize plans suggested by the other two.

From their conversation, Olek came to conclude that he was the first to learn of their tunnel plan. These three men originally wanted to keep their plans secret to lessen the risk of being discovered by the Nazis or be betrayed by another worker. However, the scope of the project required much more help than they first realized. Olek just happened to listen in at the opportune moment.

On seeing Olek listening, Moshe gestured to his friends and asked, "Should we tell him?"

They all nodded, and Moshe looked at Olek to explain. "I'm not telling you anything new, but we're all aware that once we finish our work here, they'll kill every last one of us. If we want any hope of surviving, our only chance is to escape."

Feivel then explained their plan to construct a thirty-meter tunnel, they hoped would exit beyond the minefield and the barbed wire fences. "The tunnel starts beneath the storage room used to store groceries for our meals."

Olek gave a puzzled look.

"It's the room that butts up against the back wall of the pit, next to our barracks."

Olek nodded, remembering seeing the small room.

"So, you know the room is about two meters square. When it's opened," Feivel explained using his hands. "You see all the groceries inside, but there's also a hidden compartment with a secret door at the bottom. This compartment can't be seen by the guards because it's hidden from any vantage point above. Once we open that secret door, there's a small crawl space that goes down at least two meters deep.

"Why so deep?" Olek asked.

"It has to be that deep because it needs to go below the stone wall of the pit that extends about a meter below ground level."

"Oh, that makes sense," Olek gave a nod of understanding.

"From there, we just started to dig the tunnel a few days ago." Feivel's tone of voice implied the daunting task ahead of them.

Olek interrupted again. "How did you get your tools?"

"We're using our hands mostly, and a couple of spoons we found on some of the dead bodies we dug up. Once we've dug a little way, we have to take out the sandy dirt and spread it around our bunker hut or put it in the toilets that they dispose of each day or find some other way to spread it around outside."

Olek was both curious and eager to help and asked, "How long is the tunnel so far?"

"Only a few meters or so." Chayim pointed to a spot on the floor to help Olek estimate the distance. "The problem we're having is knowing which direction to dig. It's hard to know for sure."

Olek thought, then asked, "What about a compass? Would that help at all?"

"That's what I need!" Chayim replied. "But where are we going to get one of those?"

"Some of the Gestapo guards carry a compass from their Hitler Youth days. Maybe I could try to get one." Olek rubbed his chin as he weighed the risks.

Chayim glanced at Olek, considering his proposal. "If you think you can get one without getting yourself killed, then by all means. A compass could make all the difference for us at this point."

Olek smiled. "Okay, I'll see what I can do. If I get killed, then I get out of this hellhole and speed up the inevitable. But if it gives me a chance to get out and see my girlfriend again, I'll do whatever it takes."

Thoughts of Leva occupied Olek's mind more and more each day, especially as the accumulated exhaustion and deprivation of each day took its toll on him. Was she okay? Did she still think of him, or did some tall, blond Swede sweep her off her feet? Maybe Olek was too damaged to still appeal to her. Maybe he was somehow too disturbed now because of all the killing and mayhem and chaos he'd experienced. No, Leva wasn't like that. She wasn't fickle or faithless. He knew she loved him. But what about now? Could she still love him?

Two days later, after a long day at work, Olek motioned to Chayim in the barracks that he had something for him.

"Will this work?" Olek asked, his voice giddy with excitement.

Olek handed him a square black metal object about six centimeters square and two centimeters thick. Stamped into the aluminum cover plate were the words "*Marsch-Kompass.*"

Chayim inspected the compass, his eyes full of astonishment. "How on earth did you get that?"

"Let's just say some of the guards aren't destined to be college professors." Olek chuckled.

"Do they suspect you?" Chayim wanted to know if Olek was still in any danger.

"He has no clue, and I doubt he'll report it because he's too embarrassed to admit that he lost it." Olek laughed again.

Chayim opened the compass, inspecting the magnetized needle, orienting arrow, rotating bezel, and magnifying glass.

"A friend of mine growing up had one just like this that he got when he was in the Hitler Youth." Chayim rolled his eyes as he reminisced. "He was such a piece of..." Chayim paused. "He'd brag about all the things he did in the Hitler Youth because he knew I couldn't join."

"Look who gets the last laugh," Olek joked. "Put it to good use, Chayim. I hope it will do the trick."

"I can't believe you were able to get this. It's a miracle."

Olek gave a slight nod of agreement. "Sometimes I think God doesn't care that we're suffering down here. But when things like this happen, I doubt he's ignoring us."

CHAPTER 40

3 February 1944
23,000 Feet over Bremen, Germany

Al unleashed a barrage of .50 caliber bullets at the enemy plane, hitting its right wing. Smoke billowed from the engine, and the plane dipped away to hide in the clouds.

"Two Me-109s at six o'clock high! They're diving straight for us!" Al heard Howie call out from his tail gunner position. Al could only watch helplessly as a second plane banked toward him. Bright flashes of gunfire appeared just seconds before the bullets whacked into the side of their plane. Al could hear Howie fire at the approaching pair of Me-109s, but it wasn't enough to stop them as they fired their rockets, jettisoning their tube launchers, then banking away. Al flinched as the rockets passed through their bomber formation and detonated below them. The underbelly of their plane was rocked by the concussion, fragments penetrated the ball turret. Al screamed in pain as shrapnel grazed his head, pulling away the hair on his scalp. Blood splattered everywhere inside the ball turret.

Dazed and in pain, Al was too stunned to move. His warm blood trickled down his face and over one eye. He wiped it with his sleeve so he could see what was happening around him. He blinked a few times to focus his eyes.

Captain Sterner called for a damage report. Al pushed the button. "Something hit us hard. There's major damage to the wing and fuselage. It looks bad enough—"

Captain Sterner again raised his voice and repeated his demand for a damage report, unable to hear Al on the interphone.

Al started to talk again, then he heard Sterner ask Hank or Montoya for a damage report.

Al inspected the microphone on his interphone and noticed the cord was damaged from shrapnel.

Feeling a burning sensation on the top of his head, he reached up to touch his scalp and realized a clump of his hair was missing. The blood again oozed from the wound and down into his eye.

With blood obscuring his view, he noticed the Me-109 had circled and was coming at them again. This time, the pilot of the enemy plane unloaded another barrage of bullets at *Plano's Pride,* striking the left wing.

"Damage report!" Sterner demanded on the interphone. "Barsauskas, can you see what happened?"

Al couldn't answer, but through the static, he heard Hank reply, "Something burst right next to Al, Captain. I think he's hurt."

"Montoya, check on Al," Sterner said.

"Montoya was hit too, sir." Al listened to Hank as he kept his cool and explained what happened to Montoya. "It looks bad."

"Woody, can you see anything from up there?" Captain Sterner sounded desperate for some answers.

Al heard Woody's damage report. "It looks like the tank under the wing may be on fire. Number two engine is smoking, but I can't see anything else from up here," Woody paused as he inspected the plane a little closer.

"There may be a crack on the seam where the wing connects to the fuselage, but I can't tell for sure."

Hank called out, "The whole panel is missing on both engines, Captain, but there's definitely a crack in the fuselage!"

Sterner didn't hesitate and announced, "Prepare to abandon ship! Woody, send a distress signal from our exact position. Harris, call out the coordinates while we calculate our position."

Al wiped some blood from his eyes again, relieved that the bleeding was subsiding. He looked out to see pieces of metal falling away from the engines.

"That crack is getting bigger," Woody called out. "It's not gonna hold much longer!"

Sterner declared, "Abandon ship!"

Al struggled to open the hatch door to the ball turret, to don his parachute and bail out, but he couldn't make the handle turn. He pushed and yanked, but it wouldn't budge.

Al exhaled in frustration as he pounded on the plexiglass and shouted, "Get me out of here!"

At that moment, Al heard an eerie whining sound coming from the growing gap between the wing and the fuselage. Desperate, Al continued to fight the latch on his door until he had spent all his energy. Exhausted, he exhaled deeply so he could catch his breath. Using his handkerchief to wipe away the blood from the plexiglass, he cleared a section so he could see what was happening around him.

The screeching sound continued as the plane twisted in the air. Al tugged on the latches, desperate to escape his plexiglass prison. With a sudden burst of energy, he yanked on the latches, and it flung open. He wriggled his way up, then pushed aside the hatch door and lifted himself out of the turret. The instant his legs were free, he grasped his nearby parachute and inserted his arms into the straps. Twisting himself into the harness, he pulled on the latches, double-checking to make sure they were secure. Just then, Al heard a pop, and instantly the ball turret jettisoned from the plane. Al's heart raced, his eyes bulged as he watched the plexiglass bubble tumble away. Clinging to a bulkhead, Al realized he would have died had he not escaped when he did.

Al searched for help, hoping someone else was there. As he glanced to his left, he gasped as Hank's limp body plummeted from the plane. Al covered his mouth in terror at watching his best friend fall helplessly, unable to pull the ripcord on his parachute.

Al knew what he had to do to survive. He fought the wind forces, feeling the plane begin to spin, the centrifugal force forced him to the floor of the plane, and he reached for anything to keep him from being tossed around. After a few seconds, the outward forces were too strong, making him lose his grip. Al slammed into a bulkhead, knocking the wind out of him. Gasping for air, he took in a few shallow breaths, but without warning, he couldn't fight the force of his body being pulled toward the open hole created by the missing ball turret, and he was flung from the spiraling plane.

Blacking out for a moment, the rushing wind startled him to his senses. His skin burned with the frigid air. His arms flailed as he twisted in a free fall. The freezing air sharpened his senses, and his brief parachute training seemed to click in his mind. He was suddenly aware of what was happening to him. Recalling his training, he pulled on the ripcord. A deafening whoosh erupted as a white ball of webbing, nylon rope, and dazzling white silk fabric burst from the harness on his back. Within seconds, the parachute had deployed, bursting into a massive pillow of white above his head. He felt a painful pull of the chute from his harness and under his armpits.

As he calmly drifted downward, the only sound he heard was the rippling of the silk parachute in the wind. Still a few thousand feet in the air, he scanned the German countryside, hoping to avoid landing near a collection of houses and barns below him. He scanned the fields and forest below him, looking for an escape route, but saw few options. He desperately searched to see if he could find Hank's parachute, but after looking everywhere, he saw nothing.

As he fell toward the frozen ground, he realized his descent pointed him toward a barn and a nearby tractor. Twisting and pulling wildly on the straps of his chute, he was desperate to change his trajectory; he felt as though he was being pulled toward the tractor. Bracing himself for impact, he slammed into the tractor's metal seat and gear shifter. He let out an involuntary groan as his lungs expelled all his air in an instant. Pain shot through his body as he heard a deafening pop in his back. His body was draped around the solid frame of the tractor. As he dropped hard to the frozen ground, he landed awkwardly, he couldn't breathe. Frantic, he fought to force air into his lungs, and he coughed and gasped for air.

He tried lifting his arms to assess what was causing the pain in his back, but his arms seemed too heavy to move. It was as though they were fastened to the ground. He glanced down at his contorted legs, but they seemed to dangle uselessly from his hips. As much as he wanted to stand and run away, his body remained limp.

He heard faint voices shouting in the distance. He struggled again to stand, but he couldn't move. With each attempt at moving, a shot of excruciating pain darted through his back and legs.

Wiping away the blood from his face, from under the tractor, he saw an elderly farmer running toward him wielding a pitchfork. As the man approached, his eyes wide with a mix of fear and anger, he could see the remains of the white parachute, but had yet to find the downed American flyer.

Al shouted, "I'm over here! Help me. I'm hurt."

Within seconds, the farmer rushed over to see Al twisted on the ground beneath his tractor. "*Na bitte!*" The man spat as he held his pitchfork with both hands, ready to stab Al if he made a false move.

"Help me. I'm hurt!" Al screamed in English, then in Polish. The man was unfazed, not understanding Al's desperate plea. Al knew some German from his high school days, but his mind wasn't thinking well enough to recall what he needed to say. As his body burned with pain his mind instantly remembered the phrase, and he shouted, "*Bitte helft mir, ich bin verletzt.*"

Startled, the man stepped back, surprised to hear German coming from an American.

"*Bitte helft mir, Bitte helft mir,*" Al repeated in German, then he said in English for emphasis. "Please help me. I'm hurt."

Seeing that Al couldn't move, the farmer tossed his pitchfork to the ground. He mumbled to himself as he approached Al with caution. The man bent down wanting to pull Al from beneath his tractor, but upon seeing Al's contorted body was unable to move; the man stepped back to assess the situation. Looking around for ideas, he finally concluded that Al wasn't going anywhere.

Al watched as the man walked toward the barn, and then he disappeared. He returned a few minutes later escorting a round and robust woman wearing a scarf on her head, a tattered wool coat, and rubber galoshes.

She bent down next to Al and asked in her best English, "How *verletz*... uh... hurt?"

"I can't move at all. I think I'm paralyzed." Al's voice cracked. The word "paralyzed" made him shudder.

She gave him a confused glower, then said "*Gelähmt?* she asked. "No Move? "*Gelähmt?*"

"Yes," Al answered. "*Ja, ich bin Gelähmt.*"

"I call *polizei und der Arzt* . . . uh . . . how you say . . . doctor? *Komm schnell.*" She said with unexpected kindness. She touched Al's arm and smiled, trying to comfort him.

CHAPTER 41

19 February 1944
Stockholm, Sweden

Confused and curious, Leva opened the door to see a man from the Royal Postal Service waiting patiently.

"Yes," she announced. "Can I help you?"

"I have a telegram for Leva . . ." he paused to pronounce the name. "Leva Barsauskas."

"That's me." Her eyes were fixed on the envelope as he handed it to her.

"Good day, ma'am," he said as he walked away.

Leva ripped open the envelope to read a telegram from the United States.

February 8, 1944
Government Office
Washington, D.C., USA
Miss Leva Barsauskas,
Maltesholmsvägen 1
Hässelby Slott
Stockholm, Sweden

The United States Secretary of War desires me to inform you that a report through the International Red Cross states that Staff Sergeant Algirdas Barsauskas is a prisoner of the German government.

A letter of information will follow soon from the Provost Marshal General.

J.A. Ulio, Adjutant General

Leva covered her mouth and stared at the telegram. She couldn't breathe as she thought about what it all meant.

"Babcia," she screamed

Babcia came as fast as she could from the kitchen. Leva handed her the telegram and she quickly scanned it.

"Oh my." Babcia mumbled. She put her hand on her hip, looking up at the sky as she thought about her grandson being a Nazi prisoner of war. She looked at Leva and reached out to embrace her.

Leva was determined to stay in control of her emotions, especially in front of Babcia. As they embraced, Leva hurried to wipe the tears from her eyes with the back of her hand.

"I wonder what happened," Babcia asked.

"His plane was shot down. That's my guess." Leva answered. "How else would he be captured by the Germans?"

"Oh, you're probably right." Babcia turned away as she scratched her unkempt hair, struggling to think it all through.

Leva watched her struggle as she processed the news. It's not the only time she has struggled to cope with stressful news. For the past year or so, Leva had noticed Babcia's slow decline in doing difficult tasks, like balancing her checkbook or remembering where she put her wallet or keys. It had been a frustration for both of them, so Leva had tried to protect her Babcia from too much stress.

Babcia nodded as she turned around. "I sure hope he's okay."

"At least he's alive, or else they would have said he was killed or missing, right?" Leva wanted to be reassuring but shook her head in frustration because it didn't come out that way. "What I meant to say is, we know he's alive, right?"

Babcia nodded and gave a brief, anxious smile. "That's right. But I just can't believe that my only grandson is..." She struggled to hide her tears from Leva, but the tears flowed freely despite her efforts.

Leva stepped up and hugged her again. "He'll be all right, Babcia. Before we get too worked up, let's wait until we get that letter they promised with more details." Leva pulled Babcia from their embrace but held her by the shoulders. Forcing a smile, she tried to comfort her. "We have to hope for the best, and take what comes, right?" Leva quoted one of Babcia's favorite sayings.

"I know . . . I know," Babcia's voice cracked as she answered, and then the tears came again, and they rushed down her cheeks. Babcia sat in a kitchen chair and they both sobbed, holding hands.

CHAPTER 42

20 February 1944
Ponary, Nazi-Occupied Lithuania

As Olek worked the tiresome tasks of digging up corpses, he found a friend in Itzak, a quiet, resourceful young man with broad shoulders and a quick, biting wit. They both attended Vytautas Magnus University in Kaunas, yet didn't know each other at the time. Itzak was a proud father, smiling when he talked about his two girls.

He, his wife, and two girls escaped the massacre in their Jewish village of *Užpaliai*, but they were later captured near Vilnius. Itzak was taken to the ghetto and then forced to go out each day for work. He didn't know where they had taken his wife and children. He hadn't seen them for more than two years.

Olek and Itzak discovered they shared many similar interests and experiences. They first grew to know each other while working on the screening crew. They would sift through the cremated ashes to remove any large bone fragments, gold, and other valuables. While they worked, their discussion was a welcome distraction. Often, they'd debate about their favorite professors or at least favorite classes, but they each shared a mutual distaste for the Sovietization of the higher education system that happened while they were at university.

As the burning brigade began their third week, Olek told Itzak about the tunnel project and let him in on all the details so far. Chayim, Feivel, and Moshe were the original tunnel diggers, but that number expanded to about ten, including Itzak and Olek. Digging shifts started just after dinner and lasted until nine each night. The next shift dug from three to six every morning, just before they went off to work digging up and burning corpses.

Most of the workers were unconvinced that a tunnel would be worth the effort and were far too tired to help spend their energy working on it. Having nothing to lose by trying, Olek and the others considered the tunnel as their only hope of surviving. Even though they were physically and mentally depleted each day, they hadn't given up all hope just yet.

Digging in the tunnel was exhausting, which made it even more challenging to do the highly physical work related to the corpses. Despite their fatigue, they would return from the day's work and then fulfill their assigned shift in the tunnel. Most chose to skip dinner if they were assigned to the first few digging shifts because descending into the oxygen-deprived tunnel on a full stomach usually made them vomit.

Tunnel digging shifts were no more than an hour due to the lack of oxygen inside. Lighters, candles, and matches were difficult to keep lit. The deeper the tunnel grew, the harder it was to see. It also meant that anyone digging couldn't stay inside for very long or else risk fainting due to a lack of oxygen.

As the tunnel was first being excavated, the sandy soil was both a blessing and a curse. The sand made it easy to dig, and they could use their bare hands, or a spoon or other tool contributed by one of the corpses. But the sand was also an obstacle as the tunnel roof often fell in on itself, putting Chayim's engineering skills to the test.

When the first forty men arrived, they were given the materials they needed to build a bunker hunt. It was made of dried logs covered in wooden planks and a straw roof. When the next group of forty men arrived, they were given more materials to build a second hut. Some of the wood designated for construction was used instead to help shore up the tunnel.

Feivel then convinced the guards to let them gather some of the dead pine boughs and small trees throughout the Ponary forest. He argued they needed the wood to improve their bunker huts and use it as firewood. The guards agreed. Each night, men were allowed to go out with a guard to find wood. Once inside, they stripped the logs into smaller pieces and used them as support for the tunnel.

Getting enough wood was the first issue. The next big task was cutting the wood to size while keeping the guards oblivious to it all. To mask the sound, the men would sing folk songs while the others feverishly sawed the wood. Without a real handsaw, they used what they found off the corpses: a few knives, a pair of scissors, a couple of files, and a serrated bread knife. Each night, the men cut enough boards to reinforce the portion of the tunnel dug out the previous night.

Each flat board was cut to the width of the tunnel, roughly seventy centimeters wide. The pine logs were cut to the height of the tunnel, about sixty-five centimeters high. A log was placed on each side of the tunnel to support a flat board pressed into the sandy, damp ceiling to keep it from collapsing. Through trial and error, they discovered the support braces needed to be spaced about every twelve centimeters of the tunnel.

Many of the men sat patiently on the dirt floor for Feivel to begin his nightly briefing about the tunnel's progress. Feivel gazed over the men and cleared his throat. "So, after three weeks, we just reached the ten-meter mark last night." He raised his fist in celebration. "But we still have a lot more to do."

His eyes skimmed over the group, then he bent down so Moshe could whisper a few words in his ear. Feivel shook his head and said, "I'll just tell them everything."

Moshe shrugged, and Feivel turned back to the group. "According to our calculations, we're making some progress, but we need to pick up the pace. One of the things we just figured out was how to install a light inside the tunnel."

The men nodded their approval, smiling as a rumble of private conversations speculated about how they were going to make it happen.

"So, I'd like to thank Itzak Farber and Olek Kosmen for finding a long string of wire the other day while they were out gathering firewood. How they were able to pick it up and bring it back without the guard noticing, I'll never know!" Feivel said. "We'll tap into the electricity as it comes into the toilet room. Who knows how to do that?"

A balding Russian officer raised his hand. "I'll do it. I've done electrical work before."

"Thanks, Leonid," Feivel said. "Once we get that wire installed, it will make digging so much easier. We can also turn the light off and on so we can signal to whoever's digging to know the guards are coming. It should make things go much faster since we won't have to stop and keep trying to light a candle so we can see."

With only a few men willing to dig in the tunnel, they divvied up their shift assignments and were about to leave, but Feivel made one more plea for help. "The soil from the tunnel is becoming a bigger problem. We need to keep looking for new ways to get rid of it. We need to work harder on this because if we don't hide the soil, they'll eventually figure out we're digging a tunnel. Please look for new places to hide it. If there is room under the planks of your bed, put some there. Someone suggested that we climb up and put some of it under the straw roof of our hut. That turned out to be a great idea. Someone else suggested that we put a small hole in our pants pockets, then fill each pocket with dirt and slowly release the sand from our pockets as we walk around outside. Let's give it a try. Whatever we can do, we must get it out of the way as soon as possible."

The men responded with a simple nod.

"That's all we have for tonight," Feivel glanced around the room to see if anyone else wanted to speak. "Okay. See me if you have any problems with your assignments."

The next day, Olek and Itzak were assigned to take their turn digging up corpses. This section of the burial pit was abnormally difficult. While most of these corpses were still clothed, more and more of these corpses adhered to each other due to advanced stages of decomposition. Not only was the stench more intense and sickening, but the nature of the job was more tiresome. Itzak would dislodge a body with his shovel and lift it from the pile. Olek would struggle to separate the figure from the other corpses, brushing off as much of the wet and gelatinous sand as he could. Then Olek would lift the feet and Itzak would reach under the armpits and lift the corpse to a waiting stretcher, where it was wheeled away.

Olek had spent an hour digging in the tunnel earlier that day and was exhausted. He turned away from the stench of the pit to catch his breath and stretch his aching back. As his face was turned away, he heard Itzak let out a quick inhale of surprise, then give a loud, mournful groan. Olek looked over and saw Itzak pull up three corpses that appeared to be a woman and two children. As Itzak lifted the adult woman, the children appeared to be clinging to each other. He cried out, "Oh please—not my family." He turned to Olek, sobbing, "It's my wife, Chava, and my two girls, Golda and Malka."

Itzak fell to his knees, his shoulders sagged. Crying quietly, he tenderly caressed the tussled hair of his wife's decomposing body.

"Are you sure it's her?" Olek asked, unable to grasp the scene unfolding before him. "Maybe it's just someone who looks like her?"

"No," Itzak couldn't be consoled. "I recognize their coats."

Itzak stroked the fabric of his daughter's coat, then grasped the collar to reveal some handwritten Yiddish characters. "See, it says 'Malka.'" He inspected the coat of the other small corpse and recognized his handwriting with Golda's name.

Itzak buried his face in his hands and sobbed. Olek stood by while Itzak's bitter tears flowed down his cheeks. Looking on, Olek wiped the tears from his own eyes, resting his hand on Itzak's shoulder.

"I'm so sorry, my friend. I'm so sorry," Olek said.

"Get to work," the guard's voice was loud and demanding. "Stop wasting time."

Olek gave an angry glance at the guard, then turned away without saying a word. The guard stood, infuriated that Olek would disobey his command.

"Hey, you. You heard me," the guard lifted his rifle to threaten Olek and Itzak.

"Please," Olek begged. "He just found his family. Can he take a minute? Please?"

The guard's eyes widened with disbelief, then he realized that a prisoner had recognized a corpse. The guard stared at Itzak for an uncomfortable moment, then, with uncharacteristic compassion, he turned away, leaving Itzak a minute to mourn.

A few other workers nearby noticed Itzak sobbing and the guard's unusual reaction of turning away. Olek took a few steps toward one of them and said, "He found his wife and two girls among the corpses. Their names are written inside their coats."

Gasps of disbelief were heard among the prisoners as one by one they shared what had happened to Itzak. A few workers put down their tools and approached the sacred scene. As Itzak regained his composure, he stood wiping his eyes. A few men stood to pay their respects, removing their hats and bowing their heads to honor Itzak's family.

Chayim was nearby and approached Itzak. "I'm very sorry, Itzak. I truly am. Olek and I will take care of their bodies, and I promise we'll do everything we can to give them the proper respect they deserve. Would that be okay?"

Itzak wiped his eyes, looking up nervously at the guards waiting for them to start shouting again at them.

"That would be very kind," Itzak smiled through his tears. "Thank you."

CHAPTER 43

23 February 1944
Bremen City Jail, Germany

Al rested on a gurney in a foul-smelling basement of the Bremen Jail, the first stop for all captured American airmen in this area of northern Germany. The facing wall was boarded up after a recent bombing. The deep cuts on Al's scalp burned, and whenever he moved his head, it bled into his eyes and onto the gurney. Without the use of his hands, he was at the mercy of the Nazis looking after him.

Al was startled when a short, pudgy man approached. His thinning hair was combed to cover his otherwise bald head. Wearing a white armband with the crimson cross indicating he represented the International Red Cross, he clung to a clipboard as he closed the door behind him. Asking in English but with a distinct German accent, he said, "Ve must complete zis form so vee can inform your family zat you are now a prisoner of ze sird reich. Vaht is your name?"

"Al Barsauskas." His voice was hoarse and raspy.

"Vaht is your unit?"

"I'm with..." Al hesitated, realizing he can't share information like that. "You can't ask me that question."

"Oh, I'm not viss ze military. I am viss ze Red Cross."

Al blinked a few times, struggling to clear his mind. He paused to remind himself of what to say. "I am Staff Sergeant Algirdas Barsauskas. My serial number is 433210."

"Okay," the man said with a smile. And vaht is your base in England?"

Al glared at him and said again, "I am Staff Sergeant Algirdas Barsauskas, serial number 433210."

"I don't sink you understand," the man said with some impatience. "Ve haf no vay of notifying ze military officials of your country, nor can vee inform your family zat you are alive. Do you want zem to assume you are dead?"

Al thought for a moment, then remembered the countless times he had been drilled about not revealing any information other than the basics: name, rank, and serial number.

"Vaht is your home address?" The man persisted.

Al said nothing and turned his head.

The man's voice grew more frustrated. "Vaht is your home address, Staff Sergeant? It's ze only vay ze International Red Cross can notify your next of kin about your injury and zat you are alive."

With his head turned away from the man, Al's voice grew weaker, "Staff Sergeant Algirdas Barsauskas. Serial number 433210."

The man continued to pepper Al with questions, but Al ignored him. Frustrated, the man let out an exasperated exhale and walked away.

Al fell deep asleep in the darkened room but was startled awake at the sound of people banging on the walls outside his door. He lifted his head to orient himself, blinking his eyes a few times, trying to focus. Too dark to see much, his head dropped to the gurney, making his head throb along with his back and ribs. He again tried to move his feet, but he couldn't feel if they were moving or not. Exasperated with his inability to move his legs, he tried lifting his arms, but he could only feel his shoulders flex, as he had no control of either arm.

He slept until two uniformed guards appeared and opened a door, letting in the bright sunlight. Working fast, they loaded him into a waiting ambulance where two other Americans sat next to him.

"You must not talk," one of the guards stomped his foot. "No talking."

Al noticed one man's arm was broken and disfigured. He held his arm with the other, grimacing in pain as he sat. The other man's head was wrapped in gauze, covering one eye. He glanced at Al, lifted his chin, and uttered a simple "hello."

Al nodded back and smiled but remembered his briefing about saying nothing to anyone who appeared to be an American. The Germans were known to disguise intelligence officers as injured American soldiers to gather information.

After an hour-long drive, the military ambulance stopped at a long, green military barracks. The sign above the door said *Lazerett* X-B (military hospital). As Al felt himself being pulled from the ambulance, he noticed row after row of barracks.

"Where are we?" he asked, then remembered to speak in German, "*Wo sind wir?*"

The man said, "*Das ist Stalag zehn-B.*"

"Stalag Ten-B," he said again, "*Wo sind wir?*"

"*Nördlich von Bremen,*" he said curtly. "*Keine Fragen,*" he said, wagging his finger. "No more ask."

"How far north of Bremen?" Al asked, pushing his luck. The man ignored the question but helped lift Al through the double doors and inside the building. As they set the gurney on the floor, Al looked up to see nurses and aides scurrying about, preparing to begin the admission process.

They removed Al's uniform and dressed him in a hospital gown. Next to him was a small duffle bag where they stored his uniform, boots, and coat, but all military insignias were removed. As with all new POWs, Al was given a bed bath with a disinfectant that made the skin on his face feel dry and itchy. A photographer came and took his picture as he lay in his hospital bed. Al could do nothing but wait as a gray-haired woman took her time completing an index card with Al's personal details. Afterward, Al was given a POW number that the women double-checked with the index card and a metal tag attached to a small chain. She nodded, giving a quiet "uh-huh" and strung the metal tag around Al's neck.

After a week, Al was discouraged because his legs still wouldn't move. He did, however, gain some of the mobility back in his arms. Although he couldn't grasp anything yet with his fingers, he could reach up to scratch the stitches on his scalp that were a constant irritation. If he happened to move in just the wrong way, he'd cringe in pain from the wounds that still bothered him on his back. His ribs were also quite sore, and he felt sharp pains in his stomach when he coughed.

Al was feeling stronger, and his energy levels were getting better. But he still required two brawny orderlies to help him use the toilet or manage other daily hygiene needs.

Al was one of the most difficult patients for the staff, and some days he would be left in his bed all day. Unable to use the toilet on his own, he couldn't feel when he needed to urinate. At day's end, he was wet, uncomfortable, and embarrassed. Despite calling for help, no one came. He needed the time and resources that this overworked medical staff didn't have. Al could do nothing but suffer in silence.

Near the end of February, a German doctor walked into the dorm room where Al and seven other Americans rested on their hospital beds. Each of the men was seriously injured, all with some type of debilitating injury.

"Can I get your attention?" the doctor said loudly, displaying his impressive English skills. "I have something important to tell you."

Al looked up at the doctor, wide-eyed.

"We have just learned that arrangements have been made for a prisoner exchange that will take place next week. You will be going back to your country, but we have six days to get you ready so you can travel to *Kreuzlingen*, Switzerland, in time for the exchange to occur."

Al scanned the room, wondering how they were going to transport all these prisoners on a train to Switzerland. It seemed like a massive endeavor.

"You will be leaving tonight," he said with authority. "You must do everything you can to help us get you ready."

An audible gasp rang throughout the room as the patients realized it was all going to happen that day.

"Each of you will be escorted by a nurse who will care for you until you are taken into custody by the Swiss government, which will be acting on behalf of your country. From there, they will transport you back to your country. Don't ask me any questions because I've told you all that I know."

CHAPTER 44

2 March 1944
Stalag 10-B, Sandbostel, Germany

Except for making friends with his nurse, Al was otherwise miserable during the train ride to Switzerland. For five days, they traveled at various speeds, making multiple stops in Bremen, Hannover, and Göttingen. Every major city and town was destroyed, with rubble piled up on every corner. The people seemed to be walking around in a daze.

He and his nurse chatted about everything but politics and the war. Her name was Helga, and Al grew to appreciate her dedication to her job, as well as her willingness to help him with almost anything he needed. Al and the other patients were given special rations that allowed them to eat more than just one meal a day, unlike all the other prisoners on the train.

Al could do nothing but wait and stare out the window during each long and boring delay. Sometimes they waited while they swapped out train engines. A few times, they waited while crews repaired the tracks after American bombs destroyed them.

Throughout the early morning of 3 March, the train stopped multiple times as more passenger cars were connected to their train. At sunup, each of the American prisoners had to get dressed in their uniforms, though it was a challenge for those whose arms or legs were in plaster casts or slings.

Although Al couldn't help himself, Helga dressed him. It was the first time he'd worn his uniform since he was shot down almost a month ago. He had lost a few pounds—pounds he couldn't afford to lose, given his already small frame. She cinched up his belt to the last hole, but his pants were still too baggy for his liking.

After arriving in *Konstanz* near the Swiss border, the train stopped, and a handful of German guards came aboard. One by one, they checked the identification of each person aboard, including the security guards, nurses, doctors, and orderlies. Everyone had to produce their proper papers before continuing. The process seemed to be an unexpected one, as the train staff seemed annoyed that they were delayed for nearly two hours.

At the border, the train stopped again, and the German guards marched off. That left several German escorts to remain until the exchange was complete. Anxiously, they checked and rechecked their list, making sure there were enough people to make a one-for-one exchange.

As they crossed the German border into Switzerland, Al noticed the sullen faces of the Americans instantly change, and the formerly quiet train car erupted with boisterous conversations laced with smiles and laughter.

One of the Swiss officials stepped into the car and said, "Once we get to *Kreuzlingen*, we have about seven hundred fifty passengers that need to come aboard this train headed back to Germany. We have about six hundred on our train who need to get on the other train headed to Portugal. It's going to take quite a while because each person's name has to be checked against the official list approved by both governments, and we also have to get all of you injured passengers off first. Once we get you transferred to that other train, it will likely take a few hours for this entire process to take place. All we can ask of you is to be patient. Okay?"

In less than five minutes, the train crossed the Rhine River and pulled into the Kreuzlingen station. The eager Americans leaving Germany gaped at the passengers of the train car that pulled side to side with their train.

With the windows of both trains aligned, Al lifted himself on his elbows so he could see the passengers as they passed by. Al was stunned to see their sullen faces as they looked out their window. Many wore a woeful expression, revealing the painful reality that they were leaving their safety behind and entering their war-ravaged homeland.

As the train inched along, at long last it slowed and squealed to a stop. Al heard the train engine cut off, and the incessant low rumble he had come to ignore went silent. He could now hear whispered conversations that seemed to echo in the silence.

Al couldn't tear his eyes away from looking at the people on the opposite train. Despite the awkward glances of these everyday-looking people, Al's eyes locked on a middle-aged couple that sent a wave of adrenaline through his body. His face went hot and flushed.

Al leaned in for a closer look at the couple. The man was looking down, but Al could see both of their faces.

"No," he said to himself.

Hearing him, his nurse replied. "No, what?"

"Do you see that couple straight ahead?"

"The ones to the left of that family with the dog?" she asked.

"Yes." Al squinted to make sure his eyes were properly focused. "I could swear they are the parents of my buddy Hank. He was a waist gunner on my plane when we were shot down. I've seen their photo a hundred times. It hung over Hank's bed. These people look exactly like the picture. She's even wearing the same coat in the picture." He shook his head in disbelief. "It has to be them. It just has to."

"What are the odds that your American friend would have parents who were prisoners and coming to Germany?" she asked. "That's not very likely."

"His parents were born here, as I recall him saying." Al glanced at the ceiling of the train as he tried to remember. "I think my friend even came to Germany when he was about ten years old." Al continued to stare at the couple, unable to take his eyes off them.

"I wonder if they'll let me talk to them?" Al asked, even though he knew better.

"I don't see them allowing you to get close to any of them, let alone talking to them," she said. "Why would America be sending all these people back to Germany unless they thought they were spies of some sort? And why would Germany allow them to come back if they weren't loyal Germans?"

Al thought for a moment and nodded. "Maybe you're right."

While Al continued to stare at the couple, he felt his gurney being raised. Two muscle-bound orderlies had lifted him, and Al lay flat to make it easier for them to stay balanced.

"I guess this is goodbye, Helga. Thank you for everything." Al reached out to shake Helga's hand. "You have been very kind to me."

"Please take good care of yourself," Helga said with a smile. "Work hard so you can walk again! I've seen people do it before."

As the orderlies slowly descended the stairs, Al stole one last glance at the couple in the other train.

On 4 March, as Al's train arrived near the Port of Lisbon, he could see the words *"Gripsholm Sverig"* emblazoned across the length of the Swedish luxury liner. This ship was chartered by the U.S. government to deliver repatriated American citizens from the Far East, South America, Europe, and South Africa. Painted in the blue and yellow colors of the Swedish flag, the ship left the port of Lisbon late that night. Its lights were shining bright, indicating it was on a diplomatic mission.

After waking up the next morning and eating a welcome breakfast, Al met his new nurse. She helped lift him into his wheelchair, and Al sat in his room while she convinced a crewman to allow them to use the utility elevator to get him up to the main deck so he could feel the fresh ocean air. Other American soldiers and fliers congregated there, and they shared their stories about how they were injured. Some of these men were missing limbs. Others' faces were disfigured or burned. A few were in wheelchairs, but most were using crutches or had some other injury, whether visible or not.

Each day, they would congregate on deck to chat and reminisce until it was mealtime, and most hurried back to wait in line for their much-anticipated meal. On the third day of the voyage, a teenage girl approached the Americans. She introduced herself as Mira. While she spoke English well, she couldn't hide her Polish accent. Al came to learn she was born in Poland to an American mother and a Polish father. They were living in Warsaw when the Nazis invaded Poland, and Mira and her family were forced to live in the Warsaw ghetto.

Al was curious and asked Mira, "We've heard some awful things about the Warsaw ghetto. What was it really like?"

"Horrific. No doubt about it. Many of my friends were tortured or killed. I heard screaming and just dreadful sounds going on around us. Most of the Jews were eventually loaded into cattle cars and sent to Treblinka." Mira shrugged, hiding her sadness by telling her about her experience in a casual, matter-of-fact manner.

"How did you get out?" Al asked.

The others were hanging on her every word.

"We were taken to a prison in Warsaw, where they held Jews with foreign citizenship. My mother is American, and that meant we had dual Polish and American citizenship, but the Gestapo didn't always agree. My mother argued 'til she was blue in the face trying to get us out of there. It was awful," she said. "We got out just hours before the SS guards, along with a Ukrainian and a Lithuanian detachment, came into the prison and started a pogrom."

"Lithuanians?" Al said with surprise. "I'm from Lithuania, although I'm an American now, but why are the Lithuanians helping the Nazis?"

"Because they hate the Jews," Mira speculated, "and they're willing to kill them," Al nodded with understanding. "There are plenty of those people throughout Lithuania. You said a word I didn't understand. What's a pogrom?"

"It's a Yiddish word that means destruction, but it's usually associated with an organized massacre of Jews."

"That happened when you were there?" Al asked skeptically.

"We heard about this later, of course, but it all happened just after we left the prison at about one in the morning. A few hours later, the pogrom started, but the Jews fought back with some guns they had hidden. A few days later the Nazis came in with tanks and flamethrowers. Everyone who wasn't shot or burned to death was sent to Treblinka. We can only expect they were killed there."

Al and other Americans stood in stunned silence, although many had already heard such rumors about the *Gestapo* or the *Schutzstaffel* (SS). "Where did you go after that prison?"

"We were sent to a French concentration camp in Vittel, France. It was mostly Jews who had American or British citizenship. We had some Italian war prisoners come for a while. But they kept torturing us with their threats and broken promises. We were told we were going to Auschwitz; then they changed their mind. We didn't find out we were included in this prisoner exchange until a few hours before we left. And even then, we were unsure we would make it out of Europe until the very last moment. It was terrifying and nerve-wracking." Mira's eyes were fixed on the still, blue ocean in a contemplative gaze.

"So, you're an American, but you've never been to America?" Al wanted to change the mood.

"That's right," Mira quipped. "What should I look forward to? Tell me everything."

One by one, the men chimed in with their favorite American food they were all craving. "If you get to Philly, you gotta try a Philly steak," one said.

"You get up to Rochester, New York, you gotta try a garbage plate?"

"What the hell's a garbage plate?" another soldier asked.

The soldier from Rochester began to explain, but he was interrupted by yet another soldier.

"Why would a pretty girl like this want to waste her time in Rochester when she could go to New York City?"

"I've always wanted to visit Manhattan," she said.

"You should. If you're ever there, give me a call. I'll take you for your first New York pizza. It's killer diller."

"What's *killer diller*?" Mira asked with curiosity.

"It means amazing, stupendous," he said with a grin.

Al interrupted. "You can't really be an American unless you've tried a hot dog. And no matter what kind of crapola these guys want to feed you, you haven't lived unless you had an original Chicago-style hot dog. But you have to tell them you want yours "dragged through the garden." That means with a little onion, tomato, peppers, mustard, relish, and a pickle," he said with a longing smile. "With the frankfurters made in Chicago by Lithuanian Jews, no less!"

Mira smiled at Al. "I guess I'll have to find my way to Chicago. It sounds amazing."

On 15 March, New York Harbor came into view. The deck of the *Gripsholm* was packed with 660 passengers, all wanting a view of the Statue of Liberty. After a ten-day journey, the passengers who had all suffered to some degree or another hugged as they said their farewell. Al watched from his wheelchair as the New York skyline overwhelmed his view.

Al was taken off the ship by two attendants carrying him on a stretcher. He was carried to a waiting ambulance bus filled with other Americans who were also unable to walk.

Once Al had settled in at Halloran General Hospital on Staten Island, his nurse delivered a copy of the telegram the Army Hospital had sent to Leva in Sweden. He smiled as he read it.

March 15, 1944
Halloran General Hospital
Staten Island, New York, USA
Miss Leva Barsauskas,
Maltesholmsvägen 1
Hässelby Castle
Stockholm, Sweden

The United States Secretary of War desires me to inform you that Staff Sergeant Algirdas Barsauskas was returned to military control March 3, 1944. He has since been repatriated to the United States for rehabilitation.

J.A. Ulio, Adjutant General

CHAPTER 45

4 April 1944
Ponary, Nazi-Occupied Lithuania

For the first few days after finding the corpses of his family, Itzak was inconsolable. He saw little reason to keep living. He told Olek he was going to collapse on the job so the SS would put him out of his misery. Olek dragged him out of bed and into line for roll call, despite Itzak's pleading with Olek that he wanted to be taken to the infirmary. After a few days, and with enough prodding from Olek, Itzak was finally able to get himself moving.

Work on the tunnel continued despite the constant interruptions. As the tunnel grew, removing the soil now required five or six men to be inside at the same time. As one man scooped out the loose soil, he'd kick it toward the next man behind him. The last man in the chain would empty the soil into a pile where it awaited disposal. This was tiresome work, especially with the lack of oxygen. Altogether, twenty volunteers were working on the project, all of whom slept in the second, smaller bunker hut. Those who didn't want to help were put into the larger bunker hut. This meant the details of the tunnel weren't openly shared among all the men, although most were aware that it was still a work in progress. Having these uninvolved men removed from the day-to-day details of the project also lowered the risk of them somehow revealing the tunnel's existence to the guards.

The process of digging required self-discipline and focus from these already exhausted men. While a single spoon was available for digging the tunnel, most men chose to dig with their bare hands because it was more efficient. Many would leave the tunnel with their fingertips bleeding.

The tunnel continued to make steady progress despite many near disasters. Olek was digging one night in late March, with Feivel close behind, when the tunnel roof collapsed on Olek, covering his face and torso.

Feivel saw it happen but was too far away to help. "I'm coming, Olek! I'll get you. Hang on."

Olek's face was covered with sand and dirt. Panicked, he turned his head back and forth, desperate to rid the dirt from his face so he could breathe.

"Help me!" Olek cried out again, unaware that Feivel was scrambling to save him.

"I'm here," Feivel latched onto Olek's boot. "I've got you."

Feivel pulled Olek's feet, grunting as he yanked with all his might to free Olek from the pile of soil. Bit by bit, Olek's arms were freed from under the mound of dirt. Olek was frantic as he brushed the dirt away from his mouth and nose.

"I can breathe," Olek exhaled with relief, panting as he struggled to breathe.

Once the crisis was over, Olek felt Feivel's hands let go of his feet.

"That was terrifying," Olek said breathlessly. "Thank you for saving me."

Feivel let out a relieved chuckle. "That's why I'm here. To keep you from killing yourself."

Olek propped himself up on his elbow, collecting himself after his brush with suffocating to death. Within a few moments, he began to kick the excess dirt toward Feivel and once again clear away the fallen dirt.

The next day, Chayim and Moshe were the lead men digging the tunnel when the light flashed off and on, signaling that the Gestapo guard was lowering the ladder into the pit.

"Hurry!" Chayim snapped at Moshe, frustrated that he wasn't as agile. "Hurry, Moshe! Hurry!"

"I'm hurrying as fast as I can."

The tunnel was now about twenty-five meters long, and it was a long way back to the bunker. To make their escape, both needed to turn around so they could crawl headfirst. As Moshe was taller, his lanky frame was unable to turn around, and Chayim was trapped.

"Hurry, please, Moshe!"

"I'm stuck. I can't get my feet turned around," Moshe protested.

"We've got to get out or we're going to get caught. You have to hurry."

Moshe yanked on his feet and was somehow able to free his feet from the wall of the tunnel. Once he had turned around, they both scurried along the tunnel floor on their knees and elbows. Moshe leaped from behind the hidden door into the storeroom, Chayim right behind. Both looked to see if it was safe to come out. Seeing no guards, they dashed to their beds and covered their dirt-covered bodies with their blankets.

Seconds later, the SS guard turned the corner and walked in, hollering, "You stupid cockroaches, you make me want to puke." Moshe and Chayim held their breath under their covers as they listened to the guard's expletive-laced rantings. "Everyone outside for roll call, *schnell*!"

The guard walked out ahead of the men, and Moshe and Chayim had enough time to brush off the dirt from their clothing. Once the guard was satisfied that everyone was accounted for, he climbed up the ladder. Moshe and Chayim glanced at each other, realizing they were just seconds away from disaster.

On 6 April, Olek overheard Moshe yelling at Chayim and Feivel in a corner of the bunker. "We've been digging this stupid tunnel for two months, and we're no closer than we were when we started. We'll dig until we're dead." He threw his arms in the air in frustration.

Chayim had heard similar criticisms from the other workers who mocked him and Feivel for having the audacity to think they could build an escape tunnel. But hearing Moshe complain was something new. Despite his sour disposition, he was always among the most supportive.

As Moshe complained, a few others came over to join in.

"I've had enough of this tunnel. I'm too tired to dig anymore," one of the Russians chimed in. "I think your compass is deceiving you. I think you're headed right for the guard's shack."

"Like everything German, your compass is full of lies," another said.

Chayim shot back, "We'll know in the next few days if I'm right or not. But trust me, we are so close. We can't give up now."

"I'm not going to dig one more centimeter. Count me out." The Russian lifted his chin in disgust and walked away.

"Listen to me," Chayim felt his chest fill with anger and frustration. "I've checked and double-checked our angles. I've done the calculations. We've angled the tunnel up in the right direction so it will land between those three tree stumps just beyond the fence. I promise you, we're just about there. We can't quit now."

Chayim's confidence silenced the complainers.

Olek said, "Chayim knows what he's talking about. And we all know we're coming to the end of the corpses. There's not much time left. We must keep digging or else all of this was for nothing."

"It's already a wasted effort," another Russian countered.

"It's not wasted. I promise." Olek's voice was earnest in pleading. "We're almost there. I know it. And I trust Chayim and his calculations."

The men walked away, shaking their heads in disbelief but unwilling to push the issue much further.

Three days later, Chayim and Olek were taking the last shift of the night in the tunnel. Chayim was in front, and Olek was just behind him, putting the tunnel supports in place and clearing away the dirt for the men behind them.

"Olek," Chayim said in exhilaration. "Come, quick. Look at this."

Olek leaped from his position, crawling closer to the front wall of the tunnel, and climbing onto Chayim's feet.

"Look, these are the root of the tree stumps we were aiming for." Chayim used his spoon to dig away the dirt from the clump of roots above his head. "See, that's got to be the stump on the left, and if I continue digging over here, I'll bet we'll run into the roots of the other two tree stumps."

"Are you sure?" Olek asked. "I don't want to say we're there and then come to find out that it's not where we thought."

Chayim nodded, then turned and started chipping away in the opposite direction where he calculated the roots of one of the other trees should be. After a few minutes of frenzied digging, he let out a loud, "Yes! I knew it!"

"What is it?" Olek's voice was filled with anticipation.

"It's the root base of that other tree stump." He pushed the dirt to his feet, and Olek kicked it out of their way.

"Let me see. Hang on, and I'll try to light a candle." Olek leaned in toward Chayim, lighting a match and putting it to the wick of a candle. For a few seconds, it illuminated the space while Chayim continued chipping away at the roots. The candle flickered, but Olek cupped his hand around it and struggled to keep it lit.

201

"Did you see that?" Chayim asked. "Those are the roots of a dead tree."

"I saw it. It sure is." Olek said with relief.

Chayim brushed away the sandy soil, and the tiny roots dangled freely from the top of the tunnel.

"Can you see that?"

Olek smiled. "Wait until the others hear about this!"

The candlelight went dark, but it was enough that both could attest that they finally reached the end of digging the tunnel.

The next day, Chayim had cleared away the soil between the three stumps, and Olek handed him a copper tube they had saved from a pile of garbage. Chayim pushed the tube up through the soil with all his might. Frustrated, he retracted the tube, put his lips to it, and blew with all the force he could muster. Once the tube was clear of the darker, more compact soil at the end of the tube, he returned it to the small hole and inserted the end of the tube inside and pushed again. After forcing the tube through a half meter of soil, he gave it one last push until it broke free. Within seconds, they could smell the fresh and crisp spring air. Encouraged, Chayim again blew into the tube, removing the plug of dirt at the end. A stream of fresh air filled the tunnel.

"We made it, Olek," Chayim said with jubilation. "We really made it!"

Olek reached up to Chayim, extending his hand in appreciation. "Congratulations, Chayim. You did it."

Chayim gave an embarrassed chuckle. "Thanks, Olek, but I can't say that I was always confident. I wondered many times if my calculations were right."

"You were smart," Olek said, squeezing Chayim's hand, then let go. "If you hadn't been so persistent, I think most people would have given up."

As the technical issues of stabilizing the tunnel were finally resolved, now came the challenge of organizing the escape. Feivel, Chayim, Moshe, and Olek met to discuss the plan for getting everyone out in an orderly and disciplined manner.

They agreed to organize themselves into groups of ten, with the first two groups made up of those who did the most work.

"What do you guys think about letting Itzak be the first out? Olek asked. "Before he found his family, he was right there with us helping dig the tunnel. He did anything we asked of him."

"I like that idea," Feivel said. "Do you think he'll be up for it? Do you think he'll step up so we're not having to wait for him?"

"I have no doubt he'll be up for it. He would like nothing more than to avenge his little family."

"I'm okay with it if you're okay with it," Chayim said in agreement.

After solving problems with removing their shackles, communicating with each other in silence, and figuring out who would be responsible for carrying their only set of pliers to cut the fence, they couldn't hide their excitement, as they smiled and congratulated each other.

Feivel then remembered an important detail. "So, once we make it out of the tunnel, and we've cut through the barbed wire, where do we rendezvous?" Feivel looked to Olek, who knew the area better than anyone else.

"Why don't we go north and meet at the Neris River?" Olek said with confidence. "Once you're close to the river, we should be able to see each other."

"I can't visualize what you're saying," Moshe said with a confused glower. "It doesn't make any sense to me."

"I'll be happy to draw a little map," Olek said. "But that's about four kilometers from here, or about an hour if you walk slowly. A half hour if you're running for your life."

"Shouldn't we find a place that's closer?" Moshe asked.

"I wouldn't risk trying to rendezvous anywhere near here. It has to be the river or else risk running into a guard, or someone else—"

"That works for me," Feivel couldn't hide his impatience. "We can work out any other details later. But I think we've got the important things figured out. So, one last thing, what time should we start? What time should the first man be out?"

"I would consider the moonlight and not go out when there's a lot of moonlight," Olek proposed. "We're at a full moon tonight, but in a few days the moon won't be visible until three or four o'clock in the morning."

Chayim's eyes lit up with excitement. "Passover starts on 15 April, this Saturday. Don't you think it would be poetic if we gained our freedom at the start of Passover?"

CHAPTER 46

13 April 1944
Kyusyur an der Lena, Siberia, USSR

Although the polar summer had technically begun, it still felt like the bitter Siberian winter. Having sunlight made it helpful to see what you were doing outside, but it was still dangerously cold. At night, the average temperature dipped to -23 degrees. The sun rose at 04:30 and didn't set until 20:30. In just a month, the sun will stay up all night and stay that way until 31 July.

As the winter lingered on, the ice on the Lena River was at the peak of its annual thickness of two and a half meters, making it a huge challenge to catch fish. Still, Dr. Buchinsky insisted that everyone eat some raw fish every day because cooking fish removes vitamin C. This insistence was among the biggest reasons everyone survived the scurvy outbreak and endured the most vicious months of the winter.

Dr. Buchinsky was beloved by all the exiled Lithuanians. For almost a month, he worked tirelessly to save so many of them from certain death. Before he arrived, nearly every family had someone either freeze to death or die of scurvy. As the exiles slowly recovered, Dr. Buchinsky didn't need to make so many house calls, but a few times a week, he visited Zeneta to treat a kidney infection.

"Hi, Doctor. Come in." Ugna opened the door, then stepped aside to let him step in before hurrying to shut the door again.

Ugna smiled as she watched the doctor wave hello to Mykolas and Saule. Dr. Buchinsky was drawn to Mykolas, often including him in his daily activities. He knew Mykolas had lost his father. He was even willing to act as a surrogate father, at least for now.

"I've got an errand we can do today," he said to Mykolas. "I'll tell you and your mother about it in a minute, but first I need to talk to Zeneta, okay?"

Ugna smiled as her son gave an eager nod, and he turned his attention to Zeneta. She was still bed-bound, unable to do much of anything else because she was always nauseated, and her feet and ankles were swollen to the point her boots were painful to wear.

"How are you doing today?" He lifted Zeneta's hand and removed her mittens so he could check her pulse. With his fingers, he grasped her wrist as he counted her heartbeat, keeping an eye on his watch's second hand.

"How's the swelling today?"

Zeneta hesitated, choosing her words. "Not the best."

"What about your sleep?"

"I'm lucky to get a few hours each night." She glanced at her feet as she spoke.

"And now the big question," he eyed Zeneta with a crooked smile. "Are you able to keep anything in your stomach?"

"I try." Ugna reached over and took Zeneta's hand and squeezed it.

"She really does try," Ugna said. "But it's very hard for her."

He stared directly into Zeneta's eyes. "Can you urinate?"

Zeneta paused. "About every two or three days, but it's very dark when I do."

"How much are you drinking?"

Zeneta's mind wasn't as sharp as usual, and she turned to Ugna and said softly, "What do you think? Half a liter, maybe?"

"Maybe on a good day." Ugna put her other hand on Zeneta's hand. "Most days it's a lot less than that."

"Really?" Zeneta gave Ugna a look of surprise.

"It's not much," Ugna said with an apology in her voice, not wanting to offend Zeneta.

"Okay!" Dr. Buchinsky slapped his thigh. "That's job number one right now. You've got to drink at least a liter every day. It's the only way we're going to get rid of this nasty infection."

Ugna looked at Zeneta, bobbing her head in agreement. "We can certainly try, can't we?"

Zeneta knew the pain and nausea were often overwhelming, and despite being tired and weak, she wanted to make the effort. "I'll try," she said. "I'll do my best."

"You know, even if Sikorsky gave us approval to take you to a hospital, we couldn't get you there until the river thaws." Buchinsky pointed in the direction of Sikorsky's quarters. "And that won't be for a few more months."

"I know," Zeneta said. "And I know you're doing all you can. I'll try harder to drink more."

"That's my girl," Dr. Buchinsky said.

He turned to Mykolas and said with enthusiasm, "Now, young man. If it's okay with your mother, I've got to go check some nets on the river. Do you want to come?"

"Yes!" Mykolas jumped to his feet as he answered and turned to his mother. "Is that okay, Mama?"

Concerned for her young son, Ugna asked Dr. Buchinsky with reticence. "Do you think he'll be okay? He's only nine—"

"I'm almost ten," Mykolas was insistent. "In August."

"Yes, Ugna." He chuckled. "He'll be just fine. I'll take personal responsibility for him. We need to go check the nets about a couple of kilometers away and bring back whatever fish we've caught. We'll come right back. We're going with about five other men, too, so it won't be the two of us alone."

"Please, Mama," Mykolas said, pleading with his mother. "I'll be safe."

Ugna was torn. She wanted to protect her son, but Mykolas desperately needed to have a father figure in his life. Dr. Buchinsky was such a kind man, and she couldn't deny her warm feelings for him.

"Oh, all right," Ugna said. "Just please be careful."

"We'll be a few hours. I've got some fur mittens for him if you don't think the pair that he has are good enough."

"Yes, use your mittens." Ugna took a deep sigh. "That would be great. Thank you."

As Dr. Buchinsky walked out the door ahead of Mykolas, Ugna's arms were folded, and she looked on anxiously. Mykolas turned to his mom and said, "I'll be okay. Don't worry about me. I'll be back. I promise!"

CHAPTER 47

15 April 1944
Ponary, Nazi-Occupied Lithuania

At 22:00 on 15 April, Feivel and Chayim gathered everyone together to talk about the final plan.

"I can't say this enough. As soon as one person emerges from that tunnel, there is no going back. If we get caught, they will shoot us anyway. It's much worse to die like pigs at the slaughter than to die like a jackal who fights bravely to the end."

The men nodded anxiously, listening intently to Feivel's instructions. "Also, we all need to crawl. Don't ever stand up, you got that? We'll need to crawl about two hundred meters to get to the first fence. Olek and I will tie a couple of white rags to the fence so you can find the exit. Other than that, it's all up to you to follow the plan. Good luck, everyone."

Feivel then entered the tunnel, leading the first group of ten that included Olek and Itzak. Chayim led the second group of ten, with Moshe and the rest of those who worked hard to finish the tunnel. The next group was led by a Russian partisan, they waited at the entrance until there was room for them to go in. His group had all committed to joining the partisans once they reached the *Rudnitsky* Forest.

As Feivel descended further into the tunnel, Itzak and Olek were close behind. Feivel and Itzak both had knives in case they needed to defend themselves. Olek carried a small bottle of concentrated vinegar he planned to splash in the eyes of anyone who tried to stop him.

Olek cut off Fievel's and Itzak's shackles before cutting off his own. The fourth and fifth man had a file and made quick work of the chains of their shackles, passing the file down the line so everyone could remove their shackles. While they waited, they took turns removing their shackles and pushing them aside out of their way.

As the twenty men in the tunnel waited eagerly for the escape to begin, Feivel at long last gave the go-ahead signal.

"We're going. There's no going back now!" Feivel said with anticipation, and Olek passed the word along through the chain of men. The word was quick to arrive in the bunker. A terrifying tension gripped the men waiting for their turn.

Olek watched Feivel as he stabbed the spoon into the root-covered soil and grass that covered the tunnel exit. Olek felt the rush of adrenaline once the cool, fresh air hit his lungs.

It seemed unusually black outside, with no moon on the horizon. Once Feivel crawled out of the hole, fresh dirt landed on Olek's face and shoulders. Itzak leaped out, and Olek trailed him, keeping close by holding on to his foot as they crawled over the cold, dew-soaked grass. Olek looked back and, one by one, saw the shadows of men emerging from the tunnel. His breathing increased. Each of his senses was keenly focused on the slightest abnormality of sound, light, or smell.

Feivel and Itzak crawled forward in complete silence. Olek glanced to his side to see the guards pacing the fence line, their outlines illuminated by the bright lights along the Ponary perimeter. Halfway to the fence, Olek noticed the silhouettes of the guards, unaware of their presence, and the faint shadows of men who continued to pour out of the tunnel.

In the night's silence, he heard the faint sound of a small twig cracking under the weight of someone's hand. It was like a Howitzer shell exploding in the night's stillness.

"*Achtung!*" the guards shouted. "*Achtung! Achtung!*" and a few guards raised their rifles to their cheeks and began firing randomly toward the noise.

Feivel leaned back toward the stream of men behind him, encouraging them. "Just keep going."

Olek and Itzak needed no prompting, and from somewhere deep inside they found the energy to crawl even faster. Aimless gunshots continued. Olek turned back to see some men standing to dash toward the fence. Rapid gunfire rang out as the guards began aimlessly shooting at the shadows.

"Get down," Olek said under his breath, not wanting to draw the attention of the rifle fire, but he couldn't hide his frustration that a few men had panicked.

Reaching the fence, Olek let go of Itzak's boot. Itzak instantly removed the pair of pliers from his pocket and began snipping the barbed wire fence. Grunting slightly as he pressed both hands against the handles of the pliers. Olek reached into his pocket to pull out two white rags. He had torn up a dress shirt he took from a corpse, taken just for this purpose.

"Here you go," he said to Feivel, who snatched the rag from his hand and tied it to the fence. He then turned to Itzak, "Hurry, Itzak! Hurry!"

"I'm just about finished," Itzak said, and just then the wire cracked. The segment of wire dangled loosely. Olek helped Itzak bend the section of the fence away from their path, and Feivel crawled through.

As Olek slipped through the hole in the fence, several men waited for their turn. The gunfire grew louder and more intense as the angry guards screamed at each other.

Once through the fence, Olek followed Itzak and Feivel. He could hear men's footsteps following close behind, but he didn't dare look back to see who it was or how many men had made it through.

As they continued sprinting northward, Olek heard the disheartening sound of mortar fire and could feel the compression impact on his chest. He wanted to turn around and help, but the voice of Feivel reminding him to keep going echoed in his mind.

With the gunfire a safe distance away, Feivel and Itzak stopped. Olek's lungs burned.

"Sounds like they fired mortar shells," Olek said, panting.

Feivel and Itzak turned again to run. After thirty minutes, they heard water rushing over the rocks of the Neris River. Feivel dashed to find cover under a grove of trees. "Let's stop here and see how many men made it through."

Olek put his hand on Feivel's arm and countered, "Let's keep going until we reach the other side. It's safer over there."

"I don't know how to swim," came the whispered reply.

"Me either," Itzak looked down at his feet.

"What are we going to do if you can't swim?"

"I say we wait to see how many make it here, then we'll all cross together, hanging on to each other so we don't float away," Feivel answered.

After waiting for nearly fifteen minutes, a few more men appeared out of the darkness. Olek recognized them as being from Ponary and turned to

Feivel. "Let's go now. We have eight of us. The rest will have to make it on their own."

Feivel turned around to count heads. "Okay," he said with reluctance.

"I'll wait here. I'm not going to come all this way and then drown in the river," Itzak protested.

"No, Itzak. You have to go now!" Olek's voice grew louder. "I'll go first, and you just hang on to my hand and don't let go, no matter what. I'll drag you across if I must."

Itzak let out an exasperated exhale, unable to hide his anxiety. He had come this far and had endured so much, and his freedom lay on the other side of the river. But he was about to give up on his freedom because he was terrified of drowning. It seemed like such a trivial matter, given all he had endured. Chiding himself for giving in to this childhood fear, he acquiesced. "Okay. Let's get it over with."

Olek grasped Itzak's hand tightly. Feivel took Itzak's other hand as they stepped from the rocky bank into the frigid water.

"I'm serious. Don't let go." Olek demanded.

"I won't." Itzak's voice quivered.

The chilly river seeped through the torn seams of their tattered boots, taking their breath away as the water came to their knees.

"It's not much deeper. Keep going," Olek encouraged.

Their steady breathing was replaced by swift, shallow breaths as the water came up to their necks. Feeling the powerful force of the water push on his body, Olek squeezed Itzak's hand tighter, "Go slow and keep your feet planted. We're almost there."

Itzak panicked, his rapid breathing reminded Olek of a dog panting in the summer heat. Both Olek and Feivel squeezed Itzak's hands with all their strength.

"I've got you. I'm past the deepest part. We're headed uphill now," Olek said. "Just hang on."

The water level was now to their chests, then to their beltline.

"See, I told you we'd make it." Olek looked back to see all eight men, their clothes dripping with water as they emerged from the river.

"Let's wring out as much of the water as we can," Olek smiled as he inspected his wet clothes. "We're going to be wet for a while until we can find a place to build a fire and a shelter."

Hiding in the woods by day and traveling only at night, it took them a week to walk more than fourteen kilometers. On 22 April, this ragged group of men stumbled upon a small village they hoped was *Žagarė.*

Seeing a peasant man walking next to a horse as it pulled a small wagon, Feivel approached the man and asked, "Are there any Germans near here?"

"Germans?" he said with surprise. "No Germans. No Poles. They know better than that."

"What do you mean?" Feivel was curious.

"They'll get themselves killed."

"You mean by the Soviets?" Feivel asked, but the man said nothing and kept walking.

As they continued walking into town, they encountered three men in green, scruffy uniforms and a thick leather belt with a holster. Each wore a hat with a distinctive Soviet sickle and hammer.

"Excuse me," Feivel asked politely. "We're hoping you can help us find the Soviet partisans. We escaped from Ponary. We've been trying to find them for more than a week," he explained, assuming everyone knew of Ponary's infamous reputation.

"What's Ponary? Where's that?" he asked, then his eyes widened with recognition. "Oh," he said under his breath. "Ponary!" He glanced at all eight men, unable to hide the pity in his eyes. "You need to come with me."

Feivel threw his arms around the man's neck and kissed him. Olek took his hand, tears streaming down his face. "Thank you, kind sir," Olek said. "Thank you. I can't thank you enough."

Chapter 48

22 June 1944
Kyusyur an der Lena, Siberia, USSR

<hr>

Zeneta's kidney problems continued to worsen, though forcing herself to drink more water did help ease her symptoms. Her issues could eventually go away without further treatment, but with her frail condition, her best hope was to get medical care from a kidney specialist. The nearest hospital was in Yakutsk, and it was unlikely anyone there would know how to treat her.

Getting such treatment presented many challenges. First, leaving Kyusyur was extremely difficult, as the only way to leave was by supply boat. That boat wouldn't arrive until the Lena River thawed—which wasn't likely to occur until late June or early July due to the brutal winter. The next hurdle was getting Sikorsky to approve a medical treatment somewhere other than Kyusyur, and that wasn't likely either because any trip south to Yakutsk would take a few weeks or so. Going beyond Yakutsk requires train or air travel, but that would take money. Money that was in short supply. Then there was the challenge of getting back to Kyusur before the river froze again.

Dr. Buchinsky weighed his options, and wanted to help Ugna and her children. Zeneta could sense that Dr. Buchinsky was attracted to Ugna, but he also genuinely enjoyed his interactions with Mykolas, acting as a much-needed father figure for him. Still, he saw the risks of pursuing a relationship with Ugna, given challenges like the unpredictability of war, the capriciousness of Soviet authorities, and their precarious location in the far reaches of Siberia. He approached Zeneta, admitting he wanted to get to know Ugna better, but he feared such a relationship could potentially create conflict with Mykolas and Saul, who were still holding out hope of seeing their father again.

Still, he wanted to find a way to help, suggesting to Zeneta that he was trying to find a way for all of them to escape Kyusyur. As his plan came together, he figured he had nothing to lose by trying to convince Sikorsky that Zeneta needed emergency medical care now. It was a long shot, but Buchinsky hoped to leverage Sikorsky's greed and fear.

The day they announced that the supply boat would arrive soon, Buchinsky put his plan into action.

He knocked on the door, and Ugna greeted him.

"Are you ready?" he smiled at Ugna

"Ready for what?" she asked.

"To go talk to Sikorsky about leaving here on the supply boat."

"What?" she asked, trying to keep up. "How are we going to pull that off?"

"We're going to request emergency medical leave for you and Zeneta."

"Is she that sick?"

"No," he said with a wink. "But don't tell him that."

"Okay," she replied. "If you think it will work."

As they entered Sikorsky's office, he glared at them saying. "Make it quick. I haven't got all day."

Dr. Buchinsky gestured to Ugna. "This is Ugna Petrauskas. She has something to ask."

Ugna's voice was soft. "My friend Zeneta Kosłowski is very sick. If she doesn't get medical care soon, she'll die."

Sikorsky sucked on the end of his pencil. "So? People die here all the time. Why should I care?"

"She can't work," Buchinsky interjected. "She's a liability. And it takes several people to take care of her who could otherwise be working."

Sikorsky scowled at Ugna. "And I guess you want to escort her? That's convenient."

Ugna held her composure, though her cheeks flushed with frustration.

"Sir," Buchinsky said calmly, "may I speak with you privately?"

Buchinsky tilted his head toward Ugna, silently asking her to leave. When the door closed behind her, Buchinsky leaned in and put his hands on Sikorsky's desk. "She's an old woman. She's of no use to you anymore. Let her go."

He looked at Buchinsky, and after pausing for a moment, said, "What's in it for me? And don't tell me you have rubles. I don't want rubles. They're worthless."

"I might have something of value. But the deal has to include Ugna as her escort and the children."

"Unless you're just incredibly stupid, you can't come in here and make demands. You must have something of real value. What have you got?" Sikorsky's voice dripping with disdain.

"I may have some jewelry." Buchinsky tilted his head and nodded.

"Yeah, I'll bet. Probably nothing but junk. Let's see it."

Buchinsky pulled from his pocket a small heirloom he received as a gift of thanks from Zeneta for saving their lives—a simple gold band with two modest diamonds.

Sikorsky's eyes lit up. "You'd give this up for them?"

"It's all I have."

Sikorsky paused as he thought, eyeing the ring and calculating how much he could get for it. "Okay. I'll approve the old woman. Not the others."

"That ring is worth two years of your salary," Buchinsky said. "It has to be Zeneta, Ugna, and her kids."

Sikorsky smirked. "Or what? You'll swim to Yakutsk?"

"No. But if I tell the Lithuanians you stole my family heirloom and threatened to starve us. They'll stop working. You'll miss your quotas, and Moscow will blame you and your leadership."

"You've used this trick before."

"And it worked. Production went up, and you still have your job."

Sikorsky stewed for a long moment. "Fine. But if they don't come back, I'll report them to the NKVD."

"Okay. But I'd like the ring back until the paperwork is ready."

Sikorsky hesitated, feeling the sting of Buchinsky's mistrust. "You make me want to vomit!" Sikorsky hurled the ring across the floor.

Buchinsky retrieved it calmly. "Thank you for your cooperation."

Days later, when Buchinsky reviewed the travel documents, he was stunned. "I don't know if it's his stupidity or sloppiness, but the papers don't say anything about Yakutsk being your destination. It just says your travel is authorized 'for medical treatment.' That gives you more freedom."

Zeneta leaned in and asked. "What do you mean, freedom?"

"It means you can go just about anywhere."

"Does that mean we could go... farther?" Ugna's voice raised in a question.

214

"Anywhere in the Soviet Union," Buchinsky said. "If you're up for it."

"What about Moscow or even beyond?" Zeneta asked, her eyes alight. "Maybe we could make it back to Vilnius?"

"It's ambitious. That could take you a month or so, even by train."

"We'll stop and rest along the way," Zeneta said. "We'll take it slow."

"You should be able to make it," he admitted. "But if you're planning to go to Vilnius, be warned—we don't know who controls Lithuania. It still could be the Nazis. If you try to go home... they might arrest you."

Zeneta nodded. "I know. But if I'm going to die, I don't want to be buried in this frozen waste place."

Zeneta rallied at the thought of leaving, but after boarding the river boat back to Yakutsk and on a train to Novosibirsk, her pain was growing unbearable. Her swollen legs made travel excruciating. Ugna did her best to help her, and Zeneta might not have endured the long trip were it not for her attentive care.

They arrived in Novosibirsk and made their way directly to the military hospital. The gray, crumbling building was typical of Soviet concrete construction. The mood was both cold and dark. The hospital was teeming with sick people from throughout Siberia. Zeneta, Ugna, and her children waited endlessly in the lobby, hearing conversation among Mongols, Tatars, and Russians—each voice carrying its respective dialect, worry, and weariness. The walls were streaked with grime, the floor a mosaic of muddy footprints and melting snow. The hours dragged, measured only by the slow shifting of bodies in the queue and the occasional bark of names bellowed from behind the front desk.

After nearly ten hours of waiting, Zeneta was finally seen by a doctor. Her nurse, a stocky woman with an unruly halo of hair and a warm smile, came to explain the doctor's treatment to Ugna.

"You must be Ugna?" the nurse asked after seeing Mykolas and Saule by her side. "Zeneta told me about you."

"How is she doing?"

"She's doing okay. A lot of swelling, but she's not too bad. We gave her something for the pain and a diuretic for the swelling. It's most likely Bright's disease—kidney-related."

Ugna's expression grew tense. "Can you help her?"

"She should be fine for now, but to treat Bright's disease, she'll need more specialized treatment. We can't do much for her here."

"Where can she go for treatment?"

Tatyana smiled. "In Moscow. We've arranged transport."

Ugna blinked. "You're serious?"

"Your papers authorize you to fly. There's a connection in Chelyabinsk, and you'll arrive in Moscow in two days."

"All of us?"

"Yes. You're listed as her caregiver, and your children are named on the itinerary too," she said, smiling as she eyed Mykolas and Saule playing with each other.

Ugna nearly wept. "This is the best news I've had in years."

That evening, at the airport, they were issued tickets and instructed to sleep in the waiting lounge until morning. Zeneta clutched her travel papers with trembling hands.

"I can't believe it," she whispered. "We'll be in Moscow by the weekend."

Ugna glanced down at her children, curled up on their coats on the floor, already asleep.

"And from there," Zeneta continued, "just a thousand kilometers to Vilnius. Not ten thousand."

"If we can even get near Lithuania," Ugna interjected quietly.

Zeneta tilted her head toward the ceiling, her mind fixed on getting home. "We'll figure it out. If we can make it to Moscow, we'll find a way to get home if it kills us."

CHAPTER 49

9 July 1944
Halloran Hospital, Staten Island, New York, USA

Al turned his head to see through the tiny window in the door. Someone unlocked the door to his seclusion room. He watched as a middle-aged doctor with salt-and-pepper hair and a faded white lab coat stepped through the door.

"Can you get me out of these straps, please? I'm not going anywhere," Al couldn't hide his anger and helplessness.

"I'll take them off right now if you promise not to hurt yourself."

Al took a deep breath.

"Will you be safe?" he asked again, and Al gave a slow nod.

The doctor reached down and unbuckled the leather straps from Al's wrists.

"Are you willing to talk about why you wanted to kill yourself?"

Al rolled his eyes but nodded slightly.

The doctor pulled up a chair and sat down. "You have so much in life ahead of you. You're young—"

"I have absolutely nothing to live for!" Al's voice echoed through the small room. "My father was killed. My mother is in Siberia and is probably dead. All my buddies were killed when my plane was shot down. My girlfriend just sent me a Dear John letter. I don't have much to live for. And now I can't run. I can't walk. I can barely use my arms. Hell, I can't even control my bladder. Who would want to marry a cripple like me who has to wear a diaper?"

The doctor sat quietly, listening to Al vent.

"I thought I heard that you have a sister?" the doctor asked.

"She is in Sweden, taking care of my Babcia—" he paused. "My grand-mother."

"I'm sorry to hear about your parents and your buddies, but you're not completely alone, and that's something to live for."

Al again rolled his eyes. "I've invited her to come to America many times, but she doesn't want to come. She wants to stay there. She says it's because she has to take care of my Babcia, but I wouldn't be surprised if she's just afraid of leaving the comforts of my grandmother's place. She lives in an old Swedish castle."

"An old castle, eh? That must be interesting?"

"It needs a lot of work," Al said. "She had to let go of most of her helpers because of the war."

"I assume your grandmother has some money so she can help you?"

Al nodded, annoyed by the question.

"You could go to Sweden and live with your sister and grandmother. At least you'd have your family close to you."

Al was defiant. "No. I'm an American now. I joined the army so I could become a citizen. I don't want to give that up."

"You don't have to give up your citizenship if you go to Sweden unless you want to. The real question is, who's going to help you once you're discharged? Do you have someone to take care of you in Chicago? You'll need to have somebody to help you, to look after you for a little while. To take you to the doctor. Get your medicines. Help you around the house. Things like that."

Al rolled his eyes. "I was planning to go back and marry my girlfriend, but now that she's engaged to someone else, I don't have anyone else who would do that."

The doctor stood in silence as he thought. "Well, okay. Now I'm not saying this would happen this week, but eventually, when you're ready to be discharged." He rubbed the stubble on his chin as he thought. "I'll bet we could put you on a plane to Sweden? I know it's a little risky, but we could make it work."

Al's anger subsided as he considered what it would be like to see Leva and Babcia again. "You'd send me back to Sweden? Really?"

"Possibly. I'll have to look into it further."

"And I'd go alone?"

"No, we'd send a nurse with you," he said kindly. "But we'd also have to get your sister to meet you and agree to watch after you."

"She doesn't know yet." Al's voice dropped off.

"She doesn't know what yet?"

"That I'm a cripple."

"She doesn't know about your injury?"

"All she knows is that I was sent somewhere for rehabilitation. She has no idea about all of this."

"Why haven't you told her?" The doctor seemed puzzled.

"I just didn't know how to tell her. I was hoping I would be better by now so I wouldn't have to tell her the details," Al exhaled.

The doctor glared into Al's eyes. "If she were in a similar accident, would you be upset if she didn't tell you?"

Al grimaced, realizing the flaw in his logic. He sat quietly as he thought.

"Can you write and tell her now?" He asked.

"I can't write anymore. My handwriting is—" Al paused. "It's just too hard to hold a pen long enough to write so anyone can read it."

"I'm sure one of the nurses will be happy to write whatever you want, if you're willing to let them help you."

"But how do I tell her that I smell like pee all the time? That I need help going to the bathroom. That I can't walk?"

"Your problem with your bladder is only temporary. I also think you'll get back full function in your torso, arms and shoulders. You've come a long way since you first got here." The doctor reached to examine Al's hands and arms as he spoke. "Once we noticed you were more irritable than usual, and acting more agitated and depressed, we recognized that you most likely had a kidney infection, so we immediately started you on penicillin. That infection should be cleared up in a week or so, and you'll be able to control your bladder again. If we had known earlier, we could have helped you sooner."

"I know," Al said sheepishly. "The nurse already yelled at me."

"Why do you think it's so hard for you to ask for help?"

Al struggled to shift his weight to his weakened arms and hands. After some trial and error, he sat up in his bed and rested his head on the headboard. "It's just hard, I guess."

"Would you be willing to help your sister if she couldn't walk?"

"That's different," Al protested.

"How is it different?"

Al paused, unable to offer a rational reply. "It just is. I don't know how to explain it."

"Are you worried she would say no?"

"No."

"So, what are you worried about?"

Al breathed in deep through his nose, then let out a sigh. "I don't know."

"Are you concerned that you're somehow not worthy of her time?" he asked pointedly.

Al looked away, staring at the blank wall. "No. It's just that I'm supposed to be the man of the family. Aren't men supposed to do the helping and not be constantly asking for help?" Al knew it sounded silly as soon as the words escaped his lips.

"You really believe that? That men are not supposed to ask women for help?" The doctor gave a coy smile.

"It still bothers me that I would have to depend on her, especially for things that should be private, you know what I mean."

"You're right. You're going to need help doing basic things, like bathing, using the toilet, doing laundry, and cleaning up after yourself. But I don't think it will be that way forever. Once you get things figured out, you can have a lot of independence. But to get to that point, you'll need someone to help you. And it sounds like your sister is the best person. And if she lives in Sweden, we'll figure out how to get you there."

"I'd like to go back to Sweden." Al's mind was churning as he contemplated the possibility of seeing Leva and Babcia again. "Honestly now. Don't get my hopes up. Do you really think it's possible?"

"I think so. You have dual citizenship, so I don't think you'll need a visa for Sweden. If not, we can get you a visa to be with your family because you have a life-threatening illness."

"I do?" Al asked with surprise.

"Yes. You do."

"How so?"

"Well, we're getting a lot better at treating spinal cord injuries than we did back in the First World War. Back then it was more or less a death sentence because most of men lived for about a year and a half and eventually died of an infection. We didn't have penicillin like we do now, which makes a world of difference. However, if your infection went undetected for much longer, you would have likely died from it."

"Really?" Al's eyes widened with surprise as he contemplated the seriousness of his injury, as he had never considered the potential for life-threatening complications. "No one ever told me that."

A sudden memory flashed in his mind—the week before his attempt. The nurse was changing his catheter, her face pinched with concern.

"You should have told us sooner," she had scolded, noticing the cloudy discharge. "Infection can get out of control pretty fast."

He remembered dismissing her warnings, the darkness already clouding his thoughts.

"When these infections reach your kidneys, they can affect your thinking—make everything seem darker than it is," she had explained, but he'd barely listened, the crushing weight of worthlessness was already building inside him.

Each day after that, the world seemed a bit darker. A bit more meaningless. His thoughts spiraling into despair. Where ending it all seemed the only reasonable, even necessary thing to do. It wasn't just an impulse, but a viable, logical solution that made perfect sense through the fog of infection and gloom.

"You have to be very careful because you don't have that sense of feeling to know if you have a bladder infection." The doctor stared directly into Al's eyes. "That's why you need help. You just can't do it alone. The odds will be stacked against you if you try to go it alone."

Al said with remorse, "Do you think I was feeling so depressed because of that infection?"

The doctor smiled. "It probably had something to do with it. We're just glad we found you when we did."

Al offered a reluctant nod.

"If you ever feel that sad or hopeless again, promise me you'll tell a nurse or a doctor or someone else before you go and try to hang yourself." The doctor gave Al an accusing glare. "It could also mean you have another infection, so promise me you'll tell someone."

"I will," Al said, looking down at his feet.

"I'm sure you were feeling hopeless, especially with all you've been through. But you need to know that there's always someone here to help you, to listen to you. There are nurses, volunteers, and aides. Anyone would be eager to sit and listen and help you work through your problems."

"You make it sound easy." Al glared at the doctor.

"I'm not saying your life is going to be easy. No one has an easy life. But it's easy to ask for help. There are plenty of people willing to help you. You just have to ask."

Al studied the ceiling, not knowing what to say.

"Promise me you'll ask for help before you pull a stupid stunt like that again."

Al watched his hand twitch for a moment, then he nodded at the doctor.

"Okay. I'll talk to someone next time."

The doctor looked at Al, nodded to himself, and said, "I think we can get you out of this seclusion room and out of the psychiatric ward, if you're okay with that."

"You'll let me out of the psycho ward?" Al's face brightened as he realized he didn't have to be tied down to his bed any longer. "Please! I'd love that."

"I'll let the nurse know," he said. "We'll get you moved as soon as we can, but you also have to promise me that you'll get with a nurse to help you write to your sister and tell her everything. We need her commitment that she's willing to take care of you…"

Al interrupted. "Oh, she may complain a little, but she'll love having me back in Sweden again."

"Okay, good. I'll start the wheels in motion to get you on a plane to Sweden when you're ready to be discharged."

"When will that be again?" Al asked.

"Probably in a month or so. But don't hold me to it," He chuckled. "We need to make sure your infection is cleared up and that you're strong enough to travel."

"Okay," Al looked down as he contemplated a long stay.

"One more thing," the doctor added. "I don't know what kind of castle your family has in Sweden, but you'll need to let them know you'll be in a wheelchair."

Al chuckled, "It's pretty big and has plenty of rooms."

"But what about stairs? Make sure you've got a way to the bathroom, to the kitchen, and your bedroom," he explained. "If they need to make modifications, I'd suggest you let them know now."

"Yes, sir," Al smiled. "My Babcia loves doing projects like that. I'll explain what you just told me. They'll take care of it."

Chapter 50

11 July 1944
Žagarinė, Nazi-Occupied Lithuania

Olek traveled for several days, finally making it to Vaidotai by hiding in forested areas and stealing food where he could find it. At the end of the fourth day, he hid in a grove of trees near Max's store until it was almost closing time. Olek listened as Max locked the front door, then cautiously stepped through the back door and hid in the shadows. As Max approached the back door to leave for the day, Olek stepped out of the shadows, saying cheerfully. "Hi, Max!"

Max jumped, wide-eyed and terrified, bending his ear toward the voice he couldn't recognize. "Who are you and what are you doing in my store?"

"Max, it's me, Olek!"

"Olek?" his voice lilted up.

"Max leaned forward, squinting to focus his eyes, then became speechless for a moment. "How? What on—" he stumbled. "It is you. Wow. You've lost a lot of weight. I wouldn't have recognized you."

Max stepped forward and embraced Olek. "I just can't believe it's you." His voice cracked as he reached for his handkerchief from his back pocket to wipe his eyes. "I thought you were dead. How on earth did you get here?"

"I don't have time to tell you. I need to find Mordecai."

"He's still living with Dr. Avižienis, last I heard."

"What do you mean, last you heard?"

"We don't talk much because we don't want to be seen with each other, especially if they happen to find out he's hiding a fugitive."

"How far away are they?" Olek was eager, shuffling as he waited for an answer.

"Are you crazy? You want to go see him tonight?"

"Yes. I don't have much time. Once the Russians take Vilnius, we're going to be a target of the NKVD. That means both you and me, Max."

Max shifted his feet nervously.

"You know what the Soviets did to the Lithuanians, and they'll do it again, just to get you out of their way, simply because you own a business. They don't like competition."

"What can they do to me?"

"They'll send you to Siberia. They'll send you to a work camp."

"They didn't before."

"You may not be so lucky this time," Olek said.

"Well," Max looked down and shrugged. "I can't just leave everything. My whole life is this store."

"It could all be taken from you in a heartbeat. Please, just think about it, Max. Please?"

"Okay. Okay. I'll think about it." Max nodded dismissively.

"In the meantime," Olek couldn't muffle his anxiety about Mordecai, "will you please take me to Mordecai?"

"Yes, yes, yes," Max said, trying to hide his apprehension, knowing he hadn't spoken to Dr. Avižienis for quite some time. "Let's go. It's not far from here."

Olek watched as Max locked the back door. Seeing no one nearby, they quickly walked toward a fenced pasture. After opening and closing the gate, they followed a dirt path across an open field. In the distance there was a dilapidated barn. Olek couldn't help but ask an obvious question: "Did you say they're making Mordecai stay in that old barn?"

"Yes, but they fixed it up so it's nice inside." Max seemed a little defensive at Olek's question. "Don't worry. You'll see."

Olek could see rotting wood near the foundation of the abandoned barn. Looking up, he noticed much of the roof had collapsed. As they stepped through the grass toward the back of the barn, Max knocked on the sliding door, then gave it a slight tug, and it rolled open.

"Mordecai," Max called as they walked through the opening. "Are you in here? I've got someone here to see you."

Without hesitation, Mordecai emerged from his hiding place behind an old horse cart, leaning back and forth to get a better look at the unknown visitor.

"Olek!" Mordecai beamed, tears welling in his eyes. "You came back."

He jumped into Olek's arms. As they hugged, tears flowed down their cheeks. Mordecai repeated, "You came back for me. You really did."

Max looked on, wiping the tears from the corner of his eyes with his thumb.

"I knew you'd come back if you could. I knew it." Mordecai rested his head on Olek's shoulder.

Olek grasped Mordecai's shoulders and stepped back. "Look at you. You're practically all grown up!"

Mordecai smiled proudly, then replied. "You don't look so good."

He glanced at Max, and they both broke out with a nervous laugh.

"If you had been through hell like I've been through, you'd look pretty bad as well. A couple of months ago, I was just skin and bones."

Olek then turned to Max. "Why is a twelve-year-old boy living alone in a drafty old barn?"

Embarrassed, Max said, "Dr. Avižienis said it was safer here than at his house or somewhere else in town."

"Yeah, but he's only twelve!" Olek protested, then he turned to Mordecai. "How often do you see someone? Does anyone come and see you?"

"A few times a week," Mordecai said without hesitation. "They usually come a few times, but I haven't seen anyone for almost two weeks."

"Two weeks?" Olek shouted in Max's direction.

"Did Dr. Avižienis tell you he was going somewhere?" Max asked.

Mordecai gave a quick glance at Max, not wanting to say something wrong. "No, but he said something about some Germans watching him or something like that."

"Was he afraid they were on to him?" Max's eyes widened as he stared at Mordecai.

"I don't know. Probably." Mordecai shrugged. "He was afraid to come here and told me that if he didn't come back for a while, to go see you."

"You'll need to go check on Dr. Avižienis," Olek said as he glanced at Max. "Something may have happened to him." Olek turned to Mordecai. "But you're not staying here anymore. You're coming with me."

"Really? You're taking me away from here? Where?" Mordecai's eyes gleamed, sensing something exciting was going to happen.

Max looked at Olek and blurted, "You're going to get yourself—" Max stopped and glanced at Mordecai, afraid of saying anything that would frighten the boy. "Uh...you'll have to be very careful not to, uh," he stammered. "Well, you know."

"I know. We'll be careful, Max." Olek nodded. "I've spent a lot of time hiding out in the woods lately, so I know how to get around without drawing attention to myself."

"Before you go, let's go back to my store," Max said, stepping toward the big barn door, ready to leave. "I've got a few things for you to take with you. You'll also need some cash, if for no other reason than for bribe money."

CHAPTER 51

11 July 1944
Chelyabinsk, USSR

Before boarding the second leg of their flight to Moscow, a midlevel airport official demanded to see Zeneta's paperwork.

"You cannot board this plane." he insisted. "You must wait for the next transport plane."

She looked on, confused and frustrated, knowing she shouldn't ask questions, but obey. She was relieved an hour later when they boarded a much faster and more comfortable C-47 commercial flight. This plane was a gift of the United States as part of the lend-lease act. This flight was bound for the airport in center of Moscow, rather than the military aerodrome far outside of the city.

As their plane prepared to land in Moscow, Zeneta pointed at her feet. "Not doing too badly, are they?"

Ugna looked down and nodded. "Not too swollen...at least not as swollen as they warned us about."

"Maybe I won't need to go to the hospital here in Moscow after all?" Zeneta's eyebrows jumped a few times.

Ugna smiled back. "Should we try to make it to Lithuania?" she asked, already knowing that's what Zeneta wanted.

Ugna watched as Zeneta descended the stairs without help, stepping onto the tarmac at the *Khodynka* Field in Central Moscow. As they walked out of the airport, they explored the surrounding area, hoping to find a hotel. With no clear idea of where they were going, they decided to skip a hotel and save their money and instead buy train tickets to Lithuania, or at least some place nearby like Latvia. The danger was crossing over into German territory while the Red Army was pushing the Germans out of Russia. Each day, the battle lines changed.

Tired of walking around the city, they returned to the airport terminal. Zeneta tried hailing a taxi, but she couldn't speak Russian, and the drivers quickly drove away. After a few more tries, they finally found a Polish-speaking cab driver, and they piled their bags into the car. Speeding toward the *Leningradsky* station," Zeneta asked. Do you know if we can get to *Smolensk* from this train station?"

"Yes!" the young driver said, looking back into the rearview mirror. He had an eager smile. "As long as they have resumed passenger service. We kicked the Germans out of there last October, and the train station has been repaired, so I know it's possible."

"What we're really trying to do is get into Lithuania or Latvia," Zeneta said, hoping he would offer some assistance.

"What for?" he asked. "That's where the war is."

"We know, but we're from Lithuania and we're trying to find the safest way back if it's possible," Zeneta explained.

"There's no train or bus that goes into Lithuania or Latvia. You'll have to sneak in," he said, assuming it was unlikely that two women and two children could somehow sneak into Nazi-held territory.

"We've got money." Zeneta grinned as the driver looked at her through his rearview mirror.

The man thought for a moment. "Well, if you're that determined to get there, I'd say go somewhere small where there hasn't been a lot of fighting, so the train stations aren't blown up. If it were me, I'd go to *Druya*."

"*Druya?*" Zeneta asked.

"Yes. It's right on the border with Latvia, and you can walk across the river in some places."

"How do you get there from here?" Zeneta asked.

Changing lanes as he spoke, he glanced again in the rearview mirror as he explained the step-by-step process of getting to the *Druya* station on the Byelorussian-Latvian border.

Zeneta turned to Ugna, "Can you remember this? *Smolensk, Polotsk,* then *Druya.*"

Ugna nodded.

The driver added, "I must tell you that I'm from *Druya.* I know a priest at the Church of the Holy Trinity in *Druya,* Father Abrontovich. He can help you. He knows people on the other side of the river in *Piedruja.*

"Should we trust this man?" Ugna leaned in and whispered in Zeneta's ears.

"He seems like he knows what he's talking about. What other options are there?"

As the driver slowed and came to a stop at the train station, Zeneta paid the fare and then shook his hand. "We'll try our best to get to *Druya,* so I hope I can trust you," she smiled nervously.

"I know you don't know me from Adam," he said with seriousness. "But I promise you there's no better way to make it to Lithuania. Trust me," he said. "Once you get to *Druya,* you'll be in good hands once you find Father Abrantovich. Tell him Vladimir sent you. Vladimir Sipovich. He'll know who I am. I promise."

Zeneta, Ugna, and the children smiled and waved as Vladimir sped away.

After purchasing their tickets, their trip from *Polotsk* to *Druya* added another ten hours. Much of it was due to damaged tracks and switching trains twice due to malfunctioning locomotives.

They arrived in *Druya* in the late afternoon and were thrilled to step off the train and stretch. Walking past the *Druya* cemetery, they approached a dirt path leading to a large white church. The arched gate was open, and she entered through the main door.

"Hello?" Zeneta's voice echoed through the cavernous nave. She stood with her hands on her hips.

"Nobody's home," Mykolas said.

"We've got to go find the priest." She eyed Mykolas, then turned to Ugna. "What's his name again?"

"Father Abrontovich," Ugna recalled without struggle. "The taxi driver's name was Vladimir Sipovich."

"Hello, Father Abrontovich?" Zeneta called out, her voice again reverberating against the stone walls.

Within seconds, a man approached through the vestibule. His long, white beard glowed against his ankle-length black cassock. A large crucifix hung from his neck, but his beard kept his collar hidden.

"How can I help you?" he asked in Polish.

Zeneta exhaled, not knowing where to start. "Well, I'm so glad you speak Polish." She turned to Ugna and asked, "What's the name of that cab driver again?"

"Vladimir Sipovich," Ugna said, "We met him in Moscow."

"Vladimir is in Moscow?" he laughed. "That young man is always up to something. Where did you meet him?"

"He was our taxi driver. We told him we were trying to get into Lithuania or Latvia, and he suggested we come and see you," Zeneta said as she used her hands to explain herself.

"Well," he sighed. "That's a tall order. The Soviets have guard towers up and down the river."

Zeneta and Ugna glanced at each other, crestfallen at the father's explanation.

"Vladimir said you could help us find the best place to cross the river." Zeneta's voice was pleading. "Is that still possible? We are so desperate to get to Vilnius before the Soviets reoccupy Lithuania. And it won't be long, from what we hear."

"There's so much up in the air right now. The Germans are retreating, and the Red Army is moving fast." Father Abrontovich stroked his beard as he spoke. "You'll be lucky to make it to Vilnius in a few days, and the Red Army may very well be there before you arrive."

"Will you please help us?" Zeneta asked imploringly.

Abrontovich exhaled, eyeing the two small children, he gave a weary shake of his head. He motioned for Zeneta, Ugna, and the children to follow him as he sat on a pew. His arm rested on the back while he looked at them in the row behind him. "It's a dangerous thing to cross the river. They have patrols going up and down the river all the time. The guard towers are positioned to see just about every angle of the river. You have to be careful not to draw attention to yourselves, or they'll kill you and think nothing of it. And with two young children," he paused. "It's just very dangerous."

"But Vladimir made it sound like it was easy and that you had someone on the other side in Latvia who could help us," Zeneta protested.

"Vladimir has always been one to underestimate things. He's right that I have friends over in *Piedruja*, but getting there takes planning. It takes time."

"Can you teach us so we can cross over tonight?" Zeneta asked.

Abrontovich hesitated. "Tonight?" His voice was skeptical.

"Yes. We are running out of time." Zeneta said pleadingly.

He paused, gazing toward heaven, and said, "If you want to go tonight, you're taking a huge risk. But if you insist, it won't get dark until midnight, and the sun comes up at about three in the morning. You only have about two hours of darkness. You must do exactly what I tell you, okay? You only have one chance to get it right."

Zeneta, Ugna, and the children made it to the river without getting noticed. As they stepped into the chilly water of the Daugava River, Zeneta exhaled quickly, trying to catch her breath due to the shock of the cold water. Trying not to splash and draw attention to themselves, they worked their way across the deepest portion of the river. Zeneta and Mykolas held their bags high to keep them from getting wet. Ugna carried Saule as they waded through hip-deep water. Although Saule held their clothes high, she couldn't keep them from getting soaking wet. Stepping onto the banks of the Latvian side, they dashed into a grove of trees, out of view of the

Soviet guard towers. They rested there, exhausted but exhilarated. It wasn't until late that morning that the bright sun woke them up, and their clothes were almost dry.

It was just as Father Abrontovich had described it. The bus was just where he said it would be, and it was on time. After being up all night and with the anxiety of not knowing if or how they were going to make it to Vilnius, their adrenaline wore off as they settled into their seats. Mykolas and Saule fell asleep, leaning on each other in their seats.

Zeneta smiled, loving the pastoral landscape that was uniquely Baltic in its beauty. They changed buses for the trip from *Krāslava* to *Daugavpils*. Each bus was full of families with children, headed to destinations westward, all fleeing the oncoming Soviets.

After arriving in *Daugavpils*, Zeneta approached a kind, balding ticket agent to buy their tickets to Vilnius, but he told her they could only get them to *Trakai*, roughly thirty kilometers west of Vilnius.

"*Trakai* would be fine," Zeneta nodded. "I can find my way to Ponary from there. Do you know if the trains are running?"

"Yes, but the Germans are using the local trains to evacuate, so it's hard to know if there are any left for passengers. Who knows if the train will show up or not?"

"We'll just have to take our chances. *Trakai* is only fifteen minutes from Ponary. That's a lot closer than getting dropped off in *Ukmergė* or *Utena*."

"Yes," he nodded. "But as long as you know that we'll be stopping often to see if it's safe to proceed to the next city. If at any time we learn that it's not safe, we're turning the bus around, and that's as far as you'll be able to go."

"I understand," Zeneta smiled as she handed over her money.

Zeneta knew going to the cabin in Ponary was a risk, yet despite the dangerous circumstances, it was a risk worth taking. Even though she hadn't dared tell Ugna where they were going and why it was so important, she knew her future depended on going to the cabin. Hidden in an upstairs room was a secret stash of cash, jewelry, and investments that she and Matis had squirreled away for just such an emergency. When they had no other resources left to live on, this stash was their last resort. She wondered if it was worth the risk to bring Ugna and the children, but she doubted this remote cabin would be of any military significance. She'd just have to take the risk and see what happens.

Waiting an hour in the bus terminal in *Daugavpils*, they finally boarded their bus bound for Lithuania. Once they had left the terminal, Zeneta and Ugna could hardly contain their excitement, although they were both feeling the impact of their long journey, more particularly Zeneta. Her feet had grown swollen again, forcing her to remove her shoes. Her nausea had also returned for the first time since leaving Novosibirsk. The water pills didn't seem to be working as well as before, but she didn't want to say anything to dampen Ugna's excitement.

After thirty minutes, the bus slowed at the border station between Latvia and Lithuania. Expecting to be stopped by the German guards, the bus approached at a crawl. When no German guards were in sight to inspect them, the bus again picked up speed.

"That was a bit anticlimactic," Zeneta looked at Ugna and chuckled.

A man and his wife were sitting in the adjacent seat to Zeneta and Ugna. He heard Zeneta's comment and leaned over toward Zeneta, saying, "The Germans are pulling back. I was in Vilnius yesterday—they're in full retreat."

"Are the Russians in control of Vilnius?" Zeneta asked.

"Parts of it. But it's a war zone."

"What about the area near the prison. That's where I live," Ugna interjected.

"There was a lot of fighting there a few days ago. I don't think there's much left there now. The fighting has been intense for a week, and there's a lot of rubble everywhere."

Ugna turned to glance out her window, her eyes staring blankly toward the horizon. After a moment, Zeneta touched Ugna's hand and asked, "What's got you so deep in thought?"

Ugna let out a deep sigh, searching for the best words to describe her emotions. "I was hoping there was some way to take the children back to see our home, especially after all they've been through. Maybe it would help them to go back and see something familiar. But what if everything they've loved is destroyed? It would be even more traumatic."

Zeneta gave her a light squeeze on her hand. "You're right. I think we ought to reconsider our plan. I was hoping to go back and live in our home in Ponary. It's isolated and in a beautiful forest where Matis and I were able to hide from the Soviets. But now I'm thinking we should get to safety somewhere as far away from the Soviets as possible."

"So, what are you saying? We should get off at the next stop?"

"There's a part of me that wants to just run away. But there's also another part of me that wants to go back to my home just for a moment. I have some important things there that I just don't want to leave behind."

Ugna glared at Zeneta with a furrowed brow. "What could be so important?"

Zeneta turned away, a little embarrassed, then admitted, "I know it sounds selfish, but Matis and I have a hidden stash of money and other valuables, so we have something to rebuild our lives after this is all over. It's all I have now to support myself for the rest of my life, especially without my husband." Tears welled up in Zeneta's eyes.

Ugna gave a reassuring smile. "If you think it's worth it, then we'll be there to help in any way we can."

After arriving in *Trakai* and boarding a bus bound for Ponary and other cities further north, they sat quietly as they waited for their stop. Stepping off the bus, Zeneta turned to the bus driver and asked. "When does the next bus back to *Trakai* stop here?"

"It all depends." He glanced at his watch. "But if they can stay on schedule, usually every half hour."

"Great. I think we can make it back in time. Thanks."

As they got off the bus, they each breathed in a wretched odor.

"What's that smell?" Zeneta asked aloud, not expecting an answer.

"I don't know, but it's horrible," Ugna replied, her face wrinkled with disgust.

Ignoring the smell, Zeneta motioned, "My house is this way." Ugna and her children followed her.

"The smell is getting stronger," Ugna said, feeling a wave of nausea come over her. Zeneta turned her head to identify the source of the putrid smell. "It's usually a very beautiful place. I don't know what happened since we left, but something isn't right."

Mykolas and Saule couldn't take it anymore and covered their mouth and noses as they walked. Within minutes, they followed Zeneta as she walked down a gravel driveway through a wall of trees.

"This is our cabin," Zeneta said proudly, seeing it much the same as when she, Matis, and Olek left in haste.

Approaching the door to the house, Zeneta turned to Ugna, shrugging with trepidation. "I hope everything is okay." Leaving their luggage outside the door, she twisted the doorknob. It didn't move.

"Oh, good. It's locked. Maybe Olek left to go somewhere?"

Stepping over to the rock where they hid the spare key, she grabbed the key, inserted it in the lock, and opened the door.

"Olek?" she called out. "Are you here?"

The house was musty, and the furniture was displaced. In the back room, windows were boarded, and the fridge stank of rot.

"Maybe he had to leave in a hurry," Zeneta said hopefully, not wanting to think about what might have happened to Olek.

"Maybe?" Ugna said, trying to be reassuring.

As Zeneta walked cautiously up the stairs, she let out a sigh. "Oh, good. Everything looks okay up here." She stopped and glanced around the room to see if anything was out of place. Seeing nothing, Zeneta reached toward the bookcase and pulled on the secret book. In an instant, the bookcase swung open on its hinges, revealing a dark space behind it.

Mykolas and Saule smiled, their eyes brightened with wonder at seeing a hidden room appear. Zeneta bent down to peek inside, then covered her mouth in surprise. "Oh, my heavens! Someone has been living up here. Look at it."

Ugna and the children bent down, wide-eyed with awe at seeing a two-way radio, the Murphy bed half-retracted into the wall, and several cans of food and water in the corner.

Zeneta stepped to the far edge of the small room, reaching for the edge of a throw rug to reveal a small, well-hidden door on the floor. As she lifted the door, it revealed a box with a lock needing a key. She lifted the rug from the opposite corner to reveal the lock's small key. "I'm so relieved the key is still here."

She inserted the key and twisted it. The lock gave a small clank as it released, and her hands shook with apprehension, not knowing if anything was still inside. She lifted the small door, put it aside, and peered inside, then let out a gasp of relief. "It's all here." She sighed with a smile. "All of it."

She reached in and pulled out several rolls of Swedish krona. Each roll was wrapped with paper bands that were glued at the seam. Mykolas' eyes bulged at seeing so much money. "Wow! Where does that money come from?"

"It's from Sweden." Zeneta continued pulling out rolls of money. "My husband's mother, we call her Babcia Koslowski, lives in Sweden, and she sent us this money many years ago. It's our emergency fund."

Zeneta carefully made a small pile of money rolls, coins, a string of pearls, and another necklace with gleaming diamonds.

"There should be a few papers in here too," Zeneta said as she reached in again to remove a small stack of papers with English characters.

"What are those?" Mykolas asked.

"Stock certificates. They represent ownership in a—" she stopped. "Well, anyway, we need to be very careful with them."

She reached for a worn leather purse on a shelf. The metal clasp at the top was snugly fastened, and she grunted a little as she opened it. "This should work just fine."

She reached down and placed the money and jewelry inside the purse. She folded the stock certificates, inserted them inside a hidden pocket and refastened the clasp on the purse.

"There. That's it. We can go now." She gave a relieved smile.

One by one, they turned to exit the hidden room, but they all stopped and stared at three empty vodka bottles tossed carelessly in the corner of the room. They were hidden from view when they first crawled through the opening. At the side of the bottles were some handwritten papers, the edges of the papers curled up, and a small stack of books was placed on top to try to flatten them. A single folded page fell to the floor, but she ignored it to inspect the pages and pages of notes.

"What on earth is that?" Zeneta asked as she lifted the books, and the papers slowly coiled up into a tube. The writing appeared to be Olek's handwritten notes. The penmanship was ordered, yet the text was very small, reaching both edges of the paper, so he could fit more words on each page.

Zeneta reached for the folded sheet of paper and opened it. She was surprised to see the handwriting of a child. As she read the letter, she said, "Wow. Listen to this."

> *Dear friends of Mr. Olek,*
>
> *My name is Mordecai and I am Jewish. Some horrible men were capturing and shooting Jews, and they shot me and my family over in the pits, but they did not kill me. I waited for them to leave and when it got dark, I got out of the pit and came here and hid in the shed. Olek found me and helped me get better from where the bullet hit my stomach.*
>
> *Last night two men came and took Olek away because they didn't like him. I was in this room so they didn't see me. I am scared that they killed him in the pits.*
>
> *These papers are what Olek wrote because he wanted people to know that a lot of Jews got killed in the pits. Please don't lose them because they are very important to him, so I wanted to make sure they got found because Olek is my best friend. He saved my life, and I am glad he helped me to live.*
>
> *Mordecai*

Zeneta's mouth gaped open in disbelief as she looked at Ugna, her eyes wide with panic.

With Mordecai's letter in hand, Zeneta folded her arms in an unconscious reaction to protect herself from the horrible situation that confronted them.

"Are the pits very far from here?" Ugna's voice was laced with fear.

"They're right over there," Zeneta pointed toward the window in her bedroom. "You can even see them from the balcony." She ducked her head as she stepped out of the hidden room. After opening the doors to her balcony, she scanned the forest surrounding her house. "Oh. It looks like they're gone. They're all filled in. They're just mounds of dirt now." Zeneta's voice was soft. Her mind raced as she realized the size and scale of what was likely under those dirt piles.

"I don't want to be here," she declared. "I don't know what happened here, but—" she paused. "We have to leave now!"

Zeneta hurried out of the room and down the stairs, leaving Ugna and the children behind her.

"I'll get those papers," Ugna said as Zeneta dashed down the stairs, grasping the railing to steady herself.

"Oh, Ugna," she said as she turned round. "Will you get those papers of Olek's? I can't—"

"I've got them," Ugna interrupted. "Just go."

Zeneta rushed to the door as Ugna, Mykolas, and Saule followed close behind. She closed the door, not caring if she locked it or not. Not caring if someone came and lived in the house. Or if someone burned the house down. She wanted nothing more to do with this place.

Grabbing their luggage and running, she fought the urge to stop and steal one last gaze at her once beloved summer cabin. She kept her face forward, shaking her head in disbelief, rushing toward Ugna, Saule, and Mykolas.

Exhausted from their frantic escape, they finally slowed, seeing the bus stop a short distance away. Zeneta and Ugna stopped and dropped their bags, resting their hands on their hips to catch their breath. They noticed a couple sitting on the bench waiting for the bus.

Gasping for breath, Zeneta turned to Ugna. "Well. Now where do we go?"

Ugna paused, trying to catch her breath. "Anywhere but here."

"So, you felt it too?" Zeneta asked, her eyes wide, giving Ugna a piercing gaze.

"Of course, I felt it," Ugna shuddered as she spoke. "I just want to get away from here."

"Do you want to try and go see your home in Vilnius?"

"No, let's just get as far away from here as we can."

CHAPTER 52

21 August 1944
Puise, Nazi-Occupied Estonia

Olek and Mordecai had made their way from Lithuania more than five hundred kilometers north, through Latvia to the Estonian coastline near Puise. Going by foot, train, or whatever means they could, they traveled at night, avoiding the main highways where the Germans were actively patrolling to prevent refugees from leaving the Baltics. All refugees intercepted by the Nazis were sent away at gunpoint.

Despite the Nazi patrols, thousands of Lithuanians, Latvians, and Estonians found a way to make their way westward toward Germany to escape the Soviet juggernaut.

Olek chose not to go to Germany but to travel north toward his goal of reaching Sweden. He knew the Germans still held many key parts of Estonia. Oddly enough, he felt safer being a Jew in German-held Estonia than being a Lithuanian in any Soviet-held Baltic country.

He knew that Estonian resistance fighters called "Forest Brothers" were active throughout Latvia and Estonia, but specifically in the dense forests in the northern part of the country. He hoped he could find these resistance fighters because they could tell him the best route to Sweden. Like the Lithuanian resistance, the Estonians were fighting to reestablish their independence from both the Nazis and the Soviets. But the Nazis were actively seeking out the Estonian resistance. Those they found were either executed or sent to one of over forty concentration camps throughout Estonia.

For weeks, Olek and Mordecai slept in abandoned farmhouses in Northern Estonia. They had tried and failed four times at gaining passage on a Swedish fishing boat.

Late one night, Olek and Mordecai slept soundly on a bed of straw and hay strewn on the floor of a small barn. As a small breeze whistled through the wooden slats, Olek was awoken from a deep sleep by a small commotion outside the barn. He reached over to see if the noise was Mordecai getting up to pee. Before he was fully awake, he reached and felt Mordecai by his side. Startled by a large man appeared in the shadow of the bright moonlight, Olek could see the end of a rifle pointed at his head. An angry voice shouted in a language Olek didn't recognize. Instantly, he lifted his hands, saying, "Don't shoot!" Mordecai was startled and screamed in terror.

"Please don't shoot!" Olek pleaded, his heart raced as Mordecai clung desperately to his arm.

The man's flashlight clicked, flooding a blinding light into Olek's eyes. Before he could raise his hand to protect his eyes, the light turned to Mordecai. Olek watched as Mordecai shuddered with terror, then shielded his eyes from the powerful light.

Upon seeing Mordecai's youthful face, the gun-toting man lowered his rifle. Olek tried to listen to the strange language, and recognized it was Estonian, he pointed to himself and muttered "Lithuanian. Friend."

Another man appeared from the darkness. "Are you another Lithuanian?" He asked in Polish.

Relieved that he could communicate, Olek answered, "Yes! Please don't shoot us!"

"Are you with the group waiting for the boat to Finland?" he asked Olek casually, as if they were among many others nearby who were also waiting for passage out of Estonia.

"Is it here?" Olek said, not wanting to let on that he didn't know.

"Not yet. It will be here soon, though. Why are you sleeping?" He asked quizzically.

"We got lost. We didn't know where the boat was supposed to pick us up," Olek lied.

The man slung his rifle over his shoulder as he turned to point out the location of the anticipated boat. "It's the Finnish boat to Hanko, right? That's the one you were waiting for?"

"Yes," Olek smiled, hoping Mordecai wouldn't reveal that he was lying. "We were told a Finnish boat was sure to arrive tonight."

"You better get moving. It should be here at any time." His voice was urgent and encouraging. "Just follow the dirt road to the shore. It's only a kilometer from here."

Olek stood, gathered his small knapsack, and tapped Mordecai's arm, prompting him to also gather his knapsack. "Let's go, Mordecai. We must hurry to make our boat."

"Is it this way?" Olek asked again for clarification, and the man pointed and nodded.

"Thank you," he said gratefully. "We appreciate your help."

Hearing the roar of the Baltic Sea crashing upon the shore, Olek and Mordecai heard a group of people chatting on the beach as they waited for the Finnish-bound boat to arrive.

Suddenly, a truck appeared out of a grove of trees and the driver cut the engine. The back of the truck was filled with more people eager to board the soon-to-be-coming boat. One by one the passengers jumped from the truck, collected their meager belongings, and joined the other passengers on the beach.

Moments later, two Forest Brothers stepped out of the darkness and approached the group on shore. Saying nothing, he motioned that he was going to find the boat, then he disappeared over a berm a few meters away. Minutes later, they returned and beckoned everyone to follow them.

Olek and Mordecai joined thirty other refugees who stepped carefully over the occasional rocks and driftwood on the shore. The roar of the waves crashing against the shore helped conceal their presence from potential Nazi informants.

Continuing for several minutes, Olek noticed the shadow of a small fishing boat anchored offshore and bobbing in the surf. The boat was about ten meters long and built for nearshore fishing rather than a long, arduous sea voyage across the Baltic Sea. With no mast and an inboard diesel engine, its low profile seemed ideal for traveling undetected in the open sea by the patrolling German submarines.

"Leave your luggage on the shore and we'll load it separately," a voice called out. "Step out into the water and use the ladder to climb aboard."

One by one, the group stepped with great care into the sea, avoiding the big rocks beneath the water and trying to keep their balance. Olek was behind one well-dressed woman who clung to her two young children while they clasped their hands around her neck. Olek did his best to keep her steady as she stepped toward the ladder, doing his best to keep her from losing her footing and plunging into the water. Olek offered to hold the oldest boy while she lifted a younger girl to one of the deckhands. Once she was aboard, Olek struggled to lift the much heavier boy to the deckhand. In a sweeping motion, the deckhand again reached down and easily hefted the boy aboard.

The boat's captain wore a bright yellow sea jacket and black rubber boots. Standing in the water, he handed luggage to his other deckhand on board. Stacking the luggage in the center of the boat, each pile of luggage was three or four bags high. Within minutes the entire mid-deck was filled with luggage and covered with a tarpaulin, the captain nodded his approval to the deckhand. The captain dashed up the ladder and scurried to help his crewman finalize their preparations to shove off.

After all thirty people were finally aboard and situated on the deck directly below all the luggage, they found their seats and settled in. It was a tight fit. Everyone sat hip to hip on the bench, filling both sides of the boat. Olek noticed the three portholes on each side of the boat for fresh air.

Olek and Mordecai sat next to each other, sitting beneath a porthole. Olek nudged Mordecai, "I'm glad we're near the fresh air. It's going to get stuffy down here!"

Within minutes, the boat's diesel engine roared to life, sputtering while the deckhands lifted the anchor and gave the signal it was safe to go. The boat moved forward. Olek looked out the window and could see nothing but the dark abyss in every direction.

After feeling the engine's gentle, monotonous hum, Olek and Mordecai collapsed on each other and fell into a deep sleep.

After two hours of relatively calm water, once they made their way past *Hiiumaa* island and into the open sea, the water grew choppy. The incessant motion of the giant, rolling waves made the passengers seasick. Olek awoke to the sound of a woman groaning, then jumping up to a porthole to vomit. As the smell wafted through the cabin, it caused a chain reaction of people leaping to the portholes to heave.

Mordecai was among the second wave of people who also jumped up to the porthole, heaving his last meal into the waves below.

"I'm sorry if I got any on you," Mordecai said apologetically.

"Don't worry about it." Olek put his hand on Mordecai's shoulder to try and comfort him.

As the swells continued, many passengers, including Mordecai, felt the urge to vomit every ten or fifteen minutes. Mordecai jumped up to poke his head out of the small porthole, but his vomit spilled down the wall and onto the lower deck where Olek sat. Because everyone else was sick, few were willing to complain about the horrible smell. Many couldn't help themselves from moaning or crying.

After four hours, it seemed that everyone had vomited so much that nothing was left in their stomachs. Still suffering from the urge to retch, it wasn't worth the bother to stand up. So many people had already missed the porthole. Vomit mixed with sea water and splashed menacingly on their feet. These rolling waves continued for the remaining ten hours of their journey.

At midday, Olek could see the rocky shores of Finland through the porthole.

"Look." He nudged Mordecai's elbow while he dozed. "We're almost there."

Mordecai's head popped up, groggy and feeling miserable. Gazing out the window, he asked, "Do you know where we are going?"

"I think they said we're going to some place called Hanko." Olek bobbed his head as he tried to see how far he could see the shoreline. "It's supposed to be the southernmost part of Finland. That's about all I know."

"And there's no Germans or Russians there?" Mordecai asked.

"As far as I know, all the Germans are gone. And the Russians are gone too," Olek said with restrained confidence.

"How long are we going to stay here?"

"Hopefully not too long. I may have to find a job somewhere so I can make some money for a ferry to Sweden," Olek said.

"Where are we going to stay? In the woods again?" Mordecai was not optimistic that they would be living under a roof.

"They're taking us to Helsinki. There are people there who help refugees from the Baltic countries."

"That means us. Right?" he asked Olek.

242

"Yes. Anyone from Lithuania, Latvia, or Estonia. We're all Baltic countries."

"Does that mean we'll have a place to stay?" Mordecai's eyes widened with hope.

"I'm pretty sure we'll have a place to stay for a while." Olek gave a relieved and reassuring smile. "At least until we're ready to leave for Sweden."

"How long will that be?" Mordecai asked.

"I don't know. Probably a month or so."

CHAPTER 53

22 September 1944
Kazlavas, Nazi-Occupied Lithuania

The rumors of the rapidly shifting front lines forced Zeneta, Ugna, Mykolas, and Saule to give up their goal of making it to Klaipeda in the northern part of Lithuania. With no other choice but to walk westward toward Germany, they trudged along, hoping they could make it safely to the Baltic Sea in occupied Poland, where they could somehow locate transportation to Sweden.

After a day of walking, Zeneta and Ugna decided to spend the night in the relative comfort of a hay barn. As they continued their westbound march the next morning, more people joined the procession of refugees, despite the fact they were walking further into Nazi occupied territories.

All were eager to escape the Soviets. What started as a few people grew into a throng of bedraggled souls, most were from Lithuania, but some were also from Latvia, Estonia, and Ukraine. All were reluctantly fleeing their beloved homeland, unwilling to subject themselves to another round of Soviet occupation.

As the crowd grew larger, so did the number of uniformed Nazi soldiers with their antiaircraft weapons and assorted military vehicles. They had nowhere to go but back to Germany after being routed by the Red Army. Many were reluctant soldiers, and despite being in uniform, they did what they could to befriend and protect the refugees.

By the first week of October, the huge throng of people on the main highway grew still larger, with Lithuanian refugees, animals, and German soldiers all traveling in the same direction. At times, the sheer number of people was so great that the oncoming cars were forced to slow down to avoid the throng of people spilling onto the road.

The constant threat of attack by Russian fighters forced everyone to stay on high alert. Zeneta and Ugna were constantly looking over their shoulders, scanning the skies for any sign of danger. Despite the constant threat of attack, they traveled roughly fifteen to twenty kilometers each day.

After making it to *Pruszcz* on the outskirts of *Danzig*, Zeneta found a local market where she could restock their food items like eggs, bacon, and bread. She also bought two bottles of vodka for bartering. After paying for her items, she made her way out of the market but dropped her loaf of bread. A stout farmer with leathery skin noticed her juggling her groceries and stopped to help her.

"Let me get that for you." He reached down and handed her the loaf of bread and brushed off the dust. "Probably no worse for wear."

"We've eaten bread in far worse condition."

"Haven't we all?" he chuckled. "So, are you part of that huge entourage of people walking through town?"

"Yes."

"Where are you headed? To Gdansk?"

"We thought we'd see if we could hire a boat to get to Sweden," she said with apprehension. "We just don't know if it's possible."

"From what I've heard, the Nazis mined the water of the Baltic to keep people from escaping north." He shook his head in contempt.

"We've heard that too but didn't know if it was true or not."

"I've heard that from a few people," he said.

"Do you think it's true?" Zeneta's piercing eyes looked at him with earnestness. "I really want to know, so don't sugarcoat it."

"I know for sure there are mines and German U-boats. I've also heard that survivors from bigger passenger ships were being targeted by Nazi U-boats. But I think you'd have a fighting chance if you were on a small fishing boat. You'd be less of a target."

"Honestly?" She let out an exasperated sigh. "Is there a chance we could make it, or are you just saying that to appease me?"

"It changes from day to day, to be honest. But there are still plenty of people trying to make it to Sweden. It's not cheap. A few Swedish boat captains are willing to take the chance... for the right price."

As the days passed, they continued northward toward the coast, staying west of the rubble and destruction near larger cities like Gdansk and Gdynia. They also avoided the main roads that were bursting with streams of Baltic refugees, along with even more Nazi troops retreating into Germany.

Exhausted and bedraggled, they arrived at the coastal town of *Karwia*, north of Gdansk. The town was mostly abandoned after the Nazis had targeted this and other Polish towns and villages with random raids and massacres upon arriving in Poland at the beginning of the war.

Walking past a farmer plowing his field behind a horse-drawn cultivator, Zeneta watched him closely for a moment, hoping she could ask him for help. The unusually tall man walked with a distinct limp as he led his horse through the dry, dusty soil. His gray hair and unshaven, gaunt face were unsettling to Zeneta. Yet she watched his beleaguered eyes, hoping he would be safe to approach. Seeing no other person to ask, she stepped over the plowed rows and yelled in Polish, "Can you tell me where we can find a place to stay for the night?"

The man's head jerked with surprise, squinting to better see Zeneta and three other people standing nearby.

He smiled briefly and said in a raspy voice, "I'm sorry, I'm hard of hearing."

"I said," Zeneta cleared her throat and enunciated her words. "Do you know where we can find a place to stay tonight? We're desperate."

He smiled. Most of his teeth were missing. "Try the parish church about a kilometer that way," he said, pointing northward.

Zeneta turned and was surprised to see a church's steeple with a cross at the top. "Oh. That church?" she asked.

"Yes. When you get there, it may appear abandoned because there are no windows in it. But Father Gomułka is usually there at about sundown to take care of people who show up and need a place to sleep."

"Father Gomułka?" Ugna asked.

"Yes. Gomułka. You'll see him."

"Thank you so much." Zeneta smiled back, wanting to stay and find out more about the man, but she knew the daylight was getting short.

Finding the parish church was easy because it stood out among the other abandoned buildings in this small village. Plus, it was only a short walk to the Baltic Sea coastline. As they approached the church, other refugees were congregating on the church grounds, also waiting for Father Gomułka to arrive.

Just as the farmer had said, the priest arrived thirty minutes before sundown. He wore a long, black cassock and a priest's collar, his hands clasped behind his back as he walked toward them.

"Good evening, dear friends. Gather round and we'll do our best to help you one at a time." He was missing his two front teeth, but his eyes beamed, and his countenance glowed with a sense of unmistakable confidence. He then stepped toward the refugees and greeted them warmly. As he finished meeting everyone, he turned to Zeneta first, putting her instantly at ease. "How can I help you?"

"We were hoping you could help us find the four of us a place to stay for the night." Zeneta drew Mykolas and Saule close to her.

"This is Mykolas." She smiled as she lifted her hand to his shoulder. "This is Saule," she tapped Saule's shoulder as she said her name. "And this is their mother, Ugna. I am their friend, and my name is Zeneta."

"Well, Zeneta..." He brought his arms around from behind his back to shake everyone's hand. "I am Father Gomułka." He reached into his cassock and pulled out a key ring with two ancient-looking skeleton keys.

"Follow me." He walked toward a back door and inserted the key into a rusty metal keyhole. With an audible clank, the lock released, and he opened the door and motioned for them to follow him.

"We decided to protect everything when the war started, so we removed the pews, along with the stained-glass windows, the church bell, and some of our most valuable relics, and we buried them out back in the cemetery," he explained. "Our plan has worked so far, but we are not proclaiming victory just yet." He winked as he glanced at Mykolas and flashed his toothless grin.

"Zeneta, I have a special place for you and your family." He motioned for them to follow him. "Why don't you stay here in the sacristy? It looks empty now, but I have a few blankets and some old pillows in the ward-robe," he said. "Help yourself to whatever you like."

"For families, we like to give them a little privacy," He bent down slightly and asked Saule, "How would you like some privacy?"

Saule nodded shyly, then stepped closer to her mother.

"We'd like that, wouldn't we, Saule?" Ugna replied.

"Thank you, sir." Zeneta put her hands together as if praying, wanting to communicate her sincere gratitude."

"It's my pleasure," he said with kindness. "So, tell me, how long do you think you'll need to stay here?"

"We're not sure," Zeneta answered tentatively. "We're hoping someone can tell us how to hire a boat to get us to Sweden. My daughter, son, and mother-in-law live in Stockholm."

"Well," he gave a thoughtful grimace. "Let me get everyone settled and we can meet in my office." He pointed to his little office next to the sacristy. "Just keep the door open and I'll let you know when I'm ready."

Zeneta nodded, then turned to help Ugna find the best place for Myko-las and Saule to sleep for the night.

"Can we stay here for a few days?" Saule asked Zeneta innocently.

"I'm not sure how long we'll be here." Zeneta smiled. "We need get on a boat to get to Sweden. Once we get there we can settle in for a few days. But I promise, once we get to Sweden, and we find my daughter Leva, we'll have a really nice place to stay. It's a castle."

"Really? Saule asked. "A real castle?"

"Yes. A real castle." Zeneta explained.

Saule looked at her mother. Ugna reached and caressed Saule's hair, smiling as she nodded.

Zeneta watched carefully for Father Gomułka to come back from helping the other refugees get settled. Appearing from nowhere, he unlocked his door and gave Zeneta a quick nod, beckoning her to follow.

She stepped quickly through his office door, then watched as Father Gomułka held the door for her, closing is softly behind her.

Father Gomułka studied Zeneta's face in the dim light of his cramped office, his weathered hands folded on the desk between them. The crucifix on the wall cast a long shadow.

"When you ask to find a boat to leave German occupied territories, you understand what you're asking, right my child?" His voice was low, careful. "In times like these, trust is a luxury we can't take for granted."

Zeneta nodded, her throat tight. "I know the risks, and I'm sorry if I'm putting you at risk, Father."

He rose slowly and walked to the window, peering through the curtain at the empty streets outside. "The Germans questioned me last week about 'suspicious activities' at the church." He turned his back to her. "Three families from my congregation have since disappeared. One of my altar boys disappeared after he was caught carrying a book written in Polish."

He returned to his desk, fiddling his fingers as he asked, "Who sent you to me? Tell me again."

"A farmer on the way into town. He was plowing his field, and he pointed in this direction," Zeneta replied, clutching her worn coat tighter.

Father Gomułka's eyes narrowed. "Do you know him?"

Zeneta hesitated, uncertain if this was a test. "No... he was busy plowing his field, and we startled him. He walked with a limp. I also think he was deaf."

Something in the priest's expression softened, but he wasn't finished. From a drawer, he withdrew a small group photograph and placed it before her. "Point to him."

Zeneta studied the faded image of a few dozen people posing in front of the church. Instantly she pointed. "That's him. The tall man right there."

With kind eyes and a resolute expression, the priest watched her carefully, then slowly put the photograph back in his desk drawer.

"Wait here," he said, disappearing through a side door.

Zeneta sat rigid in the wooden chair, the minutes stretching painfully. Perhaps she had failed his test. Perhaps he was calling the authorities now.

When Father Gomułka returned, he carried a small loaf of bread and two cups of thin tea. His face remained solemn, but something had changed in his demeanor.

"I know a man named Piotr," he said quietly, placing the bread before her. "He has a fishing boat that can take you to Sweden. But I must be certain before I contact him. His life—and yours—depends on it."

He looked at her with unexpected gentleness. "I want to help you, child. But in these times, caution keeps us all alive."

Zeneta felt tears threatening. "I understand, Father. Thank you."

"Don't thank me yet," he said, but the ghost of a smile touched his lips. "Now tell me everything about your family. Leave nothing out."

After listening intently to her story, sipping tea and savoring the dry bread, he asked several more pointed questions. After twenty minutes, Father Gomułka finally nodded with satisfaction.

"Very well," he said, his earlier warmth returning. "Your story is too complex to be a lie. I'll contact Piotr tonight, if I can find him."

"How much can I expect to pay?" Zeneta asked.

"It's not cheap to get a boat because it's hard to get fuel. The Germans control all sales of petrol, so it's difficult to find fishermen who can get enough fuel to go all the way to Sweden. It all depends upon whether or not you have money?"

"We have enough to get by, at least we hope so anyway."

"You'll have to pay him upfront, with cash. He doesn't want to barter for groceries or vodka. He only deals in Reichsmarks. Can you do that?"

"Yes, we can. But will he take Swedish Krona?" she asked.

"You've got Krona?" His eyes widened with surprise. "Even better. He loves Krona," the Father beamed.

"And now I get to ask you a question about trust," Zeneta asked pointedly as she smiled at the irony. "Can we trust him? We can't take any unnecessary risks."

"Oh, you can trust Piotr," Father Gomułka said with a smile. "I'd trust him with my life."

"Does he have a boat?" she asked. "Or is he just the middleman?"

"He owns the boat. He's been a fisherman all his life. So was his father, and his father's father." He chuckled at himself for sounding silly. "He knows these waters as well as anyone."

"I'm glad you have confidence in him. When can we meet him?" Zeneta asked.

"Probably tomorrow," he replied with enthusiasm. "I'll go talk to him tonight and make sure he's got fuel and when he's planning to go next. There will be only the four of you?"

"Just the four of us."

"Okay. I'll let him know. You won't be the only ones on the boat, you realize that?"

"I assumed as much," Zeneta replied.

"And you must be ready to go at a moment's notice."

"We're ready right now!" She chuckled.

Chapter 54

26 September 1944
Helsinki, Finland

Olek and Mordecai joined hundreds of refugees who had settled into an abandoned Finnish army training camp. While only a handful of barracks were livable, it was enough to give the refugees a cot, some blankets, and a small space to call their own. Many of the refugees were Estonian and Latvian young men and their families who had fled Nazi conscription. Others were political refugees fleeing the inevitable arrival of the Red Army and the return to the terror they had endured in 1940 during the Soviet occupation.

Their living spaces were separated by wool blankets attached to the drapes with clothespins. For Olek and Mordecai, these accommodations were luxurious when compared to living in the forests, on barn floors, or under some make-shift shelter. All refugees were given two meals per day, and although Mordecai wasn't fond of all the pickled fish, he didn't complain much.

Olek and Mordecai had both been given a work pass to leave the camp and help the Finnish farmers harvest their crops. From onions, carrots, sugar beets, and potatoes, they both earned a small wage that they planned to use for their eventual journey to Sweden.

As they awoke the morning of 26 September and prepared to leave for work that day, news was buzzing around camp about the armistice signed between the Soviets and the Finnish government a week earlier. It was clear something big was brewing. Olek watched three official Finnish government cars arrive at the camp. Within minutes of their arrival, the camp loudspeaker announced the cancellation of work passes for all refugees to prepare for a mandatory meeting in ten minutes.

They lined up according to their native language. The largest group of Estonians met on one end of the camp. The Latvian group is on the other end of camp. The smallest groups like the Lithuanians and Ukrainians met near the camp's main office, where a translator would relay the message in their native language. This was how they typically met for occasional meetings where they discussed camp rules, policies, and upcoming activities.

"All refugees must prepare to leave camp today at noon," a translator said to Olek and the handful of Lithuanians.

"Why?" Olek asked. "Why now? Why so quickly?"

"The Soviets have demanded it."

Olek's eyes widened with distress. "Can they do that?"

"It's all part of the armistice agreement."

"What armistice agreement?" Olek asked.

The man explained that the Finnish government had just agreed to accept the terms of the Moscow peace treaty that was originally signed in 1940. It gave the Soviets rights to annex certain Finnish territories, along with a long list of other demands. For the refugees, the most threatening of all the Soviet demands was that the Finnish government had to extradite all former Soviet refugees back to their home countries. The news was unsettling.

"What if we don't want to go back?" Olek said angrily.

"The terms of the agreement stipulate that the Finnish government must cooperate with the repatriation."

"So, you're forcing us to go back?"

"Eventually, we'll have no choice but to cooperate. That's why we're putting all of you on a train today."

"Where are they taking us?"

"To Rauma."

"What's Rauma?"

"It's a city about 250 kilometers northwest of here on the coast. We'll get you up there so we can get you on a ferry over to Sweden."

"Sweden?" Mordecai questioned. "You're taking us to Sweden?"

The man glanced at Mordecai, amused by his enthusiasm. "Yes. We're not quite sure how and when that part will happen, but we have to get you out of Helsinki now before the Soviets get here in the next few days and force us to hand you over to them so they can take you back to Lithuania."

"Is it just Lithuanians?"

"No. They want all those from the Baltics. And the Ukrainians and Byelorussians too. Everyone who was once under Soviet rule must go back."

"And what if we don't have enough money to pay for passage?" Olek rubbed his chin as he thought about what could go wrong. "Will we be stuck here?"

"The Finnish government will cover the cost of getting you to Sweden," he said with confidence.

Olek's hands were on his hips. His eyes darted back and forth as his mind raced to process it all.

"That's great news!" he replied.

"What's great news?" Mordecai asked.

Olek explained that because they didn't have to pay for passage to Sweden, they could instead use their money to travel to Stockholm and find Leva and her grandmother.

Mordecai's lips curled upward at Olek, who nodded and beamed his approval.

"Please be packed and ready to go before noon," the translator said. "The trucks and buses will be here to take you to the train station." The translator turned to the group of Lithuanians and gave a reassuring grin. "It may take you a while to get to Rauma, but you should be there by late tonight or early tomorrow."

CHAPTER 55

28 September 1944
Karwia, Nazi-Occupied Pomerania (Poland)

"It looks like the cloud cover is going to hold," Zeneta said as she turned to Ugna. They gazed into the blackness of the Gulf of Gdansk.

"Let's hope so," Ugna said, her voice uneasy. "What did Father Gomułka say about the chances of that fishing boat coming tonight?"

"He said it all depends on the moon. Piotr won't risk it if it's too bright. The German patrol boats are likely to see us."

"What about all this wind? It looks like a storm out there." Ugna pulled Saule closer as she scanned the horizon.

"I don't know. We'll just have to wait." Zeneta seemed impatient with Ugna's questions. "He said we'd see a boat with a flashing hurricane light. That would be the signal where the boat would be coming ashore."

Mykolas looked up to his mother as he asked, "What time is it?"

"It's half past midnight, Son."

Mykolas nodded with resignation but didn't reply.

"They said it could come any time after midnight or before three in the morning."

Mykolas sighed and sat down on the sandy beach, wrapping his arms around his knees while he waited.

After waiting and watching for more than an hour, Saule pointed to a faint flashing light on the horizon. "What's that light out there?"

Zeneta and Ugna both squinted to focus on the area where Saule pointed.

"I see it," Mykolas called out in a loud whisper, pointing in the same direction. "Right there. See it?"

Zeneta shook her head, looking hopefully at where Mykolas had pointed.

"There it is again," Mykolas said with exasperation. "Now can you see it?"

"I see it." Ugna gave an exasperated exhale at finally seeing the hurricane light on a boat. "I see it now."

Moments later, a small group of eight other refugees gathered near the water's edge, waiting for the fishing boat to arrive. As the unlit boat suddenly appeared, the passengers paced while the boat rushed toward the shore.

"Get in quick," the captain ordered. "Hurry!"

As Zeneta waited her turn, she asked the captain in Polish, "Are you Piotr?"

"Yes, I am," he said with urgent encouragement. "We don't have much time. There's a storm brewing, but I think we can stay ahead of it."

"What did he say, Mama?"

Knowing Saule's anxiety would cause more problems if she learned about the storm, Ugna said, "He wants us to find a seat so we can make room for each other."

Piotr jumped out of the boat to help the women and children climb aboard his small wooden fishing vessel. He tossed their luggage into the boat, knowing he would have time later to store it beneath the hull.

When the final passenger had boarded, Piotr gave a slight push to his boat to dislodge it from a sandbar. A swift motion, he lifted himself effortlessly aboard, stepping onto the ledge at the back of the boat. Then he rushed to the helm, and the engine growled as it came to life. As the boat picked up speed, it jumped over the waves. A cloud of mist blasted the passengers as the boat bounced over each wave. He slowed the engine's speed to keep from hammering the passengers on the rough seas.

Piotr had made this trip at least a dozen times. Heading northwest from *Karwia*, their destination was Karlskrona, Sweden, about a hundred and twenty nautical miles away. In calm waters, it would take about twelve hours. In rough conditions like this, it could take fifteen hours. The rough waters were not ideal for passengers, but the German patrol boats were known to stay in port with conditions like this. Another significant threat was the naval mines, but this boat's wooden hull was much less of a risk than larger vessels with a steel hull.

As Piotr had suspected, the storm cleared after an hour at sea, allowing him to pick up speed. Although Zeneta and Ugna were seasick, they weren't sick enough that they felt the need to vomit. Both did their best to sleep during the long, arduous trip.

As the passengers did their best to sleep, they were all awakened when a deafening thud hit the hull of the boat. In the moonlight, Piotr jumped from his seat to quickly inspect his boat for damage.

Seeing no obvious damage, he studied the water for any debris. As he tried to decelerate the engine, a huge explosion erupted a few hundred meters behind them. The moon illuminated the massive bulge in the water, then a blast of water shot up more than sixty meters. Piotr accelerated the boat, and he was not quite far enough away to avoid being drenched by the descending water.

Zeneta watched Piotr as he wiped the water from his face.

"Wow," he said aloud, looking at Zeneta and Ugna, who were closest to him. "Good thing we're in such a small boat."

Saule was terrified and turned to Zeneta and Ugna. "Are the Germans shooting at us?"

"No," Zeneta and Ugna both echoed in reply. Ugna caressed Saule's hair. "I think it was an underwater mine."

"You're right," Piotr answered. "The timing delay mechanism gave us time to get far enough away before it went off. Someone must be praying the rosary." He gave a nervous laugh but then bowed his head and mumbled a few words before touching his forehead, chest, and shoulders and whispering, "In the name of the Father, the Son, and the Holy Spirit, amen."

Zeneta and Saule watched as Piotr prayed, then Saule turned and whispered. "What was he doing?"

"Saying a prayer," Zeneta said as she looked at Ugna and Saule with a kind smile.

"How come?" Saule gave a confused glance.

"To thank God that we weren't hurt."

"Oh." Saule nodded, then cuddled up to Ugna to try to get warm.

CHAPTER 56

28 September 1944
Halloran Hospital, Staten Island, New York, USA

Al sat patiently in his wheelchair in New York's North Beach Airport. His nurse made the final arrangements for their flight to Sweden. Dressed in his Army Air Corps uniform, he looked over his shoulder for his nurse.

Her name was Margaret, but she preferred "Maggie." She was a young mother of two young kids, her husband was a physician, and she loved talking about her family. Although in her mid-twenties, she had gray hair that she usually pulled into a bun. She was Al's favorite nurse, and he had requested that she be given this assignment to escort him to Stockholm. Not only was she a good nurse, but she was uniquely qualified to deal with patients with paralysis. Before she became a nurse, she helped take care of her uncle, who was paralyzed during the First World War. She had worked on the paralysis wing at Halloran Hospital long before Al arrived.

"We're all set," she said, handing him his papers. "Our flight goes from here to Shediac, New Brunswick, then on to Botwood in Newfoundland, and then we go to a place called Foynes, Ireland."

"All right, that sounds like just how I would plan it," he joked. "I've never heard of any of those places."

"Me either. But I guess we're going to learn about them soon enough, won't we?"

Al scanned his papers with a bit of confusion. "So how do we get from Ireland to Sweden?"

"That's the tricky part, from what they tell me." She didn't look up as she spoke but continued shuffling through her papers. "We have to get on a BOAC flight from Foynes to Leuchars Airfield somewhere in Scotland, then—"

"What's BOAC?" Al interrupted.

"It stands for British Overseas Airways Company or Corporation, something like that," she replied, still distracted by her papers. "Then we have a BOAC flight from Leuchars to Stockholm."

"Wow. I sure hope we make it," Al said. "I'd hate to get stuck in Scotland and not be able to make it to Sweden. How long do you think this whole trip will take?"

"Probably a few days. We'll spend the day or so in Foynes, just to make sure we've got everything worked out with your wheelchair. They're not used to dealing with wheelchairs, so we may need some help carrying you onto the airplane."

"It wouldn't be the first time," Al said with resignation.

"It's a good thing we're going now instead of next week," she added. "They told me they would stop flying this route in October because it gets too dangerous with the cold." Maggie glanced at the large clock on the wall. "Well, we'd better get going."

Al pushed himself in his wheelchair. He had a small rucksack on his lap. Maggie carried her luggage in one hand and Al's bag in the other. They moved through the Marine Air Terminal, through a corridor that opened up to a ramp down to the East River. Al held on tight as gravity pulled him down the ramp, where a huge airplane with a massive wingspan floated as it was moored to the dock. A crew of sailors dressed in white was scrambling to load luggage, along with a massive pile of postal bags filled with airmail. Four sailors spotted Al and Maggie as they approached.

"You must be our passenger to Sweden," one of the sailors announced. He stood at attention and gave Al a sharp salute, then added, "Welcome aboard our B-314, the *Dixie Clipper*. Thank you for serving our country, sir."

Feeling a little embarrassed, Al returned the salute and then reached out to shake his hand. "Thank you, Sailor.

"You're in for a treat," the sailor said with a tone of excitement. "This is the same plane that took President Roosevelt to the Casablanca Conference last year."

"You're joking," Al said.

"No, sir. Once we get you inside, I'll show you around."

He summoned two more sailors to help. "We're going to lift you over that big ledge, okay?"

"Thank you."

The sailors gathered around Al, carefully lifting him inside the cabin and ducking to avoid hitting their heads on the bulkhead.

Al's bulging eyes scanned the interior that resembled a luxury train car. "Holy mackerel!"

The sailor explained as he gave Al a brief tour of the massive interior. "This was owned by Pan American Airways. Before the war, they could fit seventy passengers. Now it's a Navy plane. We don't use the armchair seats anymore, but we can take out these seats when we need room for some of the things we carry back and forth from here and England." His voice became softer. "I can't tell you what it is, so I'll leave it at that. But you can still see that it's fully detailed. Even the passenger and berthing compartments are nice." He continued to roll Al through the aisles of the plane. "Here's the galley. When the president was here, he had a chef prepare his meals from here. They even served the president caviar for his sixty-first birthday."

"Today's my twenty-first birthday," Al said with a wink. "Do I get caviar?"

"I'll have to ask Captain Cone!" he shot back. "He was the pilot for the president's flight. Maybe he saved some caviar up in the cockpit."

"That's okay," Al laughed. "It's not really my birthday. And I don't like caviar that much anyway."

After finishing the tour of the cavernous airplane, he escorted Al to his seat and helped him move from his wheelchair into his assigned seat.

"I'm going to put your wheelchair over here and secure it to the wall," he said to Al. "Just let someone know and they'll be happy to get it for you. The men's room is just past that bulkhead." He pointed to an area behind them. "Oh, and ma'am,"—he looked at Maggie sitting next to Al— "the lady's room is a bit further in the back."

"Thank you," she replied with a polite smile as she settled into her seat.

After sitting in the water for another twenty minutes, the door to the cabin was closed from outside, and the four powerful prop engines roared to life. Al couldn't hide his excitement, and he turned to his nurse and said cheerfully, "Well, Maggie, are you ready for this?"

"Are *you* ready for this?" she said with a smirk. "This is going to be a lot harder on you than me."

"I know." Al breathed in through his nose as he thought. "But once it's all over, I'm looking forward to seeing Leva again. My sister"—he turned to Maggie to make sure she understood— "and my Babcia Kosłowski. That's my grandmother. She has always been so good to me, and I wasn't always good to her. I've had a lot of time to think since I got back to the States, and I realized how much my sister and Babcia mean to me. So, I think it will all be worth it once we finally get there."

Maggie sat up in her chair and said, "I know you told me about your mother a few months ago. Have you heard anything from her since then?"

"Not a thing. Just that one cryptic letter where she said she was far from home and attended lectures about Stalin. We can only assume she meant Siberia. Where else would it be? She also said something about babysitting some children, too. It was a pretty bizarre letter." He gazed up at the ceiling briefly, hoping to find answers. "I've heard too many horror stories about people going to Siberia. Most don't survive, so I doubt I'll ever see her again." Al's voice cracked as he said it.

Maggie reached over and gave his hand a quick squeeze.

CHAPTER 57

28 September 1944
Stockholm, Sweden

Leva walked into the kitchen, expecting to see Babcia sitting in her usual place at the table with her cup of tea. Seeing the seat empty, she stopped. "Babcia," she said aloud. She inspected the stove and noticed the teapot was cold. She turned to glance out the window, hoping Babcia was somewhere outside.

"Babcia," she said, her anxiety growing as Leva searched from room to room, trying to find her grandmother. Babcia had been complaining about having headaches over the past few weeks. The headaches would come and go, so she never complained too much. Usually, she would just drink a cup of tea and feel better.

"Babcia!" she called out with more urgency. "Where are you?"

Leva walked up the winding staircase and knocked on the hefty wooden door to Babcia's bedroom. "Babcia? Are you okay?"

As she opened the door, her eyes were drawn to the bed, and she had to step closer to see if Babcia was under the thick feather blanket. The bed was empty. She noticed the light was on in the bathroom. As she approached the door, Leva covered her mouth in horror. Babcia had collapsed on the floor near the toilet.

Leva leapt to Babcia's side and screamed, "Babcia! Babcia! Are you okay?"

Leva reached down to lift Babcia's head as it seemed twisted awkwardly in relation to her shoulders. When Leva touched her face, she recoiled, sensing her soft, wrinkled skin was ice-cold.

"Oh, Babcia," she sobbed. "My dear Babcia."

A pool of coagulated blood had oozed from Babcia's ears; her mouth gaped open as it rested on the bathroom tiles. Leva noticed that a large, bluish bruise had formed on Babcia's forehead where she had hit the floor.

Leva knelt next to her grandmother, caressing her hair as she sobbed, "What am I going to do without you? I need you. I can't run this place by myself. I need you." Leva leaned over to rest her head on Babcia's back. Her unrestrained sobs grew louder as she wept.

"I can't do this," she said pleadingly. "I don't want to do this anymore. Take me with you, Babcia. I don't want to be here." Her mumbled words continued as she repeated her wish to be with her grandmother.

The doctor finished his assessment and turned to Leva.

"It looks like she had a massive stroke with intracranial hemorrhaging. She probably didn't know what hit her." His voice was cold and clinical. "I'm very sorry."

Leva's arms were folded in front of her as she anxiously chewed on her thumbnail. Her hand reached up to wipe away a tear from the corner of her eyes. She tried to speak, but her throat constricted, preventing her from talking. She gave a quick nod and turned away, so she didn't have to see her grandmother's body.

"The undertaker is here and is ready to take her away." The doctor looked at Leva with pity. "You don't have to be here if you don't want to."

"No, I want to be here," she insisted.

"Okay. It's up to you." He took his stethoscope from around his neck and stuffed it back into his small, leather physician's bag.

"Can I do anything for you?" His face was somber. "Do you need a sedative or something?"

"No," Leva's voice squeaked, and she coughed to clear her throat. "No. I'll be okay. Thank you."

"Don't hesitate to call me if you need anything. Okay?"

Leva nodded and watched the doctor leave the room. Within minutes, a tall, thin man in a dark suit coat entered the room, removed his hat, and gave a slight bow.

"So sorry, ma'am, about the loss of your loved one," he said in a deep yet soft voice. "Would you like to spend more time with her?"

"No," Leva said faintly. "Go ahead."

Just then, another younger man entered the room from the hallway, pushing a gurney. Once Leva saw the gurney, she changed her mind and left the room. Leva walked down the stairs and sat at the kitchen table to wait for the two morticians to take her Babcia away to the mortuary. She stared out the window at the tall oak trees that dotted the landscape. Her thoughts were heavy as she contemplated the long list of tasks and responsibilities that now fell on her shoulders. Exhausted from crying, she now felt even more emotionally drained as she considered what her life would be like now that Babcia was gone.

She knew she couldn't go back to Lithuania. It was far too dangerous. Her mind raced with thoughts of going to America with Al. Maybe she should just walk away from Hässelby Castle or possibly even donate it to the city. Surely they would want it because of its historical significance. But what if they didn't want it? What would it take to sell it? How long would that take? Maybe years.

She was startled back to the painful present when she heard the men grunt and struggle as they lifted the gurney down the twisting staircase. The gurney wheels banged on the wooden floor, and they stopped to catch their breath. Moments later, they lifted the gurney over the threshold of the front doors, again raising it high enough to keep the gurney level as they negotiated the steep stairway.

She stood up for a better view out the kitchen window. They thrust the gurney into the black Volvo hearse parked on the driveway. After loading Babcia's body into the hearse, they drew the white drapes to conceal the cargo they were transporting.

As the hearse drove down the long gravel pathway, she put her head down on the kitchen table and wept.

CHAPTER 58

1 October 1944
Karlskrona, Sweden

Disheveled and spent, Zeneta watched as the boat slowed, and Piotr carefully positioned the boat next to the dock in Karlskrona. He jumped out of his boat and tied it to the dock next to row after row of fishing boats already there. After retrieving their small bags, Zeneta and Ugna both gave Piotr a thankful hug for his willingness to bring them to freedom and safety.

"We can never thank you enough, Piotr," Zeneta said as she grasped his hands with both of hers and gave him an affectionate squeeze. "You are a good man."

"I try to help when I can," he said cheerfully. "I'm happy for you and your family."

"You have given us hope," Ugna added. "Hope that we'll survive. We didn't have that hope until we met you."

"It's my pleasure." Piotr smiled and returned to helping the other passengers step off his boat.

"Oh," Zeneta said to Piotr, "You said there was a train station nearby?" She scanned the cluster of buildings and houses on shore.

"It's just over there. About a fifteen-minute walk away." He pointed. "You can't miss it."

"There's also a small café in there too. I suspect your children are hungry for a hot meal." He let out a quick chuckle as he glanced at Mykolas and Saule. "I know I'm starving."

The children's eyes were wide with anticipation, thrilled with the prospect of having something other than hard sausage and bread.

"That would be great," Zeneta said. "Do you know if there's a public phone there? We need to make a phone call to my daughter."

"Yes, ma'am," Piotr replied. "It should be no problem."

"Great. Well, goodbye, Piotr." Zeneta waved as they walked away. "God bless you!"

Within minutes, they had walked the length of the dock and crossed the main road. They strolled through a tree-lined path until they reached an all-white two-story building with the words "*Karlskrona Central Station.*" At the apex of the roof, the clock read 4:45.

After finding a small café and splurging on an open-faced shrimp sandwich called *räksmörgås*, Zeneta stepped up to the ticket counter to purchase train tickets to Stockholm.

After failing to communicate with the young woman, a barrel-chested man in a suit and tie approached, and said to Zeneta in Polish, "Can I help you?"

"Oh," she said with relief. "You can speak Polish. I need four tickets to Stockholm, please. Two adults and two children."

"Okay," he answered. "But you need to know that today there is only one train that goes to Stockholm, and it left already this morning."

"This morning?" She turned to Ugna and said, "Did you hear that? No more trains today. We're stuck here for the night."

Ugna winced, then shrugged. "Nothing we can do about it."

"Okay." Zeneta turned to the man. "Put us on the first train tomorrow."

He nodded, then asked. "Which class do you want?"

"Class?" Zeneta asked.

"First class. Second class. Third class?" After explaining the difference in fares, Zeneta said with gusto, "Let's go first-class! I think we deserve it after all we've been through."

Ugna and the children giggled with anticipation.

After the clerk produced the tickets, Zeneta grabbed them from the counter. "*Tak. Tak.* Oh, by the way, can you tell me where I can find a telephone to make a call to Stockholm?"

He pointed to a cluster of pay phones attached to the wall.

"Thank you for all your help." She gave a kind grin.

"Ma'am," the man added, "you will probably need some help making your call."

"Oh really? Why is that?"

"Do you speak English or Swedish?" he asked.

"No," she wagged her head with understanding.

"The operators don't speak anything but Swedish and English."

Zeneta nodded and followed the man to the pay phone. She reached inside her bag and retrieved some coins. The man took the coins from her hand and inserted them into the coin slot. With the receiver held to his ear, he waited until the operator answered. He explained the situation in Swedish, then turned to Zeneta, "Who are you calling? Do you have their telephone numbers?"

Zeneta shook her head. "All I know is it's in Stockholm in a district called *Vällingby*, and the place is called *Hässelby Slott*." He gave a nod of understanding toward Zeneta, then drew the phone closer to his ear to listen to the operator again.

After a long pause, he said to Zeneta, "They said it's ringing, but there is no answer. She has tried it several times."

"Okay," Zeneta replied with disappointment. "I guess they're not home." She smiled at him. "Thank you. Or should I say '*tak*' for all your help?"

He smiled at her Swedish thank you and walked back to his office.

Zeneta took drew in a long breath and turned to Ugna. "Well, so much for calling Leva. Now what should we do?"

"They said there was a hotel across the street somewhere." Ugna pointed. "Hopefully, they've got a room for us."

"I'm exhausted," Zeneta answered then let out a loud exhale. "Let's go see what they say."

After getting settled in their hotel room, Mykolas and Saule went out to the local park to explore. Zeneta and Ugna had nothing better to do than clean out their worn and dirty luggage. Each of them washed their clothing in the bathtub and hung it to dry.

As both Zeneta and Ugna emptied their suitcases, Zeneta watched as Ugna turned hers upside down to shake out the dirt and dust. Surprisingly, some handwritten papers fell out.

"What are those?" Zeneta bent down and inspected a few of the papers.

"Oh, I forgot about these," Ugna smiled with a little embarrassment. "We found these at your place, remember?"

Ugna held up the papers, and Zeneta recognized them. "These are the papers Olek wrote about Ponary?"

"Yes," Ugna answered. "We were getting out of there so fast that I grabbed them as we ran. I stashed these papers in my bag and forgot about them."

Zeneta took one of the pages and skimmed over it. "Listen to this, Ugna: '12 October. By late afternoon, they marched in another big group of mostly Jews into the forest. I would guess there were at least 300 this time, and it was about half men and half women. Some appear to be the intelligentsia because they are well-dressed and appear to be well-off financially. After they shoot a group of them, they make the next group shovel dirt over the people they just shot.'"

Zeneta covered her mouth in horror. "Oh, how dreadful! And he saw it all happen from my house."

She picked up another page and scanned it over. "That's what all these papers are about. That's why that boy wrote in his letter that he wanted someone to look after these papers because they were important to Olek, remember?"

Ugna nodded as she thumbed through the papers, reading the details of the murders that Olek witnessed. She put the papers down, shaking her head. "I can't read this anymore. It's, it's . . ." she hesitated.

"We can't show these to Leva." Zeneta's mind raced as she thought about how Leva would react. "It wouldn't be good. I know Leva, and it wouldn't be good."

"I'll keep them for now," Ugna insisted. "We can figure out what to do with them once we get settled in Stockholm. Maybe there's someone there who would want them. Maybe a synagogue or something?"

"Can you imagine what the Nazis would have done if they had found these on us?" Zeneta's eyes widened with dread. "We wouldn't be here now, I can tell you that. And you can be darn sure they would have destroyed them if they got their hands on them."

CHAPTER 59

30 September 1944
Söderhamn, Sweden

In the merchant port of Söderhamn, Olek and Mordecai watched from the deck as shoremen below helped tie down their arriving ferry. More than a hundred refugees had arrived in Sweden on this ferry from Rauma, Finland. Other ferries had already arrived, and still others were yet to come. Most refugees traveling with Olek and Mordecai were Estonian soldiers or their families. Some were refugees from other Baltic countries, and a handful were Jews that had somehow escaped the grip of the Nazis.

As Olek stepped onto the platform on Swedish territory, he knelt and kissed the ground. "I can't believe we're here, Mordecai. We're safe. Finally."

Mordecai smiled at Olek but shook his head from embarrassment as passengers behind him stopped and stared at Olek, waiting for him to stand up again and keep moving.

Slowly, they progressed through the labyrinth of footpaths and corridors, coming to a large brick building. As they stepped out of the double doors, a man cupped his hands over his mouth and shouted the same message to all arriving refugees. Not fully understanding him, Olek turned to Mordecai and asked if he understood what he was saying.

"Not really," Mordecai said.

From behind Olek, a man tapped Olek on the shoulder and said in Polish, "Sorry to eavesdrop, but he's saying that all passengers are required to surrender their belongings. Once we get inside, women and young children go to the right. Men and boys to the left." He pointed as he spoke. "They have markers there to mark your luggage because they are taking all our things to be disinfected. We'll get everything back, but everything must be disinfected."

"Thank you for telling me." Olek gave a kind smile. "I appreciate your help."

When it was Olek and Mordecai's turn, they had very little to surrender except their clothes, their knapsacks, and a wallet.

"What about our money?" Olek asked, fearing he would lose the valuable cash he had been saving.

"You'll get everything back, including your money," the official insisted. "Just put all your belongings in this burlap sack. We'll give you some new clothes until everything gets disinfected."

Olek and Mordecai followed the men ahead of them into a small dressing room where everyone else was undressing. Naked and exposed, they avoided eye contact as they waited in line while the others showered.

Olek stood behind Mordecai in line. He thought to himself that he hadn't seen Mordecai completely naked before. While outwardly Mordecai had always appeared to be mostly skin and bones, he was surprised to see that Mordecai had begun the process of maturation. Still, Olek couldn't take his eyes off the large scars on his back and stomach. It had been nearly three years since Olek had nursed this emaciated boy back to health. Mordecai's enormous wound was still as shocking as the first time he had seen it. Despite the wound having healed, the residual scar tissue on his back stretched tautly over a substantial pinkish divot just below his protruding ribs.

The entire ordeal of helping Mordecai overcome a persistent infection was not a pleasant memory. Still, Olek couldn't help but stare at Mordecai and feel a deep affection for him. If this is what it felt like to be a father, it felt good. He was honored to consider Mordecai his son, having watched this thirteen-year-old young man grow and mature, especially over these past few months, surviving day-to-day in the forests.

Olek's heart ached for Mordecai, knowing he had lost his parents, grandparents, siblings, and everyone else he loved. Despite it—or maybe because of it—the boy had become a quiet yet powerful force. He was smart, yet teachable. He was hardworking, yet rarely complained. He had kept up with Olek's aggressive pace despite their having to endure hunger, fatigue, and many hardships.

As Olek reflected on all he had experienced, he nodded to himself as he thought about his good fortune of having crossed paths with Mordecai. It was impossible to imagine his life without him.

Late that afternoon, they received their clean clothes and found all their money just as they had left it.

"I was sure someone would help themselves to our money," Olek said to Mordecai. "I'm sure glad it's all there."

Mordecai gave a polite grin. "Me too."

"They said they would exchange our money for Swedish crowns. I just hope we have enough to buy train fare to Stockholm."

"Do you think we'll have enough?" Mordecai asked.

"Probably, but we'll see what kind of exchange rate they give us."

As they waited in line to be issued new identification papers, Olek's anxiety was growing more intense. He was nervous about them finding out that he and Mordecai weren't related. Would they separate them? Would they put him somewhere while they try to find his parents? Maybe they'll take custody of him while they search for a family member somewhere? If they weren't related, everything would become more complicated.

Olek looked at Mordecai and blurted, "Do me a favor, will you?"

"Sure," Mordecai said with a bit of apprehension.

"When they ask you about your last name, tell them it's Kosmen instead of Goldberg?"

"Why use your name instead of mine?" Mordecai gave a puzzled look.

"Just to keep it simple. It will make it a lot easier down the road." Olek hesitated as he searched for the right words. Mordecai scrunched his face with a glare of confusion.

"If you tell them your last name is Goldberg, then they'll assume we're not related and they may separate us. It's just safer for now. Okay?"

Olek wanted to do what was right for Mordecai. To tell him that he wanted to find a way to care for him. To somehow be a father figure, whatever that meant, since he had never been a father. But Mordecai deserved to live in a loving home. He deserved a family who cared about him. To have someone there for him to face all the challenges he was sure to face. But now wasn't the time to talk about it.

"Okay," Mordecai replied dutifully and smiled at Olek.

CHAPTER 60

1 October 1944
Bromma Stockholm Airport, Sweden

Leva paced the hallway of Stockholm's Bromma Airport. She had spent most of the day waiting for Al's flight, which was scheduled to arrive around noon. When she arrived, she learned his BOAC flight from Scotland was delayed, but they didn't say when it would arrive.

"Excuse me," Leva approached the man sitting at the BOAC flight counter. "Are there any updates about the flight from Scotland?"

"I'm sorry, ma'am," he said with a little impatience. "We are at the mercy of the weather, and the last we heard was that it hadn't yet taken off from Leuchars Airfield." He glanced at his watch. "That was about an hour ago."

"Ugh," Leva protested under her breath. "Okay. Thanks anyway."

"We'll make an announcement once we're officially notified of their departure. I promise." Leva nodded, then walked toward a wooden bench and sat. She glanced at her watch, set her purse at her side, and watched people as they walked by. With her elbow on the solid armrest, she rested her chin in her hand.

She watched as the parade of people passed by her, occasionally admiring a woman's dress or her hair. She smiled back at a small child who just happened to notice Leva looking at them. With the patter of feet on the tile floors, the low rumble of incoherent conversations, and the occasional announcement of the overhead public address system, it all combined to lull Leva to sleep.

"Leva! Wake up!" She heard a voice call her name, then a soft tap on her knee. Startled awake, she jumped in her seat, then blinked her eyes to focus on who had awoken her.

"Al!" she cried out, seeing him at eye level in his wheelchair. She leaned over and wrapped her arms around him, feeling his warm embrace that lingered for a while. As they separated, Leva saw a young woman standing behind Al's wheelchair.

"This is Maggie." Al turned to look at her. "She's a nurse from Halloran Hospital. She has been amazing, helping me survive every step of the way on this long trip."

Leva smiled, held out her hand to Maggie, and grasped it. "Thanks so much for taking care of my little brother. I'm sure that wouldn't be easy, even without the wheelchair!" She leaned over and nudged Al with her elbow and giggled.

"When did you get here? They said you hadn't even left Scotland . . ." She looked at her watch. "Three o'clock. Oh, wow, that was almost two hours ago!"

"You've been sleeping here for two whole hours?" Al chided, rolling his eyes in mock objection. "You must not be getting enough sleep in the castle."

Leva wanted to respond with a pithy reply but could only roll her eyes and shake her head.

"Where's Babcia?" Al gave a glance around as he asked. "I thought she'd be here too."

A pool of tears welled up in Leva's eyes. Her lips quivered as she tried to find the words. "I'm sorry to tell you, Al." She paused. "But Babcia died on Thursday. It was sudden."

270

Al put his hands to his mouth. He tried to speak, but his throat was tight. Tears pooled in his eyes as he watched Leva reach for her handkerchief from her purse and cover her mouth. As she cried, he reached for her hand, and he pulled her close to him to comfort her. She knelt as they held their embrace. Maggie looked on with sympathetic tears streaming down her face.

"I'm terribly sorry for you both." Maggie put her hand on Al's shoulder. "Al had mentioned he was looking forward to seeing both of you. What a tragedy!"

Leva used her handkerchief to wipe her nose. "It happened so fast. She has been working so hard to prepare for you. She hired a carpenter to come and build a ramp for you. She had someone come in and remodel one of the first-floor rooms and make the bathroom so that your wheelchair could get around. She was so happy to have a project, and getting ready for you was just what she needed. Now and then, she'd tell me she had a piercing headache, but that was all she'd say. I assumed it would go away because she didn't complain again about it. She'd tell me she had a cup of tea and just carry on like there was no problem. So, I didn't worry about it. Then I found her on Thursday morning. I still don't believe it. I woke up this morning expecting to see her at her seat at the kitchen table."

Al could only shake his head in sad disbelief. "Wow, Leva!" He looked at her with affection. "I'm so sorry you had to deal with all of it alone."

"I've just been numb, actually. Then I'd remember you were coming, and it was a great distraction." Leva gave a half smile, the tears beginning to subside.

"What can I do for you two?" Maggie asked.

"Take me to America with you," Leva chuckled. "I'd love to just walk away from it all and start fresh."

"I just got here," Al protested. "And I've been begging you to come to Chicago, and now you're ready to just leave?"

"I couldn't leave Babcia all by herself," Leva replied. "She was slowing down. Getting a little more confused. She fell a couple of times, I found out later when I saw a bruise on her arm. So, I couldn't leave her on her own."

"You never said as much in your letters." Al shrugged. "I didn't know she was having problems."

"I know," Leva sniffled, then wiped her nose again. "I didn't want you to worry about us. You were heading off to war, then when all this happened," she motioned to Al's wheelchair. "You had plenty to deal with on your own. I thought it was best to just tell you positive things instead of being negative. What could you have done? Nothing, right?"

"I suppose you're right," Al said as he shrugged. "But still, I'd have liked to have known. I guess it wouldn't have mattered, though."

"Nope. It just didn't matter in the end." Leva sat up straight and turned to Maggie. "I'll bet you two are exhausted. Why don't we get you home so you can change out of your uniform and take a bath or shower?"

"I'd like that," Maggie exhaled with a sigh. "It has been a hectic few days."

"When do you have to go back to the States?"

"My orders say I'm to return immediately, but I don't have to report to work until next Saturday. They said it's possible they may change my orders and make me go back on a hospital ship. But who knows?"

"Well, we're happy to take you around Stockholm. There's plenty to see, and the leaves are just gorgeous right now."

"I'd like that. But I'm sure you both have plenty on your plate right now. You don't have to entertain me," Maggie answered with sincerity.

"Of course, we do." Leva protested. "It's a beautiful city, and who knows if you'll ever come back. It's now or never, right?"

"I guess if I'm not imposing."

"You're not imposing," Leva smiled. "I'm insisting. We can go for a drive, and it will give us plenty of time to chat. Al and I can catch up on the last few years, and we can both keep our minds off the sad things. Heaven knows we've had our share of sadness."

"That's what I've heard." Maggie looked at Al. "He's told me about your mother. I'm so sorry."

Leva tilted her head, saying nothing, but could only nod her agreement.

Without thinking, Al blurted out, "Have you heard anything from Olek?"

She shook her head and said softly, "Nothing."

"I'm sorry, Sis." Al touched her knee, trying to console her.

"Well, we'll have plenty of time to talk." Sensing the awkwardness, Al said with enthusiasm, hoping to change the mood, "But right now, I'm starving. Let's get something to eat."

"I guess nothing changes, huh? Always hungry?"

As they left the airport and arrived at their car, Maggie helped Al get out of his wheelchair and into the front seat of the car.

"Okay, we're ready." Leva watched as Maggie closed her door and glanced at Al. "Are you okay?" Maggie asked.

"I'll be fine," Al said, unable to hide his fatigue.

CHAPTER 61

2 October 1944
Gamla Stan District, Stockholm, Sweden

Leva, Al, and Maggie left to have lunch in Gamla Stan, Stockholm's old town. Al did his best to translate for Maggie when needed, but Leva's English had improved greatly since moving to Sweden.

"I'm taking you to the oldest restaurant in all of Sweden, it's called *Den Gyldene Freden*. The locals call it *Freden* for short."

"Oh, for heaven's sake!" Maggie chortled. "That sounds so exotic."

"How old is it?" Al asked with interest.

"I think it was opened in the 1770s, something like that," Leva explained. "It was Babcia's favorite restaurant and the place where the Swedish Academy meets. They actually own the house."

"The Swedish Academy?" Al asked.

"It's the group that nominates the Nobel Prize for literature," Leva rattled off without hesitation.

"They meet here?" Al asked in amazement.

"Yes, they do." Leva smiled.

"And they'll let normal people like us in?" Maggie gushed.

"Yes, I already called them and told them we needed room for a wheelchair, and they promised to take care of us."

"Thanks, Sis. That's awfully nice of you."

It may take me a while to park because parking is next to impossible around there, but we'll work it out." Leva's voice was pleasant, she seemed happy to focus her attention on Al and Maggie rather than all her other worries.

After Leva parked and Maggie helped Al get situated at their table, the waiter arrived and explained the history of the restaurant before taking their order. "This restaurant has been here before Beethoven composed his nine symphonies and before the French Revolution."

His voice softened. "It has survived the Great Depression, the First World War, and we have every reason to believe it will survive this current world war."

Before long, they ordered and were served their gourmet meal. As they sat and chatted, Leva looked at her watch. "Oh, my heavens! It's already two o'clock, and we still have more of Stockholm I want to show you."

Maggie watched Al's tired face and could tell he had already done too much. "Are you sure you want to keep going, Al? You're looking like you've had enough for the day."

"If you want to keep going, I'll be okay," Al said, but his tone belied his willingness to do more sightseeing."

"No, I think we'd better get back. I've seen enough," Maggie said. "This has already been an amazing day. I'll never forget it."

Leva nodded. "I'll go get the car and be back in about five or ten minutes. Just keep an eye out for me."

As Leva arrived, she jumped out of the car to help Maggie lift Al into the back seat. Maggie then folded up Al's wheelchair and pushed it into the trunk.

"Okay, we're ready." Leva watched as Maggie closed her door and glanced at Al. "Are you okay?"

"I'll be fine," Al said. He sounded tired.

With the constant rumble of the cobblestone road and the lull in the conversation, Al struggled to stay awake. As Leva glanced in the rearview mirror, she smiled at seeing Al's head lean against the passenger window, his mouth gaping open as he slept.

"He's sleeping like a baby," Leva said as she smiled at Maggie.

"He's really been a trooper," Maggie replied. "But he's also prone to overdoing it, just because I don't think he wants to be a burden."

"That's what I've worried about since he got here," Leva admitted as she looked over her shoulder before changing lanes. "I'm afraid he'll overdo it and then we won't be able to get him back to America because he's not well enough."

"So that's your goal? Maggie asked. "To get to America?"

"Al would rather be in America, and I've got nothing keeping me here now." Leva said thoughtfully. "Uncle Jouzas has offered to sponsor me, which makes it so much easier to immigrate to America than if you don't have any connection there."

"When do you think you'll go?" Maggie asked.

"As soon as I can get my grandmother's estate settled. She had everything planned out, luckily, so I hope it doesn't take too long," Leva answered. "Is there any reason we should stay here? Al's okay to travel, right?"

"I wouldn't recommend that he travel in the next few months. He'll need some time to heal more." Maggie tapped her knee as she spoke, hesitant to say something that Leva didn't like.

"Oh, it will probably take us all winter to get this figured out. I'm thinking we won't leave until spring of next year. That's because I'll be by myself, and I don't think I'll be able to get us moved until spring. That is unless you want to come back and help me!" Leva joked.

"I'd love to come and help. I just don't think Uncle Sam would be too happy with me going AWOL."

"AWOL?" Leva asked. "What's that?"

"Absent without leave," Maggie clarified. "I'm still obligated to be in the army for another year because they paid for my schooling."

"Oh, I see," Leva smiled. "I still haven't figured out how we're both going to travel to America," she said with disappointment in her voice.

CHAPTER 62

2 October 1944
Stockholm Central Train Station, Sweden

"Thanks for trying, operator," Zeneta said with strained kindness. After the operator disconnected the call, she nearly slammed the phone in the cradle. "Where are they? Why isn't someone answering?"

Ugna was surprised to hear Zeneta's outburst of anger but could offer no help. "Can we take a bus or a taxi?" she asked.

"I was hoping Leva or Al would want to come here and pick us up."

"I understand, but if their telephone isn't working, there's no use in just waiting here, wouldn't you agree?" Ugna asked with caution in her voice.

"I suppose so." Zeneta looked at the clock on the wall. "It's three o'clock already. I guess we should just take a taxi?"

"How far away is it?"

"It's west of here. About twenty kilometers," Zeneta speculated. "It will likely take us half an hour or so." She breathed in deeply. "I guess you're right. We might as well get there than wait for them to come and get us."

Following the crowd, they found their way to the exit, past the huge waiting hall of Stockholm's busy train station. Saule and Mykolas looked wide-eyed at the decorative chandeliers hanging from the towering arched roof. Once outside, Zeneta quickly hailed a taxi, leaning into the front passenger side window to talk to the driver.

"Where can I take you?" the driver asked in Swedish.

"Hässelby Slott?" Zeneta replied.

Not understanding her, the driver shook his head and shrugged. "Do you speak English?" he asked.

Zeneta shook her head, then tried again to explain. She slowly pronounced the words "Hass-el-bee Slott."

"Oh, ja, ja," he replied. "*Vallingby. Ja.*" He smiled as he nodded. Seeing their luggage, he turned off his car, jumped from his seat, and used his key to open the trunk. He then stacked their luggage inside and closed the trunk.

The driver sat down, set his meter and saying nothing. In a flash he was dashing in and around oncoming traffic. Watching anxiously out the window, they sped past the bustling city. Mykolas pointed to a large, majestic building and asked Zeneta, "What's that building?"

"Probably Stockholm City Hall," she said. "It has been a long while since I've been here. Everything has changed so much."

Within minutes, they saw the traffic lights, power lines, and curbs of Stockholm quickly morphing into a rural landscape with vast expanses of rural land. Most had been plowed over in preparation for the long Scandinavian winter.

The car slowed as it prepared to turn into the lengthy, elegant driveway that took them past majestic oak trees and a manicured baroque garden.

"Wow!" Mykolas blurted as they made their approach up the private road. "Beautiful!"

They continued between the uniformly designed servants' quarters that flanked the entranceway.

Saule's eyes were wide with wonder, as she beheld the seventeenth-century castle and its royal-looking court, a stone wall surrounded the two-story building. The main entrance was a few meters high off the ground, accessible only by a grand double staircase.

"That's pretty impressive," Ugna said with as much awe as her children.

"I once thought it was pretty plain," Zeneta said. "It's not ornately decorated with all the colorful flourishes you see on many Swedish castles. But now that you say it, it does have its simple elegance," Zeneta said.

As the taxi driver drove into the circular gravel driveway, he stopped near the stairs, helped them with their luggage, and looked at Zeneta for payment. Noticing Zeneta paid him a generous tip, he looked wide-eyed at her and said, "*Tak! Tak!*"

As the taxi drove away, Zeneta turned to Ugna and said, "Well, it's good to see that Babcia's car is here. Maybe they are here after all."

"Do you want to go alone, just for now? We're happy to stay back until you've had a chance to see your children without having to explain who we are."

"If you don't mind," Zeneta said, "I want to introduce you to them. But let me have just a few minutes alone to help them get over the initial shock."

Ugna nodded. "I completely understand. Now go see your family." She smiled as she nudged Zeneta toward the stairs.

Zeneta's heart raced as she hesitantly climbed the steep, stone stairs. Her hands skimmed along the granite caps that rested upon the ornate quarried stone balusters. As she approached the arched doorway, her eyes were drawn upward as she admired the newly carved wooden doors with a large, round, iron door-knocker that was hinged to a gilded strike plate. As she lifted it, the weight of it surprised her, yet she eagerly struck it three times on the metal plate. The thunderous clanking seemed to reverberate through the entire structure.

She looked down at Ugna and her children, smiling with eager anticipation.

Zeneta heard someone on the other side of the door struggle to unlatch the lock. After a robust tug on the heavy door, the door gently squeaked open to reveal Leva's curious face. In an instant, she recognized her mother and screamed, "Mama!"

Leva leaped into Zeneta's open arms, the momentum nearly knocking both of them off their feet and onto the landing.

Leva laughed as she caught her balance. "I knew you weren't dead! I just knew it."

"Oh, I can't tell you how happy I am to see you. You'll never know how long I've dreamt of this very moment!" Zeneta buried her head on Leva's neck. As they stood and embraced, both sobbing with joy, Zeneta stepped back to take a look at Leva. "You look amazing! You're so beautiful." She caressed her face and looked lovingly into her eyes. "You have your father's gorgeous hazel eyes."

Zeneta watched Leva smile, then they embraced again.

"How on earth did you get here?"

"It's a long story," Zeneta said calmly, "But we'll have plenty of time to talk about it. Where is Al? Where's your Babcia?"

Leva turned back into the house and shouted, "Al! It's Mama. Come, quick!"

Zeneta hugged Leva again.

"Babcia passed away, Mama. It happened last week. From a stroke."

278

"What?" Zeneta gasped. "A stroke?"

"I have so much to tell you," Leva said. "And then on top of that, Al came back from America on Sunday. And... and... now you're here." Leva spoke so quickly that Zeneta looked at her with confusion.

"Slow down. It's all so much to take in." Zeneta looked at Leva in disbelief. "So, where is Al? What's taking him so long?"

"Well, Mama, that's only part of the story. There's so much to tell you. Come on in and I'll start from the beginning."

"I have a lot to tell you, too." Zeneta said with apprehension. "But first, I want you to meet my second family."

Zeneta pointed to Ugna and her children at the bottom of the stairs. "These are our new friends. They've been my family and my reason for living these past few years after your father passed away. You did get my letter about Papa, right?"

Leva blinked and gave a slight nod.

"Ugna," Zeneta called out. "Come on up here. I want them to meet you and your children."

Ugna held Mykolas and Saule by the hand as they negotiated the uneven stairs. As she reached the top, Zeneta took a deep breath and looked at Ugna. "This is my daughter, Leva."

She put a loving hand on Ugna's shoulders. "And this is Ugna. We met on the train from Moscow to Novosibirsk in Siberia. This is her son, Mykolas. He's ten. This is Saule. She's eight."

Leva held on to her mother's arm and beamed, "It's so nice to meet you. Won't you come in, please?"

As they stepped over the threshold, Zeneta helped Leva close the door until it latched. As she turned around, she heard Al shout, "Mama! It's you!"

Zeneta gasped as she saw Al in his wheelchair. With som hesitation, she rushed to embrace him. "I'm so glad you're alive and okay. You can tell me later what happened." She held him tighter and whispered in his ear. "Oh, my dear boy, I'm just so relieved that you are okay."

Tears welled up in his eyes. "I love you, Mama," he whispered to her as they held their embrace. "I thought I'd never see you again."

She felt his warm tears on her cheek. "I'm home now. "We're together," she said. "That's all that matters."

Chapter 63

3 October 1944
Stockholm, Sweden

"Thank you, Maggie," Leva said as she leaned over to hug her. "When does your airplane leave?"

"In four hours." Maggie looked toward the entryway to the airport to glance at the clock. "I've got plenty of time."

"I'm sure your two children are looking forward to seeing you come home."

"I think my mother-in-law and my husband are probably more excited," Maggie laughed. "She came from Wisconsin to help watch the kids while I'm away."

"Well, I hope you can make it home soon. But thanks for taking such good care of Al. You've been amazing."

"I am so lucky to have been here to see it all happen with my own eyes." Maggie wiped a small tear from her eye. "It was the most incredible reunion."

"I'm still pinching myself. I can't believe I got my mama back." Leva shook her head. "Frankly, I thought it would never happen."

"You have an amazing family, Leva." Maggie's voice softened. "And I'm sure you and you'll love having a houseful of people with Ugna's two children running around!"

"That's going to take some getting used to," Leva admitted. "But they're both such a good little souls, especially after all he's been through. You can't help but love them."

"I know what you're saying. I wish I could put them in my suitcase and take them home with me," she said.

"Oh, no," Leva smiled. "We get to keep them for a while. At least until Ugna can figure out what she wants to do with her life."

"Has she talked about going to America with you guys?" Maggie asked.

"It was easy when it was just me going. My uncle was willing to sponsor me, but now there's my mother and also Ugna and her kids. We have to ask him if he'll be able to sponsor all of us, but it's doubtful he'll want to take on such a big responsibility."

"What does it take to sponsor someone?" Maggie gave a questioning look at Leva.

"I'm not entirely sure, but it's basically signing a paper saying you'll be responsible for them so they're not a burden on the government. But my mother is planning to support them financially until Ugna can get on her feet."

"I don't know why I haven't thought about it until now, but why couldn't my husband and I be their sponsors? I'll have to talk to him, but I don't see that he would have a problem with it."

"Oh, wow! That would be amazing."

"I don't think I told you, but my husband is a doctor. He works at the same hospital I do, Halloran Hospital in New York. But we're both from Kenosha, Wisconsin. We're going back there after the war. We're only about seventy-five miles from Chicago. And that's where Al is from, right?"

"Is that close? I don't know how far that is in kilometers?" Leva smiled.

"Let's see," she looked up at the sky while she calculated, "I don't know how far away it is in kilometers, but in America we usually measure distance by how long it takes to get there, so Kenosha is about an hour and half away from Chicago by car."

"Is that close?"

"It's not that far." Maggie smiled. "America is a gigantic country, so we are used to long drives."

"Wouldn't that be wonderful, if we could all get together after the war?" Leva's eyes widened with anticipation.

"I already gave you my address, right?" Maggie asked. "Just send me a letter explaining everything you need. That will also help my husband, so he knows what's going on."

"I'll be happy to write, once we have a better idea of what my Uncle Jouzas is willing to do. But even if he said yes to everyone, we won't be ready to leave here for a few months, so we have time. Thanks so much for offering to help. That's amazing!"

"I can't wait. Won't it be exciting if we all get to see each other again?" Maggie clapped her hands quickly with excitement. "And I hope you don't mind my saying, but I am sure there's a divine hand in this."

"I don't know a whole lot about God and religion and things like that," Leva said. "But I have to admit, if I believed in those things, I think it's a miracle that I got my mama back. I thought I'd never see her again."

"Oh, it's a miracle all right," Maggie declared with confidence. "One hundred percent. And if I hadn't seen it with my own eyes, I would of thought it was a corny radio drama!"

They laughed, then embraced one last time.

"Thanks again for all you did for Al."

"It was my pleasure. I love your family, and I'm so happy I got to be there when your mama arrived. I'll remember it forever."

"Take care," Leva waved at Maggie as she walked away. "I hope to talk to you soon!"

Maggie nodded and waved as she disappeared.

Chapter 64

2 October 1944
Söderhamn, Sweden

Olek and Mordecai were taken to the Söderhamn refugee camp, and were given strict instructions that they could not leave without authorization. As they explored this abandoned military base, it had clearly enjoyed more prosperous days. The buildings were old and musty, the grounds were overgrown, and the barracks and lavatories were dingy and smelly. But in the rush to find a solution, the Swedish government opened this camp a few months earlier to provide for the many incoming refugees. It wasn't luxurious by any means, but it was a safe place to keep the refugees warm and fed during these cool, autumn nights.

Olek and Mordecai shared sleeping quarters, with row after row of narrow cots, straw-filled mattresses and well-worn donated blankets. Kerosene lamps glowed dimly at night, as coal rations were inconsistent, making for many cold, damp and drafty nights. Each morning, they woke to condensation dripping down the thin glass windows.

Refugees were issued secondhand clothing obtained from donation drives organized by the Swedish Red Cross and local churches. Olek wore an oversized wool coat, a pullover sweater and pair of leather shoes that were slightly too small, causing blisters on his heals. Mordecai was also given a scratchy wool coat that he could layer over his oversized cardigan sweater.

All refugees were awoken at seven, escorted to a large dining room, and instructed to eat breakfast in complete silence. Breakfast consisted of rye bread, margarine, weak coffee or warm milk. After breakfast, Swedish camp workers conducted roll call and all refugees were then lined up for their work assignments. Those who were given a work pass to go outside the camp traveled to job sites where they worked on farms, cut firewood, or handled other menial tasks. Refugees were forbidden to leave their worksite or risk losing their freedom and their work pass. Each job lasted until three o'clock, and then all returned to camp.

Olek was eager to make money, and having a work pass outside the camp allowed him to make more money than if he remained inside the camp.

At first, they helped to harvest potatoes, bending or kneeling for long hours to unearth potatoes from row after row of mounded soil. While Olek dug for potatoes, Mordecai gathered the potatoes into a tin pail, sorting out the damaged or rotted potatoes from the good ones. The cold damp conditions were often unbearable. The early morning frost was too cold for their thinning wool gloves. Olek had blisters on the palms of his hands from using a small shovel to dig for the deeper tubers.

After working in the potato fields for two weeks, they were taken to a grain processing facility. Here they helped local farmers with threshing their already harvested barley, oats and rye. Throughout the day, they would feed the raw grain into small, mechanical threshers. At first, the threshers were human powered, but after a few days, the farmer hitched up his horse, making the work far less brutal. Olek and Mordecai would take turns filling sacks of grain as the horse's hooves circled the threshing floor, separating the grain from the stalk and chaff. Each night they came home exhausted and covered in dust, only to wake up early the next day and do it again.

By the first of November, most of the farmers no longer needed workers from the refugee camp, and all work passes were canceled. Boredom
became the enemy of the refugees, but the Swedes had little to offer.

With the prospect of a long, cold winter, Olek was determined to find
a way to escape this camp. They hoped they had saved more than enough
money to take a train to Stockholm, though they wouldn't know for sure
until they attempted to purchase a ticket. The biggest question was how
they would escape the camp.

Both the main gate, and a secondary gate were manned by gun-toting
volunteers from the Swedish Home Guard. Most of the guards appeared
to be in their mid-to-late forties. Some even looked older. After watching
the comings and goings at the gate for a good part of the day, Olek noticed
that most of the guards at the secondary gate didn't seem too interested in
their assignment. Some were prone to falling asleep. Others left their post
unattended for long periods.

After dark, Olek and Mordecai hid in some nearby bushes, watching the
secondary gate closely, waiting for their one and only chance of escaping.
If they were caught trying to escape, they were sure to be placed in a locked
portion of the camp where troublemakers were kept.

When it appeared that a guard had left his post for a few minutes, Olek
whispered excitedly, "Let's go. Now!"

In a flash they dashed out of the bushes, ducking to lower their profile,
they rushed through the gate and past the empty guard building. Running
with all their might, they made it far enough away from the gate that they
stopped to catch their breath.

"Do you see anyone following us?" Olek asked as he panted.

"I don't see anyone," Mordecai replied, his hands on his hips as he
breathed.

"Okay. Good. Let's make it to that grove of trees over there, and we'll
wait for a while until we know were in the clear."

Emerging from a cluster of trees, Mordecai chased Olek into another
clump of bushes a few hundred meters away. Waiting until they were
sure they weren't being followed, Olek let out a sigh of relief. "We did it,
Mordecai!" His face beamed with joy. "I'm sure glad we're out of there,"
Olek's face beamed. "It reminded me of being in Ponary. That's not a good
memory."

Mordecai nodded, "Now what do we do?"

"We need to find the train station or a bus depot somewhere. There's got to be one nearby.

"What if we followed the river?" Mordecai asked. "Don't they usually have important buildings by the river?"

"That's very good logic, Mordecai!" Olek nodded his approval. "Let's do that."

In the dark, they followed the Söderhamnsån River eastward and came across the train tracks that led them straight to the Söderhamn station house. Just before dawn, they noticed the elegant two-story red brick train station with graceful arched windows. The colonnade entrance was etched with the numbers "1886" above the hefty double doors, indicating the year it was constructed.

Before long, people were coming and going through the main doors, still others were spilling out of the two adjacent doors at either end of the building.

"Let's try these doors," Olek suggested, hoping to avoid some of the crowd exiting the station. Finding the ticket office, he purchased their tickets to Stockholm, smiling that he had plenty of money to spare.

"We had enough to make it to Stockholm, and money left over as well." Olek said triumphantly.

Mordecai's smiled his approval, then asked, "How long is will it be?"

"About six hours," Olek replied. "That will put us in Stockholm at about three o'clock this afternoon. Then we have to figure out how to get to Leva's place."

"You don't know where it is?" Mordecai asked.

"All I know is that she lives in a place called Hässelby Castle."

"She lives in a castle?"

"Yes, her grandmother bought it several years ago. It was old and abandoned, but she had grand plans to turn it into a hotel, but then the war started."

"Is it like the castle in Camelot?" Mordecai asked seriously.

Olek giggled, then covered his mouth. "I don't think it's quite like that, but I don't know, I've never seen it."

"Is it a scary castle?"

"I don't think it is now. That's because I don't think Leva's grandmother would live in something scary. I'm sure it's all fixed up. At least the part they are living in."

"And Leva lives in the castle with her grandmother, right?"

"Yes, you're right. She and her brother Algirdas are living there."

"Will I meet him too?"

"Yes, I'm sure you will." Olek's knee bounced as Mordecai's questions made him anxious about seeing Leva again. While he fully expected she would welcome him back with open arms, still, something may have changed. Something could have happened, or maybe she met someone who might have made her avoid a relationship with him.

Just then, Mordecai interrupted his runaway thoughts. "Do you think she'll like me?"

Olek didn't quite know what Mordecai was worried about, but he guessed he was concerned that Leva might not want to be with Olek because of him.

"Yes, Mordecai. She'll like you."

"What if she doesn't?" His question implied something deeper.

"She'll like you. I'm absolutely sure of it. It might take a little time. But I'm not going to toss you out in the street under any circumstances. It's not going to come down to me choosing between you and her. I promise."

Mordecai gave a weak grin and nodded, still not satisfied that he and Olek would not be separated.

Chapter 65

Olek and Mordecai walked out of Stockholm's Central Station at three that afternoon. As they reached the street, Olek noticed a route map showing the subway metro train routes. After studying it for a minute, he turned to Mordecai.

"I think we can take the metro a good part of the way there, then there's a bus that can take us to Hässelby." He gave Mordecai an enthusiastic grin. "It shouldn't be too hard to find a castle, don't you think?"

Mordecai shrugged, and Olek replied, "Well, then, let's go!"

They made their way back into the station and found the section of the station for all the local commuter trains. They managed to find the right subway train going westward. This line had just opened a few months earlier, and a sign celebrating the new line explained their achievement of drilling a 1.3-kilometer tunnel beneath Arstaviken Bay and culminating in Alvik.

Olek and Mordecai got off the train and climbed the stairs to street level. After a few minutes, they located the waiting bus heading westward to Hässelby.

Finding a seat, they watched as they made their way westward. They jumped to the door when the bus driver shouted, "Vallingby."

As the bus drove away, Olek was feeling lost. He turned around in circles hoping to find some indication of where they should go. Seeing nothing, he approached a woman and her child. With Olek speaking Polish, she shook her head and walked away.

Olek said the only Swedish words he knew, "Hässelby Slott? Hässelby Slott?"

The woman's eyes brightened, and she nodded, explaining in Swedish and, using an encouraging tone, motioned for them to keep walking in a southwesterly direction. Olek said thank you in Polish, and she smiled.

After walking a few minutes down a small hill, they turned a corner and looked up. There was the unmistakable castle sitting majestically at the top of a small hill, nestled among a handful of majestic oak trees.

"That's got to be it, Mordecai," Olek said with excitement. "I can't imagine they'd have more than one castle way out here."

Olek practically raced toward the castle. Mordecai was gasping to keep up. Within minutes, they had arrived at the private side of the castle. They made their way through the baroque gardens, searching for an entrance. Traversing a cobblestone terrace, they stepped through a large archway that opened into the main courtyard where a massive stone staircase lead to the main entry. Olek and Mordecai stepped up to the door. Olek was about to reach for the impressive metal door knocker, but he froze. His mind raced with countless ways in which this long awaited encounter could go wrong. As they stood in the cold, Mordecai asked softly, "Are you going to knock?"

CHAPTER 66

12 November 1944
Hässelby Slott, Stockholm, Sweden

———————————

Leva and her mother were busy fixing dinner in the large, stone-floored kitchen. Tall leaded windows were fogged from the pot of barley soup simmering on the stove. The wood-burning stove glowed dimly, yet it was a pleasant source of heat in the increasingly cold and damp castle. Dried herbs dangled from the rafters as Leva and Zeneta peeled potatoes, the leftover peels filling the porcelain sink.

"I keep hearing that the Swedish government is going to cave to the Soviets." Zeneta said with disdain. "They're saying the Stalin wants to repatriate all Lithuanians…" she paused to make air quotes with her hand "or as they call us, Soviet citizens."

"I'm not a Soviet. And I'm not going back," Leva protested. "I don't care if I have to walk away from this place. There's not enough money in the world to make me stay here and risk having the Swedish government appease Stalin and force me to go back to Lithuania. I won't do it."

"The Germans are retreating," Zeneta explained. "The Allies push from the west, the Soviets from the east. I'm worried that the Soviets will be seen as liberators, and no one will believe what they did to Lithuania before the Nazis arrived."

"It's so hard to wait for our visas to be approved so we can go to America." Leva looked out the kitchen window, deep in thought. "Maybe we should also apply to Canada, just in case?"

"When we interviewed at the U.S. legation office," Zeneta paused peeling potatoes as she spoke. "They said we qualified as political dissidents. We're exempt from their immigration quotas. We just have to be patient."

"I know," Leva answered. "But what if..."

Zeneta cut her off. "We've done everything they've asked of us. We should hear from them in a month or so."

"But what if they don't allow all of us to go? What if they put you or me on a waiting list? What then?"

Zeneta didn't answer, as Leva's question was something she had never considered. "We'll just have to deal with it. There's no sense worrying about it now." Their conversation was disrupted by loud clanks on the door.

After tussling with the lock and pulling the door open, she gave a look of confusion at seeing an emaciated man at her door, along with a skinny boy standing next to him. Thinking it was another beggar asking for food, she paused to examine the man more closely. In an instant, she recognized his familiar voice as he said, "Leva!"

Standing in a stupor, she froze as it took her a moment to comprehend that she was face to face with Olek. Nearly collapsing to her knees, she held onto the door frame, and Olek jumped to prevent her from falling.

"I've got you." He wrapped his arms around her slender waist. She saw his other hand grasp the doorframe and said softly. "I won't let you go, Leva. I'm finally here."

Leva's eyes were swimming as she tried to focus on Olek's eyes. "Is it really you?" she muttered, then she gained her balance and wrapped her arms around his neck, squeezing him tight.

"Oh, Olek, I can't believe it's you. I can't tell you how much I've missed you," Leva sobbed, her tears flowing freely as she savored his embrace.

"How did you get here? Where have you been? I thought you gave up on me. You never answered my letters," Leva whispered in his ear.

"I never got a single letter from you. I sent you tons of letters, but they came back as undeliverable."

She lifted her head to look into his eyes. "I'm sorry I ever doubted you," she said through her sobs, "I thought I'd never see you again."

"I chased you at the train station when you first left Kaunas," Olek said. "I missed you by only a few minutes."

Leva shook her head with disappointment. "I'm so sorry I didn't have time to say goodbye. We were running for our lives."

"I know," Olek moved closer to her. "I know that now, but I didn't quite understand at the time."

As they stood and savored the closeness of each other, Leva heard her mother appear from behind the other side of the door. "Is that you Olek? I thought you..." Zeneta stopped midsentence, covering her mouth in shock. "I heard you were killed in Ponary."

"Just about was," Olek gave an uneasy glance. "But not quite." He turned to Mordecai standing nervously nearby. "Let me introduce you to my friend Mordecai."

Olek put his hand behind Mordecai to draw him closer. Leva watched as Olek looked lovingly at this boy, and her heart melted at seeing his affection and kindness.

"You must be the boy who left the note about Olek's papers!" Zeneta said with recognition. What's your name again?"

"Mordecai." He said softly.

"That's right," Zeneta beamed.

Leva looked at her mother with confusion. "How do you know him?"

"I'll tell you later. It's a long story," Zeneta said in a near whisper, then turned to Olek and Mordecai. "Come on in, both of you."

Leva held on to Olek as if she would never let him go. She pulled Olek inside the door, then looked at Mordecai. "Come on in, Mordecai."

She held her arms out and embraced him, but he remained stiff and awkward.

"Please come in Mordecai. I won't bite!" Leva grinned and took his hand, pulling him gently inside the door. "You must be someone very special if you're willing to put up with this guy," she tilted her head toward Olek and chuckled.

Mordecai looked at her and then back at Olek, understanding her sarcasm. "I guess he's okay," Mordecai said, giving a wry smile, "most of the time."

Leva laughed, then looked directly at Olek and asked, "Seriously, how did you ever make it here? Where have you been?" Her voice cracked as she clung to Olek's arm.

Olek explained their ordeal in fleeing the Soviets in Lithuania, Latvia and Estonia, and taking a boat to Finland. He explained being locked up in the Swedish refugee camp in Söderhamn, working in the potato fields and doing whatever they could to make enough money to purchase train tickets to Stockholm.

"We'd already walked over five hundred kilometers from Lithuania to Estonia. We didn't want to walk another three hundred kilometers from Söderhamn to here," Olek laughed. "We were taking a train if it took us a year to earn enough money. It took us a month or so, but we finally made it."

After a week, Olek and Mordecai had settled in at Hasselby Castle, helping where they could, and making plans for how to get out of Sweden and to the United States.

Zeneta and Ugna had yet to tell Olek they had his journal pages from Ponary. They opted to give him and Leva some time to reconnect before bringing up such painful memories. Zeneta called from her room, "Olek. Mordecai. Would you mind coming into my room for a minute?"

Zeneta watched as Olek came into the room with a puzzled look, Mordecai was close behind. The instant he stepped into the room, Olek noticed his papers on the bed. He looked at Zeneta and Ugna with astonishment. His mouth gaped open, unable to speak as he inspected the pages of his journal.

"How did you get these?" His expression of disbelief overcame him.

"You can thank Mordecai," Zeneta explained. "He dug up your bottles and left these papers up in our secret room at the cabin. He knew how important these papers were to you, so he wanted to make sure some-one like us would find them."

Olek looked at Mordecai with astonishment. "Is that true?"

Mordecai looked down, not knowing if he was in trouble or not. He glanced at Zeneta and Ugna, saying, "Yes, but I was only trying to help."

"You're not in trouble," Olek said. "I just didn't think I would ever see these again."

"I knew how much work you put into them, so I took them out of the bottles and hid them inside my little room upstairs."

"That's amazing, Mordecai." Olek stepped over and put an arm around his shoulders. "Thank you."

Olek continued to scan several pages of his journal entries, a pained expression crossed his face.

Zeneta inhaled slowly, then looked at Olek to explain. "We've been carrying these all over Lithuania and Poland. We grabbed them when we left the cabin. We read Mordecai's note and some of your letters, and then, when we understood what was causing that awful smell. It was just too much to fathom, so ran out of there as fast as we could go. Ugna hid these in her luggage and we forgot about them."

"Thank you for taking such good care of them." Olek smiled warmly at Zeneta and Ugna. "It means a lot to me."

"We didn't want to reopen old wounds," Zeneta added. "That's why we waited until now. I hope you don't mind."

"No, no," Olek answered. "I'm so happy that all my efforts didn't go to waste. But..." he hesitated. "I think I'll just hold on to these for now. I don't think I'm ready to remind myself of all of it right now. And I certainly don't think the world is ready to know about it yet either."

"You be the judge," Zeneta said with kindness. "It's up to you when you're ready."

Olek continued to shake his head in disbelief. "Thank you so much for saving these," he said to Zeneta and Ugna as he walked out of the bedroom. "I'm just a little overwhelmed by it all."

"Understood," Zeneta smiled. "But I hope someday you'll write a book about what you saw. The world needs to hear your story."

Olek was unsure about whether he ever wanted to look at his journal again. The memories still fresh and stinging. He looked at Zeneta and replied, "all in due time. Maybe someday when it's not quite so painful."

EPILOGUE

Zeneta, Al, Leva, Olek, and Mordecai immigrated to Chicago in March 1945, sponsored by Uncle Jouzas Koslowski, Matis's brother. Immigration was difficult—few refugees were being accepted—but because of their status as Soviet political refugees, their application was approved, along with Ugna, Mykolas, and Saule, who stayed briefly with Maggie and her husband before settling. In 1948, Ugna remarried, and her family eventually made a home in Philadelphia.

Leva, Olek, and Mordecai became U.S. citizens in 1953 and later moved to Lake Zurich, Illinois.

Olek earned a journalism degree from Columbia College and taught at Wheaton College. For decades, he couldn't bring himself to reread his Ponary journals. Each attempt triggered anxiety and frustration. In 1990, he finally reopened the sealed file folder—only to discover much of the journal was missing, including the earliest pages describing the most harrowing events of the "Holocaust by Bullets." The loss was heartbreaking, but it awakened a need in Olek to share his story. Months later, a student interviewed him for a senior project, prompting him to recount his journey to Ponary, the Nazi invasion, the tunnel escape, and his escape to Sweden. The interview was cathartic, allowing him to voice long-buried memories.

Mordecai quickly became fluent in English and he graduated high school with honors. He was married just after high school, then soon divorced. He was fascinated by cars, and he worked at Ford's Chicago Assembly Plant before earning his Ph.D. from the University of Illinois. He became a tenured professor at the University of Chicago and lives in Wheaton with his second wife, Sarah.

Leva, though unable to have children, poured her energy into mastering English and writing about her wartime experiences. After several articles were published, she began her memoir. In 1961, she was diagnosed with cancer and passed away the following year, with Olek and Al by her side.

After settling Babcia's estate and helping Al and Leva, Zeneta dedicated herself to aiding Lithuanian refugees stranded in German displaced persons camps. Many fled to avoid forced repatriation to Soviet-controlled Lithuania. Zeneta sponsored as many families as she could, continuing this work until 1955, when she was diagnosed with breast cancer. She died in 1959. Her funeral was attended by thousands of Lithuanians touched by her generosity.

When Al returned to the U.S. in 1945, he legally changed his name back to Koslowski to honor his father. He and his wife Eleanor settled in West-chester, Illinois. Al started as an admissions clerk at Hines Hospital, later earning a degree from Northwestern and rising to hospital administrator. He hoped to retire at 65. Though his children were grown, he had no grandchildren—a quiet disappointment.

Despite his work with the VA, Al's efforts to locate his bomber crew were unsuccessful. He especially searched for his friend Hank Meyer, believed to be from Utah, but never found his grave or any trace of Hank's family—or the rest of his crew.

In July of 1975, Al attended the first reunion of the 306th Bomb Group in Miami Beach, Florida. He and Eleanor attended the event. Al reconnected with a handful of people from the 306th Bomb Group, but despite all his efforts, he was unable find anyone from his plane, *Plano's Pride*.

Until the last moments on the final day of the reunion.

Al bumped into stout and robust man wearing a white shirt and tie. Puzzled by his familiar face, he checked his name badge and shouted, "Hank Meyer! Is that really you?"

"Al?" the man said. He bent down to inspect Al's nametag. In a split second, his eyebrows raised in surprise. "Al? From *Plano's Pride*? Is that you?"

"Yes Hank, I'm Al Barsauskas!

Hank's eyes bulged with delight. Al reached up from his wheelchair and embraced Hank. They hugged each other tightly and patted each other's backs. As they separated, Al smiled broadly and asked, "How are you, Hank? I thought you were dead."

"I thought you were dead, too!" Hank replied, and they laughed and hugged again. "How come your name tag says Koslowski?"

"That's my family's name," Al replied. "I had to change my name to my mother's name when we escaped Lithuania and went to Sweden. On all the military records, my name is Barsauskas," he pointed to his name tag. "But my real name is Koslowski!"

Hank shook his head in disbelief, smiling. "I've thought a lot about you," Al explained. "I even asked my congressman to find you. I almost gave up looking, but I came here because I had nothing to lose."

"I've always thought you went down with the plane," Hank said. "When we got the bailout order, I saw blood all over the ball turret and assumed you were dead."

"I got hit in my head when that rocket exploded, but it only knocked me out for a bit," Al said. "When I woke up, I crawled out and put on a parachute. When I saw you, you were unconscious, you had your parachute on, but you suddenly fell out. I was heartbroken because I thought you were dead."

"Apparently not," Hank chuckled. "What happened after you bailed out?"

"Right after I crawled out, the ball turret fell out. I just barely made it out in time. It more or less sucked me out and when I came to, I pulled the rip cord. But I landed hard on a tractor. I was paralyzed below the waist. That's why I'm in a wheelchair."

Hank shook his head. "I'm so sorry to hear that. But I can't believe you're here!"

"What happened to you after you bailed out?" Al asked.

Hank paused. "They took me to Stalag 17, and I stayed there until the end of the war."

"Oh, I'm sorry to hear that," Al said with sympathy.

"But I survived. Someday I'll have to tell you about it." Hank seemed uncomfortable with the subject. "So, tell me, Al, what happened to you after you were captured?"

"That's why I wanted to find you was because of how the Germans sent me home. Were your parents part of the POW exchange in March '44?"

Hank's eyes lit up. "Yes! That's when they went to the Swiss border."

"Yes!" Al said. "After seeing your family's photo on your bed for so long, I remember seeing an American couple on that train who looked just like them. I told my nurse I thought they were your parents. She thought I was crazy."

"You were on that same train?" Hank asked.

"Yes. I was on a stretcher from Germany, and they transferred me to another train that was headed for America. I felt so bad for those going the other way—into a living hell."

"It was hell for my parents," Hank said.

"I went back on the Gripsholm," Al nodded as he explained.

"That's the ship my parents took from the U.S. to Lisbon! They'll be shocked to hear this."

"They're still alive?" Al asked.

"Yes. Both are in their eighties and living in Utah. They lived in Germany until 1954. The U.S. government demanded that they sign some crazy oath of secrecy, saying they wouldn't tell anyone about what the government did to them. My parents refused and stayed in Germany. We finally got them back here after my grandmother died."

Al and Hank kept talking until Eleanor smiled and interrupted, "I hate to break this up, but we're going to be late for our flight if we don't leave now."

Al nodded, then turned to Hank. "Before we go, I have one important question."

"Go ahead," Hank said.

"Remember our talks about what happens when we die? You told me I'd see my family again."

"I do remember. And I still believe it. Even more than I did then."

Al's voice cracked. "That always stuck with me, Hank. I lost my mother and sister not too long ago. I really need to know that I'll see them again. Do you still think I will?"

"Undoubtedly, Al," Hank said, placing a hand on Al's shoulder. "I can't imagine a heaven without my family. I know in my heart it will happen."

"That's what they teach in your religion?" Al asked.

"Not everything, but eternal families is an important part of it."

Al nodded. "Okay. Maybe you can teach me more. I have a lot of questions."

"Let's talk by phone. I'll call you." Hank said. "But your wife is eager to leave, or you'll miss your flight."

Al looked at Eleanor and smiled. "Okay. I guess we'd better go."

He turned back to Hank. "I can't tell you how happy I am that we found each other. It's another miracle."

"It is another miracle, Al," Hank said, grasping his hand. "You take care of yourself, okay. I'll be in touch."

"You too, Hank."

Al watched as Eleanor leaned toward Hank and said gratefully, "Meeting you made this whole trip worthwhile."

"Same for me," Hank said.

As Al wheeled away, he turned back, smiled, and waved—blinking back tears.

AUTHOR'S NOTE

The Holocaust began not in the gas chambers of Auschwitz, but with mass shootings in the forests of the Baltic nations—events largely unknown to Western audiences. While we're familiar with stories from Western Europe, the experiences of Baltic peoples during World War II remain largely untold in the English-speaking world. These accounts of Soviet deportations, Nazi occupation, and desperate escapes across Europe offer crucial lessons about how quickly democracy can collapse and how ordinary people respond when caught between totalitarian regimes.

This is one of those forgotten stories—one that deserves to be remembered not just by Lithuanians, but by anyone seeking to understand how authoritarianism spreads and how people survive when their world is torn apart.

While this is a work of fiction, it is deeply rooted in documented historical events. Many scenes that may seem too extraordinary to be true—from the tunnel escape at Ponary to surviving a Soviet work camp in Siberia's Lena River delta—are based on actual accounts. The characters are composites drawn from real individuals whose experiences have been preserved in memoirs, testimonies, and government archives. Rather than interrupt the narrative flow, I've included detailed chapter notes at the end of this book for readers who wish to explore the factual foundations behind the story. These notes reveal the real people who inspired the characters, cite primary sources, and provide context for events that shaped this devastating period in Lithuanian and European history. My hope is that readers will first experience the human story, then discover just how much of what they've read actually happened.

While I've traveled to Lithuania on many occassions, I'm not Lithuanian, nor do I have any known Baltic heritage. My connection began over thirty years ago. In December 1990, I visited what was still the Lithuanian Soviet Socialist Republic. As a student journalist, I was helping promote a project that delivered aid to Eastern Europe. Lithuania had declared independence from the Soviet Union and was building relationships with the West.

During that visit, I had the rare chance to interview 95-year-old Jouzas Urpsys, Lithuania's foreign minister at the onset of World War II. On June 14, 1940, he was personally given an ultimatum by Stalin and his Minister of Foreign Affairs Vyacheslav Molotov to permit Soviet troops to enter Lithuania or face invasion. With no viable alternative, Urpsys reluctantly signed the documents. That night, Stalin required Urpsys to join him for dinner. The next morning, Urpsys was arrested and sent to a Siberian gulag, spending most of the next thirteen years in solitary confinement.

Because of these and other meaningful experiences, I developed a deep affection for Lithuania and its people. But it wasn't until decades later that I grasped the full scope of Lithuania's unique role in the Holocaust.

As I've returned to Lithuania, I've met with historians and researchers to learn the facts and uncover stories that would inform this novel. Although my characters are fictionalized, I'd like to honor the real people behind the characters of this book:

Olek Kosmen is a composite character inspired by multiple witnesses to the Ponary Massacre. Chief among them is Kazimierz Sakowicz, a Polish journalist who lived near Ponary in 1939. The Soviets had dug large pits in the nearby forest for petroleum storage—pits the Nazis later used as mass graves. On July 11, 1941, Sakowicz and his wife heard gunfire from the forest. From his attic, he secretly observed the executions and began documenting what he saw, recording victim counts, transport vehicles, and clothing details. Fearing discovery, he hid the pages in lemonade bottles buried in his yard. Many pages are still missing, but those recovered are among the most valuable eyewitness accounts of the Holocaust. His journal was published by Yale University Press in *Ponary Diary, 1941–1943- A Bystander's Account of a Mass Murder*—a haunting but important read.

Olek also draws upon the lives of Ponary survivors like Motke Zaidel, Schlomo Gol, and Yuli Farber—members of the "Burning Brigade." This group of roughly eighty Jewish and Russian prisoners were forced to exhume and burn corpses to erase evidence of genocide. Confined to a deep pit and shackled, they worked for months under horrific conditions. Aware they'd be executed once the task was complete, they secretly spent seventy-four days digging a one-hundred foot escape tunnel beneath a barbed-wire fence and minefield. On April 15, 1944, the escape began. While some were recaptured or killed, as many as twenty-two made it to freedom. The exact number remains uncertain.

Zeneta and Matis Koslowski are based on countless Baltic families—Lithuanians, Latvians, and Estonians—who were exiled by the Soviets in 1941. Men were often tortured or killed; women and children were sent to harsh labor camps in Siberia. One of the most vivid personal accounts comes from Dalia Grinkevičiūtė, a Lithuanian physician whose memoir about surviving deportation to Trofimovsk, a prison island in the Lena River delta, is now required reading in Lithuanian schools. She escaped in 1949, lived in hiding, was later rearrested, and exiled again.

Most of the other characters in this book are also composites drawn from real people and events. See the following historical notes for details.

Having traveled throughout Europe, I've visited the remnants of extermination sites, POW camps, Holocaust memorials, cemeteries, etc. These experiences taught me that history is not just about dates and events—it's about human choices made under impossible circumstances.

As we face rising authoritarianism and attempts to minimize or manipulate Holocaust history, stories like these serve as both warning and testimony. The courage of those who documented atrocities, helped others escape, and preserved evidence of genocide, serve to remind all of us that individual actions really matter, even in humanity's darkest moments

Not surprisingly, during my most recent research trip to Lithuania, I encountered an ongoing struggle over how that nation's Holocaust history is remembered—and how some are trying to manipulate that narrative. Some are trying to downplay the Nazi occupation and focus more on the victims of the Soviet occupation. Some are especially focused on minimizing or removing the role Lithuanians played in capturing and murdering Jews.

As an outsider, I have no political or cultural axe to grind, other than telling a compelling story grounded in truth and supported by the best available sources. Where the historical record was unclear, I filled the gaps with careful research and my imagination. While I respect the available documented sources, I have leaned heavily on the experiences of those who lived through these events.

I welcome your thoughts and questions at www.GaryToyn.com.

CHAPTER NOTES & SOURCES

The following notes are intended to identify the historical events, primary sources, and eyewitness testimonies that inform this novel's key episodes. From the executions and escape tunnel at Ponary, to the deportations to Siberia, the clandestine prisoner exchanges and forced labor in the Arctic, each reference provides critical context to the narrative. They also affirm the historical complexity of the period, while similarly honoring the memory of those who survived—and the victims who didn't.

Chapter 7
Lithuanian Activists Front, or "Shaulists," were members of the Sauliu Sajunga (the Riflemen Union, Lithuanian National Sharpshooters Association) who later were distinguished by their white armbands. During the Soviet occupation, they were paramilitary (civilian fighters) fighting the Soviets to reestablish Lithuanian independence. During the Nazi occupation, they played an instrumental role in the annihilation of Lithuanian Jewry, and their ranks swelled when they became anti-Semitic extremists. According to one witness, "groups of Lithuanian and Polish youths wearing white armbands appear in the streets and snatch the Jews, whom they lead off to the police stations or prison. Some of them break into the houses and haul out the Jewish males. People call them hapunes [abductors]. It was said that the price paid to the abductor for a kidnapped Jew was ten rubles." *Yitzhak Arad, Ghetto in Flames, Jerusalem: Yad Vashem and Bnai Brith, 1980), 67, https://www.jewishvirtuallibrary.org/jsource/Holocaust/firststage.html.*

Chapter 11
In June 1940, the Soviet Union forcibly occupied Lithuania. By August, it was annexed as the Lithuanian Soviet Socialist Republic. The USSR controlled the politics and the economy and aimed to eliminate all Lithuanian culture. Following Marxist principles, the USSR implemented "Sovietization" policies by nationalizing private businesses and private land and violently suppressing all dissent. Those targeted for forcible deportations included what was called the "intelligentsia," meaning anyone likely to question Soviet policies. They included school teachers, university lecturers, lawyers, journalists, military officers, diplomats, people with a family member living abroad, office workers, farmers, agronomists, doctors, and businessmen. By the end of June, approximately seventeen thousand Lithuanians were forcibly deported to Siberia to labor camps and other forced settlements.

Chapter 17
#1: The events depicted here of witnessing mass murder in Ponary forest were inspired by the experiences by Kazmierz Sakowicz. He wrote about his haunting experiences as he covertly witnessed mass executions in the Ponary forest. Forced to live near the infamous pits originally dug for storing petroleum products, he was a former journalist who meticulously documented these atrocities, creating an invaluable eyewitness account of this dark chapter in Lithuanian history. Sakowicz's profound insights and unwavering dedication to recording his experiences are among the most powerful and undeniable eyewit-

ness accounts of the initial stages of the Holocaust. *Kazmierz Sakowicz, Ponary Diary, 1941–1943: A Bystander's Account of a Mass Murder (New Haven, CT: Yale University Press, 2005).*

#2: Lithuania was the first place in German-occupied Europe where Jews were executed on a mass scale. Many people believe the Holocaust began with the gas chambers, but this is not the case. Much of the actual killing at Ponary was at the hands of Lithuanian volunteer special platoons. *The Reconstruction of Nations: Poland, Ukraine, Lithuania, Belarus, 1569–1999, p84.*

Chapter 21
Sara Prusakaitė was a Lithuanian deportee forced to work in different settlements in Olekminsk. She reports that a common survival strategy included engaging in sexual liaisons with administrators. She recalls instances where her Jewish friend "had intimate relations with her married supervisor, allowing her to receive extra food rations, (and)avoid laborious tasks." *Sara Prusakaitė, 10 November 2013; https://www.cairn-int.info/article-E_ETHN_182_0209--the-entanglement-of-historical.htm.*

Chapter 24
By 1940, Chicago Lithuanians numbered approximately one hundred thousand, making it the largest urban settlement of Lithuanians in the world and the largest concentration of ethnic Lithuanians outside Lithuania.

Chapter 26
Foreign-born US troops made a significant contribution to American victory in World War II. From July 1, 1942, through June 30, 1945, more than 100,000 foreign-born members of the US Armed Forces became naturalized citizens. *Joseph P. Harris, "The War Powers Act of 1941: Its Origins and Scope," Western Political Quarterly 11, no. 3 (September 1958): 581–94, https://military-history.fandom.com/wiki/War_Powers_Act_of_1941*

Chapter 28 Karl Jaeger, the SS commander of a Nazi killing unit that operated around Vilnius, Lithuania, has provided a detailed account of those killed each day under his command. In the report, Jaeger credits the essential help of local Lithuanians, saying four thousand Jews were "liquidated by pogroms and executions," exclusively by Lithuanian partisans. The final count of those murdered starting in the summer of 1941 and ending in November of that year is 133,346—the vast majority of them Jews." While all Nazi first-hand historical accounts should be viewed with some degree of suspicion or skepticism, many other historical sources make it difficult to completely dismiss Jeager's report as unreliable. *"The Jaeger Report: A Chronicle of Nazi Mass Murder"; see also E. Klee, W. Dressen, and V. Riess, "The Good Old Days" (New York: The Free Press, 1988), 57. See pages 46–58 for the complete report in English. https://phdn.org/archives/holocaust-history.org/works/jaeger-report/.*

Chapter 32
Communist party officials were desperate to feed their millions of starving citizens and were growing desperate for solutions. Aside from the usual defi-ciencies in the state's food delivery system, many factories and food production facilities were damaged or destroyed in the war against the Nazis. Party officials saw little risk in sending what they considered the bourgeoisie class of Lithu-anians from one forced labor camp in Novosibirsk, to another in the Siberian tundra. The aim was to see if it was feasible to develop fish-processing facilities in extreme elements. If the experiment was successful, they would invest addi-tional resources there. The settlement north of the Arctic Circle proved deadly, as a third of the exiles died during the brutal winter of 1942. *"Multidirectional*

Memory and the Deportation of Lithuanian Jews," Violeta Davoliūtė, http://www.ces.lt/wp-content/uploads/2016/01/8-ETn_St_Davoli%C5%ABt%C4%97_Multidirectional-memory.pdf.

Chapter 35

Kittel was an "unlikely executioner, with dazzling white teeth, . . . perfumed, elegant, polite, and refined." He ordered a piano be brought into the ghetto, and he played piano while the Jews were loaded onto trucks just prior to being taken to their death. When a boy was dragged out of the hiding spot with his family, the boy rushed to the piano and begged for mercy. Kittel continued playing with his left hand and drew his pistol with his right hand and shot the boy on the spot. *Ilya Ehrenburg and Vasily Grossman, The Complete Black Book of Russian Jewry, ed. David Patterson (city: Transaction Publishers, 2003).*

Chapter 38

This true account of a B-17 pilot outmaneuvering a Junkers 88 can be found in the 306th Bomb Group Mission Reports, Thurleigh, England, 13 December 1943. The pilot report stated, "As both engines (of the Ju-88) burst into flames, two series of red-yellow flares were seen to come from the enemy fighter, and it then disappeared into the haze, only forty feet off the water. We claim this Ju-88 destroyed [and is] the only claim on this mission." *Headquarters 306th Bombardment Group (H), Intelligence Report, 13 Dec 1943, Major John A. Bairnsfather, page 9, declassified per executive order 12356, 8 January 1991.*

Chapter 39

According to sworn testimony of a "burning brigade" participant Matvei Fedorovich Zeidel: "In October 1943, I was taken to the Ponary railway station and placed in a bunker. Here Germans used us for preparing firewood and burning corpses. In December 1943 we were fettered and began burning corpses. First we piled the firewood, on top of which up to 100 corpses of people were laid, poured some kerosene and gasoline, and then proceeded with another layer of corpses. Thus, we stacked about 3,000 corpses, laid firewood around them, poured the bodies with petroleum, stuck incendiary bombs on four sides of the pile and lit it up. The fire was burning for 7–8 days." *The Tragedy of Lithuania, 1941–1944: New Documents on Crimes of Lithuanian Collaborators during the Second World War—Collection of Archival Documents (Moscow: Alexei Yakovlev, 2008), https://silviafoticom.files.wordpress.com/2020/01/thetragedyoflithuania.pdf*

Chapter 42

In his sworn testimony to Soviet officials about the Ponary tunnel, Kazimir Kozlovski stated, "It was extremely hard to work in the tunnel. There was almost no air. Neither matches nor lighters would burn in the tunnel. Having worked in the tunnel for an hour – hour and a half, people were about to black out; and still, having returned from the wearisome work with the corpses, the shift, without having dinner (it was impossible to eat before working in the tunnel because one would surely vomit), descended into the pit. The work proceeded day by day, from 5 to 9 and from 3 to 6 o'clock in the morning." *The Tragedy of Lithuania, 1941–1944: New Documents on Crimes of Lithuanian Collaborators during the Second World War—Collection of Archival Documents (Moscow: Alexei Yakovlev, 2008), https://silviafoticom.files.wordpress.com/2020/01/thetragedyoflithuania.pdf*

Chapter 44

#1: FDR's secret prisoner swap program recruited ethnic Germans from Latin America, intending to use these prisoners to free Americans being held by the Nazis. The U.S. put pressure on countries like Costa Rica, Panama, Honduras, and Columbia, among many others, to arrest and detain ethnic Germans living there. They convinced these governments to send the Germans to the U.S. where they were held without charge and subsequently deported. As depicted in this chapter, ethnic Germans were swapped for American businessmen, diplomats, Jews, and other VIPs being held by the Nazis. In addition to thousands of German Americans, records indicate 1,813 individuals from Latin America were deported against their will to Europe. According to General George C. Marshall in a memo dated 12 Dec 1942 to the Caribbean Defense Command, he admits the government's intentions for many German internees: "These interned nationals are to be used for exchange with interned American civilian nationals." Beginning in early 1942, over 4,000 German Latin Americans came to the U.S. and were held in American internment camps without the benefit of due process. *"Special War Problems Division: Subject Files, 1939-1954." Entry A1 1357, Boxes 116 and 120, Declassified April 2010.*

#2: The story of Mira is based on documentation regarding the prisoner exchange at Kreuzlingen that confirms the exchange of 160 Jewish internees from the Vittel camp. The Vittel internment camp was established in German-held France in 1941, located in a resort in the Vosges Mountains near the German border. One of those prisoners was Mary Berg, her mother, father, and sister. These four American citizens held valid U.S. passports, but the German government capriciously refused to recognize their passports and threatened to ship them to Auschwitz. The Bergs were among the 160 exchanged at Kreuzlingen, as depicted in this chapter. Of the prisoners who remained at Vittel afterward, 250 were removed in May 1944, sent to Auschwitz, and gassed.

Chapter 47
The character of Itzak is based on a man known only as "Dogim," one of the active members of the escape. He uncovered the bodies of his wife, mother, and both sisters and then put their bodies on the fire. According to the sworn testimony of "burning brigade" participant Matvei Fedorovich Zeidel, "Dogim was given the right to go first. On April 15 . . . the first twenty, having taken off their chains, entered the tunnel. When it became dark, we cleared the exit from the rest of the sand, passing handfuls to each other. When the hole was large enough, we started to climb up. The night was absolutely dark. Against the sky background, the figures of sentinels were seen on the right and on the left. Maneuvering between them, we managed to creep for over 100 meters in absolute silence and suddenly there was a shot and another one. And at once gunfire spread from every direction. Despite the strong fire, we crawled to the wire and cut it in two places, as it had been planned. At least 30 people managed to escape." *The Tragedy of Lithuania, 1941–1944: New Documents on Crimes of Lithuanian Collaborators during the Second World War—Collection of Archival Documents (Moscow: Alexei Yakovlev, 2008), https://silviafoticom.files.wordpress.com/2020/01/thetragedyoflithuania.pdf*

Chapter 48
Dr. Buchinsky is loosely based on Dr. Lazar S. Samodurov, who similarly arrived from fishing on the Laptev Sea to witness so many Lithuanians suffering from starvation and scurvy. According to the account of Dalia Grinkevičiūtė, he "picked his way through each barrack, sized up the entire situation, the half-dead people, and began to work very energetically. He bravely entered into conflict with the . . . superiors who lived in warm houses, . . . dressed from head to foot in furs, wore only fur or felt footwear, ate bread, butter, sugar, and canned pork sent to the Soviet Union by the allies from America to their heart's content. The next day . . . each of us received one bowl of hot pea soup and half a kilogram of frozen fish which the doctor advised us to eat raw so as not to lose the ascorbic acid. Little by little, the starvation and scurvy started to recede. Death also receded." *Dalia Grinkevičiūtė, Lithuanians by the Laptev Sea: The Siberian Memoirs of Dalia Grinkevičiūtė (2014); Audrone Raskauskiene, "Deportation, Memory and the Self in Dalia Grinkevičiūtė's Memoirs A Stolen Youth, A Stolen Homeland and Lithuanians by the Laptev Sea," European Journal of Life Writing 3 (2014): T1–T10.*

Chapter 51
The scene of Zeneta boarding a commercial flight from the far reaches of Siberia to Moscow may seem unrealistic, but they reflect the real-life circumstances written in "Siberian Memoirs of Dalia Grinkevičiūtė" She says: "My mother frequently asked to be allowed to change her place of exile because of her serious illness, either to the Yakutsk region or the Altai region. The climate in those areas appeared to us to be milder. Her requests were refused, yet her health got worse, and she understood that she would die in Yakutsk. She was longing to see Lithuania again and wanted to be buried in her native land. In February of 1949 we escaped by airplane from Yakutsk and reached Lithuania successfully" *Lithuanians by the Laptev Sea: The Siberian Memoirs of Dalia Grinkevičiūtė; Lithuanian Quarterly Journal of Arts and Sciences; Volume 36, No.4 - Winter 1990; Editor of this issue: Violeta Kelertas ISSN 0024-5089, Copyright © 1990 LITUANUS Foundation, Inc.*

Chapter 58
The momentous Casablanca Conference held in January 1943 marked a landmark agreement between Franklin D. Roosevelt and Winston Churchill, stipulating unconditional surrender from Axis powers. Notably, before the conference, FDR achieved aviation history by embarking on the inaugural airplane trip by a sitting U.S. president. Traveling on a Pan Am Boeing 314 flying boat named the Dixie Clipper, his journey to Casablanca became the first actual Air Force One flight and the first instance of a sitting president flying internationally during World War II. Despite frail health and other challenges, he celebrated his sixty-first birthday on the return journey with a festive feast of caviar, olives, celery, pickles, turkey, dressing, green peas, cake, and champagne.

Chapter 57
The character of Piotr represents many heroic fishermen who risked their lives to carry Baltic refugees to freedom in Sweden. One of those men was Žanis Fonzovs, a Latvian fisherman, who helped refugees escape the Red Army during the Second World War. He is credited for ferrying twenty-eight boats full of people to safety. *https://eng.lsm.lv/article/society/society/silent-hero-the-fisherman-who-took-world-war-ii-refugees-to-sweden.a229382/*.

Chapter 61:
Den Gyldene Freden ("The Golden Peace"), is tucked away on Österlång-gatan in Stockholm's Old Town. It has served patrons continuously since 1722, making it one of the world's oldest restaurants still in its original location. By 1944, it had already witnessed over two centuries of Swedish history.

The restaurant was saved from demolition in 1919 when the Swedish Academy purchased it, ensuring this cultural landmark would continue to serve traditional Swedish fare. Members of the Academy, who select the Nobel Prize for Literature, have maintained a special table in the vaulted cellar dining room.

During the war years of the 1940s, while Sweden maintained its neutrality, Den Gyldene Freden stood as a reminder of enduring Swedish traditions. The restaurant's 18th-century interiors—with their rough-hewn wooden beams, copper pots, and candlelit tables—remained largely unchanged. In 1944, as the rest of Europe faced rationing and hardship, the restaurant still served its signature Swedish dishes: tender meatballs with lingonberries, herring prepared in various ways, and hearty game stews—offering a taste of normalcy in troubled times.

Chapter 64

Refugees held at the Swedish internment camp Smedsbo were required to adhere to strict regulations, including wearing designated uniforms and following a structured daily routine. They started each day at 7:15 a.m., proceeding to the dining room for breakfast in complete silence. Subsequently, they engaged in assigned tasks such as road building, repair duty, and woodcutting, remaining stationed without leave until 2:45 p.m. These regimented routines governed the lives of the refugees. *Tobias Berglund and Niclas Sennerteg, Svenska koncentrationsläger i Tredje rikets skugga (Swedish Concentration Camps in the Shadow of the Third Reich, in Swedish) (Stockholm: Natur & Kultur, 2008), 77–83.*

REFERENCES

Printed Sources

Audrone Raskauskiene, "Deportation, Memory and the Self in Dalia Grinkevičiūtė's Memoirs; A Stolen Youth, A Stolen Homeland and Lithuanians by the Laptev Sea," European Journal of Life Writing 3 (2014): T1–T10

Davoliūtė, Violeta, "Multidirectional Memory and the Deportation of Lithuanian Jews," (Lithuanian Cultural Research Institute, Vilnius, Lithuania, Ethnicity Studies, 2015) 131-150

Davoliūtė, Violeta. "The entanglement of historical experiences: The memory of the Soviet deportation of Lithuanian Jews," Ethnologie française, vol. 48, no. 2, 2018, pp. 209-224

Foreign Relations of the United States: Diplomatic Papers, the Conferences at Cairo and Tehran, 1943 – United States Government Printing Office, Washington, 196; pp 468-469

Grinkevičiūtė, Dalia, Lithuanians by the Laptev Sea: The Siberian Memoirs of Dalia Grinkevičiūtė (2014)

Headquarters 306th Bombardment Group (H), Intelligence Report, 13 Dec 1943, Major John A. Bairnsfather, page 9

Ilya Ehrenburg and Vasily Grossman, The Complete Black Book of Russian Jewry, ed. David Patterson (Transaction Publishers, 2003)

Jaak Maandi, oral history interview, 24 September 2014, Stanford University, Libraries, Department of Special Collections and University Archives, The Baltic Video Archive; source ID: 2014-KML-VE-13

Joseph P. Harris, "The War Powers Act of 1941: Its Origins and Scope," Western Political Quarterly 11, no. 3 (September 1958): 581–94

Kazmierz Sakowicz. "Ponary Diary, 1941–1943: A bystander's account of a mass murder", (New Haven, CT: Yale University Press, 2005)

Rothberg, M. Multidirectional memory: Remembering the Holocaust in the age of decolonization. (Stanford, CA: Stanford University Press 2009)

Tobias Berglund and Niclas Sennerteg, Svenska koncentrationsläger i Tredje rikets skugga (Swedish Concentration Camps in the Shadow of the Third Reich, in Swedish) (Stockholm: Natur & Kultur, 2008), 77–83

"Special War Problems Division: Subject Files, 1939-1954." Entry A1 1357, Boxes 116 and 120, Declassified April 2010.

"The Good Old Days" (New York: The Free Press, 1988), 57. See pages 46–58 for the complete report in English.

"The Jaeger Report: A Chronicle of Nazi Mass Murder"; see also E. Klee, W. Dressen, and V. Riess,

"The Reconstruction of Nations: Poland, Ukraine, Lithuania, Belarus, 1569–1999" (New Haven, CT: Yale University Press, 2003), 84

"The Tragedy of Lithuania, 1941–1944: New Documents on Crimes of Lithuanian Collaborators during the Second World War—Collection of Archival Documents" (Moscow: Alexei Yakovlev, 2008)

Digital Sources

http://www.ces.lt/wp-content/uploads/2016/01/8-ETn_St_ Davoli%C5%ABt%C4%97_Multidirectional-memory.pdf

http://www.encyclopedia.chicagohistory.org/pages/757.html

https://doi.org/10.3917/ethn.182.0209

https://eng.lsm.lv/article/society/society/silent-hero-the-fisherman-who-took-world-war-ii-refugees-to-sweden.a229382/

https://lend-lease.net/articles-en/aircraft-deliveries-to-the-soviet-union/

https://military-history.fandom.com/wiki/War_Powers_Act_of_1941

https://phdn.org/archives/holocaust-history.org/works/jaeger-report/

https://silviafoticom.files.wordpress.com/2020/01/thetragedyoflithuania.pdf

https://www.cairn-int.info/article-E_ETHN_182_0209--the-entangle ment-of-historical.htm

Other books by Gary W. Toyn

(fiction)
For Malice and Mercy: A World War II Novel (Part 1 of this book series)

(nonfiction)
The Quiet Hero: A Untold Medal of Honor Story of George E. Wahlen at the Battle for Iwo Jima

Divine Intervention: Inspiring True Stories from LDS Survivors

Life Lessons from Fathers of Faith

Life Lessons from Mothers of Faith